Hell
Dancer

WOL-VRIEY

Burning Bulb
PUBLISHING

Other Books By Wol-vriey:

The Bizarro Story of I

Meat Suitcase

Chainsaw Cop Corpse

Vegan Zombie Apocalypse

Boston Posh (Bud Malone #1)

Vegan Vampire Vaginas

Vagina Mundi

Melanie Nemesis Catchpole

Bizarro 101: A Basic Primer

Boston Corpse (Bud Malone #2)

Dr. Orgasm

Boston Lust (Bud Malone #3)

Pussy Transmission

Novellas and Short Stories By Wol-vriey

Big Trouble in Little Ass
A novella featured in
Westward Hoes

Forever Ago Sunshine
A short story featured in
The Big Book of Bizarro

Hell
Dancer

WOL-VRIEY

Burning Bulb
PUBLISHING

Hell Dancer
By Wol-vriey

Burning Bulb Publishing
P.O. Box 4721
Bridgeport, WV 26330-4721
United States of America
www.BurningBulbPublishing.com

Cover concept by Gary Lee Vincent/Wol-vriey with the following licensed image from iStockphoto LP: 55539492 © Skodadad. Author Photo: Lolade Akinsowon © 2014.

First Edition.

Paperback Edition ISBN: 978-0692688007

Printed in the United States of America

PROLOGUE

The Drake Mansion was a sprawling old house located deep in central Massachusetts, along U.S. Route 20 between Brimfield and Palmer, almost opposite the Brimfield State forest. Just before reaching St. Claire Road on the right as one drove west from Boston, there was a turnoff onto a desolate single-track road that looked like anything but the route to a half-billionaire's house. This one-lane road wound through dense forest for a mile then expanded into the wide grounds surrounding the building.

The Drake Mansion had been built in 1956. It had three floors, twelve bedrooms, four sitting rooms, and two big swimming pools out back.

The mansion's builder, Micah Drake, had been a reclusive Boston construction millionaire who'd wanted somewhere very secluded to live. Once his mansion was completed, he'd moved his wife and son out there. His wife Cherie quickly found the place too gloomy and moved back to the city, where people had a social life. She left her son with his father, however, and young Joshua Drake grew up with a deep liking of the house's gloomy ambience, so much so that he lived there his entire life after his parents' deaths.

Joshua Drake married the beautiful and equally reclusive Lauren Pullman and the couple had a son, Ellis.

Unlike his introverted father, Ellis Drake was an extrovert, and was also plagued by a deep wanderlust that made it almost impossible for him to stay home.

When Ellis was eighteen, both his parents died in a motor accident while visiting his mother's older sister down in St. Rose, Louisiana. Coincidentally, the accident occurred while Ellis was flipping through a book of magic spells while at the same time fiddling with the remote controls for a radio-controlled car, a childhood toy he'd just unearthed in the attic. The car rolled out through the patio doors and into a swimming pool; his parents' limousine somehow flipped over two other cars in the outer lanes, over the railing of the Hale Boggs Bridge, and into the Mississippi River.

The timing and strange circumstances of his parents' deaths had a profound effect on young Ellis, kindling in him a lifelong interest in the occult and arcane. Now finding himself almost as rich as Croesus, the young man began amassing—buying, having stolen on his behalf, and in some cases having made to order—every sort of magical paraphernalia imaginable. In a matter of just a few years, the Drake Mansion was chock-full of strange relics, including several that even a hardened warlock would think better left unearthed.

The house began building up an occult charge. Most of it negative.

And still Ellis Drake's occultic acquisitions continued. As did his studies in magic. But he lacked the discipline to be a truly good magician, and after accidentally doubling the size of his testicles in a ritual intended to make his penis bigger, he essentially quit magic for good.

The supernatural, however, still fascinated him and he kept on buying relics and things he shouldn't own, but now simply from a rich collector's perspective. Besides it was about now that love entered his life, and the woman he loved, Louise Chung, lived in Hong Kong and had no interest in the occult. So Ellis was hardly ever home nowadays. (Louise Chung utterly adored Ellis's huge testes, thinking them the best part of him. Most nights she went to sleep with them in her hands. He worried now that she'd have a nightmare one night and crush them like stress balls.)

But still, the occasional wrapped package of magical art turned up on the doorstep of Drake Mansion to be stored by his staff.

***

Ellis Drake had two servants: Miranda Salcedo his housekeeper, and the butler/chauffeur, Rafael Marquez. Miranda, a slim, dark, and very handsome middle-aged woman of Spanish descent, doubled as Ellis's secretary, handling his correspondence, the payment of his bills, and all purchases for the house.

Before Ellis met Louise Chung, Miranda had also been his occasional mistress.

Miranda really preferred women as lovers; she'd slept with her boss mainly to strengthen her position in his employ. (True, the super-rich Ellis already paid her an outrageous salary, but, as she quickly discovered, prostitution paid a lot extra, like the red BMW convertible Ellis had given her for her forty-second birthday, and many other sundry financial gifts she had squirreled away for a rainy day.) Spreading her legs and accommodating his masculine organ on those rare occasions when he was in the USA was hardly hard work (and was actually quite enjoyable, Ellis being very considerate in bed), and most important of all, ensured that Ellis wouldn't be thinking of hiring someone else (likely some busty blonde bimbo) to replace her as his housekeeper.

When her employer wasn't around, Miranda had the run of the mansion. Most weekends, Rafael travelled to Auburn to see his wife and kids and she had a girlfriend over.

Miranda Salcedo spent most of her free time studying black magic.

Ironically, her interest in the arcane arts had been triggered by her relationship with her employer, by the accident that swelled his testicles to the size of lemons.

"I'll have a look through your magic literature to see if there's anything to shrink them again," she'd said with deep feeling after discovering via fellatio that Ellis's balls weren't just overlarge in size, but also discharged accordingly. Ellis had always appreciated that she swallowed his come, but this time she'd seemed to be drinking a cocktail of sour gelatin laced with salt. Oh no—something *had* to be done about that. In this case bigger definitely wasn't better.

Ellis had nodded gratefully. (This was a year before he'd met Louise Chung, a beautiful descendant of one of the ancient Ming emperors, who was even better at fellatio than Miranda Salcedo, and who also adored his excessive scrotal discharge: to her mind he tasted like sweet-and-sour pork.)

Miranda's magical studies quickly established the fact that there was no fix or undo for Ellis's condition; his testicles were destined to remain swollen for life. And not just that: they would keep growing, getting larger with each passing year. (The spell that had transformed them was a curse designed by a spurned 15th Century French peasant woman, and first cast on the knight who'd ravished then abandoned her. When he'd died at the age of sixty-eight, Sir Guillaume Leduc's testicles had each been the size of watermelons and had to be pushed ahead of him in a wheelbarrow. He'd been a huge hit with the local women and had fathered many illegitimate children.)

Discovering this, Miranda had shrugged her disappointment off—Ellis was only home two to three months of the year anyway; her taste buds could cope with that. (She'd also decided to let him discover for himself that his condition was irreversible; was going to get worse, not better.) Her interest in magic had however been piqued, and she continued her studies, till now she'd become, by her own admission to her current girlfriend Sandy: "Quite the witch, bitch."

Miranda Salcedo had one current problem, however: Louise Chung. She viewed her employer's new girlfriend with deep dislike. It didn't help Louise's cause any (the women had never met, but Miranda had seen pictures of her) that she was skinny and daintily gorgeous, and also had depressingly massive breast implants. But worst of all, Ellis had suggested he was interested in marrying Louise. Miranda wouldn't have taken this seriously—Ellis had 'been interested' in myriads of women before—except that this time Ellis hadn't approached her for homecoming sex. Even when she'd suggested it, he'd refused, saying he was "trying to be faithful to Louise."

With those words, Miranda saw trouble on her career horizon. Soon, Louise would move in, and she—who'd slaved for years looking after Ellis (and she was quite fond of him now)—would be out of a job. She saw no alternative to her being sacked—Ellis would certainly let slip to Louise at some point that he'd slept with her, and women in love being what they were, Louise would then insist that he replace her with some old hag with arthritis and a club foot.

So Miranda decided the wedding wouldn't take place. It was that simple. And the easiest way to prevent any wedding happening was to kill the bride. So at the moment, Louise Mei Chung was living on borrowed time. The thin and rotted fence separating her and her funeral was just the fact that Miranda (now that her blood was aflame with jealous, righteous outrage), was still looking for the right spell to dispose of her rival with.

It wasn't just enough for Miranda Salcedo to kill Ellis's prospective bride. No, she intended to completely disfigure her first.

And in the meantime, more parcels arrived by courier at Drake Mansion from obscure parts of the world, and the building's malignance continued to grow.

Having become attuned to the mansion's psychic vibe, Miranda Salcedo paid scant attention to the increase in its magic charge. She was actually pleased: it made her spellcasting easier. She did her housework, paid Ellis's bills, made love to her girlfriend Sandy, and in between all that kept up her occult studies, searching for that elusive spell that would be just perfect to ensure Louise Chung never walked down a church aisle to an altar, and from thence into her life.

But *something* had to give. It was simply a matter of time and of toying too long with the odds of fate and probability. And there was no way to avert the coming disaster: Too many bad occult objects had been stored in too small a space for too long for evil not to make its presence felt in some tangible form.

Something very, very, very bad *had to* happen at Drake Mansion.

And it would happen very damn soon.

FRIDAY NIGHT

CHAPTER 1

Peaches

At No. 4 Applewood Drive, in Marlborough, MA, a family's worst nightmare was currently in progress.

"Fuck you, asshole," Peaches said and jabbed the fork deep into the man's left eye.

The man's lips were duct-taped over; he screamed silently as his eye burst. Clear goo spurted from it; blood followed.

Her expression serious as death, Peaches twisted the fork in his eye until it was completely ruined, a nylon bag that had once contained jelly.

Beneath her, the man—middle-aged, balding, and duct-taped to a dining room chair brought out into the living room—trembled with fear and pain. The mess from his burst eye dribbled down his face, spreading over his taped mouth before staining his clothes. He shut his other eye tight in anticipation of Peaches' stabbing it too.

Her look of deep concentration became one of amusement.

She giggled. "You can open your eye. I won't blind you. I want you to see what Cutter's doing to your wife."

The man's eye instantly popped open. (In his pain and horror he'd forgotten his wife . . . and [Oh shit, God, how could you let this happen!?] his young daughter, who these monsters had tied up and gagged and locked in the kitchen. He was wondering how in the world he'd made such a mistake in picking up a pair of hitchhikers who'd needed a ride through town. But the pair had seemed so nice and normal: the thirtyish man and his teen daughter, who'd turned out to his girlfriend.)

"You'd better watch," Peaches said, her voice becoming threatening. "If you don't, I'll pop your right eye too."

The man's good eye followed her pointing finger. His wife was bound up opposite him, her wrists and ankles also taped to the arms and legs of a chair.

Peaches laughed. Cutter was really doing a number on the woman, slicing off her right ear with his big silver hunting knife.

Cutter laughed as the wife's eyes bugged open from the pain of the knife sawing through the side of her face. "Hold still, will you, you dumb bitch? You don't want me accidentally cutting off your nose too, do you?"

Somehow she managed to shake her head. "Mmphh, mmphh!"

Cutter laughed even louder and sliced the ear fully off. Peaches knew he'd been doing it slow to maximize the bitch's pain. Cutter did lots of stuff slow. He even fucked her slow. But *that* kind of slow was great.

Blood poured from the woman's head, staining her blond hair. Cutter examined the severed ear for a moment, then flung it away. He smiled over at Peaches. "How's your old fart doing?"

She blew him a kiss. "I'm still not sure whether I want to gut the pig or not."

He caught the kiss and put it in his pocket. "Love you too, babe." Then, grin manic above his bloodstained shirt, he returned his attention to his own victim.

The bound woman stared at him in horror.

Cutter regarded her face for a long moment, then smirked. "You know, I really hate your mousy looks. You middle-aged housewives all need cosmetic surgery anyway. Let's see. First, I recommend a nose job."

"Mmmph! Mmmpph!"

Ignoring her protests, Cutter sat astride her thighs and jabbed two fingers into her nostrils. Then, jerking her nose up like that, he started slicing it off from below. He did it slowly, the blood spurting all over his fingers. Some of the blood went back down the woman's throat; she began sputtering like she couldn't breathe.

Her struggles interested Peaches. She spun around, sat on the husband's legs like she was giving him a lap dance, and watched.

Cutter finished slicing the woman's nose off. With those two big bloody holes in her face, she looked like a bleached gorilla that had run into a wall.

Cutter got up off the woman's thighs. He bent over her instead, studying her bleeding, mutilated face like there was religious truth in it. Finally, he grew bored with staring at her and straightened up. He dropped the woman's nose to the floor and stamped on it violently, his face turning all crazy.

He stomped the nose into the blue living room carpet till it looked like mince.

Then, like something had snapped in his brain, he grabbed the woman's head. She'd become woozy from the shock of abuse, but Cutter quickly slapped some awareness back into her.

"I just wanted to say goodbye," he said when her eyes had focused again.

Then he slit her throat from ear to ear, cutting back so deep through her neck that her head almost fell off. Her blood squirted all over him.

Then, his arms covered with blood, he grinned at Peaches while pointing his dripping knife at the dead woman's husband.

"You made up your mind yet, baby? You know how procrastination is the thief of time."

She giggled. "Speak for yourself. I'm still young: I got lots of time to kill." Then she got off the husband's legs and turned to look at him. He was shaking like whale blubber, his whole mass jiggling like jelly. His single good eye seemed glued open. He had a piss patch on his jeans. Strangled sounds came from behind his gag.

Peaches regarded him with interest, then smoothed his brown hair with a slim finger. "Say, Cutter, do you think he's begging for his life or cussing us?"

Cutter winced. "Darling, I don't frigging care. Now are you going to gut him or shoot him? I'm tired and we've still got the kid in the kitchen to do."

At the mention of his daughter, the man's remaining eye widened to the size of a egg. "Mmmbpph!! Mmmph!!!"

Peaches rolled her eyes. "Cutter, please pass me your knife."

He handed it over. She balanced the wet weapon in her hands for a while, still unable to make up her mind. Then after pouting a kiss at the bound man, she stabbed the knife into his throat and began slashing back and forth across it.

Cutter left her to it, just stood and watched. The knife was large in her little hand and she swung it like a sword or axe, counting on brute force rather than the weapon's sharpness to get the messy job done. Blood spurting all over her, she hacked away at the man's throat, till without warning, his head fell off his neck and over the back of the chair.

Breathing hard from the exertion of the kill, Peaches stood staring at the headless corpse for a while, then she sat on the dead man's lap again facing her boyfriend, her chest rising and falling while she got her breath back.

"Damn," Cutter said. "You didn't like him, did you?"

"I'm premenstrual," she gasped, "all sorts of stressed out."

They sat watching each other for a minute or two, then she got up and stretched. "I'm better now. C'mon, let's go kill the kid—I've something special in mind for her."

***

Pamela "Peaches" Principal was eighteen years old. Cutter was thirty-four. Both were sociopaths—serial/thrill killers.

Peaches was a cute blonde, curvy and about five-foot-six. The only things preventing her from looking more innocent than a nun were her gray eyes. Those had 'crazy bitch' written all over them.

Most people who knew Peaches concluded that Cutter had led a vulnerable and needy young adult down the path of sin and evil; but nothing could be further from the truth: Peaches was just naturally as bad as Cutter.

In her own words: "I'm his *worse* half; screw that *better* crap."

This was indisputable: Peaches was a certifiable loon in her own right.

She was initially from Elmira, New York State. She'd run away from home at age fourteen after . . .

One night her father had gotten into bed with her. (Her mother had died the previous year.)

"Daddy needs comforting from his little angel," he'd whispered gently while stroking her hair. "You understand that, don't you, darling?"

They'd began making out, caressing and kissing each other. Things hadn't gone according to plan, though. At some point in her first experience of fellatio, Peaches had bitten down extra-hard on Daddy's penis, essentially circumcising him. He'd staggered out of bed yelling, a bloody circle of foreskin dangling from the underside of his erection, while his teenaged daughter, with an equally bloody mouth, was pointing at his crotch and laughing loudly.

Peaches hadn't bitten his erection out of anger (perversely, she'd been glad Daddy was now paying proper attention to her), but simply to see what would happen if she did. (The porn she'd gleaned from the internet never showed that kind of stuff.) She'd been very pleased with the results.

But things had never been the same between her and Daddy after that. Most significantly, he'd taken to locking his bedroom door while sleeping. The bathroom door too.

Besides, she was getting bored. Her mother's death had affected her badly; her grades had plummeted in school and she wasn't going to graduate anyhow, so what was she waiting for?

So she ran off, and claiming she was sixteen to all and sundry, hitchhiked her way first down to Pittsburg, then out east to Bridgeport in Connecticut. She worked as a hooker, did a lot of drugs, and somehow survived being homeless on the streets and grew older. And grew even cuter.

But she'd finally tired of selling herself. And then, just when she was considering packing up the flesh-hustle game and traveling back home to Elmira to see Daddy again, she met Cutter.

That evening Peaches had picked up a well-dressed trick. But she'd gotten greedy. While they had sex in his car in an empty lot, she'd tried to pick his pocket.

Peaches was a crap pickpocket. The man was instantly onto her, and next thing Peaches knew, she was being slapped about like she was sparring with Laila Ali.

He had her held up over the hood, and it felt like bombs were exploding inside her head. "How dare you rob me, you skanky bitch? Eh? Fucking answer me?"

She tried to answer, but he kept slapping her silent. And he was big and really strong; one meaty hand held her in a vise-like grip while he hit her.

Damn, she thought during one of the brief interludes between slaps, when her brain didn't feel like it was being pulped, *mama always did warn me to keep my hands to myself.*

She was stunned, her hair scattered everywhere, her small breasts hanging out of her halter, one high-heeled shoe off, her skirt and panties somewhere in the man's car. And he kept hitting her. She'd have screamed for help but the lot was deserted. To either side of them were darkened windows. Worse still, the man beating her up was drunk. That was what worried her the most: that he might accidentally kill her without meaning to.

Then she saw a sign of motion behind him.

Oh, thank God, it's the fuzz, she thought. Being taken downtown and booked for soliciting—every working girl's nocturnal dread— suddenly didn't seem so bad after all. In this case, it was a lifesaver.

But then, something flashed silver in the lot lights. She saw a hand move, and next thing, the trick's neck opened up wide like a mouth spitting blood.

She stared at the blood bubbling from the man's neck, unsure whether or not she was about dying herself.

Then the body was flung aside to bleed to death on the concrete and there was a tall gangly man dressed in old denim staring at her.

"Hi," he said like nothing unusual had happened. "I'm Cutter." She felt his eyes looking her over, appraising her nubile sixteen-year-old body. "How much do you charge for anal?"

"T-t-two hundred," she'd sputtered. "B-b-but you can go free. J-j-just d-d-don't kill me afterwards."

"Kill you?" Cutter had laughed loud. "Now, why the hell would I do that, girl?"

As he unzipped his fly, something nagged at Peaches' addled mind. Finally, she remembered what it was. "You're not coming inside me except you wrap it up," she said. "You might as well kill me otherwise. I don't want AIDS."

He mused on that a moment. "I ain't gonna kill you, you fat-assed little twit. O.K., you got rubbers?"

She'd grimaced at the question. "I'm a pro. They're in my bag on the front passenger seat."

He looked in the car, found the bag, found several condom strips. "Damn, girl, you're a hard worker."

She wasn't listening; her attention was riveted on the dying man. The blood pouring from his neck had now slowed to a trickle. Something about the way he twitched out his final agonies stirred her deeply, almost sexually.

Mechanically, she let Cutter bend her over the hood of the car. She felt him kick her feet apart, heard him spit on his penis, felt it slide up her anus. Good thing those were well-lubed rubbers.

And all the while Cutter thrust into her under the lot lights, Peaches stared at the dead trick with the slit throat in his pool of widening blood. She wasn't thinking, *Serves you right, you son-of-a-bitch,* but rather: *Wow! This is so damn cool. I gotta hang out with this guy more often.*

Finding herself aroused, but unsure why she was, she stuck a hand between her legs and masturbated as he thrust into her behind.

He came, then pulled out. "Yeah, that was great, baby. You've got a real first-class ass."

Peaches hardly heard him. Her gaze riveted on the dead guy on the lot floor, she was coming herself, coming really hard, much harder even than she had on the night she'd circumcised her father with her teeth.

Yeah, she thought as she drained the dregs of her orgasm from the wet depths of her sex, *this killing thing is just great.*

Then, besides herself with excitement, she'd spun around, leapt on Cutter and kissed him hard. He'd kissed her back equally hard.

"I guess this means you won't tell the cops I killed him," he said when they parted for air.

She nodded. "Hell no, man. I'm with you from now on."

He nodded back. She could tell he was pleased.

After Peaches had gotten dressed again, she and Cutter loaded the dead man into the trunk of his car, then they took the car and left town, finally setting fire to it in a field on the way to Naugatuck and setting out on foot. Peaches completely abandoned all thoughts of heading home again. Daddy could wait.

That had been two years ago. They'd been together since then.

***

"I'm a lapsed atheist," Cutter (whose real name was Joel Miller) told Peaches the day after they hooked up.

"What the hell's a lapsed atheist?" Peaches had asked. They'd been sitting up in bed drinking beers in a motel room in Putnam.

Cutter grinned. "A lapsed atheist is kinda like a lapsed Catholic, only way more dangerous. I quit believing in God when I was nineteen; but in my mid-twenties I began thinking again that He really does exist."

Peaches sipped her beer, but she kept looking at him all confused so he explained more: "I stopped believing in God 'cos I had no explanation for the evil in the world. I mean, if God existed, why were human beings running around being so nasty to each other, right? Doing all the wars and violent shit? But then,"—with a broad grin he laid his large hunting knife on the sheets between them, then dropped his voice to a whisper—"but then, I killed a man for the first time; and at that moment, I had my revelation, I mean, *everything* suddenly made fucking sense: God *did* frigging exist. I'd distinctly felt *something* telling me *not* to kill that jerk, but I shrugged it off, said, 'why not?' and stabbed the prick anyway. And I got away with it, too—the cops never had a clue who did it. And it was worth it—killing that man I mean—it made me feel godlike, like I was God myself."

Peaches, whose entire experience of any relationship with God consisted of the "Oh my Gods!" uttered during her orgasms, nodded sagely. She understood little of what Cutter said, figured most of it was bullshit, but he had a strange magnetism that, amongst other things, kept her continually horny. And that (so long as you had someone to help scratch your itch) was a great feeling to have. They'd had sex half the night the night before and it had been good, and better still, Cutter had promised to teach her how to kill people too. And in between bouts of sweating together on the bed sheets, he'd also explained his rationale for serial murder:

"The way I view it," he'd said while stroking his chin, his pale eyes thoughtful, "is that I'm ridding the planet of people who've pissed me off. The world is full of such useless folk, and surely, before irritating me, they must have upset loads of other people, people who'll also be glad to see the back of them. Besides, I plan to get into heaven that way. See, God is certain to approve of anyone who helps Him separate the chaff from the wheat before His day of judgment, or rather, the assholes from nice, harmless folk. Now, telling good from bad people, that's the problem. Most times looks are deceptive."

Peaches spat over the edge of the bed, onto their pile of used condoms. "I don't share your point of view, Cutter. Most people are assholes anyway and deserve killing. And God? God can go screw Himself."

Cutter stared at her all worried. "Hey, careful, babe, He might get pissed off with you!"

Her face turned really angry. "Like I care. I don't give a rat's ass about what He wants, sitting pretty up there on His golden throne. He was watching me all this while, wasn't He?" She winced. Yeah, God had been watching her suck penises down here, till some days she was so full of semen she had no appetite for food, and even if she could find an appetite, her belly was too full of come anyway to have space for the food. As far as Peaches was concerned, God could go to Hell.

She said, "Screw what the Almighty wants, or helping Him out in any way. I'm gonna kill people just 'cos it's fun."

Cutter had laughed. "Oh, I just love you, babe. Yeah, let's just agree to disagree on this subject of religion and just kill a lot of folk. Alright, now that's settled, come over here and let me suck on your sweet tits again . . ."

Peaches ditched the subject. Religion was a waste of time, anyway. Life was full of much more interesting things to do. Like having one's nipples sucked on, and afterwards having one's clitoris sucked on, and then . . .

***

Now again . . .

Peaches led the way into the decapitated couples' kitchen. Their daughter was trussed up like a chicken on the kitchen floor. The girl looked about thirteen: lots of baby fat, plus she was covered in freckles and hardly had any breasts to speak of. Her mouth was duct-taped shut. The kid was sweating bullets. Her black hair was all dirty like someone had been using her as a mop.

Her eyes widened when she saw how bloodstained Peaches and Cutter were.

Peaches knelt beside her. After smoothing down the girl's rucked-up skirt, she said, "Now it's your turn, kid. You're about going to join mama and dada up in Heaven." She mused a moment. "Or maybe down in Hell. It's hard to tell where folk go after death."

Behind her, Cutter laughed. "I know you're impatient to see them again, kid, aren't you?"

The digital clock by the fridge said 10 p.m. Cutter's eyes flickered past it to the kitchen window. Outside, the moon was high, the sky black velvet sprinkled with stars like rhinestones. (It was a cool night, a good night for killing. Killing warmed Cutter's blood, made him feel truly alive.) He grinned. This house was separated from the next by a line of trees; there was no way anyone could see what was going on in here.

The bound girl began squirming furiously and flailing across the kitchen floor. In the process, she stunned herself against the fridge door.

Scratching his head, Cutter peered at Peaches. "She's got a big belly. Why don't you gut her? Spread her intestines all over the kitchen like sausage links? It's been a while since you last cut someone open."

Grinning, Peaches shook her head. She stood up. "Gutting her is too ordinary. I've got something special in mind for her."

Cutter yawned, but his eyes were interested. "Okay, but hurry it up, wilya? I wanna screw you tonight."

Peaches stood on tiptoes to kiss him. "Is sex all you think about, baby?" Then, before he could answer, she added: "Help me get her up and bring her over to the stove. I want to cook her."

Cutter went to pick up the girl. Peaches lit the largest of the stove's gas rings, then turned to face Cutter. "Hurry up, baby. I want to fuck too."

The girl had however heard Peaches' statement about cooking her and was fighting Cutter with every ounce of her strength. Peaches watched the struggle with amusement. Cutter finally tired of the conflict and stabbed the girl in the belly with his knife. She quieted down after that, like the blood dribbling from her wound was her courage flowing away. Tears of pain running down her cheeks, disbelief in her young eyes, she stared dully at her captors.

"What now?" Cutter asked.

Peaches was amused: Cutter had an erection. His penis was pressed hard against the crotch of his jeans like a rat desperate to burst out of captivity.

She pointed at the ring of blue flames on the stove. "Stick her head in the fire, Cutter. I want to see what a roast face looks like."

Gripping her by the neck, Cutter stuck the girl's head into the blue flames and held it there so the fire was cooking her face. Her eyelashes and eyebrows flamed up at once, then her hair caught alight. Her face sizzled.

The kid instantly began thrashing and pissing herself.

"Hold still, you!" Peaches said, taking Cutter's knife from him and stabbing her in the belly again. "And don't you dare kick the bucket till you're well done!"

"Hey, get me a beer from the fridge," Cutter said after a while, as the girl's eyes boiled in their sockets. "This here is damn thirsty work."

CHAPTER 2

Tanya

In the north quarter of Marlborough, Tanya Rockford dropped her bags on her motel bed. The room was small but neat. The most important thing was that there was no sign of roaches. She'd been in motels where the insects seemed landlords in their own right, including one where she'd unwitting ferried a suitcase of bedbugs back home to Boston. In the end she'd had to live at her sister's house for a week while her own house was fumigated.

But—she smiled grimly—this motel room looked okay.

She sat on the edge of the bed and turned on the TV. Same as always: another terrorist bombing in Iraq. Like they were playing musical bombers, or spin-the-bombing-wheel, or some nonsense extremist game like that.

Tanya was tired of the shitheads: If they weren't bombing Israel, or France, or Russia, they were bombing themselves, like they had a bombing quota that had to be met regardless of who the target was.

And then there were the *female* bombers. Tanya found the concept of women committing suicide/murder in the name of religion very hard to get her head around. Okay, it made some kind of sense to her for men to kill people—men liked violence anyway—but women? Double-standards or not (and she was aware she might be putting a sexist slant on her reasoning), the idea of her fellow females throwing their lives away over idealistic bullshit really pissed her off. Damn, didn't those camel-humping idiots realize there was no point doing that kind of crap? And how did they recruit those stupid girls anyway? Place an ad in the local paper that read: '*Attractive, ambitious, anti-semitic airhead wanted to blow herself up. Career prospects grim: retirement effective immediately after first mission. Payment receivable in Heaven.*'?

The newscaster—a good-looking woman in a drab gray hijab—began talking about how the terrorists were pissed off over US support for the new Iraqi government. *Yeah right, like we were responsible for Saddam Hussein too.*

Tanya muted the TV, then tuned it to a Powerpuff Girls cartoon. "Bomb yourselves to hell if you like, you jerks. I got bigger problems of my own."

She kicked off her shoes, massaged her feet awhile, then lay back on the bed, her legs over the edge, and let her mind rove.

***

Boston PD Detective Tanya Rockford was thirty-six. She was an attractive but heavyish brunette, overweight because she was "too busy to diet," as she always joked to colleagues on the force.

She was divorced, her marriage breaking up acrimoniously, with her ex-husband Randy still scared stiff of her. Tanya always laughed when she remembered how, right after she'd thrown him out of their house, Randy Rockford had tried to take out a restraining order on her, but had been too embarrassed to explain in court what she'd done to him to deserve the order, or *why* she'd acted the way she had.

So no order was every issued. Which meant Tanya could drop in on Randy whenever she felt like. And for a while she had, knocking on his front door at the most inopportune hours she could conceive of, and thrice even insisting he make love to her, or else . . .

But the fun in haunting her ex had recently tailed off. Randy had a new love now (a porno-reject-looking redhead Tanya always felt like strangling), and he was planning to marry her. Tanya knew it was time to leave him alone, let bygones be bygones. Cop or not, if she hounded him now, she'd be marked down as a stalker.

***

Tanya Rockford was currently suspended pending investigation for shooting an underage suspect.

"Suspended? Aw, c'mon, Chief," she'd protested. "What was I supposed to do? He was pointing a frigging gun at me!"

"Josh Milton is fourteen. You're lucky he survived. He's gonna have liver problems for a while though."

"His fault, Chief. The little punk shouldn't have been dealing crack . . . and packing a gun for that matter. Or pointing it at cops going about their legal business of arresting his juvenile ass." She'd winced. "C'mon, Chief, you know I didn't know he was a teen. The kid was huge and he was wearing a hoodie, there's utterly no way I could see his face in the shadows. I wasn't even going to try—not with him firing an automatic rifle at me. I just leaned through the door while he switched clips and shot back."

"I know, I know. Look, just lay low till this blows over, okay? Take a vacation. You're a good cop, Tanya, one of our best, so no way are we gonna railroad you off the force. You know City Hall's getting tough on teen killings 'cos of Anderson."

"Anderson's an A-hole, there was no reason for him to shoot that Cusack kid. I mean, the boy was unarmed!"

"You read the report? Anderson was driving past a drugstore when he witnessed a robbery in progress. He dashed in and ordered everyone in the store to freeze. The real criminals did. Sixteen-year-old Rob Cusack, though, was stoned on pot. He reached into his jacket for his wallet; Anderson thought he was going for a gun. And so we got another young stiff in the morgue."

"He probably made that up. Anderson . . ."

"Tanya, Tom Anderson's our cleanest cop, that's the problem. He NEVER—read my lips, girl—NEVER makes things up. Everyone would utterly LOVE to get rid of him, but we can't. Outside of his personality issues, he does his job and does it well. I mean, Internal Affairs has been through his life with all the toothcombs they've got, but zilch. Would you believe Anderson doesn't even download illegal mp3's from the internet? That's how damn clean he is."

"Chief, that doesn't change the fact that he's a meathead."

"Yeah, yeah, Anderson's a meathead—the whole force knows that. But he's got all of us under scrutiny. Hey, I got an idea!"

"Chief, I don't like the way you're grinning at me."

"No, no, I've *really* got an idea. How 'bout you do some work on the Cutter and Peaches case?"

Tanya couldn't say no to that. Hell no, she wasn't saying no to that.

***

Sitting there in her motel room bed, Tanya got out her case files and studied her snaps of Joel Miller, nicknamed 'Cutter' because he liked playing with knives. He was good-looking, she'd give the bastard that. His looks were likely how he'd gotten Peaches to go along with him on his murder spree. That horrible teenaged girlfriend of his— yes, that had to be Stockholm syndrome. There was a picture of the kid in the folder too. The little bitch was the all-American hometown cutie personified, so cute Christian Dior could likely bottle her essence and sell it as perfume.

Only thing was, this cutie pie had gone hard off the tracks with a vengeance.

Cutter was smart; that was the thing. He knew how to live off the grid and avoid tracking. Two full years now the pair of them had been murdering people, and they still hadn't been brought to book. Somehow the police were always too late on the scene. And Cutter and Peaches cleaned up after themselves, leaving little DNA evidence. (This was the only time in her life Tanya wished a psycho would at least occasionally rape his female victims!)

It was almost supernatural, the way Cutter and Peaches kept vanishing only to reappear again to create more mayhem.

Part of the problem was also that the pair had no apparent method to their madness, so the Fed profilers were stumped. Or, like someone had suggested, maybe there was someone sympathetic to them at FBI headquarters who kept fiddling with their forensic test results.

The Chief had some pull with the Feds. He'd done some kind of deal with them on Tanya's behalf, which meant she was now working with the FBI in an official capacity on this. The Chief hadn't specified what that capacity was, he'd just given her the phone number of someone named 'Agent Richards' and told her to call him for updates or if she discovered anything. Or he'd call her if there was something she should know. It was Richards who'd tipped her off that the pair might be in this vicinity. "If you find them, let us know and well surround them with a dragnet."

Yeah, right.

Tanya suspected the Feds really wanted someone who could work outside official channels. And who would shoot Cutter on sight without bothering to read him his rights first. *So my recommendation for this job was shooting a teenaged crack dealer? Well if that's so, they came to the right woman.*

25

Tanya was definitely going to shoot Cutter on sight. His rap sheet was a long as her legs: murder, murder, murder, murder, murder and yet still more murder. Forty-two people dead to date. No way was she bothering with arresting him. For what? So the hardworking American taxpayer got burdened with looking after him in one of the state penitentiaries where the other prisoners worshipped the ground he walked on? Only over her dead body was that happening.

The moment Tanya Rockford got Cutter in her sights, he was one dead sicko. The judge and jury would have to wait for the next serial killer to come along to hold a trial.

And she'd definitely shoot that little monster Peaches too.

SATURDAY

CHAPTER 3

Peaches

Peaches was awakened by a loud insistent buzzing. It took her a while to work out that the front doorbell was ringing.

She sat up in bed and yawned and stretched. *Damn! We've got visitors.*

She was badly hungover. Last night that kid had taken forty minutes to die—even after her eyes had burst and her face flaked off, and her hair was all charred off and her tongue was cooked to ashes, the little bitch had somehow clung tenaciously to life! Peaches had found that annoying. *Friggin' die already, wilya? What the hell are you still hanging around for? Who the hell wants a daughter or a girlfriend without a face?*

Afterwards, Peaches and Cutter had retired upstairs to the master bedroom to coke up and have sex. They'd drunk lots of beer too.

Now her brain throbbed like she had the flu. The doorbell buzzed again. She looked over at Cutter. He was passed out naked, one arm draped over the bed's edge. She shook him, he shrugged her off.

"Cutter, someone's downstairs."

"Get the door yourself."

The bell buzzed again and she heard voices. "Jimmy! Connie! Wake up! Time to go camping! The bears are waiting!"

Aw, shucks, Peaches thought. *How unlucky can one get on a Saturday morning? And Cutter clearly isn't going to be any help here.*

As confirmation, she looked over at him again. Cutter never woke up easy in the mornings anyway. His buttocks were two hairy hillocks sticking out of the bed. The bed itself was dirty with blood; they hadn't bothered to bath before having sex after killing the family. A thin line of spit dribbled from Cutter's mouth onto his pillow. Peaches winced. *Damn, now that's disgusting.*

Peaches realized she had to handle this herself. She got out of bed and quickly split the drapes and peeped downstairs. A bright blue Ford

SUV was now parked out front with a family-sized camping trailer hitched to the back of it. And the voices she was hearing indicated two people out front—a man and a woman. Another happy family impatient to head out for the woodlands.

"Jimmy! Connie! Frigging wake up, wilya!? Hey, Karen, wake up you li'l sleepyhead!"

She shut the drapes again then padded quickly to the bedside table. There she picked up a revolver that had belonged to the dead couple. It was loaded and in good condition. She laughed. *Too bad Jimmy and Connie didn't do a concealed carry with this gun; but then, some people need to die to learn the right way to protect themselves from psychos like us.*

She slipped into a wrap, then checked in a mirror that she didn't have blood on either her face or hair. Then, carrying the gun, she headed downstairs.

"Hey, Jimmy, what the hell did you two barbeque last night?" (The voice was amused now.) "Come on, open up, we know you're home—we can hear your phones ringing. Wow, that must have been quite a bender you guys had last night!"

"I'm coming!" Peaches yelled as her feet left the bottom step and she dashed into the living room.

She made her quick way past the corpses of husband and wife still taped in their chairs, the woman's noseless head lolling back on its spine. And yeah, the visitors outside were right: the roasted daughter did smell like Texan barbeque now. Combined with Peaches' hangover, the smell made her feel like puking.

The doorbell rang again. It felt to Peaches like it was ringing in her head. *Stop pressin' that damn thing already!*

She fumbled the door open, but not fully, so the carnage in the living room was concealed. She also kept her right hand hidden behind the door jamb, revolver in readiness.

"Well, hi there, girl!" a loud voice instantly greeted her.

She stared blearily at the man and woman standing on the front porch. The man was fat, the woman thin. Both were fortyish and wore uncool cotton shirts over shorts. The SUV and trailer behind them blocked off view of the road.

"We're Bob and Mildred Hasselhoff," the man explained. "We're going camping with Jimmy and Connie."

His wife smiled nicely at Peaches. "I don't believe I've ever seen you around here before, darling."

"I'm Jodi, their niece from New York. I'm staying over the weekend with . . ." Peaches realized she didn't know the dead daughter's name. Was *she* the 'Karen' they'd been shouting for earlier? Either way, no problem; all she needed was to get the pair of them inside.

Still holding the door only half open, she smiled. "Please come in. I'm sorry, we had a wild party last night, everyone's still fast asleep."

Bob Hasselhoff laughed heartily. "Yeah, don't *we* just know what that's like."

Still grinning, he stepped forward to enter the house. But his wife's eyes suddenly widened in shock. Peaches first imagined that maybe there was some blood on her hair, but then, with a strangled scream, Mildred Hasselhoff jerked her husband back by his shorts.

She was pointing down behind Peaches' legs. "Bob, Bob! Look! There's a head on the floor!" Her voice was a strangled gasp. "Oh, my God! That's Jimmy's head!"

Fuck! Peaches had forgotten about the man's severed head.

"Oh, my God, she's murdered him, she's murdered him!" Mildred whimpered as her husband bent and looked to confirm her words.

Bob too saw the head; it was lying by a corner of the sofa. He looked up at Peaches in confusion and horror. "Mildred, call 911!"

Peaches shot him. She stuck the revolver in his mouth and pulled the trigger. His brains sprayed out the back of his head and over Mildred, who just stood there transfixed.

One down, one to go, Peaches thought, already feeling the familiar rush of excitement killing always gave her. Her blood was pumping fast and she felt more alive than ever now, her hangover a memory.

Bob's head had muffled the sound of the shot somewhat. (The neighbors, most of whom were sleeping off Friday night benders of their own, later told the police that it had sounded like a distant car backfiring.) After wobbling a bit, Bob slumped forward towards Peaches. As he crumbled to the ground, Peaches had a moment of cold eye contact with Mildred over his body, before with a loud shriek, the new widow, her husband's gore all over her face, turned and dashed off down the porch steps and down the drive, streaking past their parked SUV and trailer.

Peaches kept her cool. She drew a bead on Mildred's bobbing head and pulled the trigger.

This time the 'Bang!' of the gunshot was like a peal of Saturday morning thunder. Mildred had been just about to turn the corner of the trailer and escape into the street. Now the bullet lifted her off her feet and flung her forward into the rose hedge. She hung there a moment, then crumpled to the grass.

Peaches walked down the drive and poked Mildred with a toe to make sure she was dead. Her prodding brought no reaction; Mildred lay still with blood leaking from her face.

Peaches felt relieved. *But, boy, was that loud!*

Across the street a window opened and a face peered out in her direction. The woman made a questioning gesture to Peaches. Pistol hid behind her, she waved back that everything was fine, then turned and walked calmly back into the house. She was aware of someone else also opening their window, and of two male voices conversing. She thought someone might have mentioned 911.

Damn! she thought. *There goes our peaceful weekend!*

She slammed the front door behind her, relieved that the camping trailer blocked off view of Bob's corpse from the road—the dead son-of-a-bitch was too fat for her to consider dragging him inside, and he'd be all dead weight—then she dashed up the stairs to rouse Cutter. It was only a matter of minutes before the cops came calling.

"Hey, Cutter, wake the hell up! We've got trouble! We need to be gone from here already!"

CHAPTER 4

Tanya

Tanya Rockford drove out of Marlborough with a haze of disbelief swirling like fog in her brain.

No, NO, NO!!!! What she'd just seen . . . !

Agent Richards had called just as she gotten out of the shower. Her blood had run cold as he'd told her about the murdered Hamilton family. She'd dressed double-fast, leapt into her battered brown Honda Accord and driven over there. Thank God for GPS.

And what she'd seen inside the house! The sight of roasted little Karen Hamilton, her eleven-year-old head a black lump of charcoal, had almost made Tanya wet herself with rage.

White-faced, she'd gotten details of the incident from the similarly-shocked officers at the scene—two gunshots heard, then a woman in the opposite house noticing an unfamiliar blonde girl in a bathrobe in the yard beside a camping trailer. Then, five minutes later, the same girl, now dressed in jeans and a halter exiting the house in company of a tall slim man. The pair had backed the trailer out of the yard and driven off at speed. The next passer by the house had seen Bob Hasselhoff's corpse lying on the front porch and called 911.

The local cops had no definite ID on the suspects yet, but Tanya already knew Cutter and Peaches were responsible for this latest outrage. But where were they? There was an APB out for the pair. The officers at the crime scene said the SUV and trailer had headed up north along Hosmer Street, and there were two state police Air Wing choppers out looking for it. State police STOP teams were also combing the area. They figured the killers would lay low till nightfall before trying to escape the town.

Tanya had thanked them and left. It would be pointless to tell the searchers that they were wasting their time; the pair were likely miles from Marlborough by now.

Tanya had her own theory about how Cutter and Peaches would have left town, and so she was currently headed west along Route 20 towards Worchester and Auburn. On this beautiful June morning her mood was completely ugly.

Soon the road filtered amongst trees; birches and white pine. Only one vehicle had passed her in the past five minutes, so she figured she was on the right track. *Oh, God, please let me catch those two shitheads. Oh, God, please let me find the pair and dispatch them both down to Hell where they belong.* Hardened as Tanya was, such evil stumped her: *How can anyone stick a kid's head in a gas fire and hold her there until . . . ?*

Her phone, which was lying on the passenger seat, rang. She picked it up; it was the Chief. Slowing the car, she accepted the call.

"Chief, I was gonna call you later. I've got bad news—"

"Save it. I've got worse news. The kid died."

"Huh?" For a moment the meaning of the words didn't register, then they sank in and she sputtered: "Died? How?"

"Yeah, Josh Milton died last night. How? No one knows. The doctors say maybe his wounds reopened, or a tube jerked loose, or whatever . . . Hey, you still there?"

"Yeah," Tanya nodded listlessly at the phone, the road ahead suddenly wavering before her eyes, "I'm still here."

"Okay, okay. I called to tell you not to come back to Boston for at least the next two weeks. Stay well out of town. There's gonna be a major stink over this."

"But it was *self-defense!*"

"Everyone and their one-eyed dog knows that." The Chief sounded both pissed off and sympathetic at the same time. "But the kid's got an older sister—a cousin really—who's dating City Councilor Simpson."

"Ronnie Simpson? Loudmouth Simpson?"

"Yeah, the same. And I've heard he's gonna make his election pitch for city mayor out of this, with you as the scapegoat. So just stay away. Oh, and keep a damn low profile as well. If the press can't find you, they can't hound you."

"Shit. Okay, Chief, will do. Thanks for the heads up."

"Okay, so, you were gonna tell me some bad news of your own. What was it?"

"Cutter and Peaches massacred five people overnight."

There was a long silence on the other side, during which Tanya sidled her car into a roadside shoulder and parked. A long anguished sigh trickled down the line. Then finally, the Chief said, "This has gotten way out of hand. Those two have the luck of the Devil. I mean, they're on America's Most Wanted and yet no one ever seems to recognize them? . . . How'd you figure that happens?"

"I'm on their tail at the moment, Chief. I'm playing a hunch of which route they took out of Marlborough. By my reckoning, they're headed west to New York."

"You got backup with you?"

"Er . . . no . . . Seeing as I'm working outside official channels, I thought . . ."

"Hey, now look here—don't you dare go pulling any Lone Ranger stunts, okay? Those two you're tailing are certified loons. They'll make salami out of you given half a chance. When this Josh Milton stink-cloud blows over I need you back here working for Boston, and in one piece at that."

"Sorry, Chief—"

"Oops, I gotta go; Perkins is signaling to me from the door. Seems like the good press are already here to begin assassinating your character."

"Okay, Chief . . . and thanks."

"Just one last thing." The voice on the phone dropped to a conspiratorial whisper. "You know, if you *were* to nail Cutter and the teen from hell, Simpson wouldn't have a leg to stand on. You'll automatically become everyone's darling again. So good luck, but watch your back."

The Chief hung up.

Tanya dropped the phone in her lap, then she laid her head on the wheel and cried bitterly.

She wept long and she wept hard.

Dead? That damn kid—Josh Milton couldn't just up and die like that! She'd seen his hospital pictures. Sure he was all bandaged up and piped-through in ICU, but he'd been grinning and giving his friends and supporters a defiant thumbs up. Getting shot by the cops like that had simply upped his gangsta cred. He was the man now, had the juice. And now he was suddenly dead? How was that possible?

She couldn't stop her tears flowing. To Tanya Rockford, there was a massive difference between 'life' and 'death.' While Josh Milton had been alive, she could make jokes about him being a 'no-good teen punk' or 'dope-dealing juvenile shithead' who'd deserved what he'd got. Now he was dead, however, all she felt was sadness and anger. And a whole lot of regret. The kid's death was so damned unnecessary.

She wasn't primarily concerned about Simpson's trying to use her gaffe as his stepping stone to the Mayor's office. No, she was pissed off at herself for shooting the kid (though what else do you do when someone's firing an AK-47 at you during a crack bust?), at his dumb parents for not bringing him up right (his mom was a hooker, his dad gone AWOL since the boy was four), and at society in general—social services, the school system—for closing their eyes to the kid's moral decay till it got to the level where he'd become a threat to public safety.

She sat there, her hands tight on the wheel, weeping her heart out.

She finally got over her tears. Her eyes were red from crying so much, her sparse makeup ruined. She felt completely miserable.

The boy's death was so damned needless. It wasn't meant to be like this: kids were supposed to grow up like flowers, go to school, get a life, get married, make the next generation of kids to repeat the process . . .

By stages, her emotions grew less morbid. She wiped her eyes, then stared coldly at the road ahead like it was the rest of her life. *Okay, I need to put this crap behind me. Whipping my ass to shreds won't bring Josh back to life. I need to focus on catching Cutter and Peaches.*

She put her car in motion, pulled off the shoulder, drove on between the fields and trees. As the miles ticked over, her horror at the kid's death became a grim determination to get this job done. She was taking those two down. A cold smile flickered over her lips. Like the Chief had said, success at this would silence Simpson and the press for good. She'd be able to go about her life again without enduring taunts of 'child killer' like she'd just returned from Vietnam.

That statement of the Chief's rang in her mind: "Those two have the luck of the Devil." *The luck of the Devil.* Yeah, for sure, her two targets did seem to have El Diablo watching over them.

But even the Devil's luck had to run out at some point. And she intended on being there when it did.

CHAPTER 5

Peaches

"Oh, yeah!" Cutter thrilled behind the wheel. "We lost 'em."

Beside him, Peaches grinned and leaned back in her seat. The memory of the morning's kills was like fresh dew settling on her teenaged mind.

"I told you we'd give the fuzz the slip. Those fools got nothing on me."

She laughed and patted Cutter's hand as he switched gears. "You're the man, baby."

He palmed the horn in a celebratory blast of noise. "You're damn right I'm the motherfucking man."

"You're *my* man."

He looked sideways at her. "Damn right I'm that too."

Peaches laughed. Cutter returned his attention to the road.

It was 10 a.m. The fugitive pair were in a stolen black Mazda heading west towards Sturbridge.

Peaches felt really good. It had felt great killing that couple—Bob and Mildred was it? (their names were actually irrelevant to her)—like she'd somehow leeched their vitality into herself. Even now, she could still see the shock that had flickered in Bob's eyes just after she'd shoved her revolver into his yap, that understanding that he'd just cashed his last reality check. Then, there was her memory of the bullet flinging Mildred (yeah, that was the skinny old bitch's name!) against the rose hedge, like trash going into a dumpster, or a train running full steam into Hell. No shit. And best of all? There was the memory of that kid when they'd finally pulled her off the gas range . . . Hell yeah! That one would last Peaches quite a while for thrills.

She tingled nicely all over. It wasn't anything sexual, just an 'up' feeling. She wasn't at all scared, just high, high, high, the rush of everything they'd done wiring her up like she'd just snorted the best cocaine ever made in Colombia. *Yeah, there's no way the dumb pigs will ever catch up to us; we really do have the luck of the Devil.* She gazed adoringly over at her gangly boyfriend, his eyes coldly focused on the road ahead as they cruised into Sturbridge. *Or maybe*—it was a thrilling thought—*maybe Cutter is the Devil in person.* She slapped her thighs in mirth. *Now there's a thought! I'm dating Satan!*

Cutter heard the slaps and glanced quickly sideways. "Now don't freak out, baby, okay? Don't shoot till the last minute. I'll give the signal. Just be prepared."

"Huh?" They'd just stopped at a red light. She thought he was worried about her losing it, then realized he meant the police squad car just turning in their direction from the side street on their left. She tensed slightly, tightening her grip on the gun in her lap.

The two cops drove past them without a glance, their attention on an old woman on the sidewalk who was having trouble controlling her Rottweiler. The dog was pissed off at a hissing cat on a fence and was dragging its owner along with it in its attempt to reach and murder the feline. In the rearview, Peaches watched the policemen park by woman and dog and get down. Then the traffic light turned green, the road curved, and the quartet were cut off from view.

She flicked on the radio, got Cool Country 940 out of Webster. Dolly Parton was singing, about some travelling salesman who'd swindled her out of her heart. Peaches utterly adored Dolly Parton. Well, she adored Dolly Parton's chest. And damn, those knockers were completely natural, right? Or, at least she thought they were, or they used to be back in the 70's, or . . . She frowned a minute. *Now if I had breasts like those* . . . She rolled the delicious thought over in her brain. Two career choices instantly leapt to mind: Porno actress or . . . a grin spread over her face . . . Country and Western singer! *I'd sweep the Grammys!*

She began singing along with the tune. She sang flat, making Cutter smirk in amusement.

The song ended. The lady DJ said, "We'd like to bring you this important news announcement: The Marlborough Police Department are looking for two suspects possibly connected with a multiple homicide. The pair, a dark-haired man and a young blonde woman, are believed to be driving a blue Ford SUV hitched to a camping trailer and heading north towards New Hampshire. If spotted, call 911, and don't try to engage them yourselves. Both are believed to be armed and extremely dangerous. I repeat . . ."

Cutter turned and gave Peaches his 'I told you so' smirk.

The news flash ended. Billy Ray Cyrus began crooning *Storm in the Heartland*. Lots of good tunes on today; yeah, this DJ sure could pick a playlist. What was her name again? Peaches relaxed, reliving their grand escape. *Yeah, Cutter's a damn genius for sure.*

Like the DJ had just read out, they *had* set out for the north of the town, only, about halfway up Hosmer Street, they'd come upon a used car dealership. It being Saturday, the business wasn't open yet. Cutter had driven into the car lot and parked the trailer amongst the vehicles for sale there. A quick search through the trailer turned up a spare can of gas. They'd picked out their current black Mazda from amongst the cars on display, transferred its price tag to the Ford they were dumping, fuelled it up, hot-wired it, and driven off.

As they were about exiting the lot, three police squad cars zoomed past them, sirens blaring, heading downtown.

"They're looking for us," Peaches had squeaked nervously, then a moment later, when Cutter had entered the road and turned their car to follow the police vehicles, she'd whispered in horror, "What the hell are you doing!? We should be going the other way."

Cutter had just grinned. "Trust me, baby." He'd followed the cops at a reasonable speed while explaining to her: "These are the first respondents to the call; they're not after us yet. They can't be; they're not even sure exactly what's happened."

The squad cars turned off at Applewood. They drove past them and turned right onto Route 20, with Cutter laughing, "Goodbye, pigs, enjoy rooting through our shit."

Okay, Peaches admitted to herself, *I was frigging scared then. But that's Cutter's genius, ain't it? There's utterly no way the police are gonna expect the criminals to be riding right behind them, right? It's supposed to be the other way around, them behind us? And now, they'll be looking for that SUV and trailer which was heading north, while we're off in a different direction. Yeah, Cutter's damn smart.*

The country music show ended. She surfed the other stations, didn't hear anything else she liked, turned the radio off.

"We'll have to ditch this car soon," Cutter said.

She made a face. "We're outa gas?"

"No, no. But they'll soon be looking for this car."

Peaches nodded. She looked around. While she'd been reliving their escape they'd blown through Sturbridge. A road sign announced that they were heading for Brimfield.

The town arrived as groups of houses and shops with lots of grass and greenery in between. Dogs and cats, kids frolicking on lawns, people going shopping. There were flowers and butterflies on the hedges, and birds and squirrels in the trees.

Peaches understood that to these people, this was just a regular happy day.

She kept quiet as Cutter slowed a bit and they rolled through Brimfield too. Next town (by the signs) was Palmer.

Several cars passed them, including two police vehicles. As before, no one paid them the slightest attention. Peaches, realizing the Marlborough cops had taken the bait and were looking north, almost missed the thrill of the chase. She raised her revolver to her lips, kissed its thick silver barrel. *C'mon, you city slackers, where the hell are you lot? Bonnie and fuckin' Clyde need your attention right-fuckin'-now.*

Once out in the countryside again (now there were trees literally everywhere on both sides of them like they were sailing a green ocean) Peaches said, "If we're ditching the car, we can't just leave it out in the open: that'll be a dead giveaway to our location." She mused a bit. "A place like this though, with all these trees, would be great to lose a vehicle. No one might find it for months."

Cutter nodded, clearly pleased with her analysis. "Good point, baby. Keep your eyes peeled for a side road. Then we'll walk to Palmer, steal another ride and fade from sight. I'm not sure which way to head from there, but—"

"Here!" Peaches interrupted suddenly.

They'd already shot past the turnoff. Cutter reversed.

The road Peaches had noticed was on their side, a north turning onto a single asphalt track. It was easy to see why Cutter hadn't noticed it: the turnoff was concealed by heavy overhanging foliage, shrouded by the overlapping limbs of trees.

"So here we go," he said, swinging the car onto the side road. "Let's see where this one leads."

***

At first the side road didn't seem to lead anywhere.

Driving real slow now, Cutter looked for a place where the trees thinned enough to steer the Mazda off the road and dump it, and where there was also sufficient tree cover to ensure the vehicle wouldn't be spotted from the air. But for almost half a mile nowhere suitable turned up.

"Just keep going," Peaches said suddenly. "I've got a real good feeling about this."

Cutter raised an eyebrow.

"It's a private road," she continued. "Has to be. Most likely belongs to some weirdo who hates visitors. See how it's only one lane and no one's come in the opposite direction at all since we've been on it? The house itself can't be too far away now."

"Yeah," Cutter agreed, scratching his chin. "Let's go have a look at it. Maybe we won't need to leave the area just yet." Then he smiled. "And finally, here's somewhere to leave our incriminating transport."

He steered the Mazda off the road and wound it between trees for about fifty yards. Then he and Peaches got out and did their best to bury the car beneath a covering of fallen branches.

"That'll have to do," Cutter said finally, wiping sweat from his brow. "I'm bushed."

"Me too," Peaches said. "That damn house had better be close by, or I'm gonna kill someone soon."

Cutter laughed. "You're a sociopath, baby; you're gonna kill someone soon anyway. Don't claim an excuse."

Laughing, arm in arm, they made their way back to the road. And then, keeping inside the line of trees just in case someone drove past, they traced the remainder of the road's length inward.

***

The mansion at the end of the road was big and imposing. A three-story house surrounded by a stone wall. They pushed the gate open and entered. The mansion was a monument of stone and glass. Its grounds were wide and well-tended. A few trees dotted the yard.

To the left of the house stood a detached garage with three cars in it: a blood-red BMW, a cream Cadillac, and a green vintage Bentley. There were also two Harley Davidson motorbikes in there.

Overall though, the mansion gave off a vibe of being unused.

Cutter winked at Peaches. "You're right, baby: I don't think anyone ever visits this place."

"We get rid of whoever's here now, and the cops won't ever find us."

"Never? Well, at least not before we're ready to give them the slip again."

Guns drawn, they gained entrance to the building via an unlatched side door, then padded along a short corridor.

The corridor ended in a large central hall that linked to a foyer in front. Side doors led off to a library, two sitting rooms, an ultra-modern kitchen, and a dining room. Directly opposite the corridor they'd entered by stood a short stairwell to the next floor.

Cutter nodded upstairs. "There's definitely someone home. Let's tell them we're visiting for a bit."

Peaches tugged him back as he made for the stairs. "No, baby."

He turned to stare at her. "What is it?"

"I think we oughta leave this house right now, Cutter."

"Huh? C'mon, quit fooling around. This place is per—"

"You're not paying attention," she whispered harshly. "Whoever owns this place is some kind of witch or wizard. Look at the idols everywhere!"

She was shivering. She couldn't help it. Immediately they'd stepped into this central hall, her eyes had latched onto the carvings and paintings everywhere in it. She'd never seen occult art in this sort of quantity before. They half-filled the hall like they'd been dumped then forgotten. There were carved tribal fetishes and masks, Indian totem poles, obelisks, and horrific sculptures. Paintings depicting demons, ritual murders, and occult rites hung everywhere. Stacks of musty-smelling old books overflowed from the adjoining library. A ceiling-high statue of a pig-headed oriental god stood in a corner. Also, unopened packages (or partly-ripped-open, as if just to confirm their contents) stood about, bearing post office stickers from places like Bombay, Lichtenstein, Ibadan, Sofia, and Istanbul.

Cutter laughed. "C'mon, don't tell me you're suddenly scared of some wacko's horror museum—"

Peaches cursed male insensitivity. Why the hell couldn't he see or feel what she did? The real problem here wasn't so much the objects themselves, as the horrible radiation she felt coming from them. And the artwork itself was horrendously macabre. Opposite her hung a painting of a woman nailed to a cross, only her throat had been slashed and a black snake was forcing its way out of her right nipple. *The first torment of St. Agnes the Insane (Agnes Insanus)* read the inscription. Just seeing that picture made Peaches feel like crapping her pants. It was the house, she knew—its bad 'charge' was so obvious once you were attuned to it—and . . . and Cutter . . . Cutter, her stupid boyfriend, was looking *amused*. Shit! Men!

Cutter tramped over to a life-sized statue of a werewolf with bared fangs, its body bent in a crouch as if to spring at someone.

Mimicking the monster's pose, he said, "Don't tell me you're expecting this, or them . . ." he gestured to two similarly life-sized statues of vampires, "to come to life and rip into us. Are you?"

"Don't joke about it, Cutter," she whispered back. "Let's just leave this damn place." She didn't get how he didn't sense what she did. Now she was attuned into it, the evil permeating this building was as obvious as if it was painted on the walls in blood.

Cutter mused over her request for a moment, then shook his head. "No. We're staying." He stepped away from the werewolf and stroked the *Agnes Insanus* painting, then crossed back to her side. "Okay," he said amiably. "So this place spooks you out. So you don't like horror movies. I do; the scarier the better—"

"It's not that, Cutter. I just don't—"

"Don't interrupt me, Peaches. I ain't through talking! I was saying—"

She sighed. She recognized the look in his eyes. It meant he was set on staying here, whether she liked it or not. Whether it would get them killed or not. (One thing that had kept Peaches with Cutter was how good he was at taking decisions. He never dillydallied when there was something to be done. Okay that was usually great, only not right now.)

"Look, you dickhead," she interrupted him nonetheless, staring him down. (She wasn't scared of him getting violent with her; she knew he'd never hit her, no matter how worked up he got.) "This house is a *bad* place. A *very* bad place. I can't put my finger on it, other than to say it's corrupted in some way. Whatever the case, something is *very* wrong with this fucking building. I can sense it in my bones. And if that *something* comes after us, we're not getting out of here alive."

She saw she'd almost gotten through to him. For a moment, he looked like he might give in to her plea that they leave. But then, the old 'fuck-fear' Cutter reasserted itself, and her hopes were dashed.

He waved his pistol in her face. "Fuck demons. I believe in the Father, the Gun, and the Holy Ghost, baby!"

"Don't blaspheme!" Okay, so she didn't actually like God, but in here she definitely wanted Him on their side, or if that was too much to hope for, at least not actively working against them. Still Cutter's utter insensitivity to the bad vibes around them appalled her. *Dammit, man, you really don't get how bad this place is, do you?*

Cutter smirked and put his gun away. Seeing how amused he was, she tried to rationalize her fears. *Look, there's really nothing to worry about! This is all in your head! Cutter's right . . . !* But then her gaze fell on a carving, this one of a huge rat humping a severed female head in the ear, and she almost turned and ran.

She tried one more time to get them to leave, staring teary-eyed at her boyfriend. "Cutter, please?"

"No, and that's *final*, baby." He walked over, grabbed her by the arm and forced her across the hall, then shoved up the stairs ahead of him. "Get your tight ass upstairs already, honey. We've got us some killing to do. This creepy house of yours wants blood, we'll feed it some."

***

Upstairs was less cluttered than downstairs. The stairs ended in a similar hall, but this one had more free space, its many morbid artworks either properly affixed to the walls or arranged on pedestals. A life-sized sculpture of a demon in flight hung from the ceiling at one end of the hall. Close by the right wall was a reading desk with several opened tomes on it. In the corner beyond the desk sat another oriental god-statue, this one golden and with two leering male heads and six arms.

Peaches already felt a lessening of the smothering psychic pressure from the lower floor. She was about sighing in relief when her eyes fell on one of the life-sized statues in the center of the hall.

She instantly felt cold again. She pointed the statue out to Cutter. "What the hell is that thing?"

He looked at it. It clearly freaked him out too. Then he shook his unease off and growled. "Look, keep your mind on what we're here to do, okay?"

Peaches kept her mind on the sculpture. It was of a tall and thin man in a threadbare brown suit. His skin was stark white, his hair black and cropped very short. He had a long pelican-bill of a nose. He was depicted scowling, his thin lips curled down unpleasantly. His fingers were exceptionally long and thin. In one hand, the spindly man carried a book; in the other, a long cane.

So far, except for his extra-large nose, he looked normal. But his eyes?

At this point the sculpture's realism scared her. The man's eyes were black pits in his face, almost indistinguishable from their sockets, like they'd once been full of black liquid that had leaked and become the shadows that now hemmed them in. Immobile and clearly inanimate as he was, Peaches had the impression that the man's non-eyes were searching her soul for a list of crimes to punish her for. The cane he held prodded her mind to that conclusion. She figured he had to be some kind of literary demon.

A sudden impression of implacable, unquenchable evil poured at her from the statue, making her shudder.

Then, feeling stupid, she tore her gaze from the abominable statue. *Get a fucking grip on yourself, girl, okay? You killed three people last night, two more this morning! You're a she-wolf, not some scaredy-cat!* She looked down at her revolver, forgotten since seeing the house's horrors, then fingered the knife stuck in her belt. *Cutter's right: Violence is our religion— Almighty God is a smoking gun.* She looked one last time at the demonic statue and stuck out her tongue at it. *Screw you, okay? You don't frighten me!*

Her gaze roved behind the sculpture to an oddity: a manikin onto the head of which someone had stuck a computer printout of a beautiful Asian woman's face—yes, with those slanted almond eyes she was either Chinese or Japanese. The oddity didn't end there. Someone had also stuck two large needles in the manikin: one through its arm, one deep into its belly. Peaches felt an instant return of her earlier unease. This was clearly some kind of sick magic ritual. She didn't like this; they really should leave, get their asses out of this joint now. But of course, Cutter would never agree. And so now—

Then she almost leapt out of her pants when Cutter shook her. "Hey! Take it easy, man!"

He clamped a meaty hand over her lips. "Shush! We're not alone up here! We've found the landlords. Listen!"

Calming down from being about to savage his hand with her teeth, she listened. Her ears pricked up. She nodded up at him. He took his hand off her mouth.

"Yeah," Cutter said to the background sounds of passionate female moaning. "There's some serious sex happening in one of these rooms. We just need to work out which one."

CHAPTER 6

Miranda / Sandy

Miranda Salcedo licked the bared vagina facing her. Her girlfriend Sandy squealed at the intimate contact and spread her thighs wider apart. Glazed with saliva and secretion, the salty female hole throbbed around Miranda's mouth. Miranda licked the open sex again; a slow slurp up the slit from hole to bud, another slurp back down. She worked her index and middle fingers into the vagina and slid them back and forth.

It was just approaching noon. The sun beamed in nice and warm on them.

Sandy squirmed over the blue bed sheets, seeming no longer in control of her body. Miranda swirled her tongue over the woman's swollen and glistening clitoris, while increasing the speed of her fingers in her vagina.

"Oh, yes! God, yes!" Sandy moaned in rapture.

Miranda moved her fingers some more in the wet hole, now twisting and turning them with each penetration. She licked down over the purple urethra, pausing there for a few seconds to tease it with her tongue, then removed her fingers from the vagina and sucked deeply on its folds of skin. Her fingers now rubbing Sandy's clitoris, she stuck her tongue deep inside the tangy female hole. Sandy kept moving in place on the bed, her body and legs twisting side to side in delicious pain.

Finally, Miranda straightened up onto her knees. She greased up her blue strap-on dildo with KY, sank it to the hilt in Sandy's sex, and began thrusting.

She grinned as her lover squirmed in pleasure under her. She was in a great mood this morning. All her plans were coming together at just the right time.

***

Miranda Salcedo had finally found the right kind of magic with which to dispose of her boss's fiancée Louise Chung: Voodoo.

Sandy had bought the old theatrical puppet in a Boston Chinatown store. For a face, Miranda had printed out a blown-up copy of Louise's Facebook profile picture and stuck it over the manikin's painted face.

That was that then. Last night, after a few spells linking doll and target, Miranda had made her first test: she'd stuck a knitting needle through the manikin's left arm above the elbow. An hour later, she'd telephoned Ellis Drake in Hong Kong on some pretext.

Ellis had been distraught and flustered. Louise, he explained, had suddenly developed an agonizing pain in her left arm and was practically screaming the house down. He'd been about rushing her to hospital when Miranda called; it didn't matter what it was that Miranda was calling him about, it would have to wait till tomorrow.

After offering her sympathies over Louise's condition, Miranda had hung up, after which she'd immediately picked up a second knitting needle.

"What are you going to do with that?" Sandy had asked nervously.

"I doubt Miss Chung ever had period pain this bad before," Miranda replied, then stuck the needle into the doll's belly just above the crotch. She'd winked at Sandy. "She was crawling up the walls, was she? Now she'll literally be shitting herself with agony."

Sandy winced. "Do you really need to go to this length to get rid of her?"

"She's not about leaving Ellis on her own accord, is she?" She scowled at her girlfriend. "Don't you dare go soft on me now. We're in this together."

Sandy nodded nervously. A pretty plump brunette, she felt like she'd stepped in shallow water that had abruptly risen well over her head and was now about drowning her. Okay, yes, this house did have a creepy vibe to it, but, Miranda . . . her girlfriend was serious about killing this Hong Kong heiress chick.

"Look," Miranda continued in a cold voice, "I've explained to you how it is: I've invested too much of my life in Ellis Drake to watch him go off and get married now. That'll mean the end of my employment here."

"You've already got enough money," Sandy objected. "*We* should go off and get married; forget Ellis and Louise."

"We will get married. But I intend to keep working here."

"Hell no! No way am I marrying you if you're still sleeping with him! Count me out of that. I'm a one-woman woman."

"Shut up, Sandy. I'm doing this for both of us, okay? I emptied Ellis's balls in the past. He always appreciated it. I'll just take over doing it again. *He's not* getting married." She ran a finger down Sandy's neck into her cleavage. "Speaking of testicles: did I ever tell you that Ellis's will soon be as big as your tits?" She laughed at Sandy's surprise. "Oh, they will, in just a few years; and then they'll need draining regularly."

Sandy gaped at her. "Mira, you didn't—"

"Of course I didn't, darling. He was trying to double the size of his dick." She shrugged. "I really don't know what for—he's a good six inches long already." She winked. "And clearly, Louise Chung ain't complaining . . . and speaking of Louise . . ." Miranda picked up a large ball-peen hammer and weighed it in her palm while staring at the manikin with the Chinese woman's picture stuck on its head.

Sandy shuddered at the cold look on Miranda's face. She'd seldom seen her girlfriend this ruthlessly determined. Suddenly this handsome middle-aged woman beside her seemed someone she didn't know. And now, a horrible worry bloomed in her mind: *Is this what she'll do to me if I ever leave her?*

"What are you going to do with the hammer?" she asked.

Miranda regarded the photo-faced doll for a moment, then giggled. "Why, bash her head in completely, of course, starting with her pretty face." Her giggles became full-blown laugher. "It'll be like a ketchup bottle exploding—bits of Louise's brain spraying everywhere. Too bad I won't be there to see it."

"Now?"

"No, tomorrow. When she's back from the hospital. Let the bitch suffer a lot first."

She dropped the hammer and pulled Sandy to her. She kissed her hard, dropping her hands to squeeze Sandy's big buttocks. "Right now I want some of you. It's been a whole week, darling."

Her gaze flickering over Miranda's shoulder to the voodoo manikin, Sandy allowed herself to be dragged off to the bedroom.

***

Sandy started coming. Loud, orgasmic moans wracked her body. Her large breasts wobbled. She reached up and grasped and squeezed Miranda's smaller ones, clamping fingers tight on the swollen nipples like she'd rip them off Miranda's thin frame. Thrilling at her girlfriend's grunts of delight at the sweet pain, she squeezed harder. Then she let go of Miranda's nipples—the pleasure in her sex made it impossible to hold on to them. She shuddered through her climax. The dildo entering and exiting her body felt like a Greyhound bus transporting her along a freeway of pleasure.

Above her, Miranda's lust-filled eyes stared wide as she thrust hard. "Take that, girl! And that! And this!" Rearing back like boxer about to fling a knockout punch, she slammed the plastic penis into Sandy's sex, jerked it out again, slammed it home even harder. The thrusts jerked Sandy back and forth across the sweat-soaked bed. (Miranda's own body felt like it was on fire, her vagina was a boiling vacuum that itself needed filling. But she'd get hers later. *For the moment, I'm giving Sandy the cock. And, boy, am I giving it to her!*) The sun shone brightly in on their lovemaking. She leaned forward till their noses touched, planted a sloppy kiss on Sandy's spread lips, reared back again, then rammed the blue phallus in deep. "Take this, you horny slut!"

Sandy took it, and took it, feeling her vagina crammed to bursting point. Oh, the feeling was so damn good! Her dam broke—she began coming again. Oh shit! Shit! How great this felt . . . *Oh, God! When Miranda does me like this, I can forgive her just about anything under the sun; even killing that—*

And then everything went wrong. Her eyes staring wide with passion, she suddenly saw an additional shadow fall over her. Then, a hand wrapped itself around Miranda's neck and yanked her up off the bed.

While Sandy was still wondering what was going on, the man who'd pulled Miranda off the bed put a knife to her throat and slit it. Then he flung Miranda's body back down. Miranda instantly got up again and with horrified eyes, began staggering about the room, trying to stop the blood jetting from her neck. She tried to speak, but her voice box had been sliced in two.

Laughing, the man watched her lurch about.

Sandy saw that the man wasn't alone. He had a girl with him, a teenager with crazy eyes. The girl was staring at Sandy and licking her lips.

"This one's mine, Cutter," the girl said. "I'm gonna strangle her with her own guts."

The man gave her a thumbs-up. "Fuck the bitch up, baby. Great rack on her tho'."

Brandishing a knife, the girl leapt onto the bed.

Screaming, Sandy leapt off the bed and dashed past Miranda who'd now collapsed again to a sitting position on the edge of the bed, facing the door. Miranda, her life already fading out of her eyes, reached after Sandy with numb fingers.

Almost out of the bedroom door, Sandy slipped on Miranda's blood and sprawled flat out into the hall. Before she could get up again, the girl was on her back. She tried to rise, but the girl stunned her with a hard blow to the head, so she just lay there, unable to stop what was coming.

"Nah," the teen girl said. "I ain't gutting this one. I'll have me a stab-a-thon instead." And on that note, she began stabbing Sandy deep: in the back, in the neck, in the side, in the buttocks, in the head; and when Sandy finally screamed out, leaning forward and slitting her throat, so the blood jetted sideways.

The blood spewed and spewed out of Sandy, who died making eye contact with Miranda, who, propped up against the foot of the bed, her eyes staring at nothing in this world, somehow still seemed alive.

Or, if she was dead, her corpse's lips were still moving.

***

Miranda Salcedo died with a curse on her lips. The curse was the spell that had come in the package containing the weird male figure Peaches had earlier noticed out in the hall. The *Demon Schoolmaster*, the statue was called.

Miranda had never before dared used this spell. It was both dangerous and required lots of fresh human blood. (And where was she to get that without breaking the law?) Seeing the red wetness—her life!—now splattering her bedroom floor, she saw great irony in her situation—fresh blood was the one thing she currently possessed in excessive supply. Even more of the crimson stuff was squirting everywhere from Sandy's body as that evil teen murdered her.

The girl was stabbing Sandy like a demoness, like she was possessed by the spirit of Lizzie Bowen. Sandy just lay there, bleeding, all the while looking at Miranda in confusion. Miranda wasn't even sure Sandy could see her anymore; her feeble jerking with each stab was the only evidence that she was still alive.

And then the kid went too far. Applauded by her lanky boyfriend, who was leaning against the doorway and rhythmically squeezing his hard-on, the murderous girl suddenly yanked both of the knitting needles Miranda had stuck into the Louise Chung manikin out of it.

No!—leave them in there! Miranda's mind shrilled as the needles came free, to be next hammered into Sandy's head with the ball-peen hammer.

The dual head-piercing was 'it' for Sandy.

Miranda was incensed. *This stupid little bitch has just relieved Louise of her period pains!?*

Witches never die easy, though. Miranda's hatred of the pair who'd just killed her (and her desire for revenge on them) had helped her cling to life even after she'd stopped breathing. Now, her lips moving soundlessly, she spat out the words of the animation spell.

In satisfaction, she watched her blood and Sandy's begin rippling across the hall floor towards the *Demon Schoolmaster* statue, then she toppled over sideways, dead.

CHAPTER 7

Peaches

Peaches sat on the dead woman's back, both hands clutching the steel needles stuck through her head. Bathed in brunette blood, she felt wonderful. Her vagina tingled. *Okay, I gotta get laid already.*

She looked over at her boyfriend. Cutter was gripping his crotch, which meant the killing had him all horny too. Then she looked up at his face. He was looking away from her, into the dead women's bedroom, and he looked worried. Real worried.

She looked into the bedroom too, and her euphoria of murder instantly vanished. All the spilled blood in there had now humped together into a pool on the floor and was flowing at speed out into the hall. The liquid's surface rippled like a breeze was blowing over it. Behind it, the other dead woman lay flopped over like an empty sack. Her black hair was draped over her face like curtains concealing the departure of her anguished spirit.

Cutter gaped at Peaches in horror as the trail of blood streamed past his legs. "What the bloody fuck?"

She gaped back mutely. She was equally scared. All the blood staining her hair and body was stripping off of it and plopping to the floor, to mingle with that from the woman she'd killed and flow towards . . .

Peaches groaned on realizing where the blood was all headed. *Oh, shit! Not that one!* She flung Cutter a pleading look that shrieked, *Let's get the hell out of here!?*

Cutter, though, wasn't watching her. He had his gun out again and was pointing it at the sculpture of the demonic man as the blood flowed up over it and covered it completely.

The blood vanished into the sculpture. The image came suddenly alive. The strange man blinked his black eyes, twisted from side to side, and flexed his arms. He looked around, nodding with approval.

Peaches and Cutter both gasped at the sight.

The man's skin seemed painted white, that was how pale he was. His strange black eyes foamed like boiling pools of tar. He opened his mouth in a sadist's grin. He had small pearly-white teeth.

Feeling the aura of absolute evil radiating from the man, Peaches barely restrained her urge to scream. *We're done for!* she thought.

She leapt up and grabbed Cutter. "C'mon, let's get out of here!"

To her relief, Cutter didn't attempt any macho shit now, like trying to shoot the man. He ran after her towards the staircase.

"Wait, students," the man said. His voice was hoarse, an almost froggy croak, but it had a steely authority behind it. Peaches and Cutter were already at the landing, but as if the man's voice was physically restraining them, both froze in their tracks and turned to face him.

"We were just leaving, sir," Peaches said nicely. "We'll be gone before you even realize we were here. Bye."

The man laughed. He was also freakishly tall. "Leaving? Oh? But there's nowhere to go."

Startled by his words, Peaches looked behind her. Then, with a sinking heart she gaped at Cutter. He gaped back, equally confused.

The landing and stairs had vanished. Solid wall stood there now.

They turned back to face their reanimated captor, who'd now walked over and sat on the writing desk with the opened occult books.

"What's going on here?" Cutter asked, waving his gun at the man. "Hey, don't mess with us. We're dangerous."

"Put the gun down, student."

Peaches watched Cutter do so, though he was clearly fighting the command with all his might. It was no good: with intense strain on his face, he dropped the weapon on top of a carved wooden altar shaped like a large human head with three legs. The altar's top was ridged with axe grooves. Peaches realized that the dark stains on the flat surface were blood.

Cutter straightened up again.

"Good," the man said. "One of the rules here is: 'No guns permitted in Detention.'"

"Detention?" Peaches asked. "What the hell are you talking about?"

He gave her a cold glance. "Swearing's not permitted either, you little . . ." then he laughed like crackling flames. "No, I'll relax that one. Cuss all you like."

"What is going on?" Peaches insisted. It was tiring, trying to be strong now; she felt like this supernatural son-of-a-bitch was leeching her of her free will. Sneaked glances at Cutter showed him to be in some kind of trance, like he'd not yet recovered from the command to drop his gun: his eyes were glazed over and his mouth drooped. Cutter was also slobbering spittle like he just woken up. And there was also the fact that while they'd been talking, the hall had been subtly altering around them. Everything still looked just the same, but she felt that the room's ambience was no longer just evil, but deadly.

The man placed his book down on the desk and waved his cane at them. "I am the Schoolmaster. You are both in Detention. In Detention because *you need* to be punished. Here I will determine what your crimes are." He gestured down at the female corpse by his feet, then into the bedroom at the other one. "You both clearly have been bad students." He laughed. "Everyone deserves punishment. They simply don't know it."

"So you're just going to keep us here against our will?"

"I don't need to. The school authorities—the Powers That Be— will keep you here. You alerted them that you were playing truant when you woke me from my long slumber."

Peaches understood then that the man was mad. "What do we do in Detention?"

The Schoolmaster gave her a creepy smile, and she felt like she was being sucked into his eyes. "It's simple enough: I set tests for you. If you fail the tests, you die and go to Hell. Then another set of students enter Detention and we start over again." His smile broadened. "But now, it's time to get down to the classrooms."

"Classrooms?"

"You're in school aren't you?"

Peaches nodded. *Alright, this jerk really is insane. Supernatural, but insane. All we need to do is humor him until we can somehow escape. Cutter's out of it for the moment, but . . . If there are classrooms, there have to be doors and windows out of—*

She stopped thinking because the dead women's bedroom had just altered into a classroom complete with rows of desks and chairs and a blackboard.

"Now, first things first," the Schoolmaster said. "Registration." Picking up his book, he looked sternly at Cutter with those black eyes like moonless midnight. "What's your name, student?"

"Fuck you!" Cutter yelled, rushing at the Schoolmaster with his knife raised. With admiration, Peaches realized he'd just been playing possum. *Yeah, baby, give this fool something to think about. Oh, did I so fucking hate school!*

Cutter stabbed the Schoolmaster in the eye. "Die, asshole!"

The Schoolmaster didn't flinch or bleed. Instead, Cutter gave a sudden yell of pain.

Peaches saw why: Dripping red onto the floor, the Schoolmaster's fingers were sticking out of Cutter's back.

With his right hand stuck through Cutter's body, the Schoolmaster got to his feet. "It's regrettable that occasionally a student proves hard to educate," he said while Cutter groaned in agony. The Schoolmaster effortlessly lifted Cutter off the floor and let him dangle in space, squirming like a worm on the impaling arm.

"Put him down!" Peaches screamed. No, this wasn't happening. "Fucking put him down! You can't just kill him!"

The knife was still stuck in the Schoolmaster's eye. He pulled it out with his free hand and dropped it on the floor. Peaches shuddered; there was no wound in his eye. *Oh, God, what have we gotten ourselves into?*

Cutter still dangling in midair on his right arm with blood pouring everywhere, the Schoolmaster frowned at Peaches. "This is Detention, student. *I* make the rules." He turned his black gaze on Cutter. "Now, student, tell me your name."

Blood dripped from the corners of Cutter's mouth as he formed words. "Cutter . . . sir."

"Good. Cutter is registered in Detention."

The Schoolmaster gave the barest flick of his arm. Cutter flew off his arm and smashed against the wall. He fell to the ground and lay still.

For a moment, Peaches was confused at to what the long red rope connecting her boyfriend to the Schoolmaster's hand was. Then she understood that it was Cutter's intestines: the Schoolmaster had held onto them while flinging Cutter off his arm.

Tears in her eyes, she glared at the Schoolmaster. "You killed him! You didn't have to kill him!"

"He failed the test."

"What bloody test!? You hadn't started yet!"

The tall, strange man's smile was merciless as he dropped Cutter's guts then shook the blood off his extra-long fingers. "He failed the obedience test. Obedience to instructions is part of the tests. It is also against the rules of every educational institution to attack the teachers." His lips curled into a creepy smile. "I assure you I hate losing students early. Now, what is *your* name?"

"P-P-Peaches, sir." Then scared she might share Cutter's fate if he thought she was being flippant (this was after all a school, not a nightclub), she added, "But my folks called me P-P-Pamela . . . P-P-Pamela Principal. That's my full name."

She was surprised that his grin returned; even his unseeable eyes brightened a little, their unknowable darkness somehow becoming less intense. "Principal? Your name is *Principal?*"

Then he burst into loud raucous laughter, the unexpectedness of which almost made her shit herself. He laughed a good long while, the horrible croak of his voice echoing off the enclosing stone walls and filling her head, while she stood in abject terror, realizing she was trapped for good, flinging glances at Cutter's corpse and wondering what her clearly bleak future now held. And what the hell was he finding so damn funny anyway?

But when the Schoolmaster calmed, he smiled nicely at her and said, "Hmmm, I'm delighted to meet you, Ms. Principal. It was about time that you showed up."

Peaches had no idea what he was talking about, but then he reached forward and stuck his bony fingers through the skin of her left breast and into her heart and she began screaming, screaming out for all her throat was worth.

"God no, no, NOOOOOO!!!!!!"

CHAPTER 8

Tanya

Eyes like cold steel above the steering wheel, Tanya Rockford was halfway to Palmer, driving hard after Cutter and Peaches.

The way she saw it, the reason they'd have fled this way was because of the dense network (a veritable spider's web) of interconnecting back roads leading out of the state. It would take a while to coordinate a manhunt out this way; by which time they'd be long gone again, over the state line, and vanished into New York State. *Then we start looking again.* She winced. *Thanks to Agent Richards for sniffing out Cutter and Peaches' patented brand of insanity.*

Until the fingerprint matches came in, the Marlborough cops likely still imagined they were dealing with a local crime, and were still checking which local good ol' boy sniffed too much angel dust last night and did a Jason Voorhess on the Hamiltons.

But realizing Route 20 ran almost directly past the crime scene had alerted her to its possible use as their escape route. It was just so obvious no one would consider it. The only question was: did the fugitives realize Route 20 ran all the way out of the state?

She suspected Cutter did.

She was still musing on this when, without warning, the sky turned dark and it began raining cats and dogs.

What the . . . ?

She couldn't believe it. *From a clear spring sky with no clouds to this in five seconds?*

The water blew in on her. She quickly put up the window glass and activated the windshield wipers.

The abrupt rain cascaded down in wide liquid sheets. The sky boomed with thunder and crackled with lightning, the lightning tracing intricate bright webs across the heavens. Water pounded on the roof of her Honda Accord like a clan of blacksmiths.

She slowed the car. It was becoming impossible to see the road. Or the sky. All ahead of her was a falling wall of water, like the sky was trying to wash the earth away. Rather than kill herself in an off-the-road skid, she parked beneath some trees on the right and waited. Here, the tree covering dampened the worst of the rain (just thin streams drained through their dense foliage), but the force of the deluge was bending the outermost branches almost level to the road. A large bough dropped into the road ahead of Tanya, alerting her to the danger of one crashing onto her car. She figured she'd take her chances on that happening: sheltering here beneath the trees definitely beat being out in the angry downpour.

This is no ordinary storm, she decided.

The uncooperative heavens angered her, like the Devil was conspiring to help her quarries elude justice again. *No, those two aren't getting away this time! I've got their scent, dammit. They came through here!* She was certain they had. For a moment, the Chief's warning about calling for backup came to mind. She shrugged it off. *No. If I call backup—she* blinked away tears from her eyes—*I'll never live down the 'kid-killer' accusations from the Josh Milton case. And that's something I'm not having hanging over my head for the rest of my life. This is my one shot at redemption, and I'm taking it. No one else is sharing the credit for this arrest with me—Cutter and Peaches are mine. But why on earth is it suddenly raining so hard?*

The windshield and windows were already steamed over. She wiped a patch of glass clean and peered out. Outside of the edge of gravel bordering the trees, nothing could be seen, not even the left side of the road. It was like she was in a transparent underwater tunnel.

To distract herself, she switched on the car radio.

"Good morning, folks! This is Rock 102, WAQY—" The signal blitted out into white noise. She surfed channels. Nothing.

She snapped the radio off. A sudden, unreasoning fear now gripped her. *It's like it's the end of the world. And I'm trapped in this sardine can in the middle of no—*

A loud rapping on her right startled her. She looked that way. Several shapes were pressed up against the window. The rapping continued. After checking that the safety on her gun was off, she wiped the steam off the glass. Three drenched faces stared in at her, pleading with gestures that she let them in.

Tanya checked out the faces: all were in their early twenties; besides, the girl with them was black. She sprung the locks on the doors and the trio clambered in, the girl in front, the two boys in the back. Tanya didn't really like that, they could still jump her if they wanted, but she doubted they would.

She flashed her badge. "I'm BPD Detective Tanya Rockford," she said to ensure they didn't get any stupid ideas. "What are you three doing out here in this downpour?"

The black girl shook herself like a wet rat. "I'm Sherri. The guys"— she pointed to each in turn—"are Mike and Jordan. We're students at Tufts University in Medford. We're hitching our way down to Chicopee for a research project. The rain just started all at once."

"I've never seen anything like it," Mike said from the back. "One moment the sky was all clear, the next . . ."

"Yeah," Tanya said drily. "Today, it definitely pours. Hopefully, it'll clear up before long. When it does, I'll drop you off in Chicopee."

"Hey, thanks, Detective," the girl said. Tanya figured she was maybe twenty-one, her dusky face had that youthful eagerness to it. She was slim and pretty, with her hair cut short, and was wearing a wet yellow dress. Tanya wondered which of the boys she was dating.

"No problem, It's on my way."

Outside the car, the torrential rain showed no sign of abating. It was like the world had liquefied. Like reality had melted. The sun had vanished long ago, the only lights anywhere those of the car. No other vehicle had appeared on the road for at least twenty minutes. Tanya figured they too were sheltering beneath roadside trees.

A thought struck her. She turned in her seat, so she could see all three students. "Say, maybe you guys can help me out with some police business here. Did any of you notice a couple pass this way earlier? A man and a girl?"

Mike asked, "What do they look like?"

"He's thirtyish. Handsome with dark hair; she's in her late teens, a blonde."

Mike shook his head. "Nah, I don't remember them." He looked enquiringly at Jordan. (Both young men were similarly dressed, in slacker denim. Mike was more handsome. Jordan, however, had a geek's cute innocence to him. The trio's soaked bags were piled in the foot well between them.)

Jordan shook his head. "After a while of thumbing lifts, every car looks the same to you. Why're you after—"

"I saw them!" Sherri said.

All three of them looked at the black girl.

"Where?" Tanya asked. "Where'd you see them?" She could feel her pulse racing. *So I was right, they did come this way! I'm not on a wild goose chase after all!*

Sherri said, "In Sturbridge. A trucker dropped us off there." She turned to Jordan (who, judging from the look in her brown eyes, Tanya decided was her boyfriend). "It was while we were getting bagels at that café by the traffic lights. I turned and saw this couple in a black car. I'm not sure what make it was . . . maybe a Mazda? They looked like a father and his bratty teen daughter. What struck me about them was that there was a police car headed towards them at the traffic lights, and they both looked really jumpy. Not so much nervous as like they'd both been doing uppers; I could clearly see them whispering to each other. Then the cops passed and they relaxed again."

Tanya nodded grimly. "That's them alright. Thanks for your—"

With a sound like thunder, a dislodged branch landed on the trunk of the car. All four of them stared back at the massive oak bough, then gaped at each other. Tanya could read the others' minds: *If that had dropped on the roof* . . .

"Let's find thicker tree cover," she said. "But first . . ."

She and the two young men got out and rolled the heavy branch off the trunk of the car. Tanya winced. The bough had deeply indented the metal; the trunk wasn't opening anywhere outside of an auto repair shop.

Now, standing outside in the rain, she was even more bothered by these weird events. *Why the hell is it raining so damn hard? This rain's almost supernatural in its ferocity.* Beside the car, the downpour looked solid, the falling water like melting glass, turning Route 20 into a river. The water was up over their ankles; it was a wonder it hadn't yet flooded the car. She hoped it hadn't stalled her engine, that would be the absolute pits.

They got back into the car and set off under the trees, with Sherri wiping the condensation from the windshield with an Always sanitary napkin so Tanya could see where she was going. Twice she steered the brown Honda up into the drenching to get around fallen boughs, each one larger than that which had totaled the car's trunk.

Their luck held, however; no other branches dropped on them. But (and she could practically smell her three passengers' nervousness), except they found some other shelter—a patch of relatively dry earth—it was only a matter of time before they got flattened. *But where are we going to find that in this deluge?*

Then Jordan pointed and yelped, "Over there, there's a turnoff!"

Tanya's only thought on seeing the tunnel beneath the trees was that it was drier than where they were. Only after turning the Honda onto the almost invisible road did she realize that it was *completely* dry. No rain at all had fallen in here.

She parked and they got out.

"I don't get it," Sherri said, her dark face twisted in confusion. "Why isn't the rain falling inside here?"

Jordan was frowning. "Even the runoff isn't flowing down this way; and this road's at a lower altitude than the other. Bad science."

Mike mouthed "Geek" at Tanya. She grinned through her worries. (The kid really was handsome; damp black hair and all.) If she already had her suspicions that the downpour had begun for a reason, this confirmed it. Watching the rain at the end of the tunnel falling like a transparent curtain, and the water flowing off like an invisible wall blocked it from entering this side road, was creepy.

Definitely 'bad science' like Jordan had said.

"Okay, guys, let's just get in the car and get away from here. The meteorological society can figure out what the hell's going on."

Then, after they'd all piled back into the vehicle, another thought struck her: "There's no road sign. Do any of you know where this road leads?"

All three students shook their heads. This time, Mike was sitting up front with her, Jordan and Sherri in the back.

She frowned, then shrugged. "I don't know either, but so long as we're out of that storm, we're good. We'll be okay, though; most of these west Massachusetts routes tend to link up."

"Yeah," Mike said.

Tanya set off driving. Her shoes were soaked and uncomfortable. That was less of an annoyance that the fact that they were brand new and likely completely ruined now. She tapped Sherri on the arm, then indicated that the girl pass her the spare pair of shoes she always kept in the passenger foot well. Sherri handed the brown pumps over; Tanya dropped them beside her own feet.

A mile later, they discovered that the side road led only to a large mansion in the middle of nowhere.

The front gates weren't locked. Mike got out and swung them open and they drove through.

Once inside the mansion grounds, they stood around Tanya's car awhile, staring at the huge and imposing building.

Here it was nice and sunny, just as the day had been earlier. Looking south, the sky over Route 20 seemed normal enough, except for a vertical black pillar, like a stationary twister, that Tanya was certain was the freak storm that had driven them in here. (Tanya was very angry over this delay. She worried that the fugitives might be getting away, but there was no helping it; there was no way to leave here till the storm wore itself out. Then she reconsidered: An out-of-the-way place like this was perfect for Cutter and Peaches to hide out. Only they *weren't* here: there was no sign of their black car. Sighing, she patted her gun in its hip holster. It occurred to her to call Federal Agent Richards and tell him about the black Mazda the fugitives were possibly driving . . . but no, she couldn't do that . . . she needed this catch for herself to clear her name; she needed it worse than she needed air and water.)

She pointed out the distant black portion of sky. "Okay, lady and gents, we'd best hole up here till that's gone."

Sherri nodded, turning to face the mansion. "Let's knock and see who's home."

Tanya left the car doors open so her seats would dry up. (She'd already switched her shoes; now she left the wet pair up on the hood.) The students picked up their bags. The four of them made their way up to the mansion.

The front door was open. They knocked. There was no response, so they walked in.

CHAPTER 9

Venus

Porno superstar Venus Deluxe stared moodily out the rented blue Mercedes' shotgun window.

The countryside rolled by, all green like they were navigating the Amazon River. On both sides of them were the pretty colors of flowers, orchards, and wide fields.

Venus was five-foot-four tall. She was thirty-five but looked twenty-six. As was required of a porn goddess, she was both stacked and beautiful, with soft blue eyes, a perfect nose, and those eminently kissable lips that had cost her a fortune in plastic surgery. She had mussed-up pink hair. Her 32JJ breasts were sheathed in a light blue tube top, and her coltish legs stuck out of faded denim hot pants. She was a walking wet dream, and she knew it.

But currently, she and her riding partner, porno stud Chad Cannon were lost.

Chad spun the wheel and made yet another turn that took them through yet more fields along another back road. Past tall maples and elms, and ancient oaks.

Venus looked across at him. "Man, where are we?"

He gave her a dopy grin. "Beats me."

Stoner! She utterly felt like murdering him. *I mean, how the hell does one get lost in the middle of Massachusetts in broad daylight? And Chad seems to only find those turnings that lack signs and buildings. All we need is to locate Route 20 again, right? How hard can that possibly be?*

She stared at the vehicle's dash—*The GPS!*—then sagged back in her seat. *Damn, I can't work it! I really should have paid attention when KY was explaining . . .*

Chad made a final left turning and they bumped up onto a wide road. This one too ran between trees, but it was twice as wide as the others they'd been on and also very straight. She kept her eyes peeled for a highway sign, hoping they'd stumbled on Route 20 by accident. All that would remain then was determining if they were heading towards Springfield or away from it.

She turned to look at her companion. "Hey, whatever you do, don't turn off this road, okay?"

Chad smirked back. "Don't blame me, baby. This is more your fault than mine. You're the one with the brother in Palmer."

Venus said nothing; she just sat and seethed. Yeah, Chad was right on that count. Leaving the party last night *had* been her idea.

***

Venus and Chad were in Springfield for KY's birthday bash. (KY was porn producer Evan James's transsexual girlfriend and also a major shareholder in his company Titaholics Anonymous.) KY had decided to have her party in her hometown, doing it big to show her homegirls how far she'd come from relatively shitty roots.

That was fine. Venus was a local girl too, and it was always fun to return home. So, Friday night, after they'd been drinking a lot, she'd decided to go visit her brother Rick in Palmer. Not trusting herself to drive with that much booze in her, she'd grabbed hold of Chad and they'd set off. And then, at 3 a.m. they'd headed back for Springfield to rejoin the birthday party, made a series of wrong turns, gotten lost, and slept in the Mercedes.

They'd both woken up with major hangovers this Saturday morning, with no idea where they were. And had been driving in circles ever since. Which Chad didn't appear to mind, but Venus found utterly infuriating. She couldn't recognize any landmarks (there were simply too many back roads in this part of the Bay State, after a while all the roads looked exactly the same; and her damned hangover hadn't helped any).

She'd already called both KY and Evan, both of whose phones went straight to voicemail (which likely meant KY had Evan's dick up her ass again: KY was a total harlot for early morning sex). For the umpteenth time she debated calling Rick and asking directions, but . . . he'd think she'd gotten lost because she was stoned again (and *he had* suggested that they sleep over at his place and head back for Springfield in the morning. Ouch.)

Then, just when she'd decided to call her brother anyway, and he could think whatever he liked of her, her phone went 'Battery Low' on her, and went to sleep.

There was no charger in the car. She didn't bother asking Chad; he'd forgotten his phone back in Philly in some bimbo's bedroom.

She looked over at Chad and winced at the dopey look in his eyes. Like he was here, but not quite; like he needed the ultimate pick-me-up—ten heaped scoops of instant coffee in a cup or a whole palmful of cocaine. His hands occasionally shook on the wheel; it was a miracle he'd not yet driven them off the road.

Venus grimaced. Chad Cannon should rightly be called Chad *Stoner*. Ten-inch-penis, dashingly handsome looks, and not a cell in his brain that dope hadn't fucked up like he fucked all those 18-year-old wannabe slut's asses. (She'd watched Chad interviewing those girls, with their bright eyes, virginal tits, fat asses, and no idea whatever of what being a porno actress entailed: "Oh, so you wanna be in the bizness, do you?" "Yes, Mr. Cannon." "Okay, bend over." "Alrighteee, sir! No! Stop! What the hell is that you're shoving into me!?" "Just my bizness end going into yours, baby! You're definitely in porn now! Roll the cameras, boys." "Shit, it hurts!" "Sometimes taking a shit hurts!" "Help!—I want my mommy!" "Okay, baby doll, you failed the test. Back to Louisiana with you, and wipe the poop off your cheeks before the door smacks them. Next!")

She wasn't really judging. No, lots of her porn colleagues did drugs—shit, she did them herself; she'd had lots of pot and downers last night; she even had a baggie of coke in her purse now—but Chad here took that shit to the extreme. He and Evan and KY with her big breasts and fat little dick. They did narcotics like they were helping the Pentagon test them for use against ISIS and Al Qaeda.

True, Venus herself like to party, but she preferred keeping a clear head most times. Life was business; porn was business: Venus didn't want to get ripped off. Also, she was looking to get out of the industry in five years max, and she didn't want to look back on it realizing she'd snorted all her earnings. No! She was saving her money and making investments. She wanted a nice life after retirement: a nice hardworking man who doted on her, three or four kids and a high-class boutique filled with designer clothes and jewelry . . .

She snapped out of her reverie. Chad was saying something.

"Huh?"

"Venus, what the hell is this weird storm?"

"Huh?" He was right. It had begun raining. All of a sudden and out of frigging nowhere. Chad was closing the windows against the inrush of raindrops. The sky was black as night.

Damn, she thought, *it's pouring like we're driving under a burst reservoir.* Just like that, the road ahead of them had just vanished under a waterfall. She looked back, the road behind them was getting the same drenching. She was suddenly scared: the rain hitting the car roof didn't sound like water, more like a thousand stamping Maori dancers. Left and right of them, the wind was bending the branches of the roadside trees almost to the ground. (Several trees were already uprooted and lay beside churning pools of mud.) She trembled as a massive bough snapped off its trunk and rolled across the road, making Chad stamp on the brakes.

She looked at Chad with scared eyes. "I don't like this at all. There's something very wrong about this sudden change in the weather."

"Hey, there's a turnoff here on the left," Chad said to her relief. "We'd better get in under the trees."

Once under the trees, they realized the freak storm didn't extend this far.

"We'd better just keep along this road," Chad said happily. "It's certain to lead somewhere, maybe even back to Springfield."

Venus said nothing. As the blue Mercedes rolled on down the one-lane road, she was struck by a horrible premonition that they'd both just taken the ultimate wrong turn.

CHAPTER 10

Tanya

The mansion's interior instantly filled Tanya with apprehension. Occult-themed sculpture and paintings were everywhere she looked (on her left a Salem crowd were lavishly depicted burning a witch). She quickly deduced a haphazard air to their arrangement though, like they'd been dumped without much real thought to their placement. *Dumped and forgotten, but by who? Who owns this place, anyway?*

They were just leaving the foyer, entering via double doors a large hall that appeared to dominate the entirety of the ground floor. On their left, stairs led up to the second floor.

"Wow!" Mike exclaimed, running his hands over a life-sized (and unnervingly lifelike) werewolf statue. "Even the hair feels real. Just imagine if it suddenly came to life."

Sherri shuddered and gripped Jordan's hand, her dusky face strained. "Don't say that, okay? I don't like this place. There's something foul about it."

"I feel it too," Tanya said, then instantly regretted seconding the girl's expressed fears. *I'm a police officer. Boston's finest! We don't believe anything we can't prove!* But still, she couldn't shake the creepy feeling the house gave her, like it was alive and watching them all. *No! That's bullshit. It's just a house!*

"I think we'd be much better off staying outside with the car," Sherri said.

Mike laughed. "C'mon, don't tell me you're scared of some guy's horror museum."

"Nah, man," Jordan said. "She's right: there's something messed-up about this place—it feels like more than just a kooky gallery. And where is everyone?"

Tanya yelled up at the stairs. "Hey! Is there anyone home!!"

Grinning, Mike walked over to a pair of vampire sculptures with bloody teeth. Then he picked up an old calfskin-bound book from a pile of them and flipped through its pages. "Hmmm, the one real danger I see in this place is the owner believing in all this mumbo jumbo." He grinned wickedly at Sherri. "He might attempt to sacrifice us."

Sherri, now over her initial heebie-jeebies, gave him the finger.

"Ouch," Jordan laughed. "How's that big thing feel up your ass?"

Chortling, Mike vanished behind the pile of books.

"Hey, is there anybody home!?" Tanya yelled again.

Mike reappeared from behind the book stack holding a different old volume. "Human Sacrifice: How To Do It Right And Get Results Every Time," he read off its spine. He looked worriedly at Sherri. "Guys, there's a whole stack of books like this back here, along with boxes of ritual knives. I think you're right: we should wait out—"

"Coming, students," a voice sounded from nowhere. It was in the room with them but they couldn't see who'd spoken.

Tanya looked at the others, they nodded back.

"Th-th-the air just spoke to us!" Sherri gibbered. She gripped Jordan who held her tight.

"Not the air, the Schoolmaster," the voice said.

Tanya pulled her gun. She felt scared as hell; the voice was like that of a cartoon frog. "Hey! Who's in here with us? I'm BPD Detective Rockford and I demand that you show yourself!"

"Be patient, student. I'm making a final check that your dormitory is in order and that the toilets are clean."

"Why do you keep calling us students?" Jordan asked the unseen voice. "I mean, *we are* students, but how can *you* possibly know that?"

"You're here in Detention, aren't you?" the voice replied.

Detention? Tanya decided enough was enough. To hell with bravery. She looked round at the three youths. "Okay, everyone outside to the car. Hurry."

They turned to leave, but were blocked off at the hall entrance by two people coming in through the doors. One was a tall, dark, and muscular man, the other a beautiful woman with pink hair.

"Hi," the pink-haired woman said. "I'm Venus, and this is Chad. We're heading back to Springfield and got lost. We need directions."

"Yeah," the man confirmed. "Never seen anything like it before: Some weird storm started up out of nowhere and we had to leave the road."

Venus looked reproachfully at her companion. "Not like we knew where we were to begin with." Next, she looked from face to face. "Where are we now, anyway?"

Tanya was so surprised by the couple's arrival that she almost didn't notice that the doors to the foyer had vanished behind them.

Oh, shit! she thought when she did notice. *We're really in the soup now.* She quickly looked around. The other hall entrance she'd previously noticed beyond the arrayed magical paraphernalia was gone too.

As if to confirm her fears, the voice from the air said, "Hold on, students. I'll be with you in five minutes tops."

"Who said that?" Chad asked, looking around confused. (To Tanya's trained policewoman's eyes, he seemed to be either suffering the world's worst ever hangover, or coming down off a drug binge. Venus looked wired too, but her extreme beauty concealed it a bit.)

Tapping her gun against her palm, she frowned back at Chad. "We all really wish we knew."

CHAPTER 11

Venus

Venus Deluxe liked to make an entrance. To her mind, entrances were of the utmost importance to a woman. Particularly if you worked in adult movies, you needed to let everyone realize you were there, or the other 'dolls' steamrolled over you, then you were considered 'old' and missed getting called up to make the hottest films, especially all those new-age porno flicks, the big budget sci-fi and horror ones. (Working in porn was like living in the Playboy Mansion with Hef: anything over 25 and you were practically a grandma, no matter that Hef was older than her granddad!) 'Old' was the word you never wanted to hear. (Even just being called a MILF was scary enough: it meant your wrinkles were showing.)

Looking around the hall she and Chad had just entered (and what the hell was it with all this weirdo crap everywhere, anyway?) she realized she'd made a pretty solid entrance. After making her introductions, she leaned against a pillar, her hip cocked in a way that thrust her chest out to best advantage, and took stock of everyone.

There were four people in the hall—a young black woman, two young men with a bookish air about them, and a stony-faced brunette holding a big pistol. The brunette's no-nonsense expression momentarily chilled Venus. *This one's a cop for sure, and she looks both pissed off and worried. And ready to blast someone's ass away.*

By her side, Chad Cannon was being Chad Cannon. Venus didn't need to look to know that he was flexing his muscles for the ladies' benefits. She doubted he was getting laid here though: the black girl was hanging on the arm of the blonde boy, and the cop was too distracted. Damn, the woman's eyes had just widened in shock like something odd had just happened behind she and Chad.

Then, before she could look around to see what that might be, the creepy voice sounded from hidden speakers somewhere: "Hold on, students. I'll be with you in five minutes tops."

Students? It made no sense; this didn't seem to be a school. She shrugged. Anyhow, they just needed directions back to Springfield. But, remembering the car outside with its doors open, it occurred to her that maybe these others in here were also lost?

Then her mind left her concerns. She was being noticed. The darker of the two young men was nudging the other one, the one with the girlfriend. Then gesturing at her, he whispered in the other guy's ear. Venus caught the 'Deluxe' his lips formed, then the blonde guy's eyes widened with recognition too.

Wondering how many liters of semen the pair had each deposited on their navels while masturbating to her, she pouted, then licked her lips indifferently and pretended to study a painting on the wall, while at the same time pushing her breasts out even more for their approval. Venus thrived on the attention; besides, it gave the two something to boast about to their friends: they'd once been in the same room as her.

Staring at the wall was a bad decision, though: the painting her eyes had fallen on showed a screaming woman having her guts ripped out by a bald man in a pentagram-inscribed black cloak. *The torment of Anne Johansen,* the inscription read.

Disgusted, Venus looked away, back over at her two admirers, both of whom instantly averted their eyes. Then, the next moment, she almost split her sides in laughter.

Eyes wide with disbelief, the black girl was staring at Chad's crotch.

Oops, she's checking out his dick, and Chad, trust him, isn't wearing boxers again. She confirmed her suspicions. Yes, Chad was freeballing again, his manhood hanging down the left leg of his pants like a fat sausage. And it seemed half-erect—almost out at its full ten inches—like Chad was getting turned on by the attention. No wonder the girl was gaping. Neither of the two guys had noticed what the girl had (Venus figured that was natural—as a matter of principle, only gay men checked out other fellows' junk), and the lady cop was still looking around for the source of the disembodied voice.

"Hey, show yourself," the cop said. "I know it's your house, but this isn't funny."

The black girl saw that Venus had noticed her ogling of Chad's crotch. Giggling, she looked away. She hid her embarrassment by pulling out her cellphone and saying, "Hey, you guys, I've got to call my dad. He'll be worried stiff if—"

"Put the phone down, student. No cellphones are allowed in Detention."

Detention? Venus's ear pricked up at that. A feeling of alarm set in. She looked back, and saw the door had vanished. She looked forward again in horror. "What's going on here?"

The black girl was dialing.

"Put the phone down, student, or I'll be forced to discipline you. Your recalcitrant behavior has already earned you several demerits."

"We aren't under house arrest here. I'm calling my dad."

"Okay, I warned you."

Venus made eye contact with the girl. "Put the phone down," she began whispering, but the girl had already raised it to her ear. "Hey, dad . . ." Then her dusky face turned surprised. "Hey, who's this on the line?"

The next second, her cellphone exploded.

There was a long moment when Venus stood shocked like the others, her mind refusing to process what had just happened. Like the others, she was splattered with wet pieces of the girl's face, brains, skull, and right hand.

Then, with two jets of blood pumping from her neck, the girl's headless body slumped to the floor.

Everyone seemed to unfreeze at once. "Sherri!" the blonde boy shrieked, kneeling down beside the still-twitching body. His friend and the policewoman followed suit, leaving Venus and Chad staring at each other in horror. Chad began wiping blood out of his eyes. Shuddering, Venus picked a chunk of brain out of her cleavage.

"I repeat. No phones are permitted in Detention."

The lady cop looked up from the corpse. Her face looked carved from ice. "Hey, Mystery Man, you'd better come out of hiding right now. This just became a murder investigation."

"Yes, it is about time that I attend to you all."

Venus felt frozen in place again as the air next to the dead girl solidified into the figure of a tall, tall man in an old brown suit. What scared her the most about him were his eyes: twin black pools that seemed to dip all the way into his head, like he was chock-full of darkness trying to squirm its way out.

"I am the Schoolmaster," he intoned. "For the nth time, you have all been bad and are henceforth sentenced to Detention. All of you will now please place your cellphones on this desk over here. All personal computers too."

Venus's mouth fell open in shock.

CHAPTER 12

Tanya

Speechless, Tanya watched everyone place their devices on the desk the 'Schoolmaster' indicated. They walked over there like sheep, docile and obedient, dropped their cellphones and tablets or laptops, then returned to where they'd been standing.

Everyone next looked at the Schoolmaster in confusion.

Seeing him materialize from thin air like that had knocked the fight out of Tanya herself for the moment. Terror's cold fingers stroked her scalp, making her head itch like she had chronic dandruff. She had to consciously will herself out of losing it to fear.

She regarded the Schoolmaster. *Ugh, he's so ugly*! He was tall and bony and almost balding, with skin like the surface of an uneven white wall and a huge nose; and then there were those Satan's pits he had for eyes. The expression 'non-eyes' instantly leapt into her mind— eyes that weren't really there, eyes that existed only in the viewer's imagination. Magnetic holes sucking in light.

With her cop's instincts, no one needed to tell Tanya that this man was evil incarnate: badness radiated from him like stink from seventeen scared-shitless skunks. In addition to his old brown suit, he held a cane with a curved upper end in his long fingers. He looked absurd; an eighteenth-century actor made up for the stage.

Her gaze fell to Sherri's headless corpse. There was nothing absurd about that. This freak-a-zoid was one to be very wary of.

She looked up at the Schoolmaster again.

"Yours too," he said, looking directly at her. "And put the gun down also. No dangerous weapons are permitted in Detention."

Tanya considered for a minute. They were clearly in deep shit here, and if she didn't take the chance . . . she realized the others were all watching her, willing her to shoot him. But . . . but the damn gun might explode, blow her hand off.

"I'm a cop," she said. "Why'd you kill her?"

He frowned. "I didn't. Her disobedience killed her—there are rules in here." He pointed a long finger at her. "And you . . ."

Tanya shot him twice, aiming for his head. She *had* to know. With the doors suddenly going missing, she had to be sure she wasn't passing up their one chance of escaping this place.

The bullets hit the Schoolmaster in the face. His head jerked back, but there was no damage. The bullets had apparently vanished into his body. Maybe they'd even been sucked into those horrible eyes of his.

Defeated, Tanya let her gun fall to her side. Left and right of her, she felt the others' stares. She looked at them. Chad's face was ashen, like his hangover had just worsened. Venus looked like she needed a shot of cocaine or something. Jordan and Mike were looking about for somewhere to flee too.

She gulped. *Oops, I really did it now. I'm like, so dead?*

The Schoolmaster looked irate for a moment. Then he calmed down and said, "I'll forgive you that because you're in law enforcement and acceptably concerned about public safety. Besides, if I killed off everyone in school for minor misdemeanors, I'd have no students left to take the exams. Now drop your gun and phone with the others and let's get you all registered for your classes."

Numbed, Tanya walked over to the desk and put her phone and pistol down amongst the others there. After removing and dropping her holster too, she turned back to face the room. "What n—"

About them, the room had altered into a dormitory. Severe gray walls hemmed them in on every side, their monotony broken by square windows along one wall. The dorm was long and contained twenty made beds (arranged ten-a-side across an aisle) with blue sheets. There was no other furniture. The floor was dusty; old black cobwebs dangled from the room's corners.

"Each of you pick a bed and drop your things there," the Schoolmaster said. "We're unisex here—women and men may mix up however you like. You have half an hour to settle in. After which . . ." he indicated a door with peeling green paint on their right, "you all come downstairs to the classroom for your lessons. I'll be waiting in 2B. It's along the second corridor on your left downstairs."

With that, the Schoolmaster vanished again.

For a long time no one said anything, they all stared at the green door with dread. Then Mike and Jordan (who had tears in his eyes) picked out two central left-hand beds and dropped their packs beside them. Chad just flopped down on the bed beside him and stared up at the ceiling, his face morose.

Venus crossed the aisle separating the beds and sat on one of them. Her face was pale. "Di-did you s-s-see what happened to that girl?" she asked in a quavering voice, gripping her sides like she was cold. "Ph-phones d-d-don't blow up like that and take people's heads off. And when you shot him, h-h-he—"

"Calm down," Tanya said abruptly. "Have any of you looked out of the windows yet? Our problems are way bigger than you think."

Everyone instantly found a window and peered out of it.

"Oh, frigging hell no!" Chad groaned and sank back down onto his bed.

He'd picked the same window as Venus, who gasped through her fingers and stood frozen in place.

"I'd say we're in a toilet-load of shit," Mike said slowly as he regarded the landscape outside the window.

Jordan nodded. "Yeah, dude. That we are."

Tanya was grateful that both young men had somewhat recovered from Sherri's death. Or maybe the shock was yet to set in—they didn't/couldn't yet believe she was actually dead? People didn't just die in freaky ways like that, did they? *You can freak out later, guys. Just not now . . . please!* She needed their calm to bolster hers. *Today's a complete mess: First Cutter and Peaches, then the storm, then Sherri dies, then we're trapped in here by that freak, and now*—she gaped— *now this . . .*

Outside the windows was a wide schoolyard, like for a high school, with bleachers and a softball field at its right end. That was weird enough, but . . . the schoolyard was bounded all around by a high stone wall above which Tanya could see nothing. No, she corrected herself, 'nothing' was inaccurate: Outside, around and above the schoolyard, was a thick white mist—like the building and its grounds hung suspended in a cloud—inside of which she glimpsed massive dark writhing shapes.

"Those are tentacles," Jordan said quietly.

"There are hundreds of them," Venus whimpered.

"And that black stuff mixed in with the mist looks like smoke," Mike said. "Like there's a fire burning somewhere below the mist. Although it's cold, not hot."

"Where the hell are we?" Tanya asked.

"A parallel dimension," Jordan replied promptly. "That's the only explanation. As far as I can tell from looking out of this window, this house seems exactly the same, but . . ."

"It isn't the damn same," Tanya objected. "I can feel the difference in my bones."

"I was coming to that," Jordan continued, scratching his blonde hair. (Tanya could hear the strain in his voice—he was fighting not to freak out over his girlfriend's death.) "This house seems exactly the same, but it isn't. It's some kind of 'evil twin' if you will. And it's shunted us across to its home realm."

"Which is?" Chad asked from the bed.

"The fuck if I know."

The five of them sat on two beds facing one another.

"What the hell do we do now?" Chad asked. "We're stuck somewhere, assume it's Hell—"

"A good assumption," Jordan interjected.

"—in a house surround by huge tentacles. No one needs to tell us that whatever's out there will be hungry for flesh. Our damn flesh. That thing out there is some kind of security assurance so we don't get away."

Tanya was relieved that the man seemed to be over his shock and wasn't about to prove a handsome liability. Then her gaze dipped to his crotch. *Damn, is his dong really that big? That has to be at least eight inches long and it's limp! And how come he's not wearing any underpants?* She looked up at Venus. Venus stared back at her, a paragon of scared doll-like perfection: exquisite face with its corona of mussed-up pink hair, huge breasts and all. *Big dick and big tits eh?* Tanya now remembered how Jordan and Mike had been whispering while Venus had been striking bust-enhancing poses by the foyer door. *Oh, they're both in porn! Shit! I'm stuck in Hell with two porn stars?* She rolled her eyes. *Isn't this just what I need!?*

"Yes, what do we do?" Venus asked worriedly. "That man—if he's a man—won't think twice about killing us all."

"He's a demon," Jordan said.

Tanya's eyes narrowed. "What makes you say that?"

"It's the only logical deduction. If we're in Hell, Hell is generally populated by demons."

"And . . . the damned." Mike got up and walked over to stare out of a window again at the wall and the mist over it. Then, perched on the sill, he frowned back at them. "That's something we're all forgetting," he said grimly. "If this *is* Hell, we're in deep shit. Hell is a place of *torment*. We've been brought here for some reason to pay for sins—real or imagined."

"Hell no!" Chad said. "They can't do that."

"Look here," Venus said calmly. "I don't think it's that. 'For all have sinned and fallen short of the glory of God.' I remember that from church as a kid. *Everyone's* guilty of something, so why select us?"

"The law of negative averages," Jordan said.

Venus gaped narrowly at him. "Huh? Speak English, man."

"Bad karma," Mike explained. "Bad luck."

"Oh."

Tanya cringed. *Oh yeah, this is some really impressive bad luck alright.* She couldn't get Sherri's exploding head out of her mind. *And . . . aw, c'mon, God, what is this crap? I thought you were merciful and forgiving? I didn't shoot the kid on purpose. You know that! What the hell am I doing in Hell?*

She calmed herself. She knew she needed to keep it together here or they were all lost. She was a policewoman; trained to deal with exigencies, trained to think on her feet. The two students (particularly Jordan) might likely be of some help in their escaping this place, but the porno couple were certain to be no use at all. Okay, so maybe it was an unfair stereotype—maybe Ms. Tits had a degree in rocket science and Mr. Cock could solve Rubik's cube in under a minute—but neither of the pair were currently showing any evidence of enhanced smarts. Venus looked like she'd shortly poop her hot pants. And . . . she eyed the woman's expensive croc-skin purse suspiciously. *How soon is it before they start toking up?*

Then she remembered they were expected downstairs. She checked her watch, then addressed the others.

"Okay, people, we've seven minutes left. We'd better get going early, in case this Schoolmaster, as he calls himself, is tough on tardiness."

"Hey! Before we leave here, what are we going do?" Venus insisted.

"Yeah, what?" Chad seconded.

"We play along with him for now," Tanya replied. "We've no choice but to. For one thing, we don't know where we are. For another—"

"The man, or rather, demon, is bulletproof and can make phones explode," Jordan finished for her. "Except we can neutralize his powers, we're not leaving here alive."

The others nodded. "Yeah, we go along with his ass for now," Chad agreed, courage flickering in his eyes. "We kick it later."

Tanya got up and forced a smile. "So, c'mon everyone. Let's go get registered in Detention."

Mike laughed.

Jordan frowned. "One warning: Everyone, *please* behave yourselves in class. This creep isn't fooling about."

Venus pouted at him. "Believe me, baby, we *know* that."

They left the dorm.

What the hell are we about walking into? Tanya wondered.

CHAPTER 13

Venus

Descending the stairs with the others, Venus steadfastly refused to believe that she was in Hell. *Oh, no, I've not been that bad in my life. And besides, we're still all alive, aren't we? This has to be that other place, the clearing house for Heaven . . . what's it called again?* She racked her brain for a once-familiar term when she'd been a cute Catholic schoolgirl in Our Lady of Mercy High School in Brighton, New York. *Yeah . . . purgatory! But . . . don't you need to be dead to go there too?*

Whichever/whatever it was, this couldn't be hell. No, she'd not been that bad. So she'd done lots of stuff to make her mother blush, fucked so many men on camera their faces were a blur (to date she'd made three hundred movies; she wanted to hit the big 5-0-0 before retiring, if her pussy and ass didn't quit on her first—hell, she still wanted that marriage and kids afterwards!), done a lot of drugs, and generally raised hell whenever she could. All the girls had fun, it took one's mind off the roundabout of faking orgasms on demand, sometimes with your pussy and ass so sore it felt like there was no skin down there anymore, just raw screaming flesh.

So yes, she'd done her share of playing the wild child. But unlike some other girls, she'd never been a bitch, and she'd never backbit on anyone or lied so they'd lose work. She glanced sideways at Chad and almost laughed at his maudlin face. *Wow, he's certainly wishing he'd treated lots of people nicer now, isn't he? He must be haunted by bleeding starlets' anuses.*

But . . . no! This wasn't *the* Hell, and that was that. She didn't care what Mike said about those black trails in the mist outside being smoke. (She'd worked their names out from their whispering: Mike was the hot, dark one; his blonde, geeky friend was Jordan. The butch cop was Tanya.) The trails didn't have to be smoke, did they? They could be monster farts, and besides . . . fire was *hot*, everyone knew that from the first time they burnt their fingers as toddlers. So screw Mike's 'cold fire' suggestion. She smirked at the back of his head as they reached the ground floor. *Hey, kid, stick to being handsome; leave the brains to your friend.*

They proceeded along a short dimly-lit corridor, with Tanya and Jordan checking the numbers of each adjacent door they reached.

"This is one damn abandoned school," Mike said. "Where are all the teachers?"

"Are you frigging serious?" Venus replied. "I already detest the one teacher we've met."

Mike shrugged meekly. Venus figured she could treat both young men anyhow she liked: They were fans of hers, and if she ventured to ball one of them down here, the guy would think this place was Heaven, not Hell.

Chad whispered in her ear. "Hey, I need some coke. I gotta clear my head."

Venus grimaced. Chad would be Chad no matter where they were.

"Darling," she replied sweetly, "you've seen what they do in this school to mere cellphone offenders; what do you think their anti-drug policy's like? I suspect it'll be sub-zero tolerance."

"Stop fucking with me, Venus. I know you've got some blow on you; I saw you slip it in your back pocket when the cop wasn't looking."

Venus rolled her eyes. Yes, that was another thing: *Can we later be charged in the real world for offences committed down here? Like say, a paranormal drug bust or shit?* She corrected herself: *Why do I keep imagining that we're down somewhere? Because Hell is supposed to be DOWN? This ain't Hell, goddammit! Jordan—bless his soul—already explained that we're simply in a parallel version of reality.*

To Chad she replied, "Cool your tubes, baby. Not here where the kids can see. Wait till we're inside the class, or at least out of sight of the others."

Chad huffed and frowned, but nodded. She could smell the sweat and fear on him. *I'm sure I reek just as bad; they'd better have showers in this place for when class is over. And I'm soon going to need to use the toilet too. My bladder feels like I just drank half of Lake Michigan.*

Chad was right, though: she needed to toke up herself. The sooner the better.

"Okay, this is 2B," Tanya announced, and pushed the classroom door open.

CHAPTER 14

Tanya

The classroom looked normal enough, four cream walls with louvered windows that looked out over the schoolyard they'd noticed from upstairs. Four rows of desks faced a long whiteboard to the left of which stood another desk for the teacher. On the other side of the whiteboard, shielded by the door as they entered, hung an anatomical figure.

"Everyone, make yourselves comfortable," Chad said once inside.

Tanya strongly felt the man was a primed bomb about to explode. That was something they couldn't have happening here. *We all need to pull together to survive this place.*

Everyone else had separated to desks. Chad, however, had turned towards the whiteboard and his hands were shaking like he needed a fix.

Okay, that's it, Tanya decided. *If this guy freaks out, there's no telling what his cotton-candy-haired girlfriend's gonna do.*

She strode over to Chad, intending to drag him back out into the corridor and scold him, maybe even rough him up a little if necessary, but then she saw what had him scared.

"Th-th-the figure!" he gasped at her, then darted across to the desk next to Venus's and sat down shivering.

It took Tanya all her reserves of courage not to shiver too. The 'anatomical figure' was a human corpse. A naked male corpse with a hole in his belly through which the classroom wall was visible. (His belly was completely emptied of guts.) The man's head hung down. She lifted it up and stared at his face. Her eyes widened with recognition.

It's Cutter! So the Devil's luck did finally run out!

She gazed at the dead serial killer, suspended from a metal stand by a pin through his neck, for a long time. Then she couldn't help it: She burst out laughing, so hard that the others began staring worriedly at her.

"Uh, he's dead," Venus said tightly. "What's funny about that? We might die too. Are you gonna laugh at our corpses as well?"

She shook her head, still totally unable to contain her mirth. "If you'd ever met this son-of-a-bitch alive you'd be happier than me that he's dead. At least now New England can sleep easy."

Their expressions showed they all thought she was losing it.

Next, Venus and Chad began arguing in whispers over something that he was fumbling for in her shorts' pocket. Finally he came away with it—a transparent baggie of white powder that had to be coke.

Fucking porn stars, Tanya thought, then she shrugged. *I can't really blame the guy. Seeing Cutter like this, and not knowing the punk is better dead than alive, I'd be scared out of my skin too.* In a way, it was even amusing seeing how flustered Chad was: *Damn! His huge dick must be all shriveled up like a prune now.*

Chad flung a defiant glance in her direction then scooped some coke from the baggie with a car key and snorted it up. Then he did it again. Venus was staring at him in mixed anger and disbelief. Then she crossed her arms over her big breasts and glared out of the window at the mist over the schoolyard. Tanya though she'd first whispered, "Hey, don't use it all up! Leave some for me!"

Jordan and Mike were watching the pair with interest. Tanya decided both students were cool. Maybe they'd want some coke too.

She shrugged again, then with a wide grin, turned back to face Cutter. His dead face told an entire Medieval history textbook of suffering, like he'd been all the heretics tortured and killed during the Spanish Inquisition. She felt fantastic seeing it. *So how did dying feel, asshole? How'd you enjoy having the life ripped from your damn body? Having your guts pulled out like yards of rope? Did you scream? I hope you did, I hope you screamed like a baby, like all those people you killed.* A sudden mental image of young Karen Hamilton with her roasted head filled Tanya with white-hot rage. *Did dying really hurt, Cutter? I hope it did! I hope you croaked in so much agony that you wished you'd never been born, that you cursed your mama for not aborting you!*

She remembered she was missing someone. *And where's Peaches, a.k.a. the Young Adult from Hell? Cutter, where's your damn barely-legal shackjob? Is she—*

The Schoolmaster appeared in the doorway. With a scared yelp, Tanya instantly abandoned mentally interrogating the corpse and scampered over to the desk behind Jordan's.

"Class is now in session," the Schoolmaster said, striding in and standing before the whiteboard. In his brown suit, he looked like some kind of sprouting tuber. His fathomless eyes scanned the class, taking in how they'd chosen to arrange themselves. (Venus and Chad were seated on the left of the class; Tanya, Jordan, and Mike on the right, near the door.) He waved his cane in a flourish. "Now to business. We will start by taking all your names down."

Then he sighted Chad, who on the Schoolmaster's entrance, had just lifted his head from snorting his car key again. Unfortunately, his nose was white with the sniffed powder, and while trying to wipe it off, some of the cocaine poured from the baggie out over the desk. Even then, he might have gotten away with his gaffe, but Chad, not wanting to waste the coke, bent to scoop up the spillage from the desk.

Venus was gaping at Chad; she clearly couldn't believe his stupidity.

"What's that you're doing?" the Schoolmaster asked in a terrifyingly calm voice.

"Er . . . er . . ." Chad stuttered.

Ditch it out the window! Tanya was screaming at Chad in her mind. She knew this was really bad. *Ditch it out of the window, you dick!*

The coke had however filled Chad with false confidence. "I'm powdering my nose!" he said defiantly. "What's it to you, teach?"

Tanya winced at Chad's reply. Venus gasped and buried her face in her hands on top of her desk.

In a brown flash, the Schoolmaster was beside Chad. He ripped the baggie from Chad's hand. He lifted it to his extra-long nose and sniffed its contents. His whitewashed face flushed pink with rage.

"DRUGS!!!? he screamed, so loud that Tanya had to cover her ears; the man's voice was horrible at more than just the excessive-decibel level. "YOU'RE DOING DRUGS IN MY SCHOOL!?!?"

Oh, shit! Tanya thought. *This guy is so dead.*

***

The Schoolmaster seemed to calm down. He returned to the front of the classroom and wrote on the whiteboard, 'NO DRUGS ARE PERMITTED IN DETENTION.' He turned to face them again. "To make this abundantly clear to you all, we'll have a spot of discipline." He pointed to Cutter's hanging corpse. "That student was punished for attacking a teacher, the silly fool."

He glared at Chad. "What is your name, student?"

By now, awareness the danger he was in had seeped into Chad's head. Desperately, he looked around for support, but everyone else was looking forward to the front of the class. He answered, "Chad . . . Chad Cannon."

The Schoolmaster nodded. "Good. You're now registered in Detention, Chad. Time to discipline you. We'll have a simple flogging." The severe gaze pierced Chad's brain like pins. "Now come to the front of the class and take your medicine like a man."

Chad didn't move.

"What are you waiting for? You'll survive this punishment. It's only ten strokes of the cane."

"No, I'm not doing it. You can't just flog me! Who gave you the right to do that? Corporal punishment is against the law."

He saw Venus, who'd been looking at him with pleading eyes, duck her head back down.

The Schoolmaster sighed loudly. "Chad, here *I am* the law. And *you* have just failed the first test of your detention, which is obedience to *all* the rules." He smiled coldly. "I hereby award you five demerits. This of course means that in the first series of tests, which will begin after I register the rest of the class, you will be at a disadvantage. Failure then, even of the slightest kind, might prove fatal." Then he laughed. "But then, this is Detention after all. Here, all failure proves fatal in the long run."

There was a collective sigh of relief from everyone in the classroom.

The Schoolmaster looked around at all of them, then rang a buzzer on his desk. "And now, it's time that you met my assistant."

CHAPTER 15

Venus

Venus couldn't believe Chad could be so stupid. *Oh my God, what do you have for brains? Semen? You're actually arguing with this teacher guy?* She glared at him. *And . . . and . . . and, oh shit, dude, you've wasted all our coke.*

Chad stared defiantly back at her, still too wired to appreciate the magnitude of his let off. But was it really a let off? Venus thought she'd noticed a sadistic gleam in the Schoolmaster's eyes when he'd awarded Chad his demerits, as if they'd really come around to bite him in the ass later.

And . . . what worried her more than anything else was how she'd felt glued to her seat while Chad and the Schoolmaster had been having their verbal exchange. It hadn't been a physical restraint; no, she'd not felt any unseen hands or bonds holding her in place. And also, it hadn't seemed a mental one. It had just felt like 'something' was making her assent to the Schoolmaster's judgments and decisions. At one point she'd been utterly mad at Chad for not walking forward to take his strokes and . . . she'd felt like getting up and forcing his adamant ass to the front of the class, and next, snatching the cane from the Schoolmaster and whipping Chad's butt for him.

What scared her, was that she knew those feelings hadn't come from any thoughts of self-preservation, but rather because she'd felt the Schoolmaster was right. *So, what if he'd wanted to kill Chad? Would I happily do that too?* She looked across the room at the others. The expression on their faces as they looked back at her told her they'd felt the same way.

She caught Tanya's eye. "Don't panic. Do as he says," the policewoman mouthed at her, then leaned forward between Mike and Jordan to whisper the same to them.

Yeah, that's true, Venus agreed. *We do what he says. But how much of that now is because we agreed on it as a plan, and how much of it is because this creepy place is making us want to do what he tells us to?*

She couldn't tell. She considered one final thought: *Or maybe, I just did want to see Chad get his ass whipped for acting so plain dumb.*

Then a teenaged girl walked in through the classroom door and Venus instantly felt like crapping herself.

First thing was, the girl was dragging Sherri's headless body behind her, leaving a red smear on the ground. Then, too, Sherri's corpse was now buck naked. The teen was dragging her along by one foot so her crotch was splayed open with the cleft of her purple sex displayed in its nesting of black pubic hair. Venus wasn't offended by corpse's nakedness—of necessity, while working in the adult industry she'd eaten her fair share of African-American vagina—but it was the kid's lackadaisical manner as she dragged the body after her (like it was roadkill she was cleaning up) that almost unnerved her.

Then the girl herself: She looked both dead and crazy, if that made any sense. (It did to Venus.) Like some kind of psycho-zombie. She wore jeans pants and a white halter top crusted with dry blood. She was blonde and very cute, but her mad eyes . . . Venus had never seen eyes like those before.

And . . . and there was a big hole in her left breast in the depths of which something red shone. And no, except she had an electric ticker, Venus didn't think that shining red thing was the girl's heart.

On seeing Sherri's corpse, Jordan gave a loud sigh. *Oops,* Venus thought, *that kid is shortly going to lose it, and really lose it big time.* She watched Mike bend to whisper comforts in his ear, then she looked at Tanya. Tanya was sitting shock-still in her seat, like she knew the new arrival from somewhere. Venus watched a cold, pleased smirk slowly spread over the cop's face.

The Schoolmaster stood. "Students, I'd like you all to meet Ms. Principal."

"Hi, everyone," Ms. Principal said with a loony laugh. "Please call me Peaches."

Tanya laughed coldly. "Hello, Peaches. I see your luck ran out too, thank God. It was about damn time you got your comeuppance."

"What's that in her chest?" Chad asked Venus.

"You like tits. Why don't you go have a look?" At the moment, Venus Deluxe couldn't care less about Chad Cannon. Later she'd relent, but now? Chad could go jump off the Empire State Building for all she cared. Or better yet, he should have been in one of the Twin Towers when the terrorist aircraft hit.

Chad sensed her reserve. "C'mon, Venus, don't be like that. I lost my nerve is all."

She relented. "Chad, you dickhead, you almost lost your fucking life," she whispered hoarsely, punching him in the chest. Tears weren't far off now. "We're about to all get killed here and you go and pull a bullheaded stunt like that."

"It won't happen again. I promise."

And then she was hugging him tight and crying. He was a true friend after all, had stayed with her through thick and thin. Not like some others who'd cut her loose, like Rob Stone had.

Venus detested Rob Stone now. She'd gotten chlamydia on a shoot and Rob had met her at an STD testing clinic in L.A. They'd been supposed to jet to Europe together the next day for an anal scene with Rocco X, so she'd told Rob how worried she was about being blacklisted if the news spread, and he'd told her not to worry, no one would find out. But next thing, Rob—damn him, how she fucking hated him—had gone and phoned Rocco X about her Clam infection and he'd cut her from the shoot and hadn't called her since, imagining she'd been planning to pass on her 'gooey stuff' to him. Even though she'd been planning to tell him herself and ask if condoms would be okay. But the way Rob had phrased it to Rocco, he'd made it look like Venus intended to ask that Rocco do a long cunnilingus scene so she could *really* infect him, so he'd never have kids. And he'd hinted that she'd gotten herpes too. And, ironically, it had turned out that Rob had actually had the clap all the time he was tattling on her and he'd given it to Genevieve Papillion, the French Butterfly. Oh, hell, that had been a total mess! But Chad here had stood by her through all that shit; he'd cleared up the herpes BS with her producers and hooked her up with Evan and KY and—

"What is your name?" Peaches asked from beside her shoulder.

She separated from Chad to look at the girl, then blanched. Up close, Peaches looked even deader than afar off. More insane too. She had this creepy vibe going on, like death had freed her madness to run riot. And the look Tanya had earlier given the kid marked her as dangerous territory. And if she'd been *that* dangerous when she was alive, now she'd be even more . . .

She was carrying a clipboard and pen. "Your name, please?"

Venus dried her tears, then, "Venus Deluxe," she replied simply for Peaches to note down. After saying it, she wondered if she should instead have given her birth name—Susan Wilson—but the horrible man hadn't seemed to mind Chad's giving his surname as 'Cannon' instead of 'Givens,' so maybe that wasn't a big deal down here. (*Oh dammit, there I go thinking of this place as belowground again!*) No point getting in the Schoolmaster's bad books—she could see him now, cropped head tilted in her direction, with that six-inch nose pointing at her like a compass needle! She had no idea what this registration crap was about anyway, but . . .

Her gaze had dropped from the girl's face to her chest. Shock and terror immediately smacked her in the face. Hot urine instantly squirted out between her legs.

Buried deep in the girl's chest, where her heart should be, was a clock. A black digital timepiece with large red numerals. The time was 3:15 p.m.

Shivering, she sat back and watched 'Ms. Principal' turn away and collect the others' names.

CHAPTER 16

Tanya

Tanya was shocked too. Like the others, she'd also seen the black clock in Peaches' chest. It was a gory sight: her white halter was ripped across her left breast, through the creamy flesh of which a brutal hole had been dug and the timepiece somehow inserted. And the somewhat dreamlike look on her face? Like she wasn't of this world anymore?

Okay, so she seems dead and I should be pleased. But why aren't I? Because I wanted to kill her myself? No, it's not that; I'm scared, that's it. Until the little horror is made into an anatomy display like her boyfriend she's going to keep being trouble. She winced. *Trust my shitty luck—like having her psycho teacher employer to deal with isn't already bad enough.*

In front of her, Mike was pleading with Jordan to calm down. (Peaches had just written both their names down—Mike Myers/Jordan Levine—and was walking back over to the Schoolmaster, her denim-panted ass still annoyingly sexy.) Tanya shared Mike's sentiments, but wondered *how* Jordan possibly could calm down: staring at Sherri's headless body was getting to her too in a big way. *And . . . why the hell did they strip it naked?*

She leaned forward over her desk and whispered, "Jordan, you need to be strong; Sherri would have wanted you to. We all need to keep it together and find a way out of this hell we've stumbled into."

Mike nodded. Jordan mumbled a teary, "How?"

"We'll find a way," Tanya promised him. "Trust me, we will."

Jordan nodded too. Peaches was now busy laying Sherri's dark body across a long desk at the front of the class. Tanya wondered what for. The Schoolmaster, meanwhile, was checking the registrations he'd made. His brow was furrowed, his nose practically stabbing into the clipboard.

"They're all ready, sir," Peaches announced.

"Thank you, Ms. Principal." He got to his feet and addressed the class. "Good, good. Now you're all in the school records and we can begin the testing." He looked around on them all, his dark-yet-empty gaze chilling. "Now, here are the rules of the tests: The five of you will compete in a series of challenges against each other. The——"

"All of us at once?" Jordan asked. Tanya was glad he'd spoken. It meant he was over the threatened mental crack-up, which was good, as Peaches had just stuck a long thin knife into Sherri's left breast and was slicing down her body with it.

"Yeah, is this some kind of reality show thing?" Chad added.

The Schoolmaster scowled at the two interruptions. "If this is Reality TV, Chad, where are the cameras? No, you'll be competing against each other in groups of two. The winner survives, the loser dies—it's that simple."

There were five simultaneous gasps of horror.

Tanya gulped. *There's only five of us. This leaves zero room for error. We screw up these tests and none of us leave this place alive.* And . . . Peaches had now slit her way down the left side of Sherri's body to her toes. Rather than peel the skin open, though, she shifted the knife over a quarter-inch and repeated the process all the way back up the corpse, creating a parallel cut. Then, at the top, she did the same again, once more slicing down to Sherri's toes.

She's cutting her skin into strips, Tanya realized. *But why?*

The Schoolmaster was saying, "The tests will be random and of different types. I'm an impartial judge: you'll each have exactly the same chance of success or failure."

"And failure means death?" Venus asked in a horrified voice. "What's fair about that?"

"What would you prefer? That I whip you each time you fail? As well as being a needlessly time-consuming alternative, Chad already rejected that option."

Venus gave Chad a disgusted look.

"Besides which, it would take forever to whip each of you to death."

Tanya frowned. She felt powerless and utterly hated the feeling. It felt like she was bound head-and-foot to a bed, gagged, and about being anally raped by a man with a foot-long penis. (She had the utter same sense of fatalism about this that Venus did: that nothing they tried here and now would make the slightest difference to the outcome of things.) They were stuck in this morbid 'game' as it were, until they worked out the rules that would enable them escape back to their own world.

At the front of the class, Peaches had now peeled three long strips of skin from Sherri's body and was plaiting them into a rope. Dread filled Tanya. *Is she making a noose to hang us with if we fail the questions?*

"And so we begin now," the Schoolmaster said. He looked them all over again. "We'll start over here on my right, with Chad and . . ." he checked his clipboard, then smiled coldly, "Venus."

CHAPTER 17

Venus

Hearing her name called, Venus felt the floor splitting wide to swallow her.

I'm dead. She'd never gotten great grades in high school, and had ducked college, and Chad . . . Chad for all his dope-fiend carrying on, had a Bachelors degree in Sociology. So any hard questions and she was screwed; Chad would steamroll over her and that was it. She began praying fervently that all the dope he'd smoked had really messed up his memory.

"What kind of test is it?" Chad asked.

Venus looked hard at him. The almost nonchalant tone of his voice filled her with dread. *Oh yes, he knows I'm no match for him.* Terror gripped her. She began shuddering, fighting not to pee herself again.

"A general knowledge quiz," the Schoolmaster replied. "Each question is worth ten marks. I'll ask you three each. You'll have a thirty-second time limit to provide the right answer. Whoever has the least marks at the end of the quiz loses, and is killed."

God, no, not a damn quiz. Close to a freak-out, Venus looked across at Tanya and the students. Tanya was staring back morosely at her. Anger surged through Venus as she imagined a smugness on the policewoman's face. *Go along with it, huh? That's easy for you to say! I'm about being murdered here!*

Then she saw Jordan winking at her. Then he shook his head, and touched his lips. Then he winked again. Then he almost imperceptibly stroked his heart downwards.

Venus got the 'calm down' gesture. She worked to unstir the troubled waters of her mind, slowly got hold of herself, and paid attention to the Schoolmaster. Maybe, just maybe, the kid could save her. Maybe . . . She'd almost got herself relaxed again when she noticed that Peaches, who'd been plaiting some kind of fucked-up rope with skin peeled off the black girl's corpse, had now cut the bone out of the girl's left upper arm and was shattering it with a ball-peen hammer.

"Please reduce the noise, Ms. Principal," the Schoolmaster chided.

"I'm done, sir," Peaches replied. "It's just the studs for the whip. But I've got enough bone fragments now."

The creepy smile on the girl's face as she said it made Venus pee herself again.

Chad looked at her, then looked down at her crotch. He sniffed. "Pull yourself together," he whispered harshly. "We can beat this guy."

She ignored him but managed to control her bladder again. Her crotch felt warm from the urine, but cold chills were tracing her spine like a ghost's fingers. Over at her desk, Peaches was sticking sharp slivers of bone into her whip of plaited skin, then supergluing them in place.

The Schoolmaster wrinkled his nose in disgust. "Urinating in class isn't permitted, Venus. That's three demerits for you."

What!? Demerits!? You stinking shit-filled unholy motherfucker asshole! Despite her terror and dread of the evil man, Venus felt like screaming and running over and throttling him. *What!? You Bastard!!!! How can you fucking do this to me!? I thought you said these damn tests were gonna be fair!? Here I am already about to fail and you're already taking marks away before I've even . . . !*

Jordan caught her eye again. "Calm down, will you!" he mouthed fiercely at her. She almost screamed back at him: *Don't tell me to calm down, you son-of-a . . . !* Then her rage subsided as a thought struck her: *No, he's going to do his best to keep me alive. He doesn't want his favorite sex goddess dying! He's still got more come to worship me with! Ha ha ha!*

Inappropriate as it was, the thought nonetheless calmed her. Even the sight of Peaches testing her spiky whip of human gore on Sherri's belly (and the accompanying shredding of the corpse's flesh) didn't faze her.

Peaches walked over to stand by her master. The clock in her breast had now switched to countdown format, with 0:00:30 on its display. Venus hated how the numbers were now so easy to read.

"Okay," the Schoolmaster said, adjusting his brown suit as he spoke, "we start now. Once again, remember you're both playing for your lives. Now, first questions are in Geography. Chad, you go first:

What is the capital of the state of Washington? You have thirty seconds to answer the question."

Chad made a face while his brain worked. Venus, watching the expression on his face change to bothered, began thanking the god of drugs for fucking his memory up. She couldn't remember the answer herself. Washington was the nation's capital, did the capital have its own capital?

0:00:19, the clock in Peaches' chest read when, to Venus's disgust, Chad heaved a sigh of relief.

"Olympia, sir," he replied.

Venus had never even heard of the place in her life. Peaches' clock instantly reset itself back to 30 seconds.

"Correct answer, Chad. You've ten marks. Venus, your question: Port-au-Prince is the capital of which country?"

Venus again felt like the ground was about opening up to swallow her. Yes, she'd heard of Port-au-Prince. They'd had that dictator there whose wife had had three thousand pairs of shoes . . . Imelda Marcos . . . no, no, that was the Philippines. Her cousin's maid was always cursing Imelda for having her husband sent to jail . . . *So, if it's not that dictator, where the hell is Port-au-Prince? They had a dictator too for sure!*

She looked at Peaches. 0:00:23. She looked over at the students. Jordan heaved a sigh of relief, like he'd been trying to get her attention and, face concealed behind Mike's back, mouthed something at her. She read his lips. *Ha . . . ee*

"Haiti!" she blurted out as Peaches showed 0:00:15.

"Very good, Venus. You also have ten points. Your next questions will be in chemistry. Now, Chad, what results do we get when an acid and a base combine?"

Chad looked stumped. He stroked his chin, scratched his cheek, and looked so forlorn that Venus almost felt like comforting him. *Oh, so you don't know it, brainy?* She began to think that she actually had a chance here of surviving this quiz. It was a delicious feeling.

She looked over at Jordan. He was mouthing, "Salt and water . . . salt and water." Chad hadn't noticed; his eyes were squeezed tightly shut and he was sweating as he racked his mind. Venus wasn't about telling him either. This was her life at stake here; she wasn't about committing suicide by sympathetic stupidity.

A beep came from Peaches' chest. Chad slumped like he'd been shot.

"Time's up, Chad. The correct answer is—

"Salt and water," Venus blurted out, unable to stop herself.

Chad instantly gaped at her in surprise. Then he turned to stare at the Schoolmaster. The man nodded severely.

"Yes, Chad, Venus is right. Salt and water is the correct answer. Chad, you forfeit those ten marks. Now, Venus, your question." He paused a moment, raising a speculative bushy eyebrow in her direction. "I'm impressed with you. I had intended transferring the acid-and-base question over to you, but since you've already answered it, you get another . . ."

Hearing that, Venus felt like slapping herself in anger. *How could I be so foolish? If I'd just kept my mouth shut, I'd be ahead of Chad on points now! And this is for our lives!* She was aware that Chad was staring at her in confusion, wondering how she'd suddenly grown so smart. He was sweating profusely now, strain evident on his face. *It's pussy power, dude. Maybe if Jordan and Mike were gay, they'd help you out too.* She didn't look over at the pair; there'd be utter hell to pay if Chad worked out that she was cheating.

". . . So, Venus, in one sentence, please explain to the class the function of a catalyst. A simple enough question."

Function of a catalyst? Shielding her face with a hand, she pretended to be wracked in thought and looked over at Jordan. Still ducked behind Mike's back, he was telling her something, but she couldn't make out more than "A catalyst works by . . .' The next words made no sense to her. That was the problem: this required an explanation, not a single-word answer. If he couldn't explain it to her, how could she . . .

The countdown timer beeped.

"A catalyst initiates or accelerates a chemical reaction without itself being affected," the Schoolmaster said. He frowned. "I'm surprised you missed that, Venus. No points for you either then in this round. You're both now tied at ten marks apiece. So now, onto the third round of our quiz: History and Politics. Chad, your question: What was the length of jail time Lee Harvey Oswald received for killing President Kennedy?"

Venus smiled. She knew the answer to this one. Damn, this was simple. She looked over at Chad, saw he looked worried. She covered her broadening grin with a hand. *This time I'm not jumping the gun and saying anything dumb. If he misses this, I'm free. I'm alive . . . alive!*

"He didn't receive any sentence," Chad said just as the countdown clock hit seven seconds. "He was himself killed while in court." He shrugged. "I don't remember the murderer's name though."

"Jack Ruby. But it doesn't matter. You've answered the question correctly. Good. Ten marks for you."

Venus now felt the weight of an immense pressure on her, like the ceiling was collapsing onto her shoulders. *This is it—I lose this one and this freak here is gonna kill me! Shit, this had better not be another of those explanation questions or my goose is cooked!*

"Venus, what is the connection between the 16th and 35th Presidents of the Unites States?"

Venus had no idea whatever of the answer to that. The question was so completely out of left field, it looped her out into orbit. *Hell, this is unfair, why do I get the complicated questions, when Chad . . . !* She looked at Chad, who was doing his best not to appear smug. *Oh, he knows I'm a frigging goner here.* She looked past Chad at Jordan, who was scratching his head, his brow all furrowed up. Shit. *He doesn't know either?*

Panic growing in her breasts, her heart racing, she looked at Peaches, who smiled back sweetly. 0:00:24, her clock read. Venus's mind was blank; she hadn't the foggiest clue what the connection between the 16th and 35th presidents could be.

Her eyes locked with the Schoolmaster's, which felt like she was being sucked into a vacuum inside his head.

"You've eighteen seconds left, Venus, and then I will kill you."

She became aware of movement at the corner of her eye. Jordan was signaling furiously to her. She looked at him and nodded. He began mouthing something:

Ass . . . ass . . .

Then: *Shit!* Chad caught on to what was going on and leaned forward and covered her view of Jordan, blocked him off completely with his body. She could have wept with rage. He really wanted her to be killed?

Unable to see Jordan anymore, she began wracking her brain. She had fourteen seconds left. Fourteen seconds to figure this out or die.

Now she knew 'ass' was involved. Which US presidents liked ass . . . women? *Hmmm. Ass . . . ass, buttocks. C'mon, kid. I'm about dying here, what the hell did you mean by that? What does ass have to do with the presidents of the USA? Okay, okay, I know Clinton liked Monica Lewinski's ass. So Clinton . . . then it's names right? William Jefferson Clinton. Yes, that's it!*

Clinton's middle name is Jefferson. Another Jefferson? Thomas Jefferson, but was he our sixteenth leader? And did he like ass too? Any mistresses on record?

0:00:08

Jefferson Clinton, Thomas Jefferson.

0:00:05

The tension in the schoolroom was so thick you'd need an axe to cut it. Venus could feel the others rooting for her, could feel Chad rooting against her. It wasn't just Chad sweating bullets now, her pink hair was plastered to her scalp by the fear she was perspiring out.

Then, just as she opened her mouth to give the Clinton/Jefferson answer, she remembered something her grandmother had once said, about her grandfather never being able to forgive Oswald for assassinating Kennedy. "Same thing the damn jackals did to Abe Lincoln," the old man had once lamented in her hearing, "all the good uns get killed off and the Nixons who don't give a toss 'bout anyones is left to rule us."

Ass . . . ass . . . Jordan meant ASS-ASS-INATION, not tush, you airhead! See what working in porn does to you!?

"They were both assassinated," she gushed in relief as Peaches' clock hit 0:00:02.

"That is correct," the Schoolmaster said. "US president's Lincoln and Kennedy were both assassinated in office."

She could feel Chad's angry glare on her skin, but she didn't care. Her luck seemed to be holding out. At any rate, she'd give Chad a run for his money in this quiz.

"Hmmm," the Schoolmaster said, squinting his black non-eyes. "You've both done passably well. Two correct answers each. To decide who wins or dies, we'll have a tie-breaker." He looked left at Peaches. "What do you think, Ms. Principal?"

The clock in Peaches' breast was once more telling the time: 4:00 p.m. She cracked her skin whip against Sherri's corpse, leaving another furrow of shredded flesh, then nodded. "Yes, sir, a tiebreaker sounds good. What do you have in mind?"

"It's time to conduct a semester behavior review for both students, taking their demerits into account."

Hearing that, Venus felt huge relief. Chad had five demerits, she had only three. She knew she'd be escaping by the skin of her teeth; all she needed to do now was not pee herself again, no matter what happened. If she did, that was another three demerits . . .

"And so," the Schoolmaster began, "Venus has—"

Then Chad, who'd begun shivering, interrupted, "Hey, this isn't fair! Venus cheated! She cheated!!"

Venus did the only thing she could to keep from pissing herself from fear again. She stuck a finger into her pants and pressed it down hard over her urethra. That done, she glared hot hatred at Chad, who'd now leapt up and was pointing at Jordan. "He helped her cheat! I saw them do it. You can't kill me when they cheated!!"

The Schoolmaster bent and got to whispering with Peaches. Peaches was nodding fiercely and gesturing at Venus. Venus pressed her finger down harder. She was blocking a dam down there. She was so scared and angry, it felt like the urine would squirt out of her butt instead in protest. Or squirt from the pores of her face. But she controlled herself. *If I dare pee now, I'm dead . . . but fuck Chad, my own goddam bestie sold me out. What if the Schoolmaster believes him? I'll still be dead.*

Heart beating like a drum, she waited for the man's verdict.

The Schoolmaster straightened up again; he was frowning. "A cheating charge is a serious one and not something to be taken lightly. So we'll penalize Venus too—"

Her heart sank.

"—with an additional demerit, bringing her total to four—"

Venus was beyond emotion. *I've survived. How?* Survival or not, she kept the finger on her urethra firmly in place in case there were other surprises in store.

Chad exploded. "This is a travesty! How can you let her get away with cheating? How!?"

"Calm down, Chad," Peaches said. Something horrible in her voice silenced him and made him stare gloomily at the pair.

"Yes, she cheated," the Schoolmaster agreed. "But, and this is the important bit, we *didn't catch her.*"

"But . . . but . . ." Chad spurted. Peaches silenced him with a violent gesture.

The Schoolmaster continued: "Cheating without getting caught is a one-point demerit—it shows developing mental acuity in the student, hints at brilliance, even possible genius to come in future. Cheating and getting caught is a five-point demerit, as it demonstrates that the student is stupid, which must never be tolerated. Had you outed Venus immediately you'd noticed . . . but apparently you rated her friendship over your life . . . So now, she has four demerits while you have five. You each had twenty marks at the end of the quiz. Sorry, Chad. You lose . . . your life."

"Fuck you!" Chad yelled and turned and dashed for the door, going like a bat out of hell.

"Servitors!" the Schoolmaster yelled. "Get him!"

And, just like that, out of the air between Chad and the classroom door, four black smoke-ghosts materialized. Smoke, that was all the substance they had. The black ghosts were shaped like skinny men with extra-long legs and arms and fingers and pipe-thin heads. Their bodies wavered like a wind was blowing them.

The 'servitors' reached for Chad with their foot-long insubstantial fingers. Eyes almost bugging out with fear on seeing them, he did a baseball slide between the pair nearest the door, picked himself up off the ground, and was off and running down the corridor.

The servitors' appearance did it for Venus. She decided that now the quiz was over, she could be as incontinent as she liked. The pressure was killing her! She quickly pulled the front of her panties aside, took the finger off her urethra and urinated on the classroom floor.

"That's three more demerits for you, Venus," the Schoolmaster said with a disgusted scowl, then turned away from her toward the door, through which the black ghosts were just exiting.

Venus finished peeing and began praying that Chad would get away.

CHAPTER 18

Chad

Chad ran. He ran like the hounds of Hell were after him. Three doors down from the hellish classroom, he looked back. The first of the servitors—like a wisp of animated chimney exhaust—was floating out of the doorway. He thought he made out a mouth in its aerosol-can-shaped head. Also two holes right through the head that he took to be its eyes. He turned and legged it again.

Shit! Shit! Shit! How the hell did I the fuck get into this mess!? Venus, this is all your damn fault! Oh, if only I'd never followed you off to go see your damn brother!

And she'd cheated!

The cocaine still had him overly alert, which was how he'd escaped the class. It also had him jumpy as a startled hare.

He'd reached the turning at the corridor's end. He ducked around it, then looked back. The servitors now hovered outside the classroom door, four thin black shapes in a day-lit rectangle.

The smoke ghosts started down the hallway. Floating real fast. Coming on like they knew where he was.

He gulped. *Shit, maybe the wages of porn really is death?*

***

Chad, a Clinton, Oklahoma boy from a family of middle-class academics, had graduated with honors, and gotten a good job. He'd gotten into porn because, well, he liked sex and had a ten-inch penis, and the money was good. (Though to date it pissed him off no end that the girls in porn made four times as much as the guys did [how the hell was that for sexism?] which was largely why he went so hard on those wannabe starlets he'd was always asked to interview. "Girl, if you can't stand the dick, get your pussy out of the porno kitchen!")

Chad's major problem had always been saving his money. He'd blown so much cash during his ten years in the business (wages from both acting and producing) that it gave him a headache to think about it. Sara Sin, his ex-wife, had more than once warned him that he'd be left with nothing and wind up as a bum, but instead of listening, Chad had divorced her and kept burning through his earnings. In retrospect though, that divorce was the smartest thing he ever did. Unknown to him at the time, Sara had just contracted AIDS on a Brazilian shoot. They'd been fighting a lot and not been sleeping together all that while, so she'd not passed it on to him. But her next boyfriend Tony Thicke? Both he and Sara were now blacklisted from the industry. Last time he'd spoken to Sara, she'd told him she was starting up a HIV-Positive porno site: Viral-XXX. So more power to her. Chad admired her brains. He'd always admired women with brains, which was how he and Venus had become friends; really tight friends. Venus, too, gave him good advice on investing his money which he never followed. He knew she was wisely salting her earnings away, and really wished he could be as disciplined as she was. But the call of the party was just too strong. Besides, coke and uppers never paid for themselves.

(About the only thing keeping Chad financially afloat now was his twenty percent ownership of Titaholics Anonymous. Yeah, betting on Evan James's fledgling porno company three years ago was the wisest investment he'd ever made in his life. The royalties from company product paid his bills, and would continue to do so for a long time to come, so long as he was smart enough not to go off and liquidate his shares while stoned. In this regard, he was very wary of Evan's girlfriend KY. KY was a ruthless bitch where business was concerned. Though she was a tight friend of his, she never fooled about where it concerned making a dollar. Chad knew that if KY ever sensed he was in dire financial straits, she'd offer to buy up his share of Titaholics. For top dollar, of course. But then, with his weakness for the party life, he'd burn through that money too in no time. And then, once porn was done with him, he'd be out in the cold on his broke butt: a big-dick has-been working in a gas station. So it was essential he didn't sell.)

Chad's other weakness was that he could never say no to some ass. Once a beautiful woman shook her hips at him or blew him a kiss, he was in there with a vengeance, like a rabbit. (And with the size of his member, the women fucked him in droves, only not for himself, but so they could say, "Oh, I too once had him—he wasn't bad at all." Sort of like they were huntresses collecting him as a trophy. Chad hated that. He'd ball all these utterly gorgeous beauties and next thing, they'd run off and marry some rich businessman with a four-inch wiener, claim they'd finally found 'true love,' and refuse him the time of day thereafter.)

Which was how, now, fleeing for his life, Chad had no underpants on: When Venus had knocked on his bedroom door to ask if he'd drive her over to her brother's place in Palmer, he'd been screwing Clara Cleavage. Thinking it was Evan at the door, Chad had grabbed his trousers and dashed into the bathroom, while Clara pretended to be asleep.

(Chad hadn't been about taking any chances. Evan had his greedy eyes on Clara, and had warned everyone to 'hands off, the tits are mine.' Evan was terribly possessive where big breasts were concerned, and would burn down Hell itself if thwarted. Had he caught Chad humping Clara [and Chad had been sliding his greased-up organ between her squeezed together 36MMM breasts at the time] that would have been it between Chad and Evan. [Chad would be out the company door—Evan owned fifty-five percent of the company shares, KY the other twenty-five; and KY *always* sided with her boyfriend, even in matters where she should actually be jealous.] Chad guessed Evan had to be possessive about breasts: he'd named his company *Titaholics Anonymous,* hadn't he?)

But it had turned out to be Venus at the door. Chad knew he was safe, Venus would never rat on him. Still, in his mad rush to get dressed, his underpants had gotten lost (they were actually stuck in the crack of Clara's ass), and Venus, who was drunk at the time (hence her needing Chad to drive), was in too much of a hurry to let him search for them.

***

Now, running for his life, and with his shriveled member swinging left and right in his trousers like a fat worm, Chad regretted not insisting on putting on some underwear before they'd set out last night. True, Maggie, Venus's fat sister-in-law had been speechless all night, her eyes wide as saucers while she ogled his crotch behind her husband's back, but . . .

Panicking, Chad figured his best option was trying to get outside the building. He and the others had only seen one exterior view of it, there might be gates in the other walls.

Around the next corner, the corridor led to a bolted door. He ran towards it. If it was locked . . .

It *was* locked. Fortunately, right beside it was a set of stairs to the upper floor. He dashed up the stairs. The stone landing led both to another inside passageway, and also to an exterior balcony. He looked out over the balcony.

What!? Where are we? At the end of the world?

Outside the schoolyard, the white mist lay thick over everything, like someone had smothered the world in cotton candy. Now Chad saw the tentacles outside the wall clearly—they were gray with hairy brown patches. They were also monstrous in size, each much thicker than an elephant's leg. They flickered and moved like whips, like . . . like the whip that crazy teen had made from the dead girl's skin. How could someone do that?

The black gaseous wisps still swirled amidst the endless white, only now Chad thought he knew what they were. Servitors, monster ones! He imagined he saw dim red eyes like smoldering coals in the midst of the black smoke—angry demon eyes!

A sudden noise from the ground floor startled him. It occurred to him that the servitors outside might be able to see him and could tell the ones after him where he was.

He turned and ran off down the corridor. He ducked through an open door into a storage room of sorts—an ossuary it was: shelves and shelves piled high with human skulls—ran through there into another corridor, then headed back downstairs. Then upstairs again by a different flight of stairs. Uncertain where he was, he played a cat-and-mouse game with himself to lose his ethereal pursuers.

Throughout his flight he saw no trace of the servitors, as though the smoke-ghosts had evaporated into his imagination. But still, he knew they were about somewhere, seeking to drag him back to that demonic classroom and demonic Schoolmaster.

He was struck by the clear realization now that Jordan's appraisal of their location—that they were in the same mansion as previously—was completely wrong. Everything may have looked the same from the dorm, but this place was a frigging complex—an actual school. Chad ran past empty schoolroom after empty schoolroom, and at one point past a large science lab filled with dusty test tubes and other apparatus. The only thing lacking was students. Or maybe (and the thought almost made him puke with fear), maybe the missing students were those rows of skulls he'd found in the storeroom upstairs; God knew there were enough heads in there to go around the classrooms. But if that was the case, who'd killed everyone? That Schoolmaster and teen? Shit! He panicked again and kept running.

Then, once again down on the ground floor, Chad sighted an open door right at the end of a corridor. *Oh, thank God!* The door opened into the schoolyard. Once out there, he was certain he'd find somewhere to hide.

He ran for the door. This corridor had a wet floor, likely from a burst pipe somewhere. Halfway to the door, Chad slipped, slewed sideways, and crashed into a pillar.

He was about cursing his bad luck, when he realized he'd actually been fortunate. Two massive shadows had just stomped out into the corridor. Concealed by the pillar, Chad regarded them in disbelief.

Two seven-foot-tall specimens wearing sports shorts and soccer boots stood there. Both looked like mountain gorillas: hairy gray-brown skin, huge hands with horny black nails, Neanderthal faces with ledge-like brows shadowing their eyes . . . and sharp pointy teeth.

Their amber eyes however revealed a humanlike level of intelligence, and they were speaking English.

"Did he come this way? The porno guy?"

"Maybe, I dunno. C'mon let's go play soccer."

"Yeah, screw looking for him."

"Okay. But I'm David Beckham."

"Shit! You're *always* Beckham. Okay, I'm Landon Donovan then. Us Yanks are gonna whip your Limey asses. It's the Civil War all over again . . ."

"You wish. The USA'll never win the World Cup . . . Hey! Where's our damn ball?"

"Aw, shucks! The Schoolmaster must have taken it. We need to find another one . . ."

The pair of talking gorilloids shambled off towards the open door.

Once they'd exited through it, Chad pulled a massive about-turn, rushing back at speed the way he'd come till he reached a stairway. At the moment, he had no idea where he was. He figured it didn't matter, the important thing was that, so far he'd lost his pursuers. He had to keep going, needed to keep on the move. If that corridor led to the outside, there were bound to be others.

While thinking, he'd been climbing the stairs two at a time. Now, once again on the second floor, he pushed open a door and entered.

The door opened into a set of toilet stalls. This was fortunate. He pulled his member out and pissed a long hard one in a urinal.

He washed his hands, then examined his face in the mirror for cracks in his personality. The strain he was under was obvious. *Damn, I look like dog poo! Like I've aged fifteen years in five minutes.* The coke was wearing off now. Along with the narcotic comedown, exhaustion from his flight racked his system. He needed to rest a bit, that was certain. But definitely not here in the shitter.

He pushed open the toilet door, peeked out once to ensure the corridor was clear of ghosts, then hurried across it into the room opposite.

This turned out to be a staff lounge. Two couches, some chairs, a desk with an old computer on it, a whiteboard, and a bookshelf. A coffeemaker and cups resided on a wall shelf besides tins of coffee and cream. The single dirty, barred window looked out over the schoolyard, over a set of bleachers by a basketball court.

The room was empty. Best of all, the thick coat of dust on everything showed it hadn't been used in ages.

Chad pulled a chair up by the window and sat down. He checked his watch. *Okay, five minutes rest. I can afford that—*

***

While warily/wearily watching the schoolyard wall, a memory scrolled through Chad's mind; a scene from Titaholics' recent feature *Teachers Like it Big 6*: his rock-stiff penis half-buried in Anna Likes fat behind on a staff lounge couch, while below him, she gasped like she was dying, and fingered herself to ecstasy . . .

The scene had involved Chad as a high school janitor, interrupting geography teacher Anna Likes in the staff lounge after everyone else had gone home. In the shoot, the geography teacher was a bespectacled redhead. Mousy, but with an outstanding figure.

Anna had been masturbating and moaning when Chad pushed the lounge door open. Initially flustered, she'd quickly gotten hold of herself and ordered him out of the staff lounge.

"Get the hell out of here, you pervert!!"

Chad had however stood distracted, staring at her. "I'm just here to vacuum your carpet, ma'am."

"Mr. Cannon, are you even listening to me?" Anna asked acidly. "I'm going to report you to the principal." The way she said it, it sounded more like: "I'm going to fuck you and the principal." (Anna was an utterly crap actress, but she had personality and 38E breasts.)

"Mr. Cannon, I said: Are you listening to me?"

Chad's gaze, however, was riveted to her breasts. She had on a sheer see-thru blouse. An inset bubble showed him fantasizing about ripping that blouse off and fastening his teeth on her nipples and chewing . . .

He'd become aware that she was walking around him, her red high heels flashing in the light. "You think this is all a big joke, don't you, Mr. Cannon? Just you wait; the cops'll know exactly what to do with a peeping tom like you. I'll make sure—"

Then she'd stared down at his pants and gasped at his erection.

"Oh, my gosh! Is that all yours?" she asked in an incredulous voice, scared but impressed. "Or did you stuff the principal in your pants too?"

Looking as confused as he could while she fondled him, he'd nodded nervously. Anna oohed and aahed awhile, then she knelt on the carpet and unzipped him.

She held his manhood in both hands, looking scared.

"Golly, it's so damn big, Mr. Cannon. And you do know what they say, don't you?"

"Uh no, Miss Likes. What do they say?"

She'd shed her fake modesty and giggled. "Just that us high school teachers LIKE IT BIG!"

Then she'd wrapped her soft lips around his penis and began sucking voraciously. And the scene had developed from there. It had been a red-hot one too. Lots of tit shots for the guys, a long blowjob, him giving her some oral then sinking it into her face-to-face; then he'd flattened her on the couch with her fat ass up in the air for the big anal scene, which (in an unprotected shoot like this) always had to come last before the money shot so the lady didn't pick up a bacterial infection.

"Is this big enough for you, Miss Likes?" he'd moaned while sodomizing her, forcing his penis ever deeper into Anna's anus, till he wasn't sure if the hard thing blocking its progress was a twist in her colon or her poop.

Anna flailed like a wounded snake and gasped on cue. "Oh, my gosh, yesss, clean my pipes, janitor! I need it this big!!"

"Time for lunch break, Teach . . ."

He'd pulled out of her ass just as he was about coming and ejaculated all over her face, getting most of it in her eyes.

It was odd, Chad realized, how even after all this time working in porn, he still couldn't shoot a money shot straight. The jism was intended for Anna's tongue and tonsils; it definitely wasn't supposed to go up her nose . . .

***

In shocked horror, Chad pulled his mind back to the present.

A young girl had just materialized in the staff lounge. She was floating above the floor, and Chad could see through her.

He sat bolt upright, confused. The girl looked about twelve years old, just verging on entrance into puberty. (She had just the barest impression of bumps on her chest.) Oddly, her head and shoulders were black. Not negro chocolate, but black like they'd been painted over . . . or (he didn't like to think it) . . . or burnt. Yeah, her head looked all burnt up. What little hair she had was prickly, like savannah scrub after a bad fire.

I can see through her, which means she's a ghost. Slowly, by degrees, he stood up from his chair. She floated towards him, her body passing through the desk with the computer on it. She looked upset, was shaking her head at him.

"W-w-who are you?" he asked, relieved that at least she wasn't one of servitors. Now he'd begun having serious jitters, his heart was pounding like a drum. This was all insane. Who was this kid? He remembered how Venus had pissed herself and he'd smirked. *Oh, yeah? The only reason I'm not doing the same now is 'cos I just peed; but . . . but, if this gets any weirder, I can still poop my pants!*

110

"Who are you?" he asked the ghost girl again, growing more horrified the longer he stared at her see-thru burnt face.

"You shouldn't have come up here," she said sadly. "Now the servitors will get you. If you'd just stayed downstairs . . ."

Chad wasn't listening. Black smoke had begun streaming in under the door. In a minute, the four servitors were in the room with him and grabbing on to him.

Chad discovered the servitors' gaseous appearance was deceptive. Their ethereal grip was like that of iron fingers. *Tighter than a starlet's anus,* he thought in despair as the four wispy apparitions lifted him up, well off the floor.

"Please let me go!" he pleaded with the servitors. "Let me go!"

The black gas-creatures gave no sense that they could hear him. One opened the staff lounge door. Then, each holding an arm or leg, they bore Chad off between them.

Behind them, the spectral Karen Hamilton kept sadly shaking her charred head. Then she vanished.

CHAPTER 19

Tanya

Tanya had been rooting hard for Chad to somehow escape the servitors. That would give them all hope.

The class was a heart throbbing with morbid expectation. The Schoolmaster sat regarding his notebooks, while Peaches strode back and forth between the 'students' cracking the skin whip against the floor. Tanya knew the girl was doing it just to keep everyone in line. It was working: the whip's wet crack against the desks, coupled with the slug-like squish of its retraction, and the deep furrows its bone studs left in whatever furniture it hit, had everyone toeing the line of least resistance.

Tanya glanced over at Venus. The woman looked numb, like she'd accidentally peed her personality out when she'd wet the floor just now. Her face was white, her eyes even whiter. She was leaned forward on her desk, arms wrapped around her fat breasts like she was protecting them from evil.

Tanya sympathized.

Still cracking the whip, Peaches walked past her. Tanya watched Mike regarding the teen's backside a moment, then she leaned forward and whispered to the two young men.

"Guys, keep your eyes open for something we can use. We *can* make it out of here."

"Yeah?" Mike replied morosely. "I don't see us getting up and leaving this classroom. We're like sitting ducks. I mean, did you fucking see those things he called servitors? There must be loads of—"

"Get a grip, man!" She looked quickly over at the Schoolmaster, hoping the harshness of her voice hadn't alerted him to their conversation. But, no, he was still reading. (It was odd: his eyes almost seemed to be beaming darkness onto the pages of his book.) "Listen:

112

the Schoolmaster didn't know Venus and Jordan were cheating, did he?"

"No, but what does that prove?"

Jordan said, "Dude, I get it. She means the son-of-a-bitch isn't all-knowing. He's not a god, just some demon underling." He too glanced over at the big-nosed man in the drab brown suit, with eyes too black to make out. "I don't think he even knows we're discussing him now."

Peaches turned from grinning nastily at Venus to look at the trio. "What are you three planning?"

Mike flipped her the bird. She turned away in a huff.

Jordan said, "I still can't tell if she's alive or not. That clock in her chest seems embedded in her heart like . . ."

"An infernal pacemaker," Tanya finished for him. She gestured to Venus, who left her desk on the other side of the room and hurried over to join them. She seemed somewhat recovered now.

The Schoolmaster looked up from his notes. "Stop moving about. That's an additional demerit for you, Venus."

Scowling, Venus flumped herself down in the seat next to Tanya and behind Mike. "If that prick keeps giving me demerits, I'll . . ."

Tanya wrinkled her nose; Venus reeked of urine. *Did she just call the Schoolmaster a prick? Well, at least she's spunky. We need that kinda spirit now.*

"Sorry," Venus said once she realized the others could smell her, "I left my deodorant upstairs in my purse."

Jordan shrugged it off. "Look, Venus, you really should take all these demerits you're getting seriously. They'll count against you in later tests."

In response, she bent forward and kissed him on the cheek. "I never said thanks for keeping my ass alive. Then her expression turned sly. "You guys think Chad got away? 'Cos if he did, I suggest we all make a break for it."

"A break to where?" Mike asked, pointing outside at the thick mist.

Venus shrugged. "To wherever the hell Chad got away to."

Then they all heard Chad yelling, "Put me the fuck down! Let me go!" from outside in the corridor. Venus's eyes spread wide. "Shit!"

Mike grimaced, then hid his face in his hands. "See? He didn't get away."

Next moment, Chad was carried screaming into the class, flat in midair between the four servitors. Tanya instantly noted that his kicking and flailing didn't bother the four ghosts in the least. Instead,

Chad's wrists and shins bore bruises from his attempts to wrench them free from the servitors' gaseous grasp.

"Put him on the desk with the corpse and hold him down there," the Schoolmaster instructed, rising to his feet.

Peaches had in the meantime gone back to sit on the desk with Sherri's body, where she'd been examining Cutter's suspended corpse, peering into her dead ex's face like they were both telepathic. Now, she unceremoniously shoved Sherri's body off the desk.

Sherri thudded out of sight. Peaches leapt down.

Chad was laid face-up on the desk, flat and spreadeagled. A black ghost stood at the end of each of his limbs, forcing them apart into a weird approximation of someone chained down in a four-poster bed.

"What do you think they'll do to him?" Venus asked.

"Duh? They're going to kill him?" Mike offered.

"Shush!"

The Schoolmaster, his large nose stabbing the air, approached Chad. "Now, Chad, you're going to die. That's all your fault, not mine." He looked over sternly at the others. "For each one of you, dying here in Detention is totally your own fault, remember that. You're all guilty—Ms. Principal and myself are simply trying to determine what it is you're each guilty of. Do you understand?"

The four of them nodded guiltily. Tanya didn't understand *why* she felt guilty. Guilty of what? Being alive? Breathing?

"Good." He returned his attention to Chad, running a bony finger along his nose while speaking. "Ms. Principal, the saws please."

Peaches grinned a freaky grin. "At once, sir." She ducked out of sight behind the desk. Tanya shuddered. *Dead or not, that girl is still a major psycho, and likely now an enhanced version of her previous horrible self.*

Chad, whose protests had subsided to a terrified gibbering, let out a loud howl the moment Peaches reappeared above the desk with two large carpentry saws in hand. Both saws had red discolored patches in their middles. They could just have been rusty, but Tanya didn't think so.

"No!" Chad shrieked as Peaches placed one saw across his midriff, and handed the Schoolmaster the other. "You can't do this to me!"

"But *we are* going to. The others will learn from your example: Here in Detention, friendship is meaningless."

Tanya leapt to her feet. "Don't do it!"

The Schoolmaster had just placed his saw on Chad's chest. He paused and regarded her coolly. "What is it, Tanya? Would you prefer to take his place? That too is acceptable to me."

Peaches sniggered. "Hey, cop, sit down. Don't spoil our fun."

"This isn't fun, Ms. Principal; it's discipline."

Peaches giggled. "Whatever you say, sir. She's still interrupting us."

"A good point. Now, Tanya, you either sit down and keep quiet or replace Chad on the table. The choice of fate is yours."

Tanya didn't believe it: Was Chad was actually staring pleadingly at her, asking that she take his place and be sawn in three? *Sorry, dude, no frigging way is that happening!*

Gulping, she sat down. The Schoolmaster was right: friendship didn't mean anything in this murder classroom of his.

The sawing began. With a slow and steady rhythm, the infernal pair began sinking their saws through Chad's shirt into his chest. Blood appeared, first in a thin red line, then it spurted messily over the saws, over Chad's body, over the table.

Chad, meanwhile, was screaming fit to wake the dead. An endless "NOOOOOOO!!!" that suddenly warped into wordless noise that conveyed just horror, agony, and anguish.

And they could do nothing but watch. The four servitors stood, each a static column of wavering black gas, their fingers holding Chad's limbs spread out as immobile as if they were lashed to steel girders.

Tanya, Venus, Jordan, and Mike, stared speechless. Venus began crying. Tanya had her knuckles in her mouth. The boys' eyes were so wide open . . . This was way more arresting than watching some car crash.

Then, with his saw buried two inches deep in Chad's chest, the Schoolmaster stopped. He gestured to Peaches, who'd pushed the belly skin by her saw aside and was poking Chad's innards with her fingers. (Chad was still screaming, though he sounded more like a dog in pain than a human.) Both their hands and clothes were blood-splattered.

"What's the matter, sir?" Peaches asked. "You're tired?"

"Enough sawing, Ms. Principal. He's too noisy. We should have gagged him first."

"We can use my panties as a gag," Peaches suggested hopefully. "That way he—"

"No. That is gross."

"Alright, sir. Whatever you say." Peaches meekly removed her saw from Chad's body, but Tanya could tell that she wasn't at all pleased.

Blood from Chad's body was dripping on the floor all around the desk. Now the sawing had stopped, he'd stopped screaming. Once again, Tanya read hope in his eyes. Maybe hope for a quick death, she couldn't tell.

"So what do we do now, sir?" Peaches asked.

The Schoolmaster grinned wickedly. "We make an exemplary example of him. Servitors, pull him apart limb from limb."

The statement cut through Chad's pain. "Nooo!" he mouthed silently.

"Nooo!" Tanya gasped as the four black wisps began pulling on Chad's arms and legs like they were contestants in a tug of war and he was the rope. They didn't move from their places; they simply 'hauled him in' as it were. And fast at that.

Like he was being quartered between four horses, Chad exploded apart, his arms and legs flying off his torso like missiles. Blood squirting from shoulder and hip joints, his body collapsed onto the desk.

But Chad was still alive. He looked sideways at Venus. Venus yelped in terror and fainted. Tanya caught her before she toppled sideways out of her seat. She laid Venus's head in her lap and stroked her pink hair.

Then Chad died too, the blood pumping out of him ceasing abruptly like someone had turned all his taps off at once.

The servitors dug their ghostly hands into Chad's torso and ripped it to bits, till finally there was just his head and shreds of him left on the table. (Tanya winced on seeing his penis go flying through the air and out the door; and yes, it *was* huge!) There was gore everywhere; the front of the schoolroom looked like an abattoir.

Mike lurched over and puked into the aisles between the desks. He remained bent over there, vomiting for all he was worth.

Jordan and Tanya stared at the Schoolmaster and Peaches.

"This is just a demonstration," the Schoolmaster said. "Here in Detention, we're not playing games with you."

"No, no games at all," Peaches added. "Here, we reform you until you die."

CHAPTER 20

Jordan

04:51, Peaches' timepiece read.

"Okay, the Schoolmaster said, "we'll now have a thirty-minute recess before the next test."

Jordan raised a hand, keeping his eyes off the red mess that had been Chad Cannon now strewn across the front of the classroom. (Thankfully, Sherri's body was now invisible behind the bloody desk.) "Where are the restrooms?"

He was aware of Mike and Detective Rockford nodding to his enquiry. He was even more aware of the pressure in his bladder. If he didn't relieve it soonest, he'd follow Venus's lead, and no, he wasn't having any demerits on his scorecard.

"Outside, end of the corridor to the right," the Schoolmaster replied. "All of you will go at once." He nodded at the comatose Venus, who the detective had draped over two chairs. "Except her, I guess, but then she's already gone."

Staring at the man's sadistic face, with those horrible black non-eyes like oil wells of evil, Jordan couldn't tell if he was making a joke or not. He groaned at the Schoolmaster's next words.

"The servitors will escort you there and back."

"What?" Detective Rockford said angrily.

Peaches giggled. "Not into the cubicles, you ditz. No one wants to watch your yellow river flow." Jordan cringed at the mad face framed by that dirty-blonde hair. Seeing the whip of plaited negro skin hanging around Peaches neck brought tears to his eyes. *That's my girlfriend's skin and bones, you crazy bitch. My God—how'd we fall into Insanity 101?*

The Schoolmaster said, "The servitors are to ensure you don't run away. We can't spend the whole evening looking for each of you. Also,

I don't want any stupid suicide attempts. Now run along, all of you, and make your water. Afterwards you'll go to the cafeteria for lunch, and after that return here . . ." he strode over to the slaughter desk and lifted Chad's head up by its hair, "so we can determine who's smart and who's not."

They shambled reluctantly towards the door where the four gas ghosts awaited. Jordan kept his eyes off the mess everywhere. Mike walked like he was blind to it all, slipping on spilled intestine so Detective Rockford had to grab him before he fell sprawling.

The detective was looking everything over with cold eyes. Calculating eyes. Jordan knew she was figuring out the angles and scheming their escape. He was glad of that.

Right at the door, Jordan turned back. He looked first at the Schoolmaster, then pointed to Venus. "Sir, I think it'll be best if the servitors bring her along with us."

"She's unconscious," Peaches pointed out. "And she's female; there's nothing to hold on to to help her pee."

"Yes, yes, yes, but . . ." Jordan stared coolly at the Schoolmaster. "If she wakes up when we're gone and we're not here, she'll think you've killed us all and she'll start screaming the house down. Trust me, you won't like the noise."

The Schoolmaster nodded. "Very well then. Two of you servitors carry Venus along behind the others."

"And handle her *gently*," Peaches added. "Don't break her before it's time to break her."

Two of the servitors floated over to Venus. One took her arms, the other her legs. Dangling her four feet off the floor, they carried her out the door.

Jordan exited last, taking care to keep his eyes off the pair of brown legs projecting around the end of the desk. Then at the door, he relented and looked; he couldn't help it. Aware of the Schoolmaster's and Peaches' gaze on him, he stared at Sherri. He gasped in horror. Shadowed by the desk, his girlfriend's dusky body seemed a lump of tarmac ripped from a road, the pale trench of excavated skin down its left side a white lane divider, the blood about her shoulders and breasts remnants of a micro car crash. Tears filled his eyes again. *Shit, Sherri! This wasn't supposed to happen, we were so happy together!*

Jordan felt like he'd just been shot in the heart. Drying his eyes with his sleeve, he ran past the servitors to join the others.

Mike and Detective Rockford had just reached the toilet door.

"Wait up, Detective," he said on reaching them.

She turned to him, one hand on the door handle, her brown hair shadowing her eyes. She looked tired but still full of fight. Jordan admired that.

She smiled tightly. "Just call me Tanya. We're all students again now, right? Okay, what's bothering you?" She gestured around her, then at the four black figures floating six yards away, Venus raised between them like a sacrifice. "I mean, other than everything else that's fucked up."

He panted awhile, containing his hurt. He dropped his voice to a whisper. "Tanya, you need to be careful. I suspect the next test will be something to get rid of you. The Schoolmaster knows you're thinking of getting us out of here."

"Hell, don't I know it?" She turned and entered the restroom.

"I like her," Mike whispered reflectively as she vanished into a cubicle.

"You like Ms. Psycho too," Jordan said over the sound of Tanya unzipping her pants. "Dude, keep it in your pants."

"No, no, not like that. I *really* like her. She reminds me of my big sister Kelly. Remember Kelly's a cop too."

Yeah, Mike's sister Kelly was a narc cop. Jordan didn't like her. She was cold and hard, total business; which was good, only she took it too far.

He looked back to ensure Venus was still asleep, then said, "C'mon, dude, Tanya's way nicer than Kelly. Remember when she flushed our pot?"

Mike winced. He still remembered the day his sister had found their stash of pure Acapulco gold. Seven hundred bucks worth of Mexican green down the drain. And Kelly had threatened to bust them both next time around. So from then on they'd kept their marijuana in their hostel. 'Chamber pot' Mike called it, because they hid in under his bed in an eighteenth century commode Jordan had bought at a garage sale.

"Ah, Kelly's frigging mean," Mike agreed. "Remember her boyfriend Luis ran off with another woman 'cos she worked him over with her nightstick? Broke his damn hand."

"Why would she do that?" Tanya asked, rejoining them.

"She caught him watching porn. She broke the hand he was wanking with."

Tanya frowned. "That's a stupid overreaction," she said, "and definitely no way for a policewoman to behave." Then suddenly, out of nowhere, she burst out laughing.

Jordan looked at her sharply. Seeing his scrutiny, she quickly controlled herself, her mirth altering to a cold frown of disapproval.

Wow! Jordan thought with a shiver. *It's like she actually approves of what Kelly did. Damn, maybe all policewomen are the same: Hard, cold, and mean.*

Tanya said, "Look, are you two gonna pee or not?" She tapped her watch. "We're due back in Hell in twenty-two minutes. Go, go, I'll watch over Sleeping Beauty for you princes."

Leaving her at the door, Jordan and Mike ran off to the urinals.

***

Jordan stared morosely at himself in the cracked mirror above the washbasin. His fractured reflection perfectly fit his current state of mind. He hardly felt the water pouring over his hands. No matter how hard he tried to concentrate on survival, his thoughts kept flitting back to Sherri . . .

They'd met at Tufts University, in a Statistics elective class they were both taking. One look at her with her smiling brown eyes, and Jordan was smitten. They'd hooked up and she'd been cute and smart and fun and they'd fallen in love and next week was 'meet the parents' at her house in Chelsea and the week after was supposed to see them meeting his parents in Cambridge, and next thing they'd come on this crazy trip for Mike's research project, hitching across the Bay State and . . .

We're here, he thought grimly. *We made love this morning and now she's a pile of meat back there.*

(Under normal circumstances, this would have been a fantastic day for Jordan Levine. The greatest in his life. Venus Deluxe was in the friggin' house! His favorite porn star! God only knew how many loads he'd spurted to her videos. His frequency of masturbation had greatly reduced since he'd been dating Sherri, but he'd occasionally still rubbed one off to Venus Deluxe behind Sherri's back, fantasizing about those perfect breasts, that toned belly, and those sweet vaginal lips that seemed to be begging him to dip his tongue between them . . . And now Venus was here in the same building as he was and . . .

well, with Sherri dead, he definitely wasn't likely to get it up any time soon.)

"Hey, man, let's go," Mike said.

Jordan looked at his best friend; he wiped his eyes dry.

Mike placed a hand on his arm. "I'm truly sorry about Sherri, man." He paused a moment, his expression equally glum. "Maybe, if we find a way to kill the Schoolmaster it'll be some kind of payback for her . . . for Chad too. It won't bring them back, but the bastard won't have gotten off scot free."

Jordan nodded. Yeah, killing the Schoolmaster seemed the only thing to do. It wasn't like Tanya could arrest he and Peaches and arraign them in court for trial.

He let Mike lead him back to the door.

Followed by the servitors, who still carried the unconscious Venus, they walked back to the classroom, where Peaches was waiting to lead them to the cafeteria.

CHAPTER 21

Tanya

The school cafeteria was wide, with lots of dusty tables. It had a lot of windows with a wide outside view of short grass and strange gray flowers. And, of course, the wall.

Almost like in a parody of a prison movie, they lined up and Peaches handed them trays of food.

05:04, the clock in her chest now read.

Lunch was burgers with fries, and flat Cokes. With Venus still out, her meal was collected by a servitor. Suspended on splayed-out black ethereal fingers, it looked like the tray floated in midair.

They picked out a table across the room, well away from Peaches. The servitor with the tray placed it by Tanya, who sat opposite Mike and Jordan.

I wonder what the guys think of me now? Tanya wondered. She knew she'd given off a nasty vibe by laughing at the story of Mike's sister breaking her boyfriend's hand for jerking off. But her laughter hadn't been intentional: propelled by a memory of her own, it had just slipped out. Still she disliked the impression of her it gave her two young male companions. *Sorry, boys, but that's how the bone breaks: Being a lady cop ain't easy. If we're not already callous bitches when we join the force, the criminal world soon conspires to make us that way.*

The pair didn't seem to have noticed though, which she was grateful for. Both young men sat there jabbing unenthusiastically at their fries, then shoveling them into their mouths and washing the masticated mash down with swills of the stale Coke. Tanya wondered how old the Coca-Cola was; it tasted like someone had mistaken it for wine in 1950 and sealed it in a cask to age it. It was drinkable though, and the fries were passable. None of them had yet dared try their burgers. Tanya made out definite patches of mold on the side of

Mike's top bun. *And what the hell is this meat inside them? Stuff looks like roadkill.*

"We'd better wake her up to eat," she said, pointing at Venus. The porno actress lay like a Disney princess, serene in space across the arms of the four ghosts. Utterly gorgeous in her slumber, her big breasts wobbling jelly mounds on her rising and falling chest, her nipples like cherries on cupcakes. It seemed almost a crime to rouse her.

"Okay, I'll be waiting in class," Peaches called from across the room. "Ensure you head back the same way we came. The servitors'll lead you if you're not sure of the route. Don't go off exploring; there are creatures in the corridors you don't wanna meet."

She left. Tanya watched Mike's surveillance of Peaches' departing rear, her swaying gait making her ass muscles twitch. Then, shrugging (men would be men even in the face of danger), she got up, picked up her drink, and emptied half of it in Venus's face.

Venus sputtered slowly awake. It took her a while to get her bearings, then, realizing the black ghosts were holding her up, she yelped loudly and almost fainted again. Jordan, however, quickly dumped more Coca-cola in her face, some of which got into her nose.

Sputtering furiously, she allowed Tanya help her down from the servitors' grasps. She sat at the table, dabbing at her face with a napkin.

"Welcome back," Mike said.

"Eat, girl," Tanya instructed her.

"No. I'll never have an appetite again in my life." Her eyes turned teary. "I can't believe what they did to Chad. They . . . they . . ."

"None of us has an appetite either," Jordan said gently. "But we need the energy. Without food, the brain doesn't work as good, and . . ."

Venus nodded, lifted her burger and bit into it.

"Tastes like shit," she said between bites. "But then, I've tasted shit before, so I guess this is way better, at least it's nutritious." She saw Tanya gaping at her. "No . . . no . . . it wasn't intentional, not scat; but whenever we're gonna film an ATM scene—"

"What's ATM?" Tanya asked. "When you're filming in a bank?"

"Ass-to-mouth. When you're screwing a girl's backside, then pull out and stick it in her mouth."

"Oh."

Venus took another bite of her burger, chewed, swallowed. "Well the standard procedure for those scenes is to not eat for a day or two before the shoot, stay on mainly liquids so your ass is all clean inside even before you have an enema; but some girls don't pay attention, so they're not clean, and when the guy pulls out of their butt, his dick is—"

"We get it," Tanya said quickly, feeling her last mouthful of fries about to come back up. "Hey, are you *sure* that burger is okay?"

"Positive. The Coke tastes like horse piss, but . . ."

Tanya wasn't about asking Venus how she knew what horse urine tasted like. She hoped it was merely a figure of speech. Still, she'd been their food tester. Hopefully, these burgers wouldn't give them all food poisoning; though, considering what awaited them after lunch, a toxic death might be a blessing.

Dully, she lifted her burger to her lips and took a tentative bite. (Venus was right: she couldn't tell what the meat was, but it was eatable.) She felt utterly strange, like reality dangled above her on a thread to which Satan was holding a razor. This was way worse than the Sword of Damocles. *One of us isn't going to survive this evening. Someone is going to die once we get back to the classroom. And yet, we're all sitting here eating calmly . . . But what else can we do? We can't escape the servitors. At least, not yet. Chad tried and look what it got him: he's smeared all over the floor. But there must be a way to escape this evil place! There has to be! I for one am not dying in here like a turkey in a shoot!*

The servitors had retreated a distance from the table. They wavered there, the very fact of their insubstantiality terrifying to behold. Seeing them threatened to unnerve Tanya. She clutched tightly at her sanity, clenched it to her like something of inestimable value, a purse of gold studded with diamonds. (It was only now, now in this brief respite amidst the overwhelming insanity of the day [how ironic that it was during the demon Schoolmaster's recess!], that Tanya realized an oddity: she'd so far [and it seemed to be the same with her companions] not really questioned how any of this could be happening. Normally, one questioned the onset of madness, didn't they? Maybe this omission was because everything—beginning with their weird inexplicable transition—had happened so rapidly, like a flash flood or raging tsunami. One never questioned the 'how' of a flood's occurrence when caught up in its raging. Analysis came later, after survival. But at the moment, particularly in a situation like this, where 'the other,' the accepted and known reality, had somehow vanished—she gazed out of the cafeteria windows at the swirling tentacles above the wall—and possibly vanished for good . . . up till now, they'd had no time to disbelieve what was happening to them.)

Tanya took another bite of her burger, then discarded it. Her appetite had completely vanished. Dully, she realized Mike had just eaten the moldy portion of his burger. She'd forgotten to warn him. She'd not checked hers either; she wondered if it had had mold on it too. It didn't matter. Depressed, she turned and stared out of the window, at the stone wall beyond the pleasant grass field.

She realized Venus was waving fingers at her. She turned to her, saw that Venus had finished her own food. *Damn, she sure regained her appetite fast.*

"Yeah?"

Venus pointed at Tanya's discarded burger. "Can I have that if you don't want it?"

"Sure." Tanya pushed the tray at her and returned her attention to staring out of the windows.

"Thanks. Suddenly I'm just so hungry. I hardly ate anything yesterday either, just guzzled lots of beer."

Tanya nodded disinterestedly. She concentrated on tuning the room out, tuning the servitors out. She needed to concentrate on the details of this prison they were trapped in.

Then Jordan said, "Okay, here's what we know about this place. From the length of time Chad was gone when he fled, it's quite large."

Tanya turned back to face him. Thank heavens someone else was thinking about how they could escape this damn place! "How can you tell that?"

Jordan continued: "Easy, it's like calculating a room's size from the echoes it makes. Even splitting the time into two equal halves— Chad's flight with the servitors in pursuit, and their trip back after catching him—it took fifteen minutes either way. And remember, it takes just ten seconds to run a hundred yards. So this is a *large* place."

Venus nodded between bites of burger.

"And . . ." Jordan pointed out of the cafeteria's corridor windows, "just to buttress that, we were walking about three minutes to get here, and it's a different set of corridors from those we took to the classroom in the first place. And that brings me to another point—"

"Lower your voice," Tanya said. She pointed at the servitors. "What if these things can hear us?"

"Forget them," Mike said. "There's no doubt that they *can* hear us. They heard the Schoolmaster, and he was speaking English. But they're mute, they're not about telling him what we're saying."

Venus looked worriedly over at the servitors. Tanya looked worriedly at Jordan. "Do you think so too?" Mike hadn't so far struck her as being overly brilliant, Jordan had.

Jordan nodded. "I do. The servitors give the impression of being clouds of gas that obey commands, but they lack initiative. No, they won't report us. Okay, so we also know there are only four servitors."

Venus asked, "There are?"

He nodded again. "We saw the Schoolmaster summon them. Here's the thing: at the moment, the Schoolmaster thinks he's got us under control. Except we give him trouble, he's unlikely to call up more servitors from wherever they're from." Jordan tapped the table. "Now, what else we know about this place? It has at least three floors: this one, the floor we're roomed on, and the one the landing on our floor leads up to. . . ."

"We also know for certain that there are dangerous monsters in here," Tanya said. "Peaches just told us so. That's something else to be careful—"

"All students will now return to the classroom," the Schoolmaster's frog-croak voice blared out of the air over their table. "Lateness in returning from recess should naturally attract demerits—"

"Not more demerits!" Venus spat angrily.

"—However, in light of this being a general action, there will be no such award of penalties. However, if you're not all back in class in five minutes, you will each receive two lashes of Ms. Principal's whip for each extra minute of lateness."

Tanya had a sudden vivid image of Peaches' whip tearing into her skin, and its sharp bone studs shredding her flesh. *Hell no!*

Galvanized by fear, she leapt to her feet.

"Okay, everyone," she growled, "get up and let's run back to the class. And I mean *run*."

They set off running, the servitors finding it difficult to keep pace with them.

CHAPTER 22

Venus

The classroom had been cleaned in their absence.

Venus was relieved to see it. Gone were all traces of Chad's gory passing. The floor was spic-and-span, shiny in parts like it had just been polished. The desk on which Chad had been butchered was likewise clean. Odder still, it was dry. Jordan, clearly as perplexed as she, swiped his fingers over it. The wood gleamed like it was freshly laminated.

Sherri's body was gone too; she sensed Jordan's relief at this. The gutted male body hung like an anatomy display was still there, however, killing illusions of normalcy.

And also . . .

"Our cell has a new door," Tanya whispered, nodding towards the Schoolmaster, who sat quietly, his impossibly black eyes watching them file into the room, all exhausted by their mad dash back from the cafeteria. No one wanted 'Ms. Principal' whipping them.

Venus hadn't noticed the new door. Now she did and gasped. "This stuff really is magic."

The new door in the wall stood just past the Schoolmaster's desk. It was aluminum, with a glass window as its top half. Venus noted the faintest smear of red on its bottom edge. *Hmmm. So that's how they disposed of the bodies.*

The boys were already seated. (She couldn't help thinking of them as 'boys,' they both were so fresh and cute!) Her heart pumping gratitude to Jordan, she followed Tanya back to their previous places. (She still didn't know what to make of Tanya. The brunette cop was definitely good-looking [if a bit on the heavy side], but frumpy, like she'd not had a date in so long, she'd forgotten what men liked in women. It wasn't her lack of makeup, either, but her carriage—she walked like a man herself. But Venus had also noticed Tanya appraising the boys' bodies and secretly smiling, so she knew she wasn't gay, or not completely anyway. Other than that? The lady was tough for sure. Venus could tell Tanya wasn't letting herself be dragged into a slump over this mess they were in. Venus intended on sticking close to her.)

They sat, their positions reversed now. Tanya slid in behind Mike, Venus sat at the aisle desk, behind Jordan. They waited quietly, tense with palpable dread, all temporary good feeling vanished. The reality of their bad situation had imprisoned them again once they'd stepped through the classroom door.

Shit! Venus realized. *One of us is going to die horribly in a short while. This is survival of the smartest. I'd better not wet myself again and get more stupid demerits!* That thought made her look over at the floor under her previous desk. Her mess had been cleaned up too. *But by who? I can't imagine either the Schoolmaster or that Peaches girl doing janitor work. That means we've at least one more person here to watch out for.*

The four servitors hovered by the door. Peaches walked between them into the class. She'd now wrapped her whip around her waist like a belt. She was carrying two transparent plastic cups and a small digital scale. She set them down on the freshly cleaned desk then sat on the desk's edge.

The Schoolmaster rose to his feet.

"It's time for the second test," he said, his lips set in an unamused scowl. "This time we focus on human biology. Now, can any of you tell me how much semen a human male normally ejaculates?"

"Between two and six milliliters," Venus instantly replied.

"Correct, Venus. And how many human sperms are contained in that volume?"

"About a hundred million?"

"Correct again, Venus. I'll not ask how you know so much about male biology. Now to your test." He indicated the cups and scale which Peaches had just brought into the class. "This is a group project. Venus, you pair with Jordan, Tanya with Mike. Each of you women is to sexually stimulate your male partner to ejaculation . . ."

All four of them gasped.

". . . and Venus and Tanya, Ms. Principal will give each of you a cup to collect their semen in. You have fifteen minutes, after which we'll weigh the volumes of semen collected from each young man and kill the one who has ejaculated the least amount."

They gasped louder, Jordan and Mike staring at each other in horror. Venus understood: sex had nothing to do with brains. How on earth did one *intentionally* ejaculate more than someone else?

Peaches was meanwhile whispering to the Schoolmaster. He nodded, then looked up and added, "Only one ejaculation each, please. And ladies . . . your partners aren't permitted to touch themselves—*you* have to get them off. Cheating will prove fatal."

"Losing will prove equally fatal," Peaches added. The clock in her breast switched to countdown mode again, set to 0:15:00. The red numbers flashed on and off, ready to start their fatal reduction to zero.

CHAPTER 23

Tanya / Venus

They were separated from each other. Venus and Jordan got the right side of the classroom, Tanya and Mike the left side. Both young men were ordered to remove their trousers.

"I have absolutely no interest in watching this," the Schoolmaster said and vanished. His voice floated back to them. "Ms. Principal will deputize for me. I'll be in the staff lounge upstairs."

"Okay," Peaches said from her seat on the desk. "On your marks . . . get set . . . wank, you two!"

***

Tanya had never considered herself good in bed. To her mind, sex wasn't something you were *good* at: you got in the mood, did it, enjoyed yourself immensely, then forgot about it till next time. It wasn't something you studied books on like you were going to write an exam on it. She did have friends like that, women who were constantly after the next thing to try out in bed, but she'd never been that way herself.

So now, in this situation, kneeling by the seated Mike with his flaccid member staring her in the face, she had little idea what to do.

Across the room, she saw Venus stroking Jordan's penis. (Like Mike's, his member was average-sized, like most of those she'd so far seen.)

She decided to follow Venus's lead; at worst, a hand job would only dirty her fingers.

Wincing, she took Mike's penis in her hands. It was cold and sweaty. She stroked it, pulled on it. There was no response; it remained dead. She looked up at him. His eyes were scared. *Oh hell! He'll never get a hard-on like this!* And she wasn't about losing him; she wasn't a quitter. *I'll make him come, whatever it takes.* Shedding her reservations, she got off her knees, pulled up a chair and sat in it, then kissed him. It was a timid kiss, but soon he lost his nervousness and responded to her. She broke contact and looked into his eyes. "Don't worry, okay, I'll get you off. You'll win this."

He nodded. "It's hard not to think about—"

She silenced him again with a kiss, simultaneously running her hand up and down his manhood. And now she felt it: his penis was swelling, growing in her hand into something throbbing and vibrant, something with a sexual purpose. Her eyes flashed across to Venus, who was slipping down her tube top. Intense jealously struck Tanya as Venus's breasts popped free. Her breasts were fantastic: big and round, and with perfectly situated nipples. *Damn that professional slut!* No way was Tanya taking off her shirt for Mike's benefit. She'd be too embarrassed. Her breasts sagged and she was a bit flabby about the belly, with prominent love handles.

She concentrated on kissing and fondling Mike. Time was of the essence here.

***

With Peaches watching everything and the threat of death hanging over both young men, Jordan's penis had also initially flopped between his legs like a dead fish.

Then Venus removed her top and pirouetted for him. Like she'd imagined, seeing her bared breasts had the desired effect on Jordan's manhood; it had instantly come half-erect. She'd expected that; her breasts were utterly perfect—the best that plastic surgery could come up with at the moment. She gloated at the half-swollen penis. *Okay, so far so good. All I need to do now is suck him extra hard and he'll pop his top into the plastic cup and we'll win!*

She got down on her knees and bent towards the straining penis. She touched its tip with her tongue, felt the swollen head leap towards her mouth. She sucked him into her mouth, swallowed him, slid up again, down again. (His crotch smelt all sweaty, but since when was that tabu to a porno actress?) Winning this contest was very important to her. Foremost in her mind was how Jordan was responsible for her still being alive now. So she wasn't losing him. And besides, in this arena, she didn't consider Tanya any competition. She looked over at

Tanya, saw her kissing Mike while her fingers worked his erection. *Not bad, girl, but . . . what the hell do you cops know about sex anyway, other than busting hookers?* Venus couldn't even guess at the number of blowjobs and hand jobs she given guys—both on and off screen—during her years in the adult industry, so there was no way Jordan wasn't going to 'out-come' Mike. Except . . .

"Venus?"

She lifted her gaze to his worried face. "What is it, baby?"

He sighed. "I'm not sure I've enough in me. Sherri and I did it both last night and this morning."

Venus concealed a grimace. *Shit, that's what I've been scared of, that he's earlier given it all to his girlfriend.* Then she smiled reassuringly at him. "Don't worry about it, I know where the come comes from. I'll find some more for you."

He nodded.

"Now you have to really trust me, okay?"

"Okay."

"Move your ass to the edge of the chair and spread your thighs."

Once he'd done so, she licked her index finger, then slid it into his anus and began massaging his prostrate. His eyes spread wide in shock and his erection leapt up even harder than before. Dropping her lips back down over his penis, Venus couldn't help laughing to herself. *No, I don't think little Sherri ever did this to you before.*

***

Tanya too began performing fellatio on Mike. He had nicely muscled abs and a six-pack and looked like he regularly worked out in the gym.

"Imagine there's only me and you in the room," she said, then bent over and started sucking on him. The hard penis tasted salty with old sweat, but she persevered. She was pleased when Mike began groaning with pleasure. *Oh, yes! Just come for me, baby!* Keeping one hand stroking Mike's shaft and the other fondling his testicles, she took her mouth off his erection and glanced over at Venus and Jordan. She grimaced in disgust. *Ugh! She's what . . . ?* Venus had her finger—no, it was two fingers!—stuck up Jordan's anus and was sliding them in and out while at the same time sucking on him hard and jerking on his shaft with her other hand. *The hell? No way am I doing that!*

Quickening her own strokes on Mike's penis, she looked up at his face to check she was doing okay with him.

"Tell me when you're about coming, alright?"

"Yeah, yeah," he gasped.

Tanya was shocked. Mike's gaze was riveted, not on her, but across the room on Venus and Jordan. *No, not on both of them,* she realized. *He's just watching her . . . ogling her huge tits. He's probably jerked off to Venus more times than I've booked perps! And here I am, with his dirty dick in my mouth, his smelly balls bumping my chin, trying to save his goddam life while he imagines he's screwing his fave porno fantasy?* She was utterly pissed off now. *Okay, so I've not got my kit off, but . . .* Forget it: sex competition or not, Tanya wasn't taking her clothes off in public, not for Mike, not for anyone.

Upset and angry, she nonetheless dropped her mouth back over Mike's penis. The gasps that instantly leapt from his throat were insufficient validation of her femininity; they seemed impure to her, tarnished by his lust for Venus.

The sexual challenge had been laid down. Tanya's female pride was at stake now: this was a competition she wasn't losing. No, not to some over-the-hill porno actress. *Mike, you son-of-a-bitch, you'd better come a whole bucketload for me or I'll kill you myself—the Schoolmaster won't need to.* She sucked him with a vengeance. He groaned and squirmed on the chair. He tried to help her; she slapped his hands away angrily, then growled up at him, "No cheating, you dick!"

She resumed sucking. And now, as she fellated him, Tanya's mind wandered back down memory lane:

***

Her mind flittered back to why she'd laughed when Mike had told the story about his sister breaking her beau's hand for watching porn.

Tanya had actually done something similar. Oh, she admitted it now, it was a dumb thing to do. But back then, filled with righteous indignation, she hadn't cared a bit. The ass had gotten what it deserved.

With the job she did, sex with her husband Randy had become an issue after a while. She saw too many raped women, their crotches bleeding like they were having their periods, their faces battered in like they'd been slugging it out in the octagon with Rhonda Rousey, and she really didn't feel like screwing anyone. And when she was unlucky enough to get saddled with working a pedophile case because no one else wanted the psychic burden of that crap? Her sex drive vanished back up inside her uterus for months on end.

And being married, that was one hell of a big problem.

Tanya had been working late one night, leaving her husband Randy alone at home. She and her partner had been driving through her neighborhood at 1 a.m., when feeling suddenly horny, she'd decided to surprise her husband in bed for a quick screw. (Randy was a terrible insomniac anyway; she expected he'd be reading.)

She'd quietly let herself into the house, and found him in his study masturbating to porn.

To her immense relief, it hadn't been any kiddie stuff, or even some underage Traci Lords scene. All the girls were clearly over 18 as the Custodian of Records credits attested, though most clearly bore vestiges of baby fat.

But the sight of their anuses! *Anabolic Anal Atrocities*, the video was called, and Tanya found no reason to argue with that title. It was a riotous collage of post-teen sexuality, the girls' rectums deep red chasms, and surprising poop-free too behind the terrifyingly distended rings of their anuses. Tanya had been horrified by the depths of those buttholes. And . . . Shouldn't they be filled with excrement? *Don't you kids ever eat anything, or do those male chauvinist pigs starve you too?*

The ass-to-mouth scenes had her silently gagging.

Tanya couldn't believe what she was seeing. An endless transition of young Jennas and Jaylas and Jessas and Kendras and Kaylas and Kiaras and Keishas and Kissas getting their asses stuffed. She winced: some first names seemed to practically condemn a young girl to a future career in porn.

Randy, why the hell are you watching this?

Unaware he was being observed, Randy Rockford was meanwhile blissfully having his second orgasm since she'd arrived home. The more Tanya watched him pleasure himself, the more incensed she grew that her husband—not some raincoated perv in the back of a theater—was getting off on this crap. Seeing Randy spurt to a freckled redhead spreading her buttock cheeks wide so globs of semen could seep out of her anus, Tanya had felt like smashing his head in with the grip of her gun, but she'd managed to hold back.

She'd get him for this for sure, but it had to be done especially memorably.

So, angry as hell reheated, Tanya had silently let herself out of the house again and returned to work. Back home in the morning, she'd acted sweetly like nothing was wrong. Inside, however, she was seething and plotting her 'revenge.'

Then a week later, Tanya had spiked Randy's wine with liquid Benadryl. She'd waited till he was out cold, then she'd gagged him and cuffed him hand-and-foot to the bed posts. Belly up and spread-eagled. Then, without lubing it first, she'd forced her nightstick up her husband's ass. There'd been a lot of blood, but she hadn't stopped. She'd forced it in real deep, then duct-taped it in place.

Next, while Randy was squealing in pain and trying to work out was going on, Tanya set up his laptop by their bed, then ran a playlist of her husband's porno downloads on it—*Anabolic Anal Atrocities*, *Butt Busters 11 (The Buttmost!)*, *Rectum Wreckers 29*, *Anal Expanders: Sextreme Insertions*, and some clips of big-breasted Japanese girls getting mass-ejaculated on. Then, while he'd lain there with his penis limp and his anus bleeding, she'd gotten out her vibrator and masturbated herself to orgasm to the sight of him writhing in agony.

Then the big finale: she'd gotten up on the bed, and while Randy gaped in stupefaction, she'd urinated all over his head and shoulders. And yes, she'd *really* pissed on him; she'd earlier drank a whole six-pack of beer to ensure she had enough urine available to soak him with. Just to show him how pissed off with him she was.

In the morning, she uncuffed Randy, yanked the nightstick out from his ass (she'd gagged—it really stank of shit), pointed her gun at him and growled, "Alright, now get your things and get out."

Randy had stared at her in disbelief. "What!? C'mon, Tanya."

"Get out before I kill you, you disgusting perverted prick!"

"C'mon, baby, it's just harmless entertainment. You're hardly ever in the mood nowadays . . ."

"Get the fuck out of my life! I hate you. I HATE YOU!"

She'd shook the gun at him. He'd decided she was serious (or at least crazy enough to shoot him) and padded gingerly into the bathroom to clean himself off.

After his bath, Randy painfully limped out of the house. He'd instantly started divorce proceedings. At the divorce hearings, Tanya claimed 'irreconcilable differences'; Randy claimed 'intolerable cruelty.' Randy would have pressed domestic violence charges too, but Tanya bluffed him that she'd recorded everything on her iPhone and that she'd upload it to YouTube if he dared report her. (Of course she hadn't: she was a cop; why the hell would she film herself abusing someone?) Sure she'd be fired from the force, but he'd permanently lose his dignity.

"And," she'd laughed in his face, "if I get a sympathetic judge, I'll get a slap on the wrist anyway—two weeks community service."

She hadn't really dated anyone since her divorce. One or two guys, then that frittered out. Feeling wonderfully empowered in acting single-handed against the porno industry, she'd told some lady friends what she'd done, one of whom (likely in the afterglow of passion, or as a threat, or a joke), had told her boyfriend or husband, and the rumor had gotten out and spread that Tanya was bad news. And that was all she wrote: Tanya's dating life subsequently dive-bombed.

And now, here she was, actively competing against that same porno industry. Like this bloody Schoolmaster creep had read her mind and known exactly what test she'd hate the most. Damn! Life was so unfair!

***

"Oh God, Tanya! You're so fucking awesome! I'm gonna come!"

Tanya was so deep into her reminiscence about her miserable love life that she didn't hear him.

It was only after she'd swallowed Mike's first two spurts of semen that she remembered what she was doing, and, quickly pulling her mouth off him, grabbed the plastic cup to save the rest of his come. Mike, his eyes closed, just kept spurting away.

When he was done ejaculating, Tanya spat what she'd salvaged from her mouth in amongst the rest. She swirled the semen around in the cup, groaning at the thought of how much of it she'd swallowed. But what she had left didn't seem too bad. In fact, it seemed quite a lot.

Across the room, Jordan was coming too. Tanya had to admire Venus's skill as she slipped her mouth off Jordan's penis and tilted it into the mouth of the cup. It clearly wasn't the first time she'd done this.

***

Venus kept sliding her fingers in and out of Jordan's ass while he came. Her fingers were curved upward so she was milking his prostate for all she was worth. She'd have liked to squeeze his balls as well, but she only had two hands, and asking him to hold the cup might count as cheating.

Still, when he'd finished groaning and she saw what she'd gotten out of him, she was delighted. She looked up at him.

"You good, baby? Did I do okay?"

He groaned. "*Okay?* Venus, that was the best blowjob of my entire life."

She laughed self-depreciatingly. "Don't judge too quickly. You're still young; there's lots more BJ's coming your way." She waved the cup of semen at him. "I think we beat them."

"And . . . time's up!" Peaches announced, though they'd not heard her buzzer go.

They looked over at the others. Mike seemed as destroyed as Jordan.

Venus gave Tanya a thumbs up, then her thoughts turned gloomy. *Okay, the fun's over, if it can even be called that. I'm literally holding this boy's life in my hands. I just hope I've gotten enough life out of him to keep him alive.*

***

The Schoolmaster reappeared a few moments later. "Pull up your pants, you two; you've had your fun for today."

While Mike and Jordan hurriedly did so, Peaches collected the cups.

Tanya was depressed now. She wished she'd not gotten lost in thought and swallowed Mike's first spurts. She stared worriedly at the semen she handed over, hoping it'd be enough. She didn't dare look at Mike, so instead she looked over at Venus. Venus had just gotten through pulling her top back up. Seeing the self-satisfied smile on the porn star's face as she handed Peaches her cup of semen, Tanya's heart sank. *We lost . . . dammit! I lost!*

Peaches weighed both cups, then announced. "No contest really, sir. Jordan wins by a mile. He came twice as much. ."

The Schoolmaster looked grimly at Mike. "Sorry, student, you die."

Mike let out a strangled groan.

Tanya gasped. Now she did glance sideways at Mike. He looked like he was already dead, limp and slack, his eyes unfocused like those of a zombie.

"No, no, you can't do that," she protested. "You *can't* kill him. It's *my* fault."

The Schoolmaster scowled at her. "Please, Tanya, don't let's start with that foolishness again." He smiled coldly. "Next time you blurt out any similar sentimental nonsense, I'll take you seriously and make the switch."

Tanya fell silent. Unable to look at Mike again, she instead peered across the room at Venus. Venus's face was pale with dread, every thrill at showing who the alpha-bedroom-female was had now completely vanished. Jordan was holding tight onto Venus and seemed to have tears in his eyes.

CHAPTER 24

Venus

At first Venus was struck speechless. Beside Tanya, Mike was standing like a corpse, staring at the whiteboard like he could see through it. *Poor kid, I wonder what the hell he's thinking.*

(Outside it seemed to be evening. The mist was darkening to gray. Venus couldn't see what time Peaches was at the moment.)

"Hey," Jordan said, "You can't just kill him."

"The rules here are the rules here," came the prompt reply. Venus clearly heard the insanity in the evil voice, madness distilled into rational rationale.

It was too much for her to take. Too fucking much. *Who does this supernatural asshole think he is anyway?* "And who makes these goddam rules?" she asked. "Who sets up a place like this to torture and kill innocent people?"

"*I* make the rules," the madman replied, his unholy black eyes two abysses she was falling into. "*Who* set this place up? Why, the Powers That Be, of course."

"The Powers That What?"

"It'd take too long to explain, Venus. We're wasting time anyway. And, I've already told you all: no one—none of you—is innocent. We're simply deciding what you're each guilty of. Ms. Principal, get the axe."

"At once, sir." Peaches again ducked behind the desk.

The noise of her search sounded to Venus like a pack of rats shredding paper. An unnerving sound.

"What do you intend doing to him?" she asked.

"We're going to chop off his head, then his hands."

"What!?" Venus and Tanya yelped together.

Peaches reappeared right then, plopping a double-headed axe down on the desk. The axe gleamed like it was fresh from Walmart. "Decapitation's a perfect punishment, sir," she said. "Which head are we chopping off, though—upper or lower? I mean his penis is the real offender here, sir."

Mike instantly snapped out of his daze. "Hell no! You aren't chopping my dick off, you crazy bitch!"

Eyes bulging with fear, Mike ran. With the door to the corridor blocked by the servitors, he dashed left to the new door in the wall and began fumbling with the key.

Venus willed him on, then winced. *Oh, shit!* Moving like lightning, the Schoolmaster had crossed to the desk, picked up the axe, crossed back to the aluminum door, and smacked the weapon's handle into the back of Mike's head. Krak! The escape attempt was over before it had begun: Mike slumped to the floor.

"Servitors!"

The gas ghosts floated over and picked Mike up, propping him upright between them. Blood dripped down Mike's face onto his shirt.

"He's not dead, just stunned," the Schoolmaster said. He looked directly at Tanya. "Now, the rest of you, sit down. We'll wait for Mike to wake up before killing him. It's important that he suffers while dying."

"It's better that we cut off his hands and feet first then, sir, then his head. If we do his head first—"

"This is completely inhuman," Jordan protested. In his voice, Venus heard several things: exasperation at their powerlessness to do anything against the demon facing them, relief that he wasn't the one about to be beheaded, and also the scared realization that the rest of them were only a quiz or test away from dying just as meaninglessly as Mike would once he revived.

"I'm not human," the Schoolmaster replied simply, "and neither is Ms. Principal anymore." His gaze hardened. "Now sit down or I'll be forced to start handing out demerits again."

Venus instantly sat down. Tanya was about sitting down where she was on the opposite side of the room, then she changed her mind and strode over to sit beside Venus.

Jordan, however, didn't sit. He remained on his feet, staring coldly at the Schoolmaster, his hands balled into fists at his sides.

"How can you be so utterly heartless?" he asked.

"Sit down, Jordan." The words, spoken softly, held a subtle threat.

"Answer me! Who are these damn 'Powers That Be' that created this monstrous place? Maybe we can appeal to them to let us out of here."

"Shush!" Venus whispered, tugging at his sleeve.

He shook her off. "Tell me—"

"Shut up. The Powers That Be can't be troubled with such little trifles as your pitiable lives. They've left that to me. That'll be two deme . . ." The Schoolmaster stopped and frowned. "You know what, Jordan? Seeing as you just won the last test, I'm loathe to punish you. So I'm giving you a special bonus."

"What's that?" Jordan asked acidly. "Twelve lashes of the whip?"

"No, not at all. You get to play in the schoolyard. It'll hopefully keep you out of my hair for the next hour or so." He pointed over at Mike, who at Peaches' direction, the servitors had draped over the slaughter desk like they'd done with Chad, only this time belly-down. "By that time, *his* punishment will be over. And yes, I think Ms. Principal is right—we'll start by cutting off his hands first, then his feet, then . . ."

Letting the sentence hang, the Schoolmaster walked over and pushed the door in the wall open. "Now, outside with you, Jordan."

"Hey!—What about me?" Venus challenged him. "I played the major role in his winning the contest." She wanted to leave this oppressive and claustrophobic setting. Most of all, she desperately didn't want to watch Mike getting his head hacked off. *Let Tanya cope with that mess; cops are used to blood and gore. If I see another damn death today, I'll go freaking, raving nuts.*

"No, Venus. While you did help Jordan win, you've too many demerits. Try good behavior sometime."

He grinned coldly; Peaches winked at her. "Besides," he continued, "after Mike here is dispatched, I've another quiz planned—you versus Tanya—and I don't want Jordan helping you cheat again."

Oops, Venus thought in horror, *we're not done for today?* She didn't see foresee her luck lasting through another quiz.

"Okay, Jordan, get going," Peaches said. "There ain't much to see out there, but at least you get to stretch your legs."

"Hey, dude!" Tanya whispered.

He looked down at her.

"Keep your eyes peeled for any escape routes."

He nodded then stepped quickly across the room.

Venus leaned over to the policewoman. "You really think there's anywhere to go from here? It doesn't look like it."

"We can't give up searching." She nodded over at Jordan, who was stepping out onto a sidewalk bordered by gray flowers. "There has to be a way out of this damn place. And it's just as likely to be out there as in here." She winked at Venus. "Jordan's smart, he knows it too. That's why he stopped giving the Schoolbastard lip immediately he suggested he go outside."

"I thought he was about getting himself killed."

"I thought so too." Tanya said. Then she hugged Venus, which Venus found oddly reassuring.

Across the room, the Schoolmaster seemed lost in thought in his books. The servitors wavered by the desk. Peaches was pacing back and forth, axe over her shoulder like a lumberjill.

Tanya grimaced. "That teenager is oh, so creepy. She's actually *impatient* for Mike to wake up so she can kill him."

"I utterly hate her." Venus laid her head on Tanya's shoulder. "You know, I really shouldn't be saying this, but I'm glad Jordan is the one who's gonna survive. I like Mike too, and I hate our losing him like this, but our chances of survival with Jordan are way higher." She realized she was dodging stating the obvious: once Mike was gone, it was their turn.

"I know," Tanya said. "I really did my best to help Mike beat Jordan, but . . ." She suddenly turned red with embarrassment. Venus couldn't for the life of her figure out why.

"It's about time he woke up," Peaches said, poking Mike with her axe.

"Patience, Ms. Principal, patience. It's a virtue, you know."

"Aren't we supposed to be representing the vices, sir?"

"Ah, my lovely little assistant, you still have a whole lot to learn about how things run down—"

And then a horrible screaming began outside in the schoolyard.

"Shit! That's Jordan!"

The aluminum door into the schoolyard had been left open. Venus and Tanya leapt to their feet and rushed over to peer out of it.

CHAPTER 25

Tanya

The immediate image that filled Tanya's mind was how large the schoolyard was. Beyond the concrete fringe bordering the classrooms, the yard seemed vast, like the walls were further away than their actual distance. Far off to her left, she made out rows of stunted trees—like unhealthy, oversized fungi—bordering the wall's farther reaches. Her overall impression was of a corrupted wonderland.

The loud screaming came again, killing her threatened dream state. She looked to her right, towards the sounds. Her heart leapt into her mouth when she saw Jordan.

What the hell are those things?

About fifty yards away, two gray ape-like creatures had hold of Jordan and were violently twisting his arms, hence his screaming. Tanya knew they weren't actual apes—she didn't think even gorillas grew to seven feet tall. Even stranger, they both wore shorts and boots. The creatures were hairy all over and had flat faces.

"Hey! Let him go!" Venus shouted across at them. Sensing she might be foolhardy enough to attempt some kind of rescue, Tanya quickly draped a hand across Venus's shoulders, ready grab her if she attempted dashing off. *This is way out of your league, little lady.* But meanwhile, the creatures kept manhandling Jordan, who kept yelling. He broke free, ran a few steps towards the classroom, then was caught again. Tanya heard the creatures laughing.

Jordan definitely needed help. Tanya turned back inside the classroom. Weapons, weapons! You didn't take on dangerous creatures without weapons.

Her eyes settled on Peaches' axe. She dashed over, wrenched the axe from Peaches' grasp, then rushed back to the door.

"You'll be too late," the Schoolmaster called to her, but she didn't hear.

A few steps outside the door, she froze as one of the apes twisted Jordan's head off his body. A wild squirt of blood hit the creature in the face. Jordan's head fell to the floor.

Behind Tanya, Venus made a loud noise then was silent.

The ape things flung Jordan's body away, then began kicking his head to and fro. It took Tanya some time to work out that they were playing soccer with it.

She stood there watching, her whole world contracting to just this spectacle. This was so deranged she couldn't make head or tail of it. The two ape creatures were dribbling the ball closer now, and she realized that this part of the yard was a soccer pitch. There was a goal post behind the two monsters. But had it been there a moment ago?

Then one of them took a shot in her direction. She watched the immense boot swing back, then forward again like a demonic golf club, then the contact. And then Jordan's head was shooting towards her like a bullet.

She remained rooted to the spot, unable even to duck. The head came closer, then streaked past her left shoulder, fanning her hair off her face with the speed of its passing.

A loud crash of shattering glass behind her roused her from her daze. She turned. One of the classroom windows was smashed to bits. Closer to her, Venus stood in the aluminum door frame. Tanya figured she'd not passed out only because she'd forgotten how to. She'd not even peed herself this time.

"Hey, sir, can we have our ball back!?"

The voices were so unexpected that Tanya looked back again. The two ape-like monsters stood about thirty yards away, waving towards her. They however made no attempt to approach closer to the classroom.

Gripping her axe tightly, Tanya backed away to the door. She pulled Venus into the classroom with her.

"Please, sir, can we have our ball back!?"

What was so unnerving about the request was how innocent and respectful it sounded, like two human kids were doing the asking. Still gripping the axe, Tanya gaped out at them. Even their posture was cringing and subservient.

"Please, sir, we're sorry for breaking your window. We'll play on the other side of the school from now on, honest!"

The Schoolmaster had been sitting with an annoyed frown on his face. Still looking pissed off, he waved a hand to Peaches. "Give them the damn head, will you?"

Peaches walked over to where Jordan's head had fallen and picked it up. The head had raw patches on it, indents and lacerations from being kicked about. Its left eye was missing, its lips split. All its left-side teeth had been knocked out. There was now also glass stuck in it.

Tanya watched Peaches walk out the door and across the yard to where the two ape-things stood. She heard Peaches rebuking them loudly and the pair making subdued apologies to her.

She turned to check on Venus. Venus sat shuddering, her arms wrapped around her body. She was shaking like she'd fragment.

Tanya looked outside again. Peaches was still talking to the hairy monsters. It was weird how docile they seemed with her, seeing as her head barely passed the level of their waistbands. It looked like she was the kid, and they the adults.

Tanya finally turned to glare at the Schoolmaster.

Like he sensed her eyes on him, he looked up from his book.

"What the fuck are those two abominations that just killed Jordan?" she asked, her voice cold as ice. She held the axe raised to strike, though she knew it would be futile. But if he gave her any damn lip now, so help her God, she'd . . .

"They're the Schoolyard Bullies, Crake and Logg. This is utterly my fault. I forgot they were out there."

"Forgot? How could you fucking forget!?"

"Normally they play on the other side of the school. I suspect their last ball went missing, and when I sent Jordan outside, they decided he'd make a good replacement. Like I said, it's my mistake. I always hate it when I kill an innocent student."

"Innocent? I thought you said we're all guilty."

"You're innocent until proven guilty. You, a policewoman, should know the law. But we will prove you all guilty, you can count on it."

Tanya glared hatred at the Schoolmaster, but it was no good. His impossible black eyes were too dead for her. With a loud groan of disgust, she dropped the axe on the floor and went and sat by Venus, wrapping her arms around her to comfort her.

"It'll be okay," she whispered. "We'll make it out of here somehow. You'll see."

Venus just moaned and wept against her breasts. Tanya could feel her tears soaking her shirt.

We'll make it out of here somehow. The words sounded false even to herself. She looked at the desk where Mike lay, still unconscious, then outside the door, where Peaches had joined the Schoolyard Bullies in a game of soccer with Jordan's head as the ball.

"And . . . GOAL!!! Clint Dempsey scores for the USA!" one of the Bullies suddenly yelled. "Oh yeah, ladies and gentlemen, this is a great moment in sports history. The Brits are definitely wishing they'd left Robert Green at home now . . ." The strange childlike voice raved on in deep excitement, running commentary over their game. "And now Abby Wambach of the US Women's Team has the ball, and . . . GOAL!!! Damn, the Brits are really taking an ass-whipping today!"

For the first time, Tanya really began thinking that the Schoolmaster was right, that they *would* all die in this mad place that defied comprehension.

CHAPTER 26

Mike

Mike woke up to a mixture of pain and noise. He had the headache from Hell.

What happened? He instantly remembered he was in the classroom and about to be beheaded. *Shit! But I'd made it to the door and then . . .*

The throbbing in his head reduced. The pounding noise resolved itself into two female voices.

" . . . He's not at fault for what happened to Jordan."

"I know, I know, but I just feel so crappy."

Something happened to Jordan? Carefully, Mike opened his eyes a slit; even that hurt to do. No, they weren't in class anymore: he was lying on his back in one of the beds in their dorm. The dorm lights were on. Venus and Tanya were sitting on the next bed looking at him.

Venus had tears in her eyes. "Those damn bullies," she said.

Tanya nodded. "I hate saying this, but we need to forget Jordan. He's gone. It's just you, me, and Mike left now. And we have just tonight to work out how to get out of this place. Three of us died today, the remaining three of us aren't likely to survive tomorrow. We're simply fortunate that, seeing how upset and angry we were over Jordan's death, the Schoolmaster decided to postpone the rest of his tests." She sat close to Venus and held her tight. "Have faith, girl. I tell you we'll make it out of here."

Venus nodded. "I want to believe you, I really do. It's just so hard . . ." Her chest began heaving again.

Mike opened his eyes fully, and sat up. His head instantly threatened to shut down again, but the wave of dizziness passed. He slung his legs over the side of the bed. "What happened to Jordan?"

Venus glared at him with what seemed hatred for a moment. Next, she leapt on him and began hitting him, pummeling him hard with her fists.

"Hey, stop it!" Tanya said. "You know he's not responsible!"

"I-I-I know!" And then Venus was holding him tight and weeping loudly on his shoulder and neck, her body shuddering against his. "Thank God you're alive! Thank God you didn't die!" she kept repeating.

He held her tight. It was awkward, her body squashed against him like this. She felt so soft and yielding, like his perfect woman would be. (The feel of her was even soothing his headache.) Under more pleasant circumstances he'd be delighted to have this goddess of love in his arms. But now, he dreaded her softness provoking his hardness. That would be really awkward. So while she wept, he looked first at Tanya (who regarded him back with her usual calm gaze), then out the window. It was night outside now, the mist black. There was no moon, no stars. He couldn't see the tentacles, but he sensed them, flickers of monster motion across the night.

When she'd wept herself dry, Venus separated from him. Now she was smiling weakly. "I'm glad you survived," she told him. "It's just horrible what happened to Jordan." She looked about to burst into tears again, but got a hold of herself in time.

"What happened to Jordan?" he asked again. "I was the one about to be killed."

Tanya told him. While listening to her account, Mike kept his face straight. He felt guilty for feeling so relieved.

"Where are the Schoolmaster and servitors now?" he asked when Tanya finished.

"The Schoolmaster's in the staff quarters," she replied. "As far as we can tell, it's a separate building on the other side of the school."

School. Massacre High.

"He left the servitors downstairs," Venus added.

"He did?" Mike felt fear.

"We're not getting away that way," Tanya said. "I'd better fill you in on everything: Okay, like Jordan determined, this school has three floors. The servitors are downstairs; we're in the middle; the Bullies are upstairs." She shook her head at the worried look that came over his face. "No, no, they're not permitted to come downstairs, nor are the servitors permitted up here either. The restriction applies to us too—we're safe as long as we remain on this floor. We venture either up or downstairs at our own risk."

"We think Peaches is also over in the staff quarters," Venus added. "At least we've not see her crazy ass since leaving class."

Mike digested that. "What time is it now?"

"Eleven-thirty."

"And here's your dinner," Venus said, handing him a bag of fries and a bottle of milk. "Food still tastes like you-know-what."

Mike accepted the bag gratefully. In between bites of food, he regarded Tanya. Yeah, he liked her. Not like he liked Venus. (Oh shit, Venus was something else, a walking erection-maker. His laptop was full of torrent-downloads of her movies—her girl/girl scenes were his favorites. Watching her groan and moan and eat pussy with her hair scattered everywhere like an explosion of pink ribbons got him oh so damn hard . . .) But Tanya was like a nicer version of his older sister. And way more reliable too. He could imagine his older sister Kelly in this mess. Kelly would have freaked out big time and shot up everyone and everything, winding up dead herself. But Tanya here was calmness personified. Sure, her dark eyes showed great strain, but she was holding herself together. He really admired that. And, damn, the lady knew how to give head. That, bar none, had been the best blowjob of his life. When he'd come, his balls had felt like they'd been exploding. Head like that alone was enough marrying a woman for. He grinned at Tanya over a sip of milk. Once she caught his eyes on hers, she looked away, an embarrassed smile on her face. Mike figured she knew what he was thinking. Oh, yeah, he *liked* her; she wasn't a beauty queen or particularly graceful, but she had *dignity*. She was too old though. Mid-to-late thirties? Kelly would never let him live it down if he began dating her; she'd say he had a mommy complex. But, hey, but who gives a shit if it's love, right? He looked from the dark and handsome policewoman to the beautiful, excruciatingly perfect, porn star. Yeah, Venus was hot-as-hell. Tanya, though, was a keeper. He could easily imagine himself slipping a ring on her finger.

He finished eating, finished the milk, ditched the empty bag under the bed.

"Let's do this," he said grimly. "We get the fuck out of here or die trying."

Tanya nodded. "I like your spirit."

Then Mike winced. "First though, I need to use the toilet."

Venus pointed behind him. "You gotta go when you gotta go. Outside, turn left, then third door on the right."

***

Mike sat straining on the toilet. It was a big hard turd, one of the sort that always filled him with deep respect for his gay friends. How the hell anyone could accommodate something that big in their ass always amazed him. And willingly at that, when . . . *God . . . this damn thing is ripping my ass to shreds!*

Finally, he got it out. Wincing, he looked down at the turd. It was brown and segmented like a dry creek bed. The damn piece of shit looked too small to have hurt so much. *Oh, hell, there's no way I'm ever turning gay. I'm not even bi-curious.*

He peed into the bowl, wiped with the provided tissue and pulled his pants up. Flushed. Walked out to the washbasin and cleaned his hands.

"We should start by searching this floor," he told his reflection as he regarded his face in the mirror. "We just might turn up something useful in one of the rooms."

"You won't," a voice said behind him.

Mike spun around. He gaped. *What the fuck!?!?!?*

A figure stood there. It was taller than himself and wearing faded jeans pants and a grey 'Thug Life' hoodie that hid its face. Its hands were stuck deep in the hoodie's pockets.

"Who . . . ? What?"

"I said, you won't turn up anything useful on this floor. Go back to your dorm, man. Tell Detective Rockford to come here. I wanna talk to her."

The voice from the hood was male, but young, teenish. And . . . Then Mike realized that one reason why this person towered over him was because his sneakered feet floated three inches off the floor. He also realized that he could see through him. A spirit?

"O-o-okay," he said in a rush. "I'll tell her."

"Yeah, tell her," another voice, female this time, added. "We want to see her."

A young girl suddenly appeared beside the hooded figure. Mike winced on seeing her head. And her feet also weren't touching the floor. And he could see through her too; in her case, quite clearly.

"Hey, man, what're you waiting for?" the hooded figure asked. "We've limited time to do this."

"I need to pee first," Mike said. The sudden appearance of these two had seemingly refilled his just-emptied bladder.

The figure nodded. "Okay, man."

Mike re-entered the cubicle he'd just left and unzipped his fly again. When he was done peeing, he left the cubicle and walked quickly past the two floating figures without looking at them, then made his way back to the dorm and the others.

"There's two ghosts in the toilet who want to talk to you," he told Tanya. "They say it's super urgent."

Then, when Tanya left, he lay in bed and stared at the ceiling, his brain temporarily emptied of thought. It was simply easier *not* to think. Later, sure, but not right now.

He looked over at the window longingly. It seemed almost better to just jump out of the window and end it all. What was wrong with this place?

"Don't you even dare think of it," Venus warned him. "We stick together, you hear me? If you so much as look at that window again, I'll break both your fucking legs."

He nodded and went back to staring at the ceiling.

CHAPTER 27

Tanya

In his haste to get away, Mike had left the toilet door open. Tanya walked right in.

She instantly recognized the tall hoodied figure as Josh Milton. She couldn't see his face, but the sheer size of him, the impression of youthful muscle beneath the hoodie, was ID enough. If Josh Milton had grown to adulthood, he'd have been a giant. As it was, he towered over her.

The girl ghost was equally easy to identify. With her coal-black head she had to be Karen Hamilton. (Once, when called away to a case from home, in her haste to leave Tanya had forgotten some steaks in the oven. When she'd gotten home the next morning, the steaks had been chunks of charcoal. That was exactly how Karen's head looked.)

Tanya composed herself. She saw no point in being scared anymore. This realm functioned by different rules. Here, ghosts were ordinary enough.

She nodded at the floating pair. "You wanted to see me. Here I am."

"Hi, Detective," Josh Milton said, his voice echoic in the tiled room.

"Hello," Karen added.

"Look, Josh," Tanya said, her voice breaking. "I'm sorry, kid. I didn't mean to kill you. I just shot . . ." She was on the verge of tears. There was a pressure of words in her chest, a torrent of apologies desperate to get out, but . . . she didn't know what to say, other than 'sorry, sorry, sorry.' At least he was still sort-of alive now, wasn't he?

"That's okay, Detective," Josh said. He pulled his big tattooed hands out of his pockets, folded his arms across his chest. "I was shooting at you too. Street rules, you know what I mean? A knife for a knife, a bullet for a bullet. Josh Milton ain't nobody's punk bitch."

The statement relieved Tanya a little. Leaning against a washstand, she asked. "But what are the two of you doing here?"

"You're in a really big mess," Karen said.

"Yeah, in quicksand-deep shit," Josh agreed.

Tanya sagged a bit. "Don't I frigging know it?"

"We're here to help you out of your mess," Josh said.

Now Tanya imagined she saw a face in the depths of the hoodie's shadows—skin pale as an overcast sky, with mop-like blonde hair, a juvenile mustache, and sunken dead eyes.

She felt a surge of hope. "You're saying there's a way out of this Hell?"

Josh laughed. "This ain't Hell by a long shot, Detective. You really don't wanna go down *there*. You should see what the demons are doing to Sherri and Jordan right now."

Karen's burnt face twisted up in fright. "Oh, please don't remind me of that, Josh."

Tanya shuddered. *Oh no, I'm not going down there; not ever. This is bad enough.* "O.K., I'm with you. How do we get out of here?"

(She found it hard concentrating on the floating pair. Her gaze kept slipping through their bodies and settling on the tiled wall and brass urinal fittings behind them. Then, realizing she'd lost focus, she'd jerk her vision back forward onto the ghosts again. Then the slipping would repeat. This created a strange displacement in her mind, a feeling of lateral vertigo, like she was on a rapidly tilting skyscraper and falling sideways into the world.)

The young ghost placed a meaty hand to his chin. His eyes smoldered like dead campfires under his cape. "There's a library upstairs, on the third floor. Lots of books there that you don't ever wanna read—the *Necromantica*, *Satanist's Bible*, and shit like that—"

"We're not allowed up on the third floor."

"So allow yourselves. You've no choice anyway—you need one of those books." He looked down at Karen, "What's it called again, girl? *The Big Black Book of Death*, the *Death Book*?"

"No, it's the *Codex Zero*."

"You sure 'bout that?"

"Trust me, Josh, they don't wanna read the *Book of Death*." She looked at Tanya. "If you get the *Codex Zero*, you're home free and out of here. There's a spell in it that will both neutralize the Schoolmaster and also open the portal to the human world again. And it's written in English, unlike some of the others."

Tanya thought it over. The pair didn't seem to be lying. Besides, Josh apparently wasn't angry with her, and Karen had no reason to be. (Karen had now linked her little fingers in Josh's huge ones.) There *was* a chance that this was just one of the Schoolmaster's sadistic tests, but unfortunately, this was the only chance she had. That *they* had.

"Why'd you call me over here to the toilet?" she asked. "Why not just come over to the dorm?"

"We don't like the smell or furnishings either," the little girl explained, her eyes twin blue moons in the enforced night of her face, "but there's only a few places here in Detention where we can appear: the staff lounge up here and the one downstairs, inside one of the soccer goals down in the yard, and in the store in the rear of the kitchen. And in a few more toilets."

"And why—?"

"I want you to kill Peaches for me," Karen said. "Before you leave Detention, kill the evil old witch. She ruined my life. I used to be so pretty; I hate looking in the mirror now! I was going to be prom queen and now just look at me!! And I'm going to look this way forever!!! I-I-I . . ."

The ghost girl broke down in ethereal tears. Josh wrapped an arm around her.

Beneath the darkness of Josh's hood, Tanya felt his eyes on her.

"Do it," he said. "Kill that psycho. I mean, look what she's done to this sweet kid."

"I can't agree to that," Tanya replied. "I'm a cop."

"Not in here, you aren't. In here, your badge isn't worth two cents. Do you understand that, Detective? Look, just do it, kill that damn Peaches for her."

Tanya stared at Karen, who was nodding fiercely, the tears streaming down her cheeks. *Wow, isn't this all messed up?* She did sympathize with Karen though, all burnt up like she was, with a few sparse patches of hair like scrubland on her head. And did she just say she'd be looking this way forever? *Oh, yes—if I was Karen I'd murder Peaches too, chop her into crazy little pieces and feed them to the gators somewhere. But apparently she can't, so she wants me to do it.*

Feeling incredibly conflicted ('incredibly' because she herself wondered what she had against killing Peaches, of all people), she looked back at Josh. "Okay, I'll try to dispose of Peaches. But . . . isn't she dead already? I mean, she has a clock stuck in her heart."

"Either way, she isn't dead enough," Josh said. "We want her planted underground. Deep underground, you dig?"

Karen, happier now Tanya had agreed, nodded. "We don't know if the clock is to keep her alive, or if it's there because, before he put it in, she was too tardy for the Schoolmaster's liking."

Tanya nodded. "I might just pull it out and see what happens."

"Okay," Josh said, "we've gotta be on our way; our time here's about up. Remember what we said: You go up to the third floor and get the—" He tilted his cowled head down to stare at Karen again.

She giggled. "The *Codex Zero*, silly. I wonder how you can't ever remember the names of books."

"Libraries scare me, girl. Seeing that many books in one place is like seeing a mass of sharks that wanna eat my brain. For me, Hell would be being shut in a library and made to read all day long."

Then he fished in the pocket of his hoodie and handed something to Tanya. "You'll need this," he said.

Tanya looked at what he'd given her. It was a battered Vodacom cellphone. The cellphone wasn't any kind of ethereal; it was cold and hard, real as fuck. Tanya, however, was way past considering the incongruity of its solid appearance from a spook's pocket.

She gaped at Josh in surprise. "We can call out of here?"

The ghost wheezed in disgust. "Are you serious, Detective? You know what's gonna happen if you dial anyone on that while you're here in Detention, right?"

"One other thing," Karen said nervously as she began fading. "Watch out up there, there's all kinds of monsters in this building. Don't go in front, ever. Let that handsome man do it."

"Yeah, girl," Josh agreed with a cynical laugh. "'Ladies first' is great, right? But only for parties and nice stuff?"

With that, both ghosts vanished, leaving Tanya alone in the toilet with the cellphone in her hand.

She stared at it confused. *If I can't use the damn thing to call out of here, why'd you give it to me?*

CHAPTER 28

Venus

We're off to get ourselves killed, Venus thought as she followed Mike and Tanya up the stairs to the third floor. *This is it. We're gonna die up there and the Schoolmaster won't have anyone left to test.*

At his own insistence, Mike was in front. (Tanya had protested that as a policewoman, she had the most experience in entering dangerous situations like this, but Mike had refused to hear it. Oddly, Tanya had seemed relieved by his insistence.) Venus was fine with that. She was staying several steps behind everyone else anyway. *Anyone wants to be first in line to die, it ain't me.*

However, she did admire Mike stepping up to the plate like this. Just like in the movies, the hunky macho guy stepped into the limelight at the right time, and the pretty women (okay, Karen was a bit less so) could relax and let him fight the monsters. And Mike really was handsome . . .

What the hell am I daydreaming for? We're about to get our frigging asses murdered up here! The Schoolmaster was crystal clear on that point.

And, I . . . I need to survive this! I have to. I'm not croaking just when I've gotten my career back on track with Titaholics.

***

Based in the Big Apple, Titaholics Anonymous—TA for short— never did any violent or sexually demeaning stuff. No rough stuff, period. Company owner Evan James wasn't into that crap. What Titaholics filmed was hardcore for sure, but classy: beautiful women, handsome men, nice locations, soft beds. And they were well organized; you almost thought you were working for Microsoft or the US Army. When she wasn't balling Evan, Kendra Yang—KY— looked after the girls and made sure they weren't taken advantage of

. . . Venus laughed, or rather, that they *didn't feel like* they were being taken advantage of. In this business, illusion was everything. Some of the girls had exclusive contracts with TA. She'd been offered one, but had declined it for a pay-per-fuck deal. She'd read one of the girls' contracts and almost pooped herself from disbelief. (Venus had read the small print, which Jenna Jones clearly hadn't before putting pen to paper [nor did it appear she'd noticed it afterwards].) After 10 years working for Titaholics, Jenna would be lucky to leave the company with a hundred grand in her bank account. Venus wasn't having any of that rubbish. For her, there *was* light at the end of her sexual tunnel. So far she had six hundred thousand saved up, and she planned to bank a whole lot more before her five-year-away D-day.

And now this crap had to happen. But, oh frigging yes, she was making it out of here alive. Fuck dying. She wasn't even sure who'd inherit her money. Maybe her parents? It was a moot question: she wasn't dying in here.

***

They'd reached the third floor. A long dim corridor stretched ahead.

"Okay," Mike whispered back at them. "Whatever happens, we stay together; this isn't a horror movie."

Don't worry, pretty boy, I ain't leaving your side. Venus suddenly couldn't help it: she was growing horny. She'd noticed Mike staring at her while she was fellating Jordan, and now in a delayed reaction, that look of lust, in company with the tightness of his ass ahead of her, was having its effect.

Oops. Get a grip on your damn hormones! This is neither the time nor the place for that.

But she was on the rebound after Jordan's death; she needed to lose herself in a warm body. That was one thing she got out of porn: when you felt like shit, there was always a warm body somewhere to meld with.

Then, as they started slowly down the corridor, she felt a sharp stab of pain in her groin. Then another one. She stopped walking, looked down aghast at her belly. *Oh please, not now.* Her period was an inconvenience she could do without at the moment; not with no tampons available.

The pain didn't repeat. *Ah, false alarm.* She hurried after the others.

She caught up with them outside a door midway down the hallway. Tanya had her eye pressed to a keyhole from which a mushroom-shape of light spilled. She straightened up and indicated that Venus take a look.

Venus bent to the keyhole, which revealed a bedroom. On the bed she made out three naked figures: two huge hairy ones and, squashed between them, a small pale one with blond hair. A quartet of red numbers flickered somewhere on the pale figure. The bodies humped up and down, the bed shook. A tinny voice squeaked loudly:

"Oh, Ms. Principal, your back door is so tight!"

"Yeeesss! Give it to me, Logg, and don't you dare come early like last time!"

"So tight! Aaahhh!" The figure on top humped up and down even harder.

Venus straightened up again and whispered, "Well, I guess we don't have to worry about Peaches and the Bullies tonight. That's a plus." Watching the threesome had however increased her own horniness. Which was a definite minus.

Tanya nodded. "It also means the other rooms up here are empty."

Mike had meanwhile left that door, and was gesturing to them from one farther ahead. They hurried over to him.

"The library," he said.

They slipped inside, shut the door, and flicked the lights on.

"Wow!" Venus exclaimed.

Facing them was a standard high school library, shelves and shelves and shelves of books extending across a fifty-yard-long space, with signs hung above them indicating the different topic sections. To the right of the shelves was an equally long line of reading tables. On the left of where they currently stood was the loans desk. An ancient skeleton with burnt head and shoulders sat there behind an exploded computer. Both were thickly covered with dust.

"Where do we start looking from?" Venus asked.

Mike pointed. "The occult section." The 'Occult Section' sign was just visible twenty yards off.

Tanya nodded agreement. "Yeah, it has to be in there." She looked at Venus. "Okay, come on. We'll split up and check through different shelves. We'll work faster that way."

Venus shook her head. For all her bravado, Tanya seemed worried. Venus guessed that Mike, being a man, couldn't read her, but to herself as a fellow woman, Tanya's unease stood out loud and clear. Something was *wrong* with this library. It looked normal enough, but Venus just knew Tanya was hiding something. Which meant danger. Which Venus was so, so, so not having any of. Oh no, not she.

So she said, "You know what, guys? I'll just hang around here and watch the door for y'all. How's that? Just in case Peaches and her boyfriends decide to come outside for a tinkle between trysts."

Tanya looked about to protest, then she shrugged.

CHAPTER 29

Tanya

Tanya shrugged. "Okay, little birdy. Chirp if you see or hear anything. And if they do come this way, fly over and roost with us."

Venus nodded with clear relief, then turned towards the desk with the burnt skeleton. Tanya watched her body tense with apprehension. She wondered if Venus would manage to keep her composure with that thing beside her. She doubted it. The porno queen was guaranteed to dash after them the moment a spider scurried by her.

Tanya was worried. The ghostly Karen had clearly said there was danger up here and to let Mike go ahead. She looked around. Everything seemed normal enough; so where was the danger?

She realized, however, that she'd never be able to live with herself if she sacrificed Mike, so she told him, "Hey, I don't like this place. It's too quiet, it might be booby-trapped. Keep your eyes peeled."

He didn't reply, and she couldn't tell if he'd heard her or not. She could let it go, decide she'd warned him enough, but no, she wasn't doing that: he had to know. So she grabbed hold of him. He turned to her in surprise.

"What?"

"Did you hear what I just said? There's danger up here. *Real* danger. The ghosts said there was." Then before he could question her further, she pulled him close and kissed him.

This wasn't the same kind of kiss as when she'd been trying to turn him on downstairs. No, this kiss went way, way deeper, like she sought to touch his soul with her tongue, to taste the colors of his personality. She felt his initial confusion, then he kissed her back with equal urgency. Behind them, she knew Venus was watching and wondering what was going on.

They separated, gasping.

Mike said, "Tanya, you're way older than me and being a bit of a stoner, I'm wary of dating a cop, but if we do survive this, would you mind going to a movie with me sometime?"

She laughed. "Would I? It's a date!" Then she grabbed his hand, and giggling like a little girl, dragged him into the occult section. She couldn't explain it. Maybe the danger they were in had heightened her emotional sensitivity, but she'd never felt so strong a connection to anyone before, and that in so brief a time of knowing them.

Mike began pointing out the different shelf divisions. "Here's European Occultism, Modern Occultism, Native American Occultism, Negro and Voodoo . . ." He looked at her in confusion. "Where do we find *Codex Zero*?"

Tanya regretted not asking the ghosts for the author's name. She'd not realized the Detention library was this extensive. This occult section alone spanned ten full shelves.

"You know," she said after some consideration, "I don't think we're looking for something recently printed. I may be wrong, but since the original codices were unbound manuscripts, we should just check for where the very old texts are kept. All those leather-bound musty tomes."

He nodded his agreement.

The shelves completely hid them from Venus. Tanya stepped out into view for a moment and waved to Venus. Venus waved back. Tanya was surprised: Venus looked resolute, like she wanted to run over and join them between the shelves, but was holding herself back from doing so.

She returned her attention to Mike. Together, they scanned the titles on the shelves hemming them in, then moved on to the next aisle. Being with Mike now, with their new connection, Tanya felt content, if not happy. Things were looking up; they knew the codex was in here. They just had to find it.

But the ghosts' admonition troubled her mind . . .

The fourth aisle they checked had an 'Old and Restored Manuscripts' section.

"Eureka," Mike said and began scanning the books' spines.

Tanya now began feeling like they weren't alone, like something was watching them. Standing with her back to Mike, she checked the book titles with half her mind. The other half of her intelligence fenced with a prickly feeling like spiders crawling through her hair. She imagined she heard a soft rustling noise from somewhere, but each time she looked up or around, there was nothing.

"Here it is," Mike said. "The *Codex Zero*."

Relieved, she turned toward him. He handed her a small bound book, about the size of a comic book. She flipped it open. Its pages were yellow with age; they seemed to have only recently been compiled into book form. After confirming that it was indeed written in English, she nodded to Mike. "Thank heavens. Now let's get out of here."

She was reaching a hand toward Mike to pull him out of the aisle, when something fell over him.

The thing was amorphous and transparent, like a nylon bag filled with water. In its interior floated a single large blue eye. (Tanya later realized that it had been lying on top of the shelf with the *Codex Zero*, watching them and deciding which of them to attack. It had chosen Mike simply because, being a man, he was bigger.)

Mike was smiling at her as the thing covered him. For a surreal moment, he seemed sheathed in plastic—her shrink-wrapped knight. Then, all of a sudden his face and body turned bright red, his skin, hair, and clothes all vanished, and his muscles and bones began showing. All the while, Mike stood watching Tanya, his expression frozen as if paralyzed until his face dissolved away. Then with a sudden explosion of red inside the creature, his body split into bits inside the transparent wrapping. Next, the creature collapsed to the floor, its body now full of suspended bones. It wobbled there, red mess obscuring its blue eye.

Tanya had frozen stiff as she watched Mike die. She became aware of a loud high-pitched noise around her. She never realized she was the one screaming until she felt something soft clamped over her mouth.

"Shut up!" Venus whispered. "You'll bring Peaches and the Bullies running!"

Then apparently, Venus also saw what was left of Mike inside the creature, because she gasped loudly.

Tanya was only half aware after that of Venus taking the *Codex Zero* from her hand and dragging her back to the library door, then down the stairs to their floor.

CHAPTER 30

Venus

Shit, she set him up! Venus raged inside herself. *The cold bitch set him up! I just knew something was wrong with the way she was acting up there!*

Venus was utterly disgusted. She glared over at Tanya, who lay in bed staring at the dorm ceiling just like Mike had done a short while earlier. Tanya looked dead, her face was completely devoid of emotion.

But . . . all of a sudden Venus was confused. She'd seen Tanya kiss Mike and also seen her face after Mike's death, and . . . and that scream? It had been a wonder the Schoolmaster himself hadn't heard it over in his quarters.

No, Venus decided, *a woman can't fake that sort of emotion; its intensity was honest. And the way she looks now, like the bottom just dropped out of her world? Yes, she really did care about him.*

She regarded Tanya now with intense sympathy. It helped her keep her mind off what she'd seen on the library floor. That thing that had eaten Mike? It had looked like some kind of single-celled organism— an amoeba or paramecium—that she'd learnt about in school ages ago. But one so BIG?

Venus wondered why she hadn't freaked out herself, how she'd remained calm enough to get Tanya out of the library. (Ugh! The disgusting monster had even stuck out pseudopods in her direction, extending liquid tentacles towards Tanya and herself like it wanted to eat them too!) *Is it because I've resigned myself to dying here? Is that it? I hope it isn't. I really don't want to die in this horrid place.* She glanced at the *Codex Zero* (Tanya had been about dropping it when she'd grabbed it from her). *And we've got our out now. Only, I can't figure this out alone.*

She looked over at Tanya. The cop still lay motionless, staring at the ceiling. Once, Tanya's gaze flickered over to the window, ironically the same one Mike had been staring at earlier when she'd deduced he'd been considering suicide to end everything. *Shit, I even put her in the same bed!*

She hurried over to the window and latched it shut, then sat on the sill with her feet on the bed to her right. *Okay, what do I do now?*

Her belly twinged painfully again. She pulled the crotch of her hot pants aside and swiped herself between the thighs. Her fingers came away clean. A relief. She hoped they'd have escaped from here before she needed to pad herself. (She was quite regular, and always planned ahead for her monthly crisis—she had a pack of Kotex over in Springfield in her overnight case.) There was tissue in the toilets, but it would soak up quickly and make a mess.

And what (she'd always wondered) was the point of periods anyway? All that bleeding just to announce another wasted egg? (She'd read somewhere that at one a month, the average woman had 450 periods in her lifetime.) *I want to be pregnant!!!* That was the reason why she'd hated having The Clam so much. Chlamydia messed with a woman's pregnancies. And Venus wasn't having that. Her family— the doting husband and beautiful kids after her retirement—weren't up for auction. She was having them, period. Hell would freeze over twice before she gave up on that dream. She wanted a normal, 'boring' life. And she was having it, no matter what.

But that was tomorrow, and a half-decade-away tomorrow at that. Now she needed a solution.

She picked up the *Codex Zero* and flipped through it. *Damn, there's lots of spells in here; at least eighty or a hundred pages of them. Too many of them to read through alone. I might miss something, and*—she checked her watch: 1 a.m.—*time's running out fast for us. There's only two of us left now, which equals just one more of that pedagogic sadist's tests . . . and then, whoever's left will be killed anyway.*

Filled to the brim with a sudden desperation, Venus stared over at Tanya again. Try as she might, she could only think of one way to rouse the policewoman from her fugue, if only temporarily.

She began stripping. *I need to fuck her awake. It might not work, but I'm definitely going to give it my best shot. Tanya, baby, your cop ass is mine tonight!*

CHAPTER 31

Tanya

Tanya felt Venus undressing her: unbuttoning her shirt, sitting her up to slide it off, undoing her bra, lowering her back down to the bed; and then undoing her belt and unzipping her pants . . .

A corner of her mind registered that Venus was naked too. That part of her mind warned her of what was likely to happen now, even asked her if she wanted it to happen.

It didn't matter to Tanya. Nothing mattered now. She felt comatose but awake, a hospital patient being tended by a naked nurse. That was all.

Watching Mike die had leeched her of willpower. She'd forced herself to be strong too long and now something had broken inside her.

She felt Venus get into bed with her, felt Venus's body pressed against hers. Soft fingers touched her face, turned her face towards Venus's. Soft lips pressed against her own; a wet tongue probed between her lips and teeth, stroked her own tongue first gently, then possessively. One part of her mind screamed that she didn't want this. But if not, what did she want? This was something after all—feeling penetrating her numbness—way better than nothing. She'd never before felt desire for another woman, didn't even now, but this was . . .

She shut her eyes and imagined Venus was Mike. She kissed him deeply, just like she had upstairs, but with passion now that they were naked together. She wanted his body inside hers, sliding through her wetness.

The soft lips on hers burnt like fire. Slowly they descended, licking her neck, lingering in the crevice over her breastbone, then sinking to her breasts. There, the lips teased her nipples, sucking hard on first

165

one then the other engorged teat. Under their expert caresses, she felt her body come alive, warmth penetrating the numbness now enveloping her like that creature had enveloped Mike . . . No! Mike wasn't dead! He was the one touching her now, the one loving her!

The lips on her breasts were replaced by fingers, as the wet mouth sucked on her skin, descending her body to her sex.

The fingers now left her breasts and parted her sex, spreading her wide. The tongue penetrated her, licked her in and out, then swept up to suck on her swollen bud. Yes! She was a flower, a pink sunflower ablaze at noon. A flower dripping sweet nectar.

Then soft thighs pressed against her cheeks and flesh nuzzled her nose. The smell of musk filled her head. *Oh, Mike!*

She opened her eyes. There was no hard penis there, instead a shaven dripping vagina stared back at her like a weeping black eye.

Her fantasy dissolved, consumed by the sexual flames now burning her up. This was no hard male body atop hers, but a soft *female* one, all luscious curves and sweaty musk. No stiff maleness hovered over her face, seeking solace between her lips, but rather, a pulsating, hungry woman-hole hung there—a sexual mouth demanding to be fed with erotic sensation.

It had been ages since she'd last even touched herself intimately, and—oh, damn these porno actresses!—Venus was expert at what she was doing with her lips and fingers.

Tanya lost all her reserve. She lifted her mouth to Venus's sex. Grabbing Venus's buttocks with both hands, she dug her tongue into the pleading vagina. She sucked on the vagina; its juices were tangy, with a faint hint of iron to them. She overlooked its slight taste of urine. She licked the urethra, began sucking hard on the swollen clitoris.

And all the while, she could feel Venus's tongue between her legs, weaving its spell of sexual magic on her sex. The sorcery of their joined bodies was so intense that the world, already a numb haze for Tanya, vanished completely. With her eyes shut, all she could see inside her head were the colors of bliss.

Then her orgasm hit, and her eyes popped open. And she trembled and moaned and felt herself shedding her horrors out into the void, into the mist that surrounded Detention.

She lay back gasping and panting, her heart racing. She could feel again! Her heart and soul ached badly, but she felt stronger than before.

"Oh fuck!" she gasped, her first words since returning downstairs. Then she realized the sweet pleasure wasn't over, that the magic was continuing between her thighs. Venus had slipped two fingers into her sex and was working her from within now. Tanya tried to pleasure Venus in return, but she couldn't concentrate. So she lay back and let Venus love her and purge her again.

And then, as her second orgasm ebbed away, the tears came. Tears of sadness, tears of self-recrimination over her not being careful enough upstairs. A torrent of tears raged from her eyes. *Oh, Mike! Mike! Mike!* she thought as she cried. *I wish I'd died instead of you!*

And Venus was with her all through her sorrow; holding her tight, holding her close and whispering that everything would be alright now, that they'd make it out alive.

And suddenly Tanya realized that she believed that again. She remembered that they'd found the *Codex Zero*.

Oh yes, now we've a real chance of leaving here alive.

Feeling like herself again (though a sad, weakened version of herself) she leaned up on her elbow and kissed Venus, chastely this time. There was no sexual desire left in her now. She understood what Venus had done and why she'd done it, and she was grateful. She realized she'd had a really narrow escape upstairs, not just physically, but mentally too. She knew she'd be okay now, Venus's quick sexual intervention would prevent her having lasting emotional scars. (She knew that was how some policewomen wound up cold bitches. They saw so much horror every day that they didn't dare love anyone; in one second the man or woman you cared for more than anything in the universe could be shot dead and your heart would be torn out of your chest and you'd be left floating free in nowhere-land.)

"Thanks," she told Venus with sincerity, "I needed that."

Venus grinned. "Feeling better now?"

"Do you really need to ask? It's been ages since I've been done that good. Wow, they *do* teach you girls well in porn."

She saw Venus was looking nervously at her, like she was embarrassed by what she was about to say. "Tanya, I know you're upset over Mike's death . . . hell, I'm upset too, but we need . . ."

"Yeah, I know," she said, her voice cold. "We need to crack the damn schoolyard code. Pass me my fucking clothes."

Venus giggled. "Hon, you've got your *fucking* clothes on."

It took Tanya a moment to get the joke. "Girl, just pass me my damn clothes, will you? And definitely put yours on, too. I won't be able to think straight with your huge breasts staring at me."

CHAPTER 32

Venus

Once they'd dressed, they got down to work. It was 2:30 a.m.; they were both well aware that every second counted now.

Watching as Tanya pored coldly over the pages of the *Codex Zero*, Venus doubted she'd converted her to lesbianism. It had, however, been great fun making her moan and groan like that. *The way she creamed my mouth with her love juices when she came? She was like a dam bursting, like she'd not been laid in six months!* (Venus had herself come during their sexual encounter, her orgasm an explosive release of fear and tension. She felt relaxed now.)

She was glad her plan to bring Tanya back to her senses had worked. It would have been the absolute pits if the policewoman had wound up a basket case, crawling the walls and twitching. Or numb like a morphine addict.

A thought struck Venus then. *Oh, you fool, you've gone and done it again, haven't you? Been too fast for your own good? Shit, how didn't you see that? If Tanya had been non compos mentis by morning, you'd win the next test with ease!*

Hell no! She forced the horrible thought from her mind. True, she'd not considered Tanya's emotional collapse as representing an advantage for herself, but that was too awful to even contemplate doing. *I'm not any kind of bitch, and I've passed up some wonderful chances in the adult industry to become one. Okay, so I cheated against Chad, but that was because I didn't know head or tails where that quiz was concerned. But in this case, there's no way I'm taking advantage of Tanya!*

But how easy would that resolution prove to keep? *This place has the awful characteristic of turning us against each other. I mean, upstairs earlier, I thought Tanya had set Mike up.*

Tanya looked up from studying the *Codex Zero*. "I think I've found the spell."

"Where? Where?" Elation thrilling in her breasts, Venus instantly huddled closer.

Tanya spread the pages of the book flat and stabbed at a diagram with a finger. "It's written in horrible old English—thee's and ye's and all that sorta crap—but I can make it out . . . the essence of the thing is simple enough to understand. And it appears simple to perform too." She frowned. "There's one other spell to unlock the outside world again, but that one requires a human sacrifice."

"Ugh. What do we need for this one?"

"Just a black pentagram. After drawing one, we stand inside it . . . and there's a spell to recite. It's not in English though."

"Not in English? Lemme see that." Venus snatched the codex from Tanya. Lips pursed, she tried to decipher the spell, "Manax feedle slaq klas noom . . ." She shot Tanya a confused look. "What the hell is this? Transcribed Arabic?"

Sighing, Tanya took the codex back. "I've no idea what the words mean either. So long as they work though, we're good. I'll just pronounce them phonetically; it's hard to go wrong that way."

"So what are we waiting for? Let's do this!"

"Not so fast, girl. There's a problem: What do we draw the pentagram with? The book is emphatic that it must be black and the star encased within a *double* outer circle; other than that any material can apparently be used to make it—wax, coal, crayons, ink . . . Venus, what are you looking for?"

Venus had gone to rummage through her purse. She produced the stub of an eyebrow pencil.

Tanya shook her head. "That's way too short to draw anything with. We won't even get one circle done." Then musing, she took the stub from Venus and examined it. "And this is brown, not black. Are you trying to get us killed?"

"Sorry, my mascara bottle's almost empty too." Then a thought struck her: "Killed? We could *die*?"

"So what's new? We'll die anyway if we don't do it."

"Tanya . . . why does the pentagram have to be black?"

"It doesn't say." She laid her finger on a line of old cursive writing which Venus had trouble deciphering. "It just says, 'This art ye black spell. Take heed that there be nothing crimson on ye caster of ye spell; neither of crimson adornment, nor red markings of ye body, nor scarlet jewelry, no matter how trifling. And if ye witch be on her monthly curse, there be danger of ye Compress. Ye black spell abhors crimson. Ye spell cain't ne'er be cast by a crimson-tressed sorceress, 'cept she dye her hair black, or shave it off . . .'"

Venus heaved a massive sigh of relief. *Thank goodness my hair's still pink.* She was naturally a blonde anyway, but KY wanted her with flaming red hair for the shoot for Titaholics' new calendar. (Venus was due at the beauty salon on Monday. She'd postponed going this past week because she'd been busy helping KY with the preparations for her birthday party. She was supposed to get her nails—all plainly varnished now—done crimson too.)

Tanya said, "This bit about the 'monthly curse' worries me. That clearly means our periods. I just finished mine a week ago. When's yours due?"

"Too soon. It's already given me advance warning, but I'm not flowing yet, think I'll still keep for a bit longer. I'm quite regular—I'd bet on tomorrow evening. You read out something about 'ye Compress.' Does the text tell us what it is?"

Tanya shut the codex and slipped it under the mattress. She stood up. "No. All we know is that it'll be dangerous for either of us to be bleeding while the spell is in effect."

Venus also got up. "In that case, the sooner we cast the spell, the better. So we need something black to write with. Where do we look?"

"First we check Mike and Jordan's bags."

They checked. Their search yielded two pencils, a blue ballpoint, and a large green marker.

Scowling, Tanya dropped the marker in her pocket. "Right size, wrong color." She nodded to Venus. "We'll search all the rooms on this floor. Hopefully, we'll find something. You know, if we just had a cigarette lighter, we could torch some wood and use the charcoal to draw with. Or even burn some paper or cloth."

"Shit! Chad had a lighter in his pocket! Okay, let's check the rooms. I really hope we find something."

Searching the entire floor took them an hour. They ransacked every room, opened every cabinet, looked under beds, inside toilet cubicles . . . (They spent five full minutes in the ossuary stacked with human skulls, first perplexed as to where the hundreds of displayed heads had come from, and then, once they'd decided the skulls were those of previous Detention students, terrified that theirs might shortly be added to the collection.) Once, they even knocked a hole through a wall into a hidden recess. They searched . . . everywhere.

They found nothing.

"I don't frigging get this!" Venus said finally. "There's loads of paper, an excess of wood, and piles of colored crayons like this place was once a kindergarten, but not a single black one?"

Tanya shook her head. "And not a single lighter or box of matches either."

"Hey!—There's sure to be matches downstairs in the kitchen."

Tanya smiled. "Yeah, let's go."

They ran for the stairs. On reaching the stairway landing, however, they instantly made out the wavering black ghost down at the foot of the steps. Its rod-thin head tilted up towards them, letting them know it had seen them, but it made no attempt to climb the stairs to reach them.

"Fucking asshole servitor," Venus growled. "We're not getting downstairs."

"Damn. I guess this also rules out using the other stairways?"

Tanya spun briskly on her heel and began walking back toward the dorm. Venus lurched after her and pulled her back. "Hey, look! I know where there's charcoal to spare. Way more than we need even."

"*What?* Where?"

Venus nodded emphatically. "Yes, yes, there is. It's upstairs. Remember the librarian skeleton with the burnt head? Its wooden chair got burnt up too, both the arms are charred black. We just need to make a trip back upstairs and fetch the chair."

Tanya gaped at her. "How're are you just remembering this?"

Venus shrugged. She honestly couldn't tell how she'd forgotten the library with both their lives at stake, except that maybe her mind had blanked it out because of her horror over Mike's death.

"Come on!" Tanya was already climbing the stairs.

Venus dashed up after her. Then Tanya abruptly stopped climbing, and Venus bumped into her back. Tanya went sprawling.

"Sorry. Why'd you—"

"Well, hello, old ladies," a horribly familiar voice said above them. "Where are you two both headed at this ungodly hour?"

Venus looked over Tanya, who was getting up again. Peaches was staring down at them from the third floor landing. The girl stood there akimbo like the evil warden on some 'women-in-jail' movie poster, cracking the haft of her bone-studded skin whip against her left palm.

The sight of the hated teen felt like a bomb going off in Venus's head. She was unable to believe that their escape was about to be thwarted. The clock in Peaches' chest read 03:42.

"Well, answer me," Peaches said in a put-on adult voice. "Where are the two of you going? You know you're not allowed up here." Her brow wrinkled up like she was thinking. "Will one of you answer me? If you don't talk, I'll be delighted to award you both lots of demerits for insubordination."

Tanya said nothing. She stood glaring at Peaches like she'd love to murder her in cold blood.

Venus completely sympathized; she couldn't stand Peaches either. The girl was a distillation of all the conceited teens she'd attended high school with. And her wild and crazy eyes? Venus didn't understand how in the world anyone could look insane 24/7, even after just having hot sex. And when they weren't on drugs.

Controlling herself with an effort, she replied, "We're looking for Mike. We woke up and he wasn't in bed. We've been checking all the rooms on our floor. We think something might have got him." The lie had come to her on the spur of the moment. She was relieved: It was a good, credible story, particularly if Peaches and the Bullies had already found Mike's remains.

Peaches frowned. "So *that* was the noise we heard. I first thought a vetzer was running amok in the rooms. She turned and cracked her whip along the corridor. "Hey, Crake, Logg, get your hairy asses over here. Double quick!" Then, looking back down at Venus and Tanya, she smirked. "Oh, something got Mike all right. The handsome fool snuck up here and tried to steal one of the Schoolmaster's prized manuscripts . . ." she grinned, "but a *gloop* ate him." She frowned again. "Unfortunately, the gloop also ate the stolen manuscript. So the boss is gonna be furious."

The Schoolyard Bullies had now arrived. One of the gorilloids stood on each side of Peaches. To Venus, they looked much like the bigfoot reconstruction she'd seen in a documentary: all hair and muscle and smell (which Peaches didn't seem to notice, but then she'd been screwing the pair earlier). This close to the Bullies, Venus clearly read the low intelligence in their brown eyes. Massive as they were (and their heads almost scraped the ceiling), each face showed the mental age of a child—say a fifth grader, definitely a preteen. *Shit, they probably thought having sex with Peaches was a PE game.*

It now struck Venus that Tanya hadn't said a word since sprawling flat on the stairs. She glanced at her, worried that the cop was having an emotional relapse. She calmed a bit: Tanya's eyes were cold hard marbles in her handsome face. Venus realized she was considering the angles: attack or retreat? Venus didn't see an attack accomplishing anything.

"Should we kill them, Ms. Principal?" the Bully on Peaches' left asked. "They're trespassing, right? And that's not allowed, is it?"

"Yes," the other Bully agreed. "And if we kill them we'll have spare footballs to play with."

Letting the whip trail behind her like a brown tail, Peaches began pacing back and forth across the landing. Venus's eyes tracked the girl's motion like she was trying to hypnotize herself. Despite her insistence on being brave, the skin-whip terrified her by the sheer inhumanness that it represented—turning a person's remains into an instrument of torture. True, Peaches hadn't so far used the whip on anyone, but that definitely wasn't from lack of intent.

Venus felt her bladder tensing to void itself, and almost let it do so. Surely she couldn't get demerits for peeing here?

She was very worried now. *Will Peaches let us be killed here? Surely if we turn and run, the Bullies won't chase us downstairs. Or will they?* Out of the corner of her eye she estimated the distance to the lower landing. Three leaps and they should be clear. Keeping her eyes on the Bullies, she stepped closer to Tanya, preparing to haul her down the stairs at the first sign of a threat.

Peaches stopped pacing and shook her head at the Bullies. "No."

"Awwww!"

Venus gushed out air in relief.

Peaches favored she and Tanya with a cold grin. "Okay, old ladies, you aren't technically on the third floor yet so the Bullies can't rip you to shreds, and besides, the Schoolmaster'd really hate me if I let you be butchered tonight, so for the love of dick, get both your old asses downstairs and back to bed."

"We wanted books from the library," Venus protested. "I'm insomniac." It seemed cruel to be forced to give up their quest now.

Peaches slashed her whip over their heads like a lasso. Venus could tell she was just dying to use it on them, but didn't dare. "Get back to bed right now before *I do* let the Bullies have at both of you! Frigging scram! And yeah, that's six demerits each."

Venus looked at Tanya. Tanya still wasn't saying anything. She just nodded towards the second floor then set off down the steps.

After a moment's longing glance down the hallway behind Peaches and the Bullies, Venus followed suit. Walking back to their dorm she felt like her last chance at survival had just been snatched away from her.

"I guess we don't get charcoal then," Tanya said quietly.

Venus felt her frustrations building up to an explosion. "Why didn't you say anything there back on the stairs?"

"It was all I could do not to attack that little brat. I wanted to grab her and shake some sanity into her scrambled brains. But I was concerned that if I did charge her, she'd whip me, and the spilled blood would prevent the black spell from working." She grimaced. "And we can't have that happening, can we? We both need to watch out that we don't pick up any wounds. We get any red on us, and . . . that 'Compress' thing the codex speaks of?"

"Oh." Venus hadn't thought of it like that. She still didn't know what 'ye Compress' meant, but it sounded bad. *Maybe the ceiling will fall and crush us to death?* She was impressed too by the toughness in Tanya's voice. *And . . . you were 'concerned?' Honey, I LOVE how you just avoided admitting that you're as scared shitless as I am!*

In silence, they entered the dorm and sat facing each other on neighboring beds. Outside, the sky was lightening; the huge tentacles were once again becoming separate entities from the mist.

"What now?" Venus asked glumly. "We need a plan. In four or five hours we'll be in class again, and you know what that means."

"All hope isn't lost yet. Peaches bought your story about Mike going off exploring on his own."

"How does *that* help *us*?"

"It means they don't know *we* have the codex. They think the monster . . . the gloop, she called it . . . ate it too. So, if we can find something black to write with, we can still cast the spell." She yawned. "Venus, let's both sleep for an hour and a half. It's 4 a.m. now. I'll set my alarm for 5:30. Then we'll keep a watch on the third floor and try to sneak back upstairs to the library once Peaches and the Bullies have gone downstairs."

Venus mused on that. It seemed a good plan. She felt her hope rekindled: this would work, it had to. All they needed was a little luck.

"Also," Tanya added, "if that doesn't work, if accessing the library again fails, remember we go to class by ourselves. We'll leave early and head for the cafeteria—I'm sure I can find it from here. Even if there's no matches in there, we'll burn some wood on a gas ring in the kitchen and use that. We'll draw the pentagram in the kitchen."

Tanya set her watch, then lay back, arms folded behind her head. Venus watched her for a minute, then got into bed beside her.

"No, it's not sex," she said, laying her head on Tanya's breasts. "I just don't want to sleep alone tonight."

SUNDAY

CHAPTER 33

KY

I

"Dammit, Evan," KY said as the countryside rushed past their car, "where the hell could Chad and Venus have gotten to? I'm beginning to think they're dead or something."

Evan James, owner of Titaholics Anonymous, took a hand off the silver BMW's wheel and wagged a finger at her. "Nah, baby, they're around here somewhere."

KY didn't think so. "Darling, it's annoying as hell to be out here this morning driving back and forth looking for those two. It's 11 a.m. We've been searching for three hours straight now, driving up and down back roads. This is our *fourth* trip down to Brimfield. Shit! All I came out here to do was have my birthday party, and see what happens?"

Evan took his eyes of the road and winked at her. "Take it easy, baby. There's sure to be a logical explanation for their not coming back to the house." He squeezed her thigh, running his hand up under her red dress towards her penis, which she always liked.

Not today though. She pushed his hand away. "Yes, something logical like a car crash."

"Don't be so morbid, baby," Clara called from the backseat.

KY looked back at her. "What else can I be? They've been gone since my party on Friday night. Venus's brother said that despite his asking them to sleep over at his place, they drove off drunk in the middle of the night. C'mon, Clara, this is Sunday morning and we still can't even get them on the phone? It's like they've vanished off the face of the planet, been abducted by aliens. Two of America's top porn stars."

Clara shrugged. "We're still looking, baby, aren't we?" She leaned forward between the front seats. "Evan, darling, are you *sure* you didn't have a fight with Venus over something? I know she gets quite a temper sometimes."

"No, I didn't fight with her." Evan slowed as they reached a fallen tree, the top branches of which projected into their half of the road. "Our last discussion was about Tuesday's shoot for the calendar. We were cool about it; she liked the ideas, wanted to discuss your office girl-on-girl scene. KY was there, she can confirm it. They were discussing hair colors. KY was saying she wanted Venus as a redhead femme fatale."

Clara looked inquisitively at KY, who nodded. She shrugged again and leaned back in her seat, got out her compact and began checking her makeup.

KY, her mind filled with dark imaginings, watched Clara admire herself. That was all she was really doing: being narcissistic; her makeup was flawless.

Even this early in the day, Clara Cleavage looked fabulous, total porn star chic: the straight blond hair parted on the left; the retroussé nose and red lipstick; and the skinny, practically anorexic body in tight ripped-denim pants and stacked blue tube top. And, god, was that tube top stacked! KY couldn't help the sudden surge of delicious envy that rushed through her: Clara's huge beasts were feats of antigravity, round globes like soccer balls on her chest. And her nipples? Those were something else too. Erected, each was half a thumb long.

Yeah, Evan was definitely onto a winner if Clara signed an exclusive deal with TA. That word 'exclusive' was the problem though: Ms. Cleavage was in so much demand in the adult industry that she'd be a complete fool to sign exclusively with Titaholics. (Clara was a genuine porno A-lister; a top draw in any movie.)

And even if they somehow did persuade Clara to sign with them, it would cost them an arm and a leg to keep her. Though not exactly smart herself, Clara had a good agent, one who took his time to actually read through her contracts. Including all the small print.

Unlike half the girls—sex-mares really—in TA's stable.

KY thought about that. She did feel sorry for the girls. Some of those contracts (most of which she'd drafted herself by copying and pasting from online legal samples) were like white-slavery deals.

But . . .

It's a dog-eat-dog business, ladies. You all learnt to read in school, didn't you?

Okay, KY knew it wasn't right to screw the girls over that way, but . . . well this current gig of hers with Evan James's company was her second chance at big time success. It was a grand scene for her. She'd blown her first shot at fame and wasn't going down the same drain again.

At least not by my own making, anyway. I'm not screwing myself over for nothing. She got out a tiny bottle of cocaine from her purse. "I've earned this," she said, sticking a straw into the bottle and lifting it to her nose. "We all have." After snorting her fill, she held the straw up to Evan's nose so he could take a hit too.

"No blow for me, baby," Clara said, when KY offered her some. "It's too early in the day. Right now, I need to mellow out." She got out a joint from her purse and lit up.

The green countryside flowed past. KY settled back in her seat and tried to concentrate. It was almost impossible; her worries rumbled like thunder through her head. Chad Cannon and Venus Deluxe had better turn up fast. And nothing had better have happened to them. Two of America's favorite porno stars vanishing, or worse yet, dying, would raise a huge stink. Enough to crash Titaholics. And KY had too much riding on Titaholics for that to happen.

II

Kendra Yang, a.k.a. KY, had once been the darling of the adult transsexual movie scene.

KY, originally from Springfield, MA, was five-foot-eight and wafer-thin. She had long black hair and was breathtakingly beautiful, with such disarming feminine grace to her that it was hard to believe she'd been born Kenneth Ming Yang, and that she still had the male plumbing to prove it.

Her penis was short and thin, her breasts huge. Her breasts were 34G and topped with large brown nipples that rode up high, surrounded by wide dark aureole. She'd insisted on having big nipples.

(She'd also wanted even bigger breasts, but her plastic surgeon, Dr. Meyer, had warned her that they'd look freakish on her little frame.

At her porno peak, KY been way, way, way hotter than Joanna Jet, Natalia Coxxx, Thailand's Long Mint, Alexis Livingston, or even tranny big-dick legend Suzanna Holmes. She was constantly in demand, screwing till the shoots had blurred into one endless orgy. Porno kingpin Joey Silveira said she was cuter than Bailey Jay. She'd worked with Joey in *Next Shemale Idol* and *Rogue Adventures*, done the *Transsexual Prostitutes* series, done several *Transsexual Babysitters* DVD's. Then there was all the web-page content she'd shot for sites like Shemale Yum and Grooby Productions. She'd done shoots in Brazil, Canada, England, France, Japan, South Africa, Germany, and Italy. She'd had her own website, slavering fans . . . just everything. In the shemale porn market she'd made good money. (And there was quite a bit to make: Despite being considered a niche market, transsexual porn was actually more popular than lesbian porn.)

She'd made even more money moonlighting as an escort. Working as an escort took KY around the world, including into the bedrooms of the presidents of two countries. They fucked her, she fucked them, they paid her, she squirreled away large sums of money. She'd have banked even more if she'd not converted so much of her earnings into Andean rocket fuel and sniffed it. Somewhere along the endless sexual trail KY had gotten a *heavy* drug habit. It was her way of coping with the soullessness of a lot of her work. She found it impossible to be both depressed and high at the same time.

But it was working as an escort that ruined KY. Her downfall came in Thailand, where she'd been invited to a private party, hired from her website for a roomful of naked but hooded women and men.

There'd been several other transsexual escorts there too.

The party had been a blast. Massive amounts to eat and drink and bowls of drugs everywhere: hash, coke, speed, meth, miscellaneous uppers and downers, vials of morphine, pre-filled needles of heroin, in short everything required to blow one's mind. There'd been enough opium available to sink the Titanic all over again. They'd all fucked her a lot and she'd herself creamed several guys butts. Someone had been whipping a giggling woman, and they'd all been laughing.

Then the host had dared her to be fisted by Big Ball, who was a giant. She'd giggled, "O.K., you're on!" and gotten out her lube. Once she'd seen the size of the giant's hands, however, KY had had second thoughts; she'd been terrified that he'd snap her anal ligaments. But aware of her fear, the giant Thai been extremely gentle when fisting her. With a cowled woman stroking her penis while Big Ball did her, KY had ejaculated extra hard to that fisting, squirting her semen almost two feet up in the air, with the giant hand in her ass feeling like it was in deep all the way up to her stomach.

Everyone around was laughing and yelling encouragement to the three of them.

But afterwards . . .

The next day had been overcast and had lent a stately beauty to the city of Bangkok. Leaving her hotel, KY had decided to go for a walk by herself. Somewhere amidst the throngs of bustling people in the heart of the city, she'd decided to cut through a quiet alley to reach the next street. Halfway through the alley, she'd heard her name called.

She'd turned. "Yes . . . ?"

"Greedy American slut!" the voice spat. Next, liquid fire splashed in KY's face. She'd been drenched with acid. She collapsed to the alley floor screaming, while her attacker—a tall woman in a red dress—calmly walked back to vanish into the crowd.

An ambulance arrived for her thirty minutes later; apparently her attacker had called for it. By then KY's head was a total wreck, most of the hair and skin on its left side burnt off. And she was completely blind in her left eye.

The Thai police told her she'd gotten off 'lightly': two German T-Girls who'd attended the same party had both been found with their throats slashed from ear to ear. One of the dead girls had also had her testicles cut off; the other had had both legs broken. Police leads suggested KY and the German transsexuals had been victims of the Thai ladyboy mafia, who'd viewed the three as muscling in on their turf. A previous escort visit KY had made to the country earlier in the year had created widespread alarm among local T-Girls about a threatened 'foreign invasion.' So the ladyboy mafia had decided to make an example of her.

Next, the doctors showed her a photo of what her face looked like before they'd bandaged it up. She'd fainted at the sight—it had been a garbled mess of meat. Her left eye looked like a squashed white bug.

That was almost it for KY.

The next twelve months of her life were a blur of reconstructive surgery: Consulting rooms, doctors and nurses, operating theaters, waking up groggy from the anesthetic; drips, bandages and bedpans; skin grafts, hair transplants, nose and lip jobs . . . The surgeries to rebuild her face cost her everything she'd saved. Everything she'd amassed working in the porn industry, all the money salted away over years of getting screwed day and night, went into getting her looks back. A whole year of her life gone down the drain. At one point, she developed complications from a hair transplant which led to her having more surgery.

She had lots of support from her friends. Her parents had disowned her years ago—not because she was transsexual, but when she started doing porn—so she never told them. The producers and directors she'd worked with all told her to 'get well and come back to work soon.'

Porn never stands still. People need content to fantasize and masturbate to. And that content must be created endlessly. New shemale stars—new intersex flesh to fantasize too—were being born every day on the plastic surgeons' operating tables. By the time KY returned to the biz, she'd become old news. There were lots of new girls, beautiful Asian faces with hyper-inflated breasts and stiff penises bi-curious men and women longed to suck on.

It didn't matter. The surgeries had been a complete success. Though left with a prosthetic left eye, KY was breathtakingly gorgeous again. (She now tended to let the hair on the left side of her head fall over her artificial eye, completely covering it. She was blind on that side, anyway, so what did it matter?) She also had that plastic doll-toy look everyone expected of porno actresses.

She wanted to get back into making sex films, but she was wary of herself. She knew how much she loved drugs; it would be easy to get stoned and make some wrong moves and crash her career revival before it even got off the ground.

She got tons of escort offers—some for massive amounts of money—but turned them all down. She was out of that scene for good. She *was* sorely tempted to dive back in, but one near-death experience was warning enough. While in hospital, making her rounds of the surgical tables, she'd heard reports of three other girls getting murdered on their sexual travels; two in Italy, one in Japan. Even Brazilian legend Susanna Holmes had lost an eye in an Italian acid attack. The international T-Girl escort circuit seemed full of jealous bitches now.

She concentrated on her website for a while, but that didn't really pull in so much money anymore. Her fan base was dispersing; there were simply too many younger and kinkier alternatives.

Then she got a movie call: twenty grand for a single film centered entirely on her. With her bank account almost exhausted, it seemed to be the way to go about things now. Play the legend card, dig in and work through her slump. A screw or two a month would be great for her confidence too.

She accepted the movie offer. The amount of money she was being paid for the shoot—even for a 'Legend's Deal' as they put it— should have alerted her that something was amiss, but Monk, the director making the film, was an old friend of hers, so KY figured she had nothing to worry about.

The shoot began normally enough. The cast was herself, two guys she'd not worked with before, and Luna Real, another transsexual. (She'd had personal differences in the past with Luna Real, but this was business. The porno maxim was 'Bitch off-screen all you want; but once filming starts, act professional, bitch, or you're out of the profession.')

The script was classic 'Tranny Surprise': Two guys on holiday picking up two pretty girls in a bar and taking them upstairs to their hotel room, where they discover the ladies' 'something extra.'

In addition to Viagra, there was an excess of drink and drugs available. That was another red flag KY should have noticed: usually when porn filmmakers got you doped up they wanted something extra-special from you; either a hardcore scene you'd never to consent to do if sober, or one for which you'd demand a lot of extra pay.

But she needed the money, so they'd gotten on with filming.

At first, everything went great. In two hours they'd gotten most of the day's shoot down, then everyone took a short break before doing the money shots.

KY wondered what that was all about. Monk assured her there was no problem. "We're just rechecking some footage. Lou thinks we might need to reshoot that blowjob scene in the bathtub."

(Monk was a tall fat man with hippie-length brown hair held down by a headband. He both had oily skin and sweated a lot, so he used tons and tons of deodorant and perfume. He always wore Hawaiian shirts and shorts and sandals like he was on holiday.)

Then Monk handed her an unfamiliar blue drink. "To rehydrate you," he said. "It'll make your skin glow and you'll come harder too."

Everyone else was drinking similar drinks, so KY accepted and drank hers too.

Suddenly, KY began giggling a lot. She also found herself thinking that everything people said was the funniest joke ever. Even when the cameraman, Lou, was worriedly saying, "C'mon, Monk, you don't have to ruin her like this! She's a friend of ours, goddammit!" she thought it was hilarious. What was he so upset about?

She walked over to Lou and tried to kiss him. He evaded her wet lips and shook his head, then told Monk, "Hey, film it yourself, I'm not doing it," and stomped off, not to return.

KY laughed herself silly. "What's with the sourpuss?"

"Oh, nothing, baby. Fuck that uptight son-of-a-bitch!" Then he yelled at the door. "Hey, asshole! You dare walk out on me? Fine! *I will* film it myself, and I'll also see to it that you never ever work in this industry again, capisce!!!?"

KY accepted another glass of the blue drink, which made everything seem even funnier to her. Then the shoot resumed.

This time, there was a knock on the bedroom door and four more people entered. Three buff men and a curvy dark woman. That made seven in all, excluding KY.

She laughed. "Ah, the more the merrier!"

Monk directed the action from behind the camera. "Okay, KY baby, now here's how we're gonna do the shoot, okay? First you take out your glass eye . . ."

She popped it out without a second thought. Giggling, she rolled it between her fingers. "Oops, it's looking at me!"

"Okay, now, stick it up Ronnie's ass."

Ronnie obediently bent over. KY pushed the prosthetic eye—flat and curved like part of a broken ceramic plate—up his anus . . . an easy entry.

"Now suck it out again. Just like you're felching him."

KY did that too. She was aware of the camera zooming in on her empty socket, and of someone brushing her hair away from her face and clipping it back, so the gaping hole was clear for all to see.

"Okay, now, lick the eye clean and stick it up Joe's ass; we'll go around all the guys."

So that's what she did. It was great fun, watching her eye pop out of the men's anuses, then licking it clean again. There was occasionally shit on it—the last three men to join them hadn't had enemas first. And meanwhile, the usual sex and horseplay was going on all around her. The original 'Tranny Surprise' shoot had now degenerated into a full-blown orgy with KY as the centerpiece attraction. She watched entranced as one guy sucked another guy's erection so deep into his throat it looked like he was performing a magic trick. Viagra had her penis harder than a bone and someone was masturbating her hard and fast. She sucked her eye out of someone's ass, then felt the telltale pressure in her scrotum.

"God, I'm gonna come!" she gasped.

"WAIT!" Monk barked in excitement. "Okay, Lucy, get on your back and spread your damn legs extra-wide; we can't have any mistakes here—I gotta get all of this. KY, now I want you to stuff your glass eye up Lucy's pussy, then I want you to fuck her with it inside her. Then, you come inside her and use your tongue to catch the eye creampie."

That was how it went: Giggling like mad, KY shoved her eye into Lucy's vagina, fucked her till she came, then pulled out and licked the creampie—eye and semen—up into her mouth.

"Okay! Great! Great! Great!" Monk screamed with delight. "Okay, now, KY, swallow your eye! Swallow it! Don't worry—you'll shit it out later!"

KY swallowed her eye. It tasted really fishy, which she liked. She had a surreal 'am I dreaming this?' moment when the ceramic oculus stuck in her throat like a recalcitrant *Arabian Nights* fishbone and she blanched, gagging for air; but then, using the deep throat relaxation technique she'd perfected for handling overlarge penises, she got the eye past the asphyxiating obstruction and swallowed it fully, and the world refocused again as an endless circus with everyone around her as the clowns.

Damn, this was great fun! She laughed and laughed and laughed.

And she needed to come again, the Viagra still had her hard as stone and her balls ached badly. One of the guys—Mario—was lying on his belly. She lay on him and stuffed her cock up his ass and began thrusting. He had a really slack ass and it took her forever to get off.

Once she'd had her orgasm, she was pulled off Mario and unceremoniously rolled over.

"Okay, now," Monk said, his voice dripping with glee, "we'll have a combined bukkake and golden showers scene. Remember I told you all to come with full bladders . . ."

KY laughed and laughed and had the time of her life while the six men all jerked off and ejaculated into her vacant eye socket. Monk filmed the eye overflowing with white semen. Then they flushed their semen out with piss. Monk filmed that too—KY's eye as a lake brimming with urine. Then, finally, Luna Real squatted over KY's face and shat a long, watery, almost diarrheal poop into KY's empty eye socket. The excrement bubbled up and spilled over her face onto the bed.

"Always keep an eye out for the Brazilian shit, you uppity Chinese bitch," Luna grunted while emptying herself.

And KY found that the funniest thing ever.

***

Monk and the porno crew packed up. Luna, Lucy, and the stunt cocks were dismissed. A still furiously giggling KY was cleaned up, dressed, and dropped off at home.

Still finding everything utterly hilarious, she finally dropped off to sleep.

The drugs she'd been fed wore off the next morning. Then she remembered what she'd done. The cold shock of horrified realization set in. *Oh, shit, shit, shit! Oh, God, please tell me I didn't go that far!*

Her empty eye socket began itching, a clear sign she was stressed out. *Shit, I swallowed my eye? How am I ever going to poop it out? Will I need surgery?* She parted her left eyelids and carefully scratched the angry scarred flesh in there. Then she sniffed her fingers. A smell of semen, urine, and feces assailed her nostrils. *Shit! I should have known when I saw Luna Real there, with all those scat vids she does. Ugh—I should kill Monk for this! How in the blazes did I fall for this? If Monk releases that video . . .* She could see her carefully reconstructed future falling apart like a cottage hit by ten wrecking balls at once. She'd be a total laughing stock, utterly unable to show her face in public.

If that movie got out, she'd be ruined for life, finished.

She instantly called Monk. Like he'd been expecting her to do so, he picked up on the second ring.

"Hey, KY baby, did you sleep well . . . and have the giggles worn off yet?" His voice was sardonic, challenging.

KY began weeping profusely. "Monk, how could you? We're friends, how could you do this to me?"

"Nothing personal, baby. It's just business. This DVD, once released is gonna make me a hell of a lot of money. I'm calling it *KY's Eye to Ass Story*."

The tears flowed from her single eye. "You drugged me, you son-of-a-bitch! I'll go to the cops!"

He laughed. "So go. I didn't force the drinks down you. You haven't a leg to stand on. Besides, the film will be out next week, way before you can drag me to court. We're editing now. It's all Lou's fault—that wimpy bastard. I'll ensure he's blacklisted . . ."

Next week? KY felt some hope. Maybe she wasn't about becoming the laughing stock of the adult industry after all. Maybe she could stop the movie's release.

"How much?" she asked coldly.

"What?" He'd clearly not expected the question.

"How much will it cost me to buy the film from you? That includes all the original files too."

"You couldn't afford it." His voice was amused.

"How much, you son-of-a-bitch?"

"Hey, hey, watch your tongue, okay?" But he was clearly intrigued enough to play with her. She imagined him now, a cat with her as his mouse, letting her imagine she had a chance of gaining her freedom before digging his nails back into her hurting flesh again.

"Two hundred grand," he said finally.

She gasped in horror. "Two hundred thousand dollars? That's extortion. You only paid me twenty for the shoot!"

"You were screwing *me* then, now the condom's on the other cock." He laughed. "C'mon, KY, give it up. We both know you haven't got the money, okay? Besides, I don't know what you're worried about anyway. I'm about making you world famous."

She couldn't even weep anymore; she was that enraged. If they'd been in the same room, she'd have clawed his eyes out with her nails for saying that. "Don't do me any more favors, asshole."

"Okay, if you want to trade insults, this conversation is over. I'll get back to work editing—"

"No, no, wait. I'll find the money."

"You can't get that kind of money."

"I'll find it. Just give me a week."

"You've got two days."

"Three."

"Two. Today's Tuesday. You get me two hundred grand in cash by Friday morning or I'll release your latest DVD to the public. And, wow, won't that be a fantastic comeback? Come . . . back . . . get it?"

He hung up. KY sat staring across her dim living room, out at NYC. It was late November, the chill well in the air, the trees all barren and gray. It might have been drawing towards Christmas for others, but she saw no cheer ahead for herself.

She already knew she couldn't raise the money. *Two hundred grand? Where the hell am I supposed to find that?* She had twenty-five thousand in the bank. By frantically calling around her friends, she might be able to borrow another fifty or sixty. Okay, say seventy-five, tops. Which made a hundred thousand. But Monk was demanding two hundred G's. Which meant he was intentionally pricing her out of the market; he had no real intent of letting her buy the movie back.

On that realization, KY went to the bathroom and ran the bath. She'd never be able to live with herself once the world saw that stupid slut Luna Real take a shit in her face. *I've been through too much already; I'm not going through the mill again! I'll be finished in more ways than one!*

So she was going to end it all now.

Grim and determined to die before being dishonored, she went to the kitchen and got her sharpest knife.

Two deep slashes and I'll be history. She laughed. *And Monk wouldn't dare release the movie then. Everyone would realize what had happened.* At least she hoped he wouldn't. It would be horrible to become a laughing stock even after death. *But at least I won't know about it then . . . or care.*

She checked the water in the bathtub. It was nice and hot, with wisps of steam rising off the water surface. Just right to die in. She shook in some bath salts, inhaled deeply their sweet scent.

Then her cellphone rang. She considered not answering it, then did, intending to switch it off afterwards.

It was Chad Cannon. "Hey, KY baby, have I got a business proposal for you! You need to be in on this! Hey, look, we're in your neighborhood right now, can we come over?"

He sounded too enthusiastic to refuse. Dully, she postponed killing herself till she'd heard what Chad wanted. "Yeah, sure, you guys can come over right away." She peered through the bathroom door at the steaming tub. "No, it's cool. I was about taking a really long bath, but no problem, it'll wait. I can always reheat the water."

Still, since she was expecting male visitors, she couldn't let them see her like this. A lady always had to look good for the guys, even if they were all turds in disguise. Quickly, she reentered the bathroom and thoroughly washed out her shitty eye socket. She popped her spare prosthetic eye in, then went to her bedroom and put some makeup on.

Chad brought Evan James over.

Evan, a Brazzers cameraman, had split with the company and was looking to set up his own outfit, calling it Titaholics Anonymous. He was both looking for backers and recruiting staff, and Chad, who was already on the team, had said he thought Kendra Yang—*the* transsexual legend—might be interested too.

"Sure I'm interested," KY said. And she was. If only this fantastic offer had come yesterday, before she'd gone off with Monk for that goddamned shoot. This was exactly what she needed and wanted now. But she knew if she accepted the job, once Monk's *Eye to Ass* DVD hit the online stores, Evan's Titaholics would drop her like a hot potato.

She decided to be honest with them. She was going to kill herself after they left anyway, so what did it matter? *At least they'll have nice memories of me. And Evan* (who she thought was impossibly sexy; just her type of hunky guy) *might even come to my funeral.*

So, tears flowing from her single brown eye, she said, "I'd love to join Titaholics, Evan, I honestly would. But see, I've got this huge problem. So huge it's about to fucking kill me."

He leaned forward, alert and interested, which she considered a major selling point in his favor. "What problem?"

She explained: "See, there's this DVD about to come out . . ."

She was surprised at the rage in Evan's eyes as she poured her heart out to him. Then, when she was done, he said, "I think we can fix this for you." He looked at Chad. "You still got Hexwood's number?"

Chad nodded. "Right here, man."

Evan assured her everything would be fine: Mr. Hexwood was a very persuasive man who would go along with her to have a little chat with Monk.

That evening KY called Monk again. "I've got the money."

His surprise was obvious. "That fast? How?"

"I hawked my ass to a Saudi sheik; what do you care? Look, what matters is I've got the two hundred grand. In cash. Do you want it or not?"

"Sure I want it," he said quickly. "Come on over."

"Monk, I'm coming over with my lawyer. He's insisting you've got to sign a release form handing everything we recorded yesterday over to me, along with all the rights to them. That way we'll know you've erased everything except the copies you give me."

She could practically hear the dollar bells jingling in Monk's brain; Christmas had clearly come early for him. "Yeah, whatever you say. For two hundred grand, girl, I'd sign away my rights to entering Heaven . . ."

He'd given her his home address and hung up.

***

Mr. Hexwood was a muscular Negro with unreadable eyes and a plaited beard. Wearing a black suit and coat and carrying a brown attaché case, he met KY outside Monk's apartment building.

Mr. Hexwood nodded to her, then said in a Barry White baritone, "Now, Miss Yang, it's most important to me that you keep quiet about whatever you see happen inside Mr. Monk's apartment. Without that assurance, I can't help you. Do you understand?"

She nodded. The man's eyes scared her.

"Good, very good. Some of it might seem a little scary, but it's all for your good, okay?"

She nodded again. He grinned. He had a gold tooth. They entered the building and rode the elevator up to Monk's apartment.

Monk let them in. He was dressed in his usual Hawaiian holiday getup and headband, and was sweating as heavily as usual; even on this cold NYC night, his floral shirt had damp patches under the armpits. He shook hands with Mr. Hexwood and indicated that they sit. He sat opposite them, across a dirty coffee table. He was fidgety. KY could see that. She just hoped he'd not suddenly pull a gun on them.

KY had no idea how this was going to work out. She had only two hundred dollars in her handbag, and to her knowledge, Mr. Hexwood had no money at all on him. The other thing she had with her was a brown envelope containing the contract releasing the movie to her. The contract was one she'd hastily assembled from searching across the internet. It contained every restriction on Monk's using the footage of her that she could find online. It should be binding. Of course, there was the problem of making him sign it . . .

But then things got *very* weird.

"Okay, down to business," Mr. Hexwood said, taking the envelope from KY and spreading the contract on Monk's coffee table. "Miss Yang says you've reached an agreement to sell her the rights to the movie *Eye to Ass Story*."

"Yeah, that's right," Monk said slowly. "A deal's a deal. I'll sell it to her—she can have everything. But I wasn't born yesterday, okay? So far I ain't seen no green."

Mr. Hexwood nodded. "Yes, that's true." He looked at KY. "Please give him the money you have with you."

KY looked at him in horror. "What? I've only—"

"That's okay. It'll prove sufficient."

His voice was surprising confident. (She wondered if this was one of those mafia-type scenes: maybe he had a gun on him, maybe he was about to make Monk an 'offer he couldn't refuse'?) So KY took out the two hundred dollars from her handbag and laid it on the contract on Monk's coffee table. "Here's your money, asshole."

Monk stared at the two hundred dollars, then glared at KY. "What is this shit? I said two hundred *thousand*, you dumb bitch. Are fucking hard of hearing as well as visually impaired?"

KY cringed. This wasn't going well at all.

Mr. Hexwood, on the other hand, said, "Please calm down, Mr. Monk, and sign the contract."

"Calm down, my ass!" Monk leapt to his feet, his face purple with rage. "You two idiots are going to regret this!" He spun to face KY. "And you, you one-eyed tranny gargoyle, I'll bury your ass so deep in shit, you'll need a frigging mine excavator to dig it up. I'll make sure you're the laughing stock of—"

That was as far as Monk got. Suddenly, he grabbed his chest as if in intense pain. Then he began choking and coughing up blood. He stood there, wavering in front of his chair, a stream of blood dribbling over his lips and down his chin.

Scared, KY looked over at Mr. Hexwood. "What's the matter with—"

She gasped. Mr. Hexwood was holding a doll, about action-figure sized, with a photograph of Monk's face stuck to its head. Mr. Hexwood was also twisting a golden needle in the doll's chest.

"Shit," KY said, looking from Mr. Hexwood to Monk and back. "You mean all that voodoo stuff in the movies is for real?"

Monk was still coughing up blood.

"Just one more pin to assure you that this ain't coincidence, man," Mr. Hexwood said. Leaving the first gold pin in place, he stuck another one into the doll's left hand.

KY froze in shock. Like he'd suddenly developed stigmata, blood had begun dripping from a hole in Monk's left hand. Monk managed to lift the hand and look at it, then he collapsed back into his chair and sat there, jerking like he was dying and staring imploringly at KY.

"H-h-h-help m-m-m-me!" he pleaded. His voice was scary to hear.

KY laughed. It felt great to be on the doling-out end of things for once. "Hey, Monk! Speak louder, you asshole—I can't friggin' hear you!"

Blood was now dribbling like snot from Monk's nose; his Hawaiian shirt was a soaked red mess. "Pl-pl-please . . . st-st-stop h-hi-him. I-I-I-I'll s-s-s-sign anything!!!"

She looked at Mr. Hexwood. "I think he's serious."

Mr. Hexwood grinned. "Yeah, I think he is." He pulled both pins out of the doll.

Monk immediately stopped bleeding. He sat staring at them both, then without speaking, he leaned forward to collect the ballpoint pen Mr. Hexwood was holding out to him.

"Careful you don't get blood on the contract," KY said. "That took me all day to put together."

Monk put the pen down, then wiped his hands clean of blood with his headband.

He picked up the pen again.

"Hey, wait!" KY said again just before he signed.

Monk looked at her in fear. "What now? I want to get this over with."

She pulled the contract towards herself, then got out an eyebrow pencil from her handbag. "I made a mistake on this: I've got two hundred grand written here. It should be just two hundred bucks."

After she'd crossed out the 'thousand' and signed over it, she passed it back to Monk, who signed above it too, then initialed and signed the whole contract.

"Now that wasn't so hard, was it, Mr. Monk?" Mr. Hexwood asked with a cold smile on his black face. "Now here's a warning, man. If you either attempt to renege on this contract, by releasing the movie under another name, or if you don't erase all your files of it . . ." he raised his eyebrows at Monk, who was shivering now, "or if you ever so much as try to harm Miss Yang here . . ." He tapped the doll. "And this time, man, it'll be permanent. Remember that: permanent agony like you just felt. You dig me, man?"

Monk nodded, his eyes wide with fright.

Mr. Hexwood took his leave of them. Monk immediately made copies for KY of his edits, then while she watched, he deleted all the original files.

"You're fucking sure that's *everything* you've erased, you scumbag?"

"Y-y-y-yes!" Monk was sweating bullets in the cold night air. He'd changed out of his bloodied Hawaiian top. His fresh floral shirt was already soaked through with perspiration. His dousing of deodorant hardly hid the smell of fear reeking from him.

KY almost felt sorry for the asshole. "It had better be, Monk, baby. You know what to expect if it isn't. And I'll ask him to stick pins in the doll's eyes and dick too."

"It is! It is!"

She left the scared and trembling pornographer.

Walking down to catch the subway home again, she wondered what she'd do with the recording she'd just copied. (Maybe it would work as motivation to do less drugs in future?) It was utterly gross stuff, watching Luna Real's ass spreading wide while the shit trickled down into her eye socket . . .

So help me, God, I'll murder that bitch if she ever comes back from Brazil!

She shuddered with deep gratitude to Evan James for restoring her dignity. Her life would have been over if he and Chad hadn't showed up. (KY was Chinese enough for saving face to be supremely important to her.)

She was utterly relieved to be free to live her life again. It was only later, when she was safely back home and the elation of her narrow escape had worn off, that the full scary import of what she'd witnessed

195

occurred to her. *I just saw a black guy work voodoo on someone. Voodoo? Shit! That stuff is for real?*

***

What happened next was that KY (who found Evan's roughish dark looks irresistible), and Evan (who was totally smitten by her huge breasts), fell head over heels in love. It helped that they both shared a predilection for drugs: they hardly ever had differences of opinion. Sex wasn't a problem: Evan didn't mind KY's penis, and he hardly used her ass anyway, generally preferring to hump her between the breasts. The only potential problem at the start was Evan's big-tit fetish—once he saw a fresh set, he *had* to slide his manhood between them. KY shrugged it off. She decided he could screw all the breasts he liked. She'd soon realized that Evan *needed* her, and she knew he knew it too.

She shut down her own website and invested what money she had left in Evan. And it was now that she discovered her talent for business organization.

Titaholics flourished, winning several AVN awards in its first year. (Charlee Cummings had won Best New Starlet; and Kendra Loki, Marbella Massive, Curvaceous, and Jade Neverland had walked away with the award for Best All-Girl Group Sex Scene, from Titaholics' feature *Smells Like Teen Pussy*.) Subscriptions to their website already rivalled those of Club Jenna. KY sold Evan on Wicked Pictures' idea of signing exclusive contracts with promising starlets (like Wicked had done with Chasey Lain and Jenna Jameson), and so shortly, in additional to the regular pay-per-screw deal with the general pool of porno stars, they also had a stable of hot busty sluts no one else had access to. And now everyone and their favorite vibrator wanted to work with Titaholics, even the girls who didn't have big breasts.

To cap things off, they'd just launched the Titaholics line of sex toys, which was already turning into a major money-spinner.

KY was delirious. She had her life back again. Her Thai acid experience and its sad *Eye to Ass* epilogue could finally be laid to rest. She had money in the bank, huge respect in the adult film industry, and best of all (so long as she cast a blind eye on Evan's 'titaholism') she'd found true love. What more did anyone want from life?

But she was aware that all it would take for them to lose everything was just one little screw-up. A screw-up like this inexplicable disappearance of Chad and Venus.

Chad owned twenty percent shares in Titaholics; that was the problem. If anything bad happened to him—if he died, for instance—the police would start investigating whether KY and Evan had killed him over profits. Then they might get their legal departments in to start checking out the contracts the girls had signed. And then . . . someone was certain to blow the whistle on how unfair they were.

Titaholics would get blacklisted for unethical business practices. The anti-porn feminist lobbies would come calling with guns. And then . . .

Kendra Yang could just see the porno empire she'd slaved to build with Evan come crashing down about their heads.

And it would all be Chad and Venus's fault.

III

"What's with all the fallen trees anyway?" Clara asked for the umpteenth time as the silver BMW sped along Route 20.

KY seriously considered the question. Clara meant the collapsed trees on both sides of the road, most looking like they'd been plucked wholesale out of the ground. (The coke was hitting KY good now, her head was as clear as the blue sky overhead. The crisis they currently faced didn't seem half as bad as it had ten minutes ago. Clouds of sweet marijuana smoke also puffed forward over her head from Clara's lips as she waited for a reply.)

"Has to be the storm," she replied.

"What storm?"

"Didn't you hear about it?" Evan queried from the driver's seat. "It was on the news yesterday, some freak weather occurrence blowing at a hundred miles an hour that happened here at around noon. Like a stationary twister. It lasted just thirty minutes then vanished."

Clara puffed out more smoke. "And it did this much damage? That's weird."

"Yeah, it is weird," KY agreed. "Weird as hell." They were in the region of the Brimfield State Forest, so there was greenery everywhere, but the fallen trees were all in the same three hundred meter stretch of road. "There's huge tree pileups at both roadsides, but except for the top branches of a few trees, none have fallen across the road." Then a worried thought cut through her coke high. "Hey, guys, you don't think those two got caught up in the storm, do you?"

"Please, baby, don't start that now," Evan said. He glanced over at her. "Please, O.K.? We'll find them both safe and sound."

"Yeah, well, alright," KY grudgingly agreed.

"You must admit she's got a point though," Clara said. "A storm of that magnitude—one that uprooted trees this big—could easily fling a car through the air and into the forest."

"Shit!" Evan gasped. "Don't you dare start supporting her!"

KY could see he was worried now. So he thought she might be right? And how'd Clara come to that conclusion? (KY didn't really like Clara, mainly because she knew Evan intended to fuck her . . . well, fuck her breasts anyway. But . . . Clara Cleavage was great *business*, and it was imperative to keep her sweet; so KY wasn't raising any stink over Evan's planned mammary philandering.)

A massive sense of foreboding settled over KY.

"Okay," Evan said, "here's what we'll do: We'll drive down to Brimfield looking for them one more time—"

"Southbridge," KY said quickly. "Let's at least go that far. It's only five miles further on."

"Okay, we'll drive to Southbridge. Then, if we don't find them there, we'll head back to Springfield and file a Missing Persons report. We've put it off long enough." He frowned behind the wheel. "I'm starting to share Clara's opinion—maybe that freak storm *did* blow them off the road. Anyway, the fuzz can search the countryside with choppers."

"I just hope we're not too late," KY said.

"Please, darling, stop saying that!"

"I can't help it, Evan. I've a definite feeling that something horrible happened on this stretch of road. And I can just feel it in my bones that Chad and Venus got caught up in whatever it was."

"Girl, I really frigging think the coke's getting to you," Clara said from the backseat. She was stretched out and mellow now, her voluptuous body draped across the BMW's leather upholstery, her huge breasts looking like at any moment they'd roll sideways off her chest. She leaned up a bit, poked her joint forward between the seats.

"What you need, KY baby, is to chill out like me. Here, have some weed."

KY hated her at that moment. "Keep that fucking thing away from me!"

"Hey, calm down, will you!" Clara pouted, then took another hit of her joint and puffed marijuana smoke everywhere.

Evan drove on.

CHAPTER 34

Tanya

Nothing this morning had so far gone to plan.

First off, Tanya and Venus had both overslept. Completely exhausted after Saturday's horrors, neither of them heard the alarm go off.

Tanya was woken by loud, off-key singing. The words of the song seeped into her dreams like gangrene eroding a soldier's legs:

We're dancers in Hell,
Strippers burning up in our cells,
And no matter how loud we shout,
There just ain't no water to put us out.

Hell Dancers, that's what we are,
Don't speak of angels here, we're all fallen stars,
Pawns in these sick games of Lucifer's.

There's no escape, we're sure gonna pay,
Try hard as we like, we cain't get away,
We're all gonna roast here past judgment day,
So shake your ass, whore, and don't you dare pray.
Almighty God's looking the other way,
'Cos you're his damned sheep that wandered astray.

Hell Dancers, that's what we are,
Pawns in these sick games of Lucifer's,
We must entertain the dark Morning Star.
Hell Dancers, bay-beeeee . . .

The singer was really bad; she sounded like a demonic dog howling. Tanya jerked awake and looked around for the source of the horrible sound.

Then she groaned. *Oh fuck, no!*

Peaches broke off singing on seeing Tanya was awake. Tanya groaned louder on realizing they'd overslept—the clock in Peaches' left breast read 06:41.

"Can't one even get some damn shuteye around here?" Venus growled, unwrapping herself from Tanya's arms and rubbing her eyes. "What in the world was that god-awful racket?"

Peaches looked offended. "You don't like Slain Jane?"

Venus winced. "Spare us the concert; we'll buy her CD. And, by the way, what are you doing in here now?"

"Almost time for class," Peaches said. This morning, she was dull-eyed and looked somewhat confused. Also, she wasn't carrying her dread skin whip.

Tanya got out of bed and stretched. "So why not wait till then?"

"The Schoolmaster says I'm to keep you two locked in here." She pointed out into the corridor.

Tanya winced as a servitor floated into view. "Oh, hell, is this really necessary? We're nervous enough as it is."

For the first time since they'd arrived in Detention, Peaches appeared flustered, enough so to be polite for once. "Sorry, old ladies, the boss's orders. He's really mad about something this morning. Woke me up and began calling me all sorts of names."

Most of which I'm certain are well deserved, Tanya thought. In addition to this throwing a massive monkey wrench into their previous plans, she remembered she'd promised the ghostly Karen that she'd kill Peaches for her. Looking at the teen now, though, murdering her didn't seem realistic. Tanya didn't dare attack Peaches right now. If pulling that clock out of her chest didn't kill her, things would just become a whole lot worse for Venus and herself. She'd also likely have ruined their escape plans for good.

So no, I bide my time. But till when? What if I can't kill Peaches before leaving? Is Karen's ghost going to start haunting me out of spite?

Peaches said, "So on the Schoolmaster's instructions, you two aren't allowed out of this dorm until he calls for you. He doesn't trust you after last night."

Last night. So he's lost his damn manuscript. So what? Last night I lost a young guy I'd begun falling for. A twinge of pain stabbed her heart. *But, hey, I've an odd feeling about this—like the Schoolmaster is actually angry over something else. Peaches has to have told him she caught us on our way up to the third floor. But even then, all he had to do was set a guard on the stairway landing to keep us away from there.*

Peaches added, "He says it's for your own protection."

"Protection from what?"

"I dunno. You can ask him yourselves once in class."

Tanya looked over at Venus, wondering what the other woman was thinking. Now, this morning, she felt odd. *I actually slept with her last night? Made love with her?* In the light of day, the act seemed ridiculous, sacrilegious even. Strange bedfellows indeed. Still, she was grateful to the porno actress; the memory of what they'd shared made her blush and tingle between the legs.

She smiled weakly at Venus, then asked Peaches, "And what about when we need to pee?"

"Use those empty milk bottles from last night's dinner."

"Hey, what about some breakfast? Our brains need food."

"Afterwards, old ladies."

"I'm hungry now." (A lie. She was too worried to be hungry, but they needed an advantage here; any they could get. They needed out of this damned room.)

"You should be, with all that exercise you did last night."

Tanya frowned. *Does she know we had sex? We didn't really clean up afterwards; do we still smell of lust?*

Peaches left. She left the dorm door open, clearly so Tanya and Venus could see the servitor floating in the corridor.

Tanya wheezed. "Well, there goes Plan A and B."

Venus nodded dully. "Plan C is?"

Tanya nodded at the closest window. "Out that way?"

They walked over and had a look outside. In the breaking dawn, the schoolyard wall gleamed sickly like it was draped with a curtain of mold. Above it the tentacles swirled thick.

They looked down. Two black smoke ghosts hovered right under their window.

"There goes Plan C too," Venus said miserably. "Tanya, what are we going to do?"

Tanya got the *Codex Zero* out from under her mattress. "One thing we're doing is taking the relevant pages with us when we leave here." She flipped through the book and ripped two sheets out. She folded those and packed them inside her bra. The rest of the codex she stuffed back under the mattress.

She turned to Venus, who'd begun sniffling. "Don't cry, girl. We'll make it, you'll see."

Venus dried her eyes and got out a comb from her purse. She began teasing her pink hair, working to make some sense of the mess it had tangled into while they'd slept. Tanya sort-of remembered herself playing with Venus's hair, wondering at its expensive silken texture, running her fingers through it after Venus fell asleep. *So maybe I'm the one who disarrayed her, or was it during our lovemaking?* She thought that that second time when Venus had been eating her, she'd gathered up her hair in handfuls while she was coming.

She decided it didn't matter. She watched Venus make the best sense she could of her hair, then watched her put some makeup on: eyeshadow, mascara, lip-gloss. Though expert, Venus's actions were mechanical. To Tanya's mind, she was clearly going through the ritual of a habitual action to take her mind off the horrors that awaited them.

Tanya, though, found her actions entrancing in the extreme. *Yeah, she looks great. I can see why all the guys wank to her. And those breasts! Yum-yum! Okay, but I'm definitely not doing it again; it'll feel weird as hell eating hair-pie in my normal frame of mind. But that once? Damn, she's an utterly wonderful memory to have.*

She was still savoring that nice emotional glaze when Peaches came to collect them both for school.

***

"He went to *Heaven*—the little shithead went to *Heaven!*" the Schoolmaster screamed at them, his voice the croak of a million pissed off toads. "HOW DARE HE GO TO HEAVEN!!!"

The Schoolmaster was incensed beyond belief. He strode back and forth across the classroom, smacking his cane loudly against his palm. "That sneaky son-of-a-bitch got away from me!"

He glared at Tanya and Venus, who were both seated at front desks. The ferocity of his gaze made them both shudder. Now, the sunken black pits of his eyes visibly sucked light out of the room, making the air about his face dark.

Mike went to Heaven? Tanya felt pleased for him. *After the horrible way he died he deserved that at least.* Her burst of joy was tempered by the sudden nasty look the Schoolmaster flung her way. For a moment it seemed like the flesh of his face had been sucked into the wells of his eyes; his head was bare bone with a buzzard's beak.

"Sir . . . ?" Peaches said. Since delivering them to the classroom, she'd been silently pacing, again dragging her whip behind her like a tail.

"Yes, Ms. Principal, what is it!?"

"Sir, so Mike went to Heaven, so what? We win some, we lose some."

"Ms. Principal, I'm not in any mood to banter boring banalities with you. What is your point?"

"Sir, why don't we just make these two pay for his crimes?"

That calmed him a little. "Ah, that's a wonderful idea. Yes, yes, yes, that's exactly what we'll do." He eyed the trembling Tanya and Venus nastily. "And now that you mention it, Ms. Principal, I have exactly the right test for them both. Something very fitting. No, there'll be no more grand escapes from *my* Detention. Heaven? How dare that little pipsqueak go to Heaven!?"

***

Thirty minutes later found Tanya and Venus in a world of trouble and terrifying danger.

Oh shit! We're fucked! Tanya had no idea what to do anymore. *How in the universe do we escape this?*

She and Venus were now suspended above a stone pool full of gloop, the type of amorphous creature that had dissolved Mike to death. The gloop floated and squirmed over each other in their pool, their transparent bodies wobbling like unstable gelatin. All their blue eyes were focused up on the two woman. Tanya counted ten of the gloop in the pool, which the servitors had rapidly hollowed out of the classroom floor. The pool filled half the classroom; the student desks were now all stacked against the walls.

Tanya and Venus were enclosed in a black dome, a metal-mesh bowl inverted over a metal base. The pool completely encircled the dome. Their prison's black floor was made from a framework of rods welded to form a grill. The rods (arranged in sets of triangles) were quite thin, the floor more space than metal.

"All the better to see you through," Peaches quipped on noticing Venus's terrified glances down at the gloop.

Inside the dome, Venus and Tanya were separated from each other by a metal-mesh wall running through its middle. Affixed onto this at breast height, one on either side, were two panels, each fronted by a scrambled face. Tanya recognized the design: it was a sliding tile puzzle, the sort where one had to unscramble an image by sliding its pieces around. The puzzle was square in shape, and composed of seven rows both across and down, with one empty space so the puzzle pieces could be moved about inside the frame.

"What's this about?" Tanya asked the Schoolmaster, who sat on his desk by the whiteboard.

"A simple IQ test, in which you compete against each other. All both of you have to do is unscramble that image of my face. Once you do so, the panel will open up, giving you access to a switch behind it."

"And then?" Tanya asked with bated breath.

"Pressing the switch will drop your opponent into the pool of gloop. So, students, time is essential here: whoever finishes the picture puzzle first, wins. Either Venus will die messily, Tanya, all the flesh dissolved off her bones, or you will."

In the opposite half of the cage, Venus yelped in alarm. Tanya felt cold all over. This was beyond inhuman. "You're setting us up to kill one another?"

He smiled. "This test also researches the human self-preservation instinct. You and Venus are friends now. Your suffering here in Detention has forged deep bonds of trust between you. But now those bonds mean nothing, do they? You're not going to let her kill you, Tanya, or are you?" He laughed. "Though I do remember you being of a self-sacrificing bent. Maybe that's even why you joined the police force? Anyhow, now we'll see how altruistic you really are. Here's your chance to throw away your life for your fellow woman."

Tanya couldn't reply. She could only stare at Venus, who stared back at her in equal horror. This was the utterly worst test ever. Below them both, the pool of gloop swished about in hungry anticipation of one of them landing in it.

The Schoolmaster got to his feet. "You have an hour for this, though unscrambling the picture should at most take twenty minutes. Remember, only one of you can win." He crossed to the classroom door, then snapped his fingers at Peaches, who leapt up from her chair and followed him, her rump wagging side-to-side like a puppy's. "Ms. Principal and I are off to the library to search for a missing codex of mine. There's the slim chance that your thieving friend Mike didn't die with it last night, and it went missing somewhere in the library, maybe even slipped underneath one of the bookshelves. Anyway, we'll see." He made an expansive gesture at their cage. "And no slacking is permitted. Have a pity party if you like, an extended farewell party even. However, if we return and you've not yet solved the puzzle . . ." He pulled a black remote control device from his suit. "I'll drop you *both* into the pool."

He walked out the door. Tanya heard his footsteps echoing away down the corridor. Then they paused and his voice floated back. "Ms. Principal!"

"Coming, sir!" Peaches had remained framed in the doorway. Her breast-clock read 0:59:22.

Tanya imagined she saw sympathy in the teen's eyes. But then Peaches waved brightly. "Okay, old ladies, see one of you later." She dashed off after the Schoolmaster, leaving the four black wraiths guarding the classroom door.

Tanya was confused. "Shit, Venus, what the hell do we do now?"

She realized it was a stupid question: opposite her in the other half of the round cage, Venus, her eyes bugged out with fear, was already frantically attacking the picture puzzle.

"What the fuck?" Tanya growled sourly. "I guess that asshole's right—even friendship with benefits means nothing in here."

And I'm wasting time. If Venus gets his face unscrambled first . . . The aftermath didn't even bear considering. After a scared look down at the waiting gloop, she began sliding the sections of the face-puzzle left and right, up and down.

The lyrics of Peaches' creepy song returned now to haunt her. Now they sounded almost like her epitaph:

Hell Dancers, that's what we are,
Don't speak of angels here, we're all fallen stars,
Pawns in these sick games of Lucifer's . . .

How right, Tanya thought glumly. *How absolutely frigging right.*

CHAPTER 35

KY

On their way back from Southbridge, they'd stopped in Brimfield for lunch at a roadside café. Evan and Clara were over at the counter ordering cappuccino and sandwiches. KY, not really in the mood for food, was sitting at the table they'd picked, musing on her feeling of doom. Her head hurt a bit, a comedown from the coke; she should have used a little more before leaving the car.

Opposite the café was a traffic light. Farther down the road a woman was walking her muzzled Rottweiler, though to KY, it looked like the dog was walking the woman, the way it kept dashing back and forth, with her helplessly trailing after it. She seemed to have its leash cuffed to her wrist. KY wondered why she'd ever bought such an undisciplined dog. The Rottweiler appeared to be particularly pissed off with a ginger cat that sat on a hedge across the road hissing at it. It was doing its unsuccessful best to drag its owner over there.

"Okay if I join you?" a deep baritone voice said through KY's thoughts.

She looked up at the speaker. It was a black man with deep-set eyes and a plaited beard.

"I'm sorry," she said, "the table's already taken. My friends are over at the . . ." Then she recognized the face. "Mr. Hexwood?"

Nodding, he sat down.

"B-b-but . . . I-I-I heard you were d-d-dead." After he'd helped her out with Monk, she'd only seen Mr. Hexwood once more: at the Titaholics launch party. There, she'd set him up with Maxi, a raven-haired beauty with the largest breasts in the room, and the largest ass too. (Maxi's huge O cups had those banned polypropylene string implants that just kept growing . . . and growing.) Maxi was wearing a reinforced bikini top, hot pants, and thigh-length boots. Mr. Hexwood had found it impossible take his gaze off her; his eyes drank in her immense bosom like they were siphoning out milk through the creamy, delicately-veined flesh.

"Greatly appreciated, Miss Yang," he'd grinned while leaving the party with Maxi, his gold tooth flashing in the light. "Really greatly appreciated, mama."

She'd winked back, then whispered out of Maxi's hearing, "Enjoy yourself. This is absolutely nothing compared to what you did for me."

And now?

Mr. Hexwood, wearing his trademark dark suit, and carrying the same brown attaché case she remembered from the night at Monk's flat, laughed. "How'd they say it, mama? Rumors of my death were greatly exaggerated."

She let it go, even though Evan had told her Mr. Hexwood had been shot to death down in Brooklyn, that he'd caught a stray bullet in the neck while driving through Crips turf.

She looked over at Evan and Clara, wondering what was keeping them. Clara was arguing with the man tending the sales counter. Apparently he'd spilled their cappuccino while gaping at her huge breasts.

She returned her attention to Mr. Hexwood. "So, man, what brings you up here to Massachusetts?"

"I came to see *you*, Miss Yang," he said.

"You came to see *me*?" Her pleasant surprise at seeing him again evaporated. Oh, shit. If he'd come all this way just for her . . .

He nodded grimly. "Word on the street is that you're worried about Chad and Venus going missing."

She nodded. "They vanished two days ago, man. And you know the hell that'll be unleashed if they're not found, right?"

"Chad's dead," Mr. Hexwood said.

KY gasped. Her inscrutable Chinese features froze in shock, though the news was somehow less of a surprise to her than she'd have expected it to be. "He's dead?"

"Yeah, stone cold. You don't want to know how he died." Frowning, he leaned across the table, and took KY's fingers in his own. "Venus is still alive . . . for now. With her at the moment it's touch-and-go. She might escape the danger, or she might not."

"But where is she?"

"She's in Detention, mama."

A rush of hope surged through KY. "C'mon, man, who's got her? Can we get the police to free her? She went with Chad to buy dope and the pushers got rough, right, and detained them?" Somehow, she knew that had to be the case. Chad was like Evan and herself, a total dope-fiend. Venus, on the other hand, was way more restrained, so it had to be Chad who'd gotten them into trouble. It just had to be.

Mr. Hexwood smiled sadly. "The police can't help Venus where she is."

"But you said—"

"Detention isn't on this Earth. We can't affect it."

The color drained from KY's face. "You're saying there's nothing we can do to save Venus?"

"She might escape. She's got a good friend there. But they're both in huge danger, and about to stab each other in the back."

KY couldn't make sense of the words. She glanced over at the counter. Evan and Clara were headed over to the table with trays. She looked back at Mr. Hexwood, then gasped aloud.

What?

He was fading from view.

"Hey, what's happening to you, man?"

The fading negro laughed and tugged on his plaited beard. "I lied about something: I really did die back then down in Brooklyn. But I'm still around somewhere. Hell, Miss Yang, I'm around in lots of places. I'll see you around, mama."

KY was really tired now. "But . . . but what about Venus? What do I do to help her? I can't just leave her in danger."

Mr. Hexwood was a mere flimsy outline now. "You've no choice, mama. It's her karma: she'll either survive or not." The ghost grinned broadly. "Oh yeah, and thanks again for hooking me up with Maxi. A brother ain't really lived till he's had that kinda hot T and A. I mean, I got so much wood that night, I almost became my own forest; you know what I'm saying!? Hell, the lady almost made dying worth it."

He winked out of view. KY yawned and practically collapsed over the table. Mr. Hexwood's baritone floated through her mind one last time. "You'll shortly be making a trip somewhere, Miss Yang. Maybe, just maybe, you'll be able to help Venus. Keep your eyes open . . ."

And then she felt Evan shaking her. "Hey, baby, wake up, we're here!"

"Yeah, sleepy head," Clara's voice seconded. "Don't tell just one joint's gone to your head like that."

KY opened her eyes. *What . . . ?*

She was still in the car with Evan and Clara. Out along Route 20, with forests on both sides.

Clara was laughing. "Damn, girl, you're a total wuss. I thought you had a good head for pot."

KY realized she'd been dreaming. *None of that was real?* But, coming on the heels of her current worries, the dream really bothered her. Particularly what Mr. Hexwood had said about Chad being dead.

Then she became aware that the car was now stationary, parked by the roadside. "Hey, why'd we stop?" Last thing she remembered, they were headed back from Brimfield towards Palmer again. They'd given up the search for good, were on their way to hand matters over to the Springfield cops. Then Clara had offered her her joint again, and she'd accepted. And then . . .

Clara explained: "Evan wants to do a photo shoot with both of us."

KY glared at her boyfriend. "A what? Evan, are you out of your mind?"

"Calm down, baby. Just look around you. The light's frigging fantastic. It'll be the best ever. I'll have you two girls on the hood of the car and—"

"Evan, if the cops catch us, we'll be booked for indecent public exposure."

"Cops drove by thirty seconds ago, baby, right before we stopped. So they won't be back for a while. And there's no other cars on the road, so . . ."

KY listened and let herself be persuaded. The dream had her all moody though, so she perked herself up with some coke. Clara stuck to pot. KY worried some more: if the cops did bust them out here for nudity, an additional drug possession charge would be a total bummer. Okay, she thought Clara did have a bust to her name down in Memphis, was it? And Chad had been done twice for coke, years ago; but she herself had remained clean.

Oh well, she thought. *I'll just go with the flow of things. I guess if it happens today, it happens today.*

***

Evan had parked the BMW in a break amidst the tree carnage. The storm had eroded the roadside soil, but the tops of the fallen trees provided ample cover from prying eyes.

He explained: "Any cars coming on our side of the road won't see us till they're past. And since we're shooting on the hood, most of those on the opposite side'll miss us too."

KY opened the door on her side. "How long have we got to do this?"

"Ten, fifteen minutes tops. Any more and we'll be pushing our luck; the cops might return." He got out, walked back to the trunk and got out the case with his camcorder, then returned whistling. "Okay, darlings, get naked already. Clara, keep your boots on, let's make it look a little kinky-like."

"Whatever you say, baby, it's your money."

"Wow, this daylight's just fantastic. And the vivid green everywhere . . ."

Shoving her forebodings to the back of her mind, KY stripped off and got up on the BMW's hood. It was pointless arguing with Evan about this. One thing she knew was that he had an almost perfect eye for making great porn. She'd learned to go along with him on stuff like this—his instincts were hardly ever wrong. If Evan said this was a great place to do a shoot, she wasn't about disagreeing with him. (Titaholics didn't normally film 'shemale' stuff; she figured he intended using this as a special bonus 'Kink Feature' for their online subscribers.)

She lay back on the hood and waited. It was hot in the midday sun, but a cool breeze washed over her, tingling her breasts and penis.

"Stroke yourself, KY," Evan instructed. "I need you with a hard-on."

She did like he said, stroked herself, her fingers floating over her penis. The hood dipped as Clara leaned on it, still dragging marijuana smoke deep into her lungs.

"Ditch the cigar already, woman," Evan said testily. "Except you plan on appearing in court, I'll have to edit this bit out." Clara giggled and puffed a cloud of smoke at him. He shook his fist at her. "C'mon, we ain't got time for smokes and jokes here."

KY kept stroking herself. It was feeling good now, something to really take her mind off the day. She stopped fondling her erection and stretched out her hands to Clara. Suddenly she wanted to suck on Clara's large breasts.

Clara dropped the joint and stamped it out. She bent low over the hood and took KY's erection in her mouth. Evan stood to one side of them, camcorder up on his shoulder, capturing it all.

Clara gripped KY's penis about the root and licked up and down its engorged shaft, slipping her mouth over the purple head and sucking hard. The sensation was driving KY out of her mind.

"Okay, now let's have some stroking tit action on her dick."

Her lips curling in a wet smile, Clara pulled KY closer so her legs dangled over the front of the BMW, then she secured KY's erection between her breasts. With the penis trapped in that tight tunnel, she began sliding her breasts up and down over it. She was so heavily endowed that KY's glans was invisible, only the bottom of her penis showed. KY shuddered with pleasure as the breasts rose and fell.

"Great, great!" Evan said. "Okay, Clara, get up on the hood too. Lie down. KY baby, now kneel over her and work on her tits. No, not so damn fast. Go *slow*, savor those tits like they're packed full of the sweetest milk and honey. The guys watching at home need to feel this, you know, feel it right down in their balls. They're the ones who pay our salaries; we gotta give 'em value for money. And, Clara, honey, give me more feeling when she's squeezing you. Bigger boobs is better, yeah? Bigger boobs equals more enjoyment for both of you. So squeeeeeze those tits . . . make sweet love to them." He had a quick look up and down the road to confirm that the police were nowhere in sight, then continued. "Yeah, that's gooood . . . !"

It went on like that, with Evan talking them through the scene. It was fast and impromptu, no storyboards or rehearsals. The recording would be noisy as hell, but KY knew Evan would later edit out their voices and replace them with a smooth R&B soundtrack. They'd also overdub a synchronized 'moan and groan' track, reinserting gasps of pleasure at strategic points in the film. She looked down at Evan's crotch; a hard-on strained against his pants. She licked her lips. Damn, that thing would be so hard now; she wished they were back in their bedroom so he could plumb her ass with it. That was the thing about Evan, show him big breasts and he was on fire. The bigger the breasts, the harder his erection. So with Clara's bared chest as their stimulus, that penis would feel like a crowbar now. Damn, she hoped it didn't break.

She lay on her back again, and Clara squatted over her face-to-face, rising and falling on her erection. Clara had her back arched, her breasts thrust out. It was a tricky position to maintain on a car hood, but her huge boots helped her balance. The hood bobbed up and down as they screwed.

KY raised her eyes from Clara's flushed face to stare up at the sky. A flock of birds were passing overhead, headed south. KY thought it would really funny if the birds right now decided to take a collective shit on the car. *Wow, would that be something to catch on film!* She looked back down, concentrated on the shoot. Evan was right by her head now with the camera, angling it for a shot of their slick joined crotches. Oh, God, this felt so good! She felt her balls tingling, felt the telltale signs.

"Money shot approaching," she warned giddily.

Clara stopped moving up and down on KY and struck a pose. She grinned at Evan. "How'd you want me, baby?"

Maybe it was just all the pot she'd been smoking, but KY admired that about Clara: how cool she was. Over the industry grapevine she'd heard that Clara Cleavage was a total pro; she knew what was expected of her and delivered it, not like some girls who bitched their way through shoots like their mother was Queen Elizabeth Taylor and this was Hollywood. KY had worked with lots of them, the royal anal pains.

Evan took a moment to consider Clara's question. "We'll do an overhead shot on your breasts." He winked at KY. "Okay, baby, hold that jism in a moment, I've gotta get up on the hood myself. . . . Now, Clara, you kneel here on my left with your boobs held out. KY, baby, sit on the roof with your legs either side of her . . . No, no, no, that's not gonna work. Okay, yeah, I got it: KY, you stand with your back to the windshield. . . . Clara, you kneel *here*. KY, you wank hard and fast and splooge all over her breasts. Spread that thick white girl-cream left and right, okay?"

You could really only do one money shot per scene, if you wanted the guy to shoot a good load, that was. KY stood up on the hood, with Clara kneeling before her like a worshipper, her massive breasts held up like a sacrifice she was offering. KY focused on those breasts, both taut orbs like bleached watermelons, letting their plentiful tracings of delicate blue veins hypnotize her.

"Oh my God, yes!" she groaned as her orgasm hit her. Her legs trembling, she squirted her semen all over the breasts spread below her. "Holy fucking shit!"

"Yeah, yeah, honey! This is great!" Evan enthused, getting it all down on camera.

CHAPTER 36

Rafael

Rafael Marquez, butler-chauffeur to Ellis Drake, owner of Drake mansion, was driving back from his weekend trip to his family in Auburn. He was driving Ellis's white Toyota sedan, which both he and Miranda Salcedo, Mr. Ellis's housekeeper cum secretary, were allowed to use as they pleased. He had the radio on at low volume, tuned to WAMG 890—La Nueva Mega Boston—which was pumping out Tex-Mex music. Apparently they were having a memorial weekend for Tejano music queen Selena.

Rafael, a short and darkly handsome man in his mid-thirties, had left his wife and kids early today because he was worried. He'd been calling Miranda Salcedo since yesterday morning without a response. He'd first thought she'd simply put her phone on silent, or gone out for a drive with her girlfriend Sandy and forgotten it at home. Then, he'd thought that maybe she'd lost or misplaced the device. So he'd both emailed her and sent her a Facebook message.

Still no response. So now back to the mansion he was headed to see what the matter was.

Since reaching the Brimfield State Forest, Rafael had been wondering at the slew of fallen trees everywhere. He'd heard about the storm on the radio, but this . . . this looked like a giant child had been playing with the trees. He drove past a Bureau of Forestry van, by which two men stood looking perplexed and talking into a radio.

Rafael shook his head and drove on. He had to get to the mansion quick. He'd not imagined that the devastation the storm had caused was this bad. True, the border of collapsed trees didn't appear to extend in much farther than ten meters from the road, but . . . with Miranda's not picking up his calls since yesterday . . . what if the storm had hit the mansion? Miranda might be hurt. He refused to conceive that she might be dead. She was a competent woman (if a little overambitious), and she and he got along just fine.

The song on the radio ended. The DJ began saying something Rafael didn't quite catch so he turned up the volume. ". . . The Massachusetts State Police are still looking for two fugitives, suspected to be Joel 'Cutter' Miller and Pamela 'Peaches' Principal, responsible for the deaths of five people in Marlborough on Friday night and Saturday morning. The pair are believed to be driving a stolen black Mazda with license plates . . ."

Rafael turned the sound down again. *The world is just crazy*, he thought. *Here I am, just now listening to Selena who got shot by that crazy Saldivar woman, and now two more idiots have gone and murdered—*

He'd just reached a gap in the fallen trees on his right, and peered into the space. What he saw in there . . .

It wasn't the fact that Rafael saw two naked women being filmed atop a silver BMW that made him lose control of the steering wheel. Nor even the fact that one of those women had a stiff penis.

No. It was the sheer size of the kneeling woman's breasts. Those huge twin orbs, their creamy white flesh freshly glazed with semen, riveted his gaze.

Rafael couldn't stop looking at that ravine-deep cleavage. Before he knew it, he'd skidded off Route 20 and into the trees on his left.

Thankfully, he'd been driving with his seatbelt on.

To a loud screeching of brakes, he hit a toppled hickory trunk. There was a loud bang, and the airbags inflated, and next thing, Rafael sat stunned amidst a deluge of green leaves, with images of immense breasts whirling around in his head.

CHAPTER 37

KY

Bang!

KY had been about waving wickedly to the driver of the white Toyota, when it lost control and skidded off into the trees. For that moment, time seemed to slow down for her.

Then she looked in turn at both Evan and Clara. Evan's mouth hung open, his eyes staring in shock. Clara, her hands still holding her breasts up, looked slightly calmer.

KY looked over again at the white car now half-submerged in the sea of fallen greenery. Alarm bells began ringing in her head. *If that guy is dead, we're screwed—stabbed up the ass with a whaling harpoon!* She could already see the damning headlines: "Man Dies In Car Crash After Sighting Porno Shoot On Highway." Or worse: "Porn Really Does Kill!!" Or: "Clara's Cleavage Kills Man!"

The best thing to do now would be simply to get back in their car and scram. Yes, just beat it, be gone from here before the police arrived. But, she cringed, what if the man in the car was hurt? Worse still, what if he died of his injuries? *We'd have practically murdered him, wouldn't we?*

She leapt down off the hood, slipped her feet into her sandals, and penis wobbling left and right, ran across the road.

"Wait!" Evan called after her. "Put some clothes on first!"

What damn clothes!? She didn't look back. A moment later she was by the car, pushing a way through the hickory branches obscuring the driver. Her feet slipped on the muddy ground as she worked her way inward. Panting, she now remembered that dashing across the road like that when you're blind in one eye wasn't a smart thing to do—she could have been knocked skywards by an oncoming car.

Reaching the front of the white vehicle, she was relieved. The windshield wasn't cracked. The airbags had deflated and the driver looked okay. He was breathing heavily and appeared dazed, but he wasn't bleeding anywhere that she could see, and he didn't seem to be in any pain.

He turned to her. He was handsome, thirtyish, and looked Latino.

"Are you okay?" she asked worriedly.

He grinned weakly back. "Yeah, I think so." Then his eyes widened. "Holy shit!"

He was looking past her. KY turned and saw that Clara had joined them. And that she too hadn't bothered to put on any clothes first. KY rolled her eyes. *Well, at least she wiped my jism off her boobs before crossing the road.*

For a long moment, the man goggled at Clara's breasts, then he shut his eyes like he had a headache. "Damn, you ladies should put some clothes on. You could cause an accident!"

"I think we just did," Clara said, pushing past KY to the vehicle door. "C'mon, man, let's get you out of the car."

Clara pulled the door open and the man got out. For a moment he stared at KY's penis. Embarrassed, she stepped back and looked around for Evan. Now without the camcorder, he'd just reached the opposite side of the Toyota. He stood there, staring in disgust at the ground by the hood.

"What's the matter, baby?" she called over to him.

"Front axle's busted."

Clara was holding the driver up, rubbing her naked breasts hard against him. KY wasn't sure if that was therapy, or whether she was trying to make up to him for the crash. One thing was sure though, he looked quite happy squashed up against her like that. KY figured he had a stiffie for certain now.

She walked around to Evan and saw what he'd meant. The front wheel on that side lay almost parallel to the ground. Behind it, the broken axle was stuck into the ground like the wheel was a flower growing from it.

"Hey, man, we're sorry about the crash," Evan said (which KY thought was the right thing to say). "Look, no problem, we'll pay for the repairs."

"Thanks," he said. "My name's Rafael. I was on my way—"

"We're heading back to Springfield," KY interrupted. "We'd better take you to a hospital there: you might have whiplash or a concussion." She flicked off a bug that had strayed from a leaf onto her arm. She was relieved: this looked far from becoming the disaster she'd feared. Clara's 'tit-therapy' on Rafael seemed to be working magic: the man was smiling weakly and breathing fast. *No way now is he going to slap us with a lawsuit. But can he even do that? Maybe he can; you can sue people for just about everything nowadays. Oh, whatever, let's just get his ass to a hospital.*

"Yeah," Evan agreed, "the doctors need to check you out. I'll come give Clara a hand helping you over to our car."

"I can manage just fine," Clara called back, to which Rafael nodded agreement.

Then Rafael said. "I can't go to the hospital just yet."

KY groaned. *Oh no, he is going to make a mess of this for us.* "Look," she said, "we know you're feeling okay, but you do need to see the doctors—"

"No. I've an emergency to attend to first."

Clara laughed. "Man, *you are* an emergency."

"No, not like that. I was rushing home—it's near here—to check if the storm had damaged the building. The housekeeper . . ."

Listening to him explain, KY realized there was only one thing to do.

Evan clearly shared her opinion. "Okay, man, let's go to your place first. Then once we're sure that everything's cool over there, we'll proceed to the ER."

"Thanks," Rafael said. He reached into the Toyota's backseat for a carryall. "I'll call for a tow truck from the mansion."

Evan took the carryall from Rafael. The four of them started back towards the road.

A gray SUV slowed to let them across. The driver, a corpulent redhead in a gaudily patterned sundress, pursed her lips tight at the sight of the two naked women. Particularly at the size of their breasts.

KY could just tell she was thinking: *Professional sluts, that's what you two are. All implants and no brains except in your asses.*

Still, once she noticed the crashed car, the redhead rolled down her window, which KY thought was real decent of her. "Do you need any help?"

"Thanks, but I'm really okay," Rafael replied her. "I live just around the corner, and they're taking me home." The naked Clara pressed tighter against him as if to ensure he kept feeling okay.

KY blew the obese woman a kiss. Waving back, the redhead now noticed KY's penis. Her eyes almost popped from her skull at the sight. Once they were out of the road, she drove off like the devil was after her.

KY had to laugh. It was fun to freak squares out like that. *Get hip with the modern age, lady. Nowadays, us chicks have dicks too.*

They quickly piled into the BMW and drove off too. There was the off-chance that the fat woman might tell the police what she'd seen. KY sat up front with Evan, Clara and Rafael sat in back. KY pulled her dress down over her head then looked back. Rafael had his head on Clara's chest now. The man looked groggy but pleased, like he was in Paradise. She grinned. Maybe he *was* in Paradise; maybe he got off on big breasts just like Evan did.

Then, in a flash, KY remembered what Mr. Hexwood had told her in her recent dream: "You'll shortly be making a trip somewhere . . . maybe you'll be able to help Venus. Keep your eyes open . . ."

"Slow down now, buddy," Rafael called from the back at that moment. "You'll hit the turning any second now, on the right. Yeah, here it is. The mansion's about a mile further on."

Evan turned the BMW onto the single-track road that appeared suddenly as though from nowhere. Entering it—rolling into that dark vale of shadows—felt to KY like they were slithering down the throat of an immense black and green snake.

KY sat still as a stone as the car rolled down the road. *This must be the trip Mr. Hexwood spoke of. B-b-but Mr. Hexwood is dead! How could he speak to me if he's dead? I dreamt that! God, this really isn't making any sense to me any more. What is going to happen next today?*

But . . . he did say Venus was still alive and I might be able to help her. But he also said Chad was dead . . .

Like always happened when she was utterly stressed out, her left eye socket began itching then, right behind the eyeball. Always behind the eyeball, where she couldn't scratch without taking her eye out.

And she wasn't taking her goddam prosthetic eye out here, not with Rafael in the car. No frigging way. Appearances had to be maintained.

CHAPTER 38

Venus

Venus was terrified. Staring at the scrambled face on the mesh dividing her from Tanya, she felt faint. The fingers that slid sections of the picture back and forth in front of her seemingly worked on autopilot, disconnected from her brain. They seemed not to belong to her even, seemed rather part of someone else who was trying desperately to free her.

She was sweating profusely, drenched in horror, a horror reinforced each time she looked down between her feet at the pool of gloop.

The gloop swirled restlessly about under the black cage. Transparent as water, they looked like large melting ice cubes stirring themselves up in a drink. Rows of tiny feelers like liquid hair rippled across their collective surface.

Venus had already urinated once on them. The concentrated amber liquid had formed a yellow puddle on the surface of the gloop, then it vanished. She hated being this scared, peeing all over the place like a baby, but it couldn't be helped.

I'm not gonna die! Venus sensed the gloop's hunger and it terrified her further. Six blue eyes were packed together in a tight circle right underneath her. *Just waiting, waiting for me to drop.*

She managed to repossess her mind. *NO! I'm not dying here, I've got way too much to live for once I survive. I've got my whole future planned out! All that money saved up. I can't . . .*

She forced her thoughts off the creatures below that waited to dissolve her if she couldn't finish the puzzle first. Her gaze snagged on the classroom windows.

Outside was depressingly familiar: brown wall, gray tentacles. A grassy expanse of nothing, with smears of blood and a battered human skull once used as a football. Today like yesterday. No hope. No future either, except to die like a fly. Venus looked inside again. Two servitors flickered past the classroom door. That too was depressing.

She reconsidered her situation. If Tanya . . .

Tanya. Venus peered through the mesh at the other woman. The cop's handsome face was cold, her eyes focused on the puzzle. She was terribly scared too; Venus could tell: Tanya's lips trembled and her right eye twitched. But the movements of her hands on the panel were sure and steady, she wasn't just randomly sliding the tiles. No, she was taking her time, working out where each one went before moving it.

Venus knew Tanya knew she was watching her, but she didn't say anything. What could she say? *Sorry I'm trying to kill you?*

This was sick. Tears filled Venus's eyes. She looked away before Tanya might notice, and stared at the puzzle facing her.

So far, working on trial and error, she'd unscrambled the top third of the picture. The Schoolmaster's empty eyes glared at her, terrorizing her afresh . . . like the night when Evan's squeeze KY had staggered into Venus's dark bedroom at 2 a.m., stoned out of her skull and holding her prosthetic eye out in front of her like it was a compass. Waking up to a noise in the middle of the night, and not immediately remembering where she was (she was druggy herself, tripping on acid), and then seeing the hole in the left side of KY's face, Venus had screamed herself silly before Chad had rushed in to calm her and drag the giggling KY away. And now Chad was dead, and the students too, and . . . *and . . . I'm next.* Chad's death hurt her no end. One of the first things she'd learnt in porn was that 'a man with a big prick tends to be a big prick,' all ego and show and nothing else. Most big-dicked guys were nothing but that . . . dicks. But Chad—when he wasn't pulling macho bullshit like scaring off aspiring starlets—had been her friend. Okay, so he'd been a prick too, but a nice prick . . . sometimes at least.

She snapped out of her reverie and attacked the puzzle again. It was a brain-numbingly slow process—it almost gave her a migraine to figure each step out, and her deep fright meant she kept making mistakes—but she somehow unscrambled the picture to halfway. Now the Schoolmaster's immense nose had joined his horrible eyes to stare at her.

Her thoughts began wandering again. She quickly called herself to order. *Oh no, I can't keep zoning out. If I do, Tanya just might finish first. I need to keep my head together. There's only half of this thing left to do now.*

She stole a glance at Tanya. This time Tanya *was* looking at her. Their eyes locked, then Tanya looked sadly away. There were tears in her eyes.

Venus tried saying something to her, but the words locked in her throat. Trembling with disgust at herself she stared at the half-completed picture puzzle. Now the tears came, and ran down her cheeks. *I hate this. Last night—barely seven hours ago—I was making love to this woman to restore her spirits so we could escape from here together, and now . . . now I'm trying to kill her? This place is utterly evil. Oh, this is Hell alright.*

She no longer harbored any doubts on that score.

She felt a moment's deep regret that she'd not simply left Tanya to have her nervous breakdown, then shrugged it off. (On that thought, her groin twinged painfully, as if in sympathy with her folly.)

She stole another glance at Tanya, and shuddered. Tanya had a cold smile of accomplishment on her lips. She took a hand off the panel and ran fingers through her brunette hair. Then, after licking her upper lip, she resumed work on the puzzle.

Venus realized she was done for. *Tanya's almost finished this!* Desperately, she looked around to see if there was any way she could save herself from falling out once the bottom of the cage opened. But no, she didn't see how she could. The metal mesh was too fine to slip her fingers through, not to mention her toes, and the cage bottom—all those stupid connecting triangles making her dizzy like she'd faint or lose her mind—was hinged at the middle of the cage and latched just outside the dome's circumference. Once Tanya pressed that switch, the cage bottom would fall and she'd have no support for her feet at all. Straight down into the gloop she'd go.

Like they sensed her fear, the gloop were swirling and swishing impatiently. And Venus now realized that there were more gloop eyes massed beneath her than there were under Tanya.

And that's not 'cos I've got better boobs, I'm sure.

She was about returning her attention to the scrambled picture again when a cockroach flitted down from the roof of the cage at her.

She swatted at the bug, knocking it off course so it fell to the cage floor.

She stole another quick glance at Tanya. Now the policewoman looked angry. Then she began furiously attacking the puzzle. *Oh, she's made a mistake*, Venus realized. *So, I've still got time. But how much longer?*

Venus had sort of gotten a hold on her terror now. She was still scared but had herself mostly under control. She forced her mind back to her own puzzle. *Okay, this piece goes in here, and this one should be here; but, first I need to move all these out of the way. Shit! This thing is worse than Rubik's cube. Damn the Schoolmaster!*

She leaned back to consider the picture. She'd now gotten the left side of the Schoolmaster's mouth done, but getting the right side in place would require her scrambling up that side of his head again.

She understood now what Tanya was so pissed off about. Apparently, she'd gotten most of the puzzle done herself, only to also discover that, in order to get the last few pieces in correctly, she had to mess the picture up and start all over again.

Mightily relieved by that thought, Venus bent back to work.

Then a flicker of motion caught her eye. It was that damned roach again! The blasted thing was inching its way across the bottom of the cage. She realized she'd hurt it when she swatted it. It couldn't fly anymore, could only drag itself along.

The roach wobbled a moment on a black steel rod, spreading its wings to stabilize itself, then it crawled off towards the edge of the cage. Venus raised a foot to stomp it; she hated bugs. Then . . .

What the . . . ? Suddenly, watching the cockroach's slow progress along the cage floor, she felt giddy again. Not with fear this time, but with excitement.

She forgot about stomping the bug. The gloop and their staring eyes also vanished for Venus, all she could see now was the cage floor. Those connected triangles. Tracing the cockroach's motion in a straight line showed Venus that the cage floor . . .

Suddenly dizzy with delight, she let out a whoop of joy, then looked at Tanya. "Hey!"

Tanya was already staring at her in confusion. "C'mon, don't tell me you're happy to die now?"

Venus shook her head. "No, no, no! We're not about dying! We're both outa here already!"

"Huh?"

"Look down at the floor of the cage! We're both standing on a black pentagram!"

CHAPTER 39

Tanya

"What . . . ?" Tanya looked down. She saw that Venus was right: viewed in a particular way, the lines of the connecting triangles did form half of a five-pointed star in her side of the cage. *Black* metal lines meant a *black* pentagram. Exactly what they needed, except for . . .

She looked quickly around the cage's circumference. *Oh, God, thank you! Now I know that you're up there for real!* The cage floor was edged with a double ring of metal—the pentagram was inside a double circle.

Venus was right: They were gone from here already!

A glance at her watch revealed that they'd been working at the picture puzzles for twenty-five minutes now. There was no time to waste. True, they had an hour, but the Schoolmaster or Peaches might come back to check on their progress, and worse still, decide to hang around and watch.

She quickly pulled the pages with the magic spell out of her bra. She began rehearsing the spell in her head.

Tanya was utterly relieved that she'd not have to kill Venus. She'd finished the puzzle twice already, but each time, just before sliding the last piece into place, she'd glanced at Venus, seen how distraught she was, and realized that she couldn't do it. She couldn't kill her. It wouldn't be any different from murder.

So the first time she'd messed up the Schoolmaster's portrait completely again and started over. The second time . . . she'd just left the last puzzle piece out of alignment. She wasn't slotting it home until she saw Venus smile with the gleeful knowledge that she was going to get Tanya first. Then Tanya would feel justified in letting her die.

But now? Now, she was glad she'd waited. Neither of them would be dying today.

(She'd spent the intervening minutes since solving the puzzle the second time trying to work out the mystery of the cellphone the ghosts had given her last night. She was still completely stumped as to its purpose. It had to be for something, but what?)

"How's it going?" Venus whispered across, her face expectant.

"Just a little longer now. I'm rehearsing the words in my head, so I don't screw the spell up, or who knows where the hell we'll wind up. Keep watch on the door. If you see or hear anything—I don't mean the servitors—"

"Yeah, sure, but hurry, please!"

Tanya went over the spell two more times. It was just four lines and should take ten seconds maximum to recite. There was a tricky bit right at the end that was quite a mouthful, but she figured if she slowed the words down on that line, or read the whole thing slowly, they'd not have any mishaps.

Her gaze dropped to the pool of gloop. Oddly, there were less of their blue eyes on her side of the pool; at least eight of the things were packed under Venus. Absurdly, her feminine vanity felt slighted: *Come on, what does she have that I don't? The little monsters aren't boob freaks too, are they? Or is it that they want her to pee on them again?*

She looked out at the servitors. There was no danger there. The black ghosts showed no sign that they knew anything was amiss.

"Okay," she told Venus, "time to get our butts out of here." Then her gaze fell on the cryptic admonition written above the spell: *And if ye witch be on her monthly curse, there be danger of ye Compress. Ye black spell abhors crimson.*

Her face creased up with worry. "You're not bleeding yet, are you?" she asked Venus.

Venus first looked confused. Then when she understood the question, she quickly pushed the crotch of her hot pants aside and stuck two fingers up herself. Tanya watched her work the fingers deep into her sex.

Venus brought the fingers out again. They were wet but clean. Both women simultaneously sighed with relief.

"That check was a moot point anyway," Venus said, drying her fingers on her top. "Do you really think I was remaining back here even if my period *had* started?"

Tanya conceded her point. Anywhere else was better than being trapped here in Detention—her gaze zipped outside to the schoolyard wall and the tentacles overhead—this realm of freakish insanity. Her one other worry concerned Venus's hair: *Is pink a shade of red or not? I don't know, but we'll shortly find out what the spell thinks. We're stuck with that one anyway; another moot point. It's not like we've a hairdresser here to un-dye it.*

"Yeah, sorry, you're right," she told Venus. "Okay, time to go. Let's do this."

She took a deep breath, then began reciting the spell. To her surprise, the strange words rolled easily off her unpracticed tongue, like the spell was helping her cast itself:

Manax feedle slaq klas'iss noom .
Noos, noos! Fiikk maya Fiikk!
Agga agga luk, maya, riss'iss' Ima,
Maya, maya, namilokusitamoi. H'niss'sutar. Noos!

What kind of a language is this? Tanya wondered as that last 'Noos!' exploded from her lips with a violence she'd not intended.

Then she gasped. The black floor of their cage was dissolving, flickering and thinning into gas like it was becoming one of the servitors. The vanishing floor still felt solid beneath her feet, but for how long?

She looked over at Venus, who looked terrified again. "Shit, we're going to drop into the gloop!"

Already, the gloop were reaching up towards them, extending transparent pseudopods in their direction, seeking to snare their bodies before they even struck the pool.

But next thing, the bottom of the cage disappeared completely along with the questing gloop, and suddenly Tanya and Venus were both falling down into a round dark hole.

They landed ten or so feet down, their fall cushioned by air.

They were at one end of a dark arched tunnel. Tanya had no idea how long the tunnel was, but right at its far end, she could make out a light; and most important, there seemed to be green flashing amidst the light. That could only be trees, right?

She helped Venus up. She was relieved that the spell hadn't taken exception to the color of Venus's hair.

They stared at each other, relief and joyful smiles on their faces.

"We made it," Venus said.

"Almost," Tanya corrected, shaking the pages of spells at her. "We've *almost* made it. There's nothing in here on how to lock the portal now that we've opened it."

"We can't lock it?"

They looked up. The circular chute they'd fallen down was comprised of smooth black stone. Silver rungs traced one side of the ascent/descent. Above the chute, the domed top of the cage hung in ominous darkness.

Tanya pointed the rungs out to Venus. "We need to be far gone from here before Peaches and her boss return."

Venus nodded, her face indicating a return of anxiety. Tanya stuffed the codex pages back in her bra again, then they set out for the faint light ahead.

✳✳✳

The tunnel walls were seamless, without even the ghost of a crack in them. Their black stone glimmered gently, somehow providing enough light to see by.

Tanya and Venus walked as fast as they could, but the black tunnel had a strange resistance: its air was thick and syrupy.

"This is hard," Venus said after a while. "I feel like I'm swimming in an upright position."

"Yes," Tanya agreed. There was a definite force impeding their motion through the tunnel. Like the gravity in here was stronger than normal. She was reminded of movies of astronauts walking on Mars. She felt the pressure coming from the sides and from above as well. It wasn't threatening to squash her, just letting her know that something about this tunnel was off.

She glanced at her watch. "I'm getting bushed too, but we need to keep moving. We've ten minutes left before the Schoolmaster's due back in class." She pointed back towards the chute they'd dropped through. In five minutes, they'd covered a mere hundred yards. Way too slow! She looked forward again; the exit seemed a mile off, at least. Not far away by any true reckoning, but with the tunnel's strange hindrance to motion it could as well have been down in Texas.

They kept walking, but it was hard going; the tunnel's resistance never slackened for a instant.

Tanya spent the time thinking. *One thing's for sure: the moment we're out of here, I'm calling Federal Agent Richards and telling him about this place. He'll never believe the real story of what happened, nor will the Chief, but once I tell them Cutter and Peaches came this way, the feds will deploy men to the mansion for sure. The building's a death trap! I won't be responsible for other innocents falling into this hell it links to. Detention? More like Massacre High! And screw taking credit for this bust anymore, my reputation can go to hell for all I care— Josh Milton's forgiven me, that's the most important thing.* She frowned. *Young Karen's gonna be mad though that I didn't off Peaches for her, but that can't be helped now . . .*

She glanced at Venus. The woman seemed to be holding up alright. *Just a bit more, girl. Slow and steady does it. Step by step by step and we'll be out of here before we know it.*

Venus began looking strained. "Let's rest a minute," Tanya said finally.

Venus sank gratefully to the floor. Tanya turned around and attempted walking back towards the opening in the tunnel's ceiling. It was just as hard. She stopped and stepped towards the tunnel walls, then back again. It was the same. The pressure was everywhere.

She looked down at Venus, who was holding her belly and grimacing. "You okay?"

"This pressure . . . it feels like . . ." Then her eyes widened in horror. "Oh, crap!"

Following her startled gaze, Tanya spun around. A small figure was just dropping from the chute leading to the Detention classroom.

"It's Peaches," Tanya remarked dully. She felt trapped. And like a trapped animal, she felt utterly desperate.

She expected to see the Schoolmaster drop down next. But no, it didn't happen, there was no Schoolmaster. No Schoolyard Bullies or servitors entered the tunnel after Peaches either.

Peaches began running towards them, a motion of limbs and evil intentions.

"This is odd," Venus said. "How come she's all alone?"

"The spell was supposed to neutralize the Schoolmaster, which would also neutralize the—"

"Hey!" Venus interrupted her. "And . . . how come she can move so fast in here when we can hardly walk?"

"We'll ask her when she arrives." Tanya pulled Venus to her feet.

"What now? We run?"

"The tunnel won't let us flee, so we fight. I'm tired of running."

"We can't kill her."

"We're definitely gonna try anyway. That little psycho isn't stopping us getting out of here."

Peaches was close now. Tanya felt in her pocket for the cellphone the ghosts had given her. She had a definite use for it now.

Peaches reached them. She had the skin whip draped about her neck. She looked pissed off. The countdown timer in her left breast read 0:04:21, meaning she'd returned to the class early.

"Hey, what did you two do to the boss?"

"Do what . . . to who? What are you talking about?"

"The Schoolmaster. He just suddenly went all stiff and froze into a statue again. And the servitors all vanished."

Again? So he was a statue once? And the servitors vanished, did they? That's utterly fantastic news.

"So what's that got to do with us?" she replied. "Maybe his batteries ran down."

While Peaches stared at her incensed, Tanya pulled the cellphone from her pocket and began entering her Boston apartment number into it.

"Stop that!" Venus warned her. "You're going to blow your head off."

"So what? I'm not going back with Peaches."

Peaches wasn't saying anything now. She was watching Tanya in confusion.

"Don't do it!" Venus shrieked. "Let's just leave her!"

"You two aren't going anywhere!" Peaches shrieked back. "You're both coming back to Detention with me this instant, and waiting for the Schoolmaster to wake up!" She unslung the whip from her neck and cracked it threateningly. "And that's five demerits each for smuggling a cellphone into class!"

Tanya laughed, then pressed the 'Call' button. She waited till the call connected, then quickly leaned forward and stuck the cellphone deep into the hole in Peaches' left breast, wedging it behind her clock.

"It's for you," she said, "from little Karen Hamilton." Then she turned and dove at Venus, knocking her to the floor.

There was a VERY loud explosion and the tunnel filled with smoke.

When they got up again, there were bits of Peaches strewn up and down the stone passageway. A plaited snake, her whip lay undamaged along one side of the tunnel. There was no blood, though, just ash and smoke. One of the teen's hands had fallen on their right. Tanya stared at it and shuddered: the pale fingers were still clenching. Still shuddering, she looked back down the stone corridor. Peaches' separated arms and legs were all moving in states of undead motion. Tanya wasn't sure what would happen if someone attempted putting her back together.

She wasn't waiting around to find out either. (At least, it appeared she'd finally worked out what the cellphone was for.) Quickly, she looked herself over to ensure she'd not sustained any cuts. Then she looked at her companion, nodding towards the exit. "Come on, Venus, let's get back to the real world."

Venus, however, was staring down at her crotch, which was now soaked red, and from where a thin line of blood dribbled down her right thigh. "Tanya, we're in trouble—my period just started. "

Tanya gaped at her in horror. The black spell had that clear warning about menstrual blood: it would trigger the 'Compress,' whatever that was. With Peaches, she'd suspected the kid had been dead so long, her blood had all either drained out or dried up by now. And she'd been proven right.

But now, here Venus was, bleeding. A second line of blood had just joined the first, streaming down Venus's left leg to below her knee, its bulblike tip the head of a red liquid snake seeking the floor.

Tanya had no words. She was confused. *But . . . but how could she have started so suddenly? She was dry when we escaped the cage. It can't have been the shock of hitting the floor, can it? I don't think that's possible . . . so . . . is it the pressure in the tunnel?*

The pressure. Already, she could feel a change in the nature of the forces at work in the tunnel: both a sharp increase in its pressure, and also something else, something horrible she had no words to describe.

Was this the dreaded Compress starting?

There was nothing else for it. She grabbed Venus and pulled her towards the light at the tunnel's far end. Paradoxically, it was easier going now, even though she knew something had just gone badly wrong, and was still going wrong around them.

Venus left bloody footprints behind her.

Running for all she was worth, Tanya just hoped they'd make it out to safety before whatever awful thing was going to happen did so.

CHAPTER 40

KY

"Hey, ain't that Chad and Venus's car?"

KY looked up from snorting a hit from her coke vial. They'd just driven through the gates of the immense old mansion at the end of the road.

She looked at the car. "Yeah, looks like. What the hell would they be doing here though?" In addition to Chad and Venus's blue Mercedes, there was another car parked in the yard, a battered brown Honda Accord with all its doors open. The Honda also had a pair of woman's shoes on its hood, which she found odd. The cocaine had begun working now; her head felt clear again. For the moment she was free of uncertainties.

Evan parked facing the mansion, then turned to look at Rafael. "Who lives here?"

Rafael raised his head from their cushion on Clara's breasts. "My boss, Ellis Drake." Then he sat up and looked out of the windows and saw the two cars. His eyes widened in surprise. "This is very strange; we *never* have visitors." KY watched as he turned to regard the extensive garage on the mansion's left side. "All the cars except mine are accounted for, so who . . . ?"

Clara laughed. "Don't sweat it, darling. Trust me, we've been looking for these two slackers since yesterday. You've done us a huge favor by helping us find them. We were just on our way to file a Missing Persons report."

Evan pushed the driver's door open. "Yeah, man, you've no idea what we've been through."

Everyone got out of the car, and waited while Evan walked over to examine the rented Mercedes. They watched him pull open the front door and peek inside it, then shrug.

KY did another hit of coke. Only now, it didn't work its magic. As the powder exploded in her brain, she had a vision of disaster. And she heard Mr. Hexwood's dream words: *Keep your eyes open . . .*

She had the sudden horrible feeling that this wasn't over yet. Not by a long shot.

Evan joined her. She frowned worriedly at him. Preoccupied with his search, Evan missed her concern. Instead, he pointed ahead, at Clara, who, still naked as sin, was ushering Rafael towards the mansion building, her body pressed against his. KY covetously regarded Clara's svelte body and huge breasts.

"I don't envy that guy," Evan whispered to her. "Concussed or not, he's got the world's hardest dick at the moment."

"Ask Clara to take care of him then," KY whispered back. "She really seems into him; I don't think she's faking her concern anymore. Maybe he reminds her of an old boyfriend. So ask her. If she balls him before we leave, we'll have a guaranteed Titaholics customer for life."

Evan laughed. "Yeah, I'm gonna do that. The guy won't believe his luck getting a porn star in the sack. And we do owe him for his bust-up ride anyway."

Then his eyes widened, and he laughed.

"What?"

"I think I got the car crash on film. Maybe we can get him to sign a release letting us use it."

Still laughing, he strode off after the pair, who were just about ascending the front porch steps. (Ahead of them, the mansion door lay open, revealing a dark, almost black interior.) "Hey, Clara, baby, wait up! I need to talk to you for a second."

"What's the matter, baby? Can't it wait? I gotta get Rafael inside, he's looking stunned again."

Evan was still laughing. "No, this is fucking serious, really fucking serious . . ."

KY didn't hurry after them. Her worries had now returned in full force. *I already know Chad's dead . . . and Venus? Keep my eyes open . . . for what?*

She felt a sudden chill in the air. Startled by it, she looked up at the mansion. As she did so, the building seemed to project disaster at her, its old stone walls and windows and its pillars throwing a cloak of darkest evil over the entire grounds. And over the people. It felt to KY like, for the briefest of instants, the fabric of reality had warped completely, and then had almost reverted back to normal. Almost, but not quite. Watching the mansion now, KY felt totally creeped out.

The dark, brooding, heavily overcast sky—the clouds masses of grey shadows like the silhouettes of demons—heightened the feeling of evil.

Rafael was meanwhile sitting in a shaded area of the wide stone porch, his back against a pillar. He looked tired, but was grinning weakly. His eyes were fixed on Clara's bare ass, whatever emergency he'd been in such a hurry to investigate temporarily vanished between those egg-like buttock cheeks.

Evan and Clara were over by the mansion's front entrance; he was whispering to her. KY watched their exchange carefully, curious as to how it would come off.

Clara at first rolled her eyes, but then she began giggling, and then she turned and winked at Rafael, who looked away in clear embarrassment.

I'll bet he's married, KY thought, unable to determine the telltale glint of gold on his left hand from where she stood. Not that she imagined any man, no matter how faithful to his wife, would turn down what Clara Cleavage was about offering him. The nipples on those immense breasts were going into Rafael's mouth the moment Clara shoved him through a bedroom door. Then her thoughts turned bothered again: *And this is so weird—why are we all waiting outside the house anyway? We're supposed to be inside it and looking for our two missing friends, aren't we? But no, we're all standing outside here, staring and chatting like we're having a picnic! Hey! —what the hell's going on here!?*

Her dead eye was itching like mad again. Again, deep in the socket where the only way to scratch it would be to take the prosthesis out. Hell no, there was no frigging way she was taking the eye out here! And now the coke had her all jumpy. Her good vibes had flipped over into bad ones. Instead of feeling clear, her mind felt murky, corrupted by the mansion.

Convinced that she needed to warn the others of looming danger, KY headed for the front porch.

CHAPTER 41

Venus

Venus and Tanya raced towards the light.

Running for all she was worth, Venus winced in pain. *The Compress? Well I feel damn well compressed alright! Ouch!*

Her vagina kept leaking blood. She looked down at herself and winced. *I look like I'm having a miscarriage.* Her legs and feet were painted red with blood, the crimson liquid ceaselessly dribbling down her thighs. Behind her lay a long line of red footprints.

Tanya looked at her. She read the utter horror in the policewoman's eyes over her condition. "Are you alright? Maybe we should stop and see if there's something we can do. You're bleeding like . . ."

"Like I'm having my entire period at once? I know; it feels that way too." She forced a wan smile. "Don't worry, I'll make it." *So long as I don't bleed to death first.* But she couldn't tell Tanya that. They had to keep going on, run for all their lives were worth.

The pressure in the tunnel was unrelenting. It hit them both from all sides, a force like giant hands trying to squash them to pulp. But they weren't squashed, all that happened was that the tunnel grew wider.

And Venus's vagina squirted out yet more blood. She felt the tunnel pressure like a hand clenching her womb. It hurt like hell, but it was a sustained hurt now, a torment her body had gotten used to. It felt like her body was liquefying to emerge from her sex.

Strangely now, even running slowly and out of breath, they moved faster by the moment, accelerating like the floor propelled them, like gale winds blew them forward.

Like, Venus thought with fear, *like the tunnel itself wants to be rid of us!*

The opening ahead was soon clearly revealed as a large arched doorway.

"That's the mansion's front entrance," Venus gasped in the pauses between wetting herself with blood. "We've made it. Those are people outside talking. I know that guy: That's Evan James, and that looks like Clara—"

"But why's it still so far off?" Tanya asked.

Venus had the same question. The door was near, but yet, as they ran towards it, it seemed to recede. And there was something else happening now; something frightening . . .

As they approached the door, it was growing bigger and bigger over them, larger and larger. And yes, they could both see people out there, but they were all giants, immense in size. Venus felt like how she imagined an ant did when faced with a mountain.

She gaped at Tanya, who was gaping back. "Are we getting smaller or . . ."

"Let's just get outside," Tanya gasped. "I can't take much more of this pressure."

At that moment, a wind from behind blew them both off their feet and out through the front door of the mansion, where they landed flat on their bellies. The merciless pressure on their bodies instantly cut out. They lay there panting, partly concealed by shadow.

Shit! Venus realized, looking around her in horror. *We've been shrunk!* "Tanya, the tunnel shrunk us!"

Tanya said, "Well now we know what the Compress is—we've been miniaturized. We're the size of roaches now. We need to alert your friends up there . . ."

Roaches? A new fear filled Venus. *Oh crap, and we're lying on our bellies! What if someone thinks . . . ?*

She made to leap up and run.

But it was too late. A woman shrieked, "Bugs, Evan, stomp 'em!!!" and next thing, a wide black thing was falling over Venus.

"NOOOOOO!!!" she screamed, throwing her hands up to ward it off, but the black thing kept coming down. And next, her whole being—her body and mind—exploded into pain, the pain of being squashed and ripped apart, of her flesh and bones being smeared left and right in a paste over the ground. And in those seemingly unending moments of excruciating agony before she died, Venus could hear

Tanya screaming in agony too as she also was viciously squashed to death by the people on the porch.

CHAPTER 42

KY

Just as she reached the porch, KY heard Clara yell, "Bugs, Evan, stomp 'em!!!"

She instinctively cringed. She hated bugs too, particularly the large creeping ones. She watched the pair stomp the two insects—like pale truncated worms they'd looked—on the porch into unrecognizable messes. Clara's chunky boot in particular made a really gory shredding of the insect she'd picked to kill: there was blood and meat smeared for half a yard. When she was finally done, Clara was sweating fiercely and breathing hard. Evan had also finished killing the other bug. He began scraping his shoe clean against the porch edge.

Clara didn't bother with cleaning her boot. She sashayed over to Rafael, who'd been watching the stomping with some distaste (*Likely 'cos he'll have to clean up the porch later,* KY thought), and pulled him delicately to his feet.

"Now, how about you and me go inside, darling? I've something physical I want to discuss with you."

Doing his best to conceal a grin (and covering his immense erection with his hands), Rafael staggered off through the mansion door after her.

That settled that then. KY saw Evan was motioning to her. "Hey, come inside, baby, what are you waiting for out here?"

And that was when the spell wore off. Or *was it* a spell? She couldn't tell. But suddenly the evil she'd sensed about the mansion seemed to switch off. Like a cancer gone into miracle recession, it vanished.

Vanished as though it had been waiting for something to happen. But waiting for what? Then her gaze fell on the two bug-smears on the porch, and she realized now that with the spell the mansion had cast over them dissolved, there was something really odd about those smears.

She climbed the stone porch steps, her eyes glued to the twin messes up there.

Evan noticed she was looking at the bug smears. "Damn," he said, "now ain't that a real strawberry mess."

She agreed. A real strawberry mess indeed. But there was something unusual about that strawberry mess.

Don't look! A voice screamed in her head.

But she felt drawn to. On her right, the mess Clara had been grinding her boot into was completely unrecognizable as anything other than red bleeding meat smeared everywhere.

Meat. That was the problem word for KY, the image that gnawed at her already frayed nerves. The dead bugs shouldn't look like *meat.* Insects, when stomped, usually splatted into gooey yellowish messes.

She bent closer to the other, less destroyed mess which lay directly in her path. Why was it bleeding—or rather, had bled—the blood squirting everywhere like someone had punctured then stomped on a plastic ketchup bottle? Had Evan accidentally stomped on a baby rat? Ugh! The image of an exploding baby rodent utterly horrified KY.

Don't look! the voice screamed again in her head. This time it sounded like Mr. Hexwood's voice.

Still, she felt impelled to see what that splash of dismantled red contained. It was dead for sure. Definitely dead: Evan had flattened the shit and life out of it.

She bent towards it, her sense of accomplished disaster increasing by the second. She knelt over the mess.

"What the hell are you doing with that?" Evan asked. "C'mon, baby—"

"Wait!" she snapped at him, her voice unintentionally sharp. "Something's wrong here."

"Kendra, babe, it's bug guts."

She prayed he was right, but knew he wasn't. Staring at the two messes—those horrible strawberry messes—a primal horror nagged at the back of her mind. The dread urged her to believe . . .

"I don't believe it. KY, you're almost sticking your nose in that pile of bug-mess!"

But she noted that he'd not stomped away into the house in disgust. So maybe Evan too sensed what she did. Or maybe he just thought she was out of her mind, paranoid from too much cocaine. *I wish I was tripping, Evan; you've no idea how much I wish I was just tripping. Chad's dead; I bet you don't even suspect that, do you? I can tell you why I'm in no hurry at all to enter the house: it's 'cos I already know there's no one in there. I know something I don't wanna know . . . but I have to know for sure.*

DON'T LOOK!!! the voice in her brain screeched a third time, loud now as an air-raid siren. But she had to know, she had to see. She had to.

A tiny piece of the nearer puddle of red mess had broken off. Was that tip-of-a-matchstick-little thing a hand and fingers? Could it be? How was that even possible? Magic or a miracle? Or a curse?

The mess. The strawberry mess. Like jam with seeds in it, only in this case the seeds were . . . it looked like there were bones in it . . . tiny little bones . . . and were those clothes? Could that be a microscopic set of pants?

And that other thing that's detached, that looks like it's got pink fur on it? God, please let it be a baby rodent's head, or even some doll's hair or thread the bug got tangled up in! Oh, God Almighty, please let it be that!

Vaguely aware of Evan's bemused gaze on her, she picked up the little bloody object.

It was about the size of a pea and all white on one side, the other being covered with that odd pink fur that had caught her attention, though the fur was all bloody now.

The porch there was in shadow, so KY stood up and held the pea-sized thing up to the sun to make it out better. Cursing her half-blindness, she squinted hard to see it clearly, to be absolutely sure her mind wasn't tricking her.

Until there was no doubt.

Oh, no! This shit wasn't real. It couldn't be . . . this couldn't be happening!

Once KY realized that the tiny furry oval she was holding was actually Venus's severed head, reality prolapsed around her. With a loud scream of horror, she fainted.

CHAPTER 43

Rafael

Clara was fellating Rafael in the mansion library, her lips bobbing up and down over his erection. He sat in a chair with his pants down about his ankles and was moaning loudly. His eyes were fixed below her head on her breasts. *Oh, my God, how can anyone have breasts this glorious? Oh, we should have gone upstairs to a bedroom!*

Clara lifted her mouth off his penis. "Oh yeah, come for me, baby."

She dipped her head back down. Rafael moaned some more. He *was* about coming. A few more slurps of her tongue would finish him off.

The library was the first room off the dim hall, on the right as one entered the mansion. Once inside the building, Rafael had instinctively steered Clara into it without bothering to turn on the hall lights. Now, hidden amidst Ellis Drake's endless stacks and shelves of musty occult literature, and with the smell of arcane learning tickling his nostrils, he felt like he was dreaming, like he'd fallen into the middle of an erotic fantasy, one conjured up by the spells in these ancient tomes surrounding him: First the two nude women atop the car, then his accident, then Clara—this paragon of tits—squeezing herself against him. And now here he was, with this ultimate woman of women— beautiful beyond belief, willowy but with breasts like balloons buoying her up—sucking him off with delicate expertise.

Oh, I never want to wake up from this dream. He was amazed that he'd held off his orgasm so long. It seemed an impossible feat. All through the ride here, with his head pillowed on her breasts, his penis had been so stiff it had hurt. He'd been scared he'd ejaculate in his pants. Her breasts were simply sumptuous, large and pneumatic enough to have prevented the Titanic from sinking.

A scream sounded outside, then there was silence. He looked down worriedly at Clara, hoping she'd not stop. She slipped her mouth off his erection, and while masturbating him expertly, winked. "Don't you worry, darling, we're finishing this. KY's a frigging drama queen anyway. She likely just saw another one of those horrid bugs."

She dipped her mouth back over his penis. He sighed as she slid her tongue up and down his rigid organ. She flicked her tongue over the crown; his thighs trembled uncontrollably. She ran her tongue through the slit in the crown. Unable to control himself, Rafael thrust up, ramming himself against her pearl-white teeth.

She laughed, then locked her lips tightly around the head of his penis and sucked hard on it. He got the clear impression that she liked him for some reason, and actually *wanted* to pleasure him; that she wasn't just doing this because Evan had asked her to put him in a good mood. (He knew their names now: Evan had introduced everyone properly on the drive over.)

Clara deep-throated him. Stars exploded in Rafael's mind. His testicles sucked up like they were about vanishing into his belly and his anus contracted like before a hard shit. Then he gasped as tingles of electricity sped down his legs and his penis felt like it was being electrocuted.

He sat staring at her bobbing head. "Oh my God! Oh, holy fuck!!!"

Immediately the first spurts of his come struck her tongue, Clara slipped her mouth off his turgid organ and finished him off with her hand, caressing his slick shaft so he spurted all over her breasts. Her other hand gently squeezed his testicles, ordering them to empty themselves completely.

It was everything Rafael had ever dreamed off. Dazed, he watched her rub his semen into the creamy white skin of her massive mammary glands. He felt like he could die in peace now, having accomplished everything a man needed to in life.

Clara sat back on her heels, grinning and licking her lips. "Okay, that's taken care of you for the moment. By the time we've found the others, you should have recovered enough to give me a good hard ride in a bed."

Rafael bent forward and kissed her. "Oh yeah. Oh yeah, baby!"

The library door opened and Evan peeked in, obscured from view by a stack of literature about the Antichrist. "Hey, are you guys in here? KY's fainted and I need somewhere to lay her down."

Rafael quickly pulled his pants up. Then he and Clara left the library. Evan stood by the door, cradling the unconscious KY in his arms. He had a pained look on his face.

"What happened?" Clara asked while Rafael went over to turn on the hall lights.

"I think too much blow. She started examining that bug-mess on the porch and freaked out."

Rafael flicked the light switch. The hall burst into brilliance.

"Wow!" Clara exclaimed. "This is some really freaky place you've got here. What the . . . ? That werewolf looks so frigging real, and those vampires . . . Damn, I've never seen such a large collection of horror stuff in my life."

"Me neither," Evan agreed. Then he grunted. "Hey, man, she's really heavy. Where's the nearest bed?"

Rafael gestured to a door. "You can put her in the—" His voice froze in his throat. *Oh my God!*

"What's the matter, baby?" Clara asked on seeing his suddenly startled expression.

Rafael couldn't reply. Eyes bugging out of his face, he pointed to Clara's left, where part of a black girl's head—her left cheek and eye, an ear with a gold earring, and a clump of hair—sat on top of a large carton.

"Don't tell me," Clara said in horror. "It's not some Halloween mask?"

"It's real," Rafael said slowly. "There's blood everywhere." He pointed the red stains out to her. In addition to the blood, all of which seemed to come from the head (there was no body in sight), there were chunks of face and brain strewn about.

On seeing the mess of gore, Clara began shivering. When she spoke, her voice was tremulous: "Rafael, is *this* the emergency you were rushing home to deal with?"

He felt as confused as she looked. And as horrified. He shook his head. "I really hope not."

He ran to the foot of the stairs. "Miranda! Miranda! Sandy! Are you women okay!?"

Then he remembered Evan and turned back to face him. "You'll have to lay KY down here on the rug, man. Somewhere away from all the blood. Clara can stay with her while we search the house.

Something's terribly wrong. We need to get upstairs and see if Miranda—the housekeeper—is alright."

"And our friends too," Clara added.

"Yes, them too."

Evan found a clear spot in the middle of the hall and carefully set KY down.

Rafael waded through the hall's array of paraphernalia looking for a weapon. "Unfortunately all of Mr. Drake's guns are upstairs."

"This'll have to do then," Clara said, handing him a short African spear. Then her gaze fell on a chunk of reddened jawbone with some teeth in it and she gasped and looked away.

Rafael hoped she wouldn't faint. Or maybe it would be better if she did?

"We should call the police," Evan said, picking out a hatchet from a rack of them. "This dead girl was clearly murdered."

Rafael nodded. "But the blood's long dry, so she wasn't killed today. Let's check through the house first. Hopefully, no one else is dead."

He looked up the stairs. "Hey, Miranda! Sandy!!"

No reply again. This wasn't looking good at all.

With Clara watching them with her hands over her mouth, they ascended the stairs.

At the second floor landing, Rafael just froze and stared. Behind him, Evan drew in breath sharply.

What faced them both was a scene from a nightmare. Miranda's girlfriend Sandy Baker lay naked and belly down on the hall carpet with two knitting needles stuck through her head. Both needles were so firmly fixed in her skull that their tips (one of which skewered her right eye) had Sandy's face raised three inches off the floor.

Rafael could see that much from the stairs. When he got over his shock and walked closer, he saw that Sandy's lifeless body had also been mutilated—stabbed and slashed what seemed to him almost a hundred times—till her flesh now hung in shreds off her torso, off her buttocks, and off her thighs.

But there was an oddity here . . .

"Man, why isn't there any blood anywhere?" Evan asked. "I mean, with this much stabbing?"

Rafael didn't . . . couldn't reply. He'd just looked left into Miranda Salcedo's bedroom. *Oh, shit, no!*

Horrified, he dashed into the bedroom and knelt beside her body.

Miranda lay on her side on the floor, with her hair over her face and a deep, yawning gash across her neck. He touched her. She was stiff with rigor mortis, and like Sandy, stank slightly.

She'd clearly bled to death, but where was all the blood? There was none in the room. Not a single drop.

That fact scared Rafael even more than the fact of Miranda's death. It meant supernatural forces were at work here. Rafael wasn't really superstitious, but when one lived in a house full of occult relics, after a while a respectful fear of the unknown seeped into one. And what had Miranda been up to with that manikin out there? (Rafael *had* noticed it.) The manikin had the boss's fiancée's face stuck on it. He knew Miranda fiddled about with magic, but . . . *Was she trying hex Louise Chung?*

But those were questions for later. He got up and turned to face Evan, who stood framed in the bedroom doorway, his face lily-white with horror.

"Let's look for your friends," Rafael said. "I pray they survived this massacre. Then we call 911."

Evan nodded and left the doorway. They walked back to the stairs.

Then at the landing, Rafael turned again. He'd just noticed something else: one of the statues in the hall was missing.

It was that odd one, the creepy one. The *Demon Schoolmaster* it was called. Rafael had never liked the damn thing. It had been shipped to the house from Alaska a year ago, and Rafael had hated it right off the bat, with its sunken black eyes that somehow seemed to be judging him for offences he'd not yet committed.

Rafael had additional reason to detest (and fear) the sculpture. Several times since the Schoolmaster statue had been in the house, he'd had nightmares of a hellish realm—a high school—where, assisted by monsters, the Schoolmaster reigned supreme, tormenting captured people in classrooms and murdering them afterwards.

Detention, the realm was called.

The killers must have taken the statue, he finally decided. *Thank heavens the damn thing is gone. But why kill Miranda and Sandy and that girl downstairs over something so worthless? If they'd met me at home, I'd have gladly handed it to them. Along with half the crap in this house.*

"Good riddance to bad rubbish," he said aloud.

"What was that?" Evan asked nervously. "Good riddance to what?"

"Just a piece of crap that's been stolen, man. Just a piece of useless junk." He frowned. "C'mon, let's hurry up with searching the house. Clara must be getting really scared downstairs."

Scared and horrified themselves, they hurried off.

EPILOGUE

The Massachusetts police never solved the mystery of why there was no blood around either Miranda Salcedo's or Sandra Baker's corpses. That aspect of the case still remains open to conjecture.

The cops were more successful, however, in determining who had killed the pair. Wanted sociopath Joel 'Cutter' Miller's fingerprints were found on a knife found on the floor of the second floor hall, and which was determined to be the one used to kill Miranda. Similarly, his girlfriend Pamela 'Peaches' Principal's fingerprints were also found on a hammer up there. The hammer had clearly been used to bash two steel needles through Sandra Baker's head. A further recovered knife (determined as being responsible for Sandra's multiple stab wounds) also had Peaches' fingerprints on it. The black Mazda reported as stolen by the couple in Marlborough was also found out in the woods bordering the Drake Mansion.

Case closed.

But that was the easy-to-resolve part of the mystery. Where were the two serial killers, Cutter and Peaches? No one ever saw them again. Nor did anyone ever find Detective Tanya Rockford, who'd been pursuing them, and who'd clearly tracked them down to the Drake Mansion.

The police to date have no idea either of the fates of porno actors Chad Cannon and Venus Deluxe.

The one person who had any kind of testimony about what had happened to Venus, was KY, who, once she revived from her faint, had a nervous breakdown and had to be locked up in the Rockland Psychiatric Center for eight months. No one believed KY's tale of Venus having been shrunken in another realm and then stomped to bits by her boyfriend, Titaholics Anonymous owner Evan James. (Porno actress Clara Cleavage refuted this version of events anyway, calmly explaining that, on the contrary, she and Evan had actually stomped on two crawling insects.) The fact that KY also claimed a mysterious dead New York negro, Mr. Marlon Hexwood, had told her in a dream that Chad had also died in that same out-of-this-world place where Venus had been shrunk only sped up the psychiatrists' decision to have her committed. And anyway, by the time KY was in any fit state to talk, Mr. Drake's butler Rafael had cleaned up the mess, and the constant coming and going of the police—ambulance men, detectives, forensics—in and out of Drake Mansion had obliterated any remaining evidence, mingling it with the sand from their endless stream of feet.

And Venus's miniaturized head? Discarded in the gravel by the porch edge when KY fainted, it was eaten by a hognose snake that night.

So what do the Massachusetts State Police know for sure?

They know that Sherrelle Jackson, aged 20, of Chelsea, MA died in the house, apparently when her cellphone exploded. Her head was in there. Her parents collected the fragments of her head and buried them.

But what became of Sherrelle's body, and of her two hitchhiking companions—her boyfriend Jordan Levine, 22, and Michael Myers, 21—no one has the slightest idea.

Ellis Drake's butler, Rafael Marquez, has his suspicions as to where all the missing people vanished to, but he's never shared them with anyone.

He doesn't want to wind up in the padded cell next to KY's.

***

Rafael Marquez had intended resigning from his employment at the Drake Mansion after witnessing the massacre there, but his phone conversation with Ellis Drake (who hadn't returned from Hong Kong for the investigation), put an end to his plans. After expressing his sincerest sympathies over the carnage at the house (and his outrage over Miranda Salcedo's performing voodoo on his fiancée), Ellis offered Rafael a quadruple raise in salary and a special bonus of any brand-new sports car of his choice to stay on at the mansion.

Even in cases where one knows better than to ask, money always talks. And money is loquacious, always has a lot to say. In Rafael's case, it was yelling loudly.

Rafael gratefully accepted the raise. And regretted it almost instantly he'd hung up the phone.

I really should have left this evil place, he thought.

***

Up till now, even with the Schoolmaster statue long gone from Drake Mansion, Rafael still has nightmares about the evil realm called Detention. And now, in Rafael's nightmares, the evil madman has an assistant, a teen named Ms. Principal. Pretty, yes, but with wild and crazy eyes, and a digital clock embedded in her left breast. Ms. Principal always carries a whip plaited from human skin and studded with sharp shards of wet bone.

Rafael's worst nightmares are the ones in which he hears the Schoolmaster and Ms. Principal discussing their 'school.'

"Well, Ms. Principal, I do say it's been ages since we had any new intake here."

"Yes, sir. It's a drag having to wait for *them* to unlock the school doors."

"Patience, Ms. Principal. Patience is a virtue."

"But it's *so* boring, sir. Can't you speed up the rate of admissions to Detention?"

"I wish I could, but the Powers That Be don't allow it."

"How about if we do it on the sly, sir? We don't tell them. We can catch people like Rafael here—who live in the mansion—and transport them over to our side."

"Hmmm. But if it's found out, there'll be repercussions."

"Sir, how the hell will anyone know we abducted anyone? You and I aren't going to tell them. And the students sure as hell won't. The dead tell no tales, right? We could start with the butler, you know. He's certain to be guilty of a lot of stuff . . ."

"We just have to determine what it is," the Schoolmaster finishes for her.

The demonic pair always laugh loudly at that, then Ms. Principal asks: "So what do you think, sir? Should we start enrolling students in Detention on our own recommendation or not?"

Rafael Marquez, butler of Drake Mansion, never hears the Schoolmaster's reply to this. It is at this point that he always wakes up . . . wakes up covered all over in sweat and doing his utmost best not to scream.

Sometimes he succeeds.

The End.

ABOUT THE AUTHOR

Wol-vriey is Nigerian, and quite tall.

He currently resides in a state of uneasy stalemate with his threatening-to-thin-beyond-redemption hair, and believes there actually are things that go bump in the night.

Wol-vriey recycles the ridiculous into reasonable reality for the reader.

His WEIRRRD philosophy?

WEIRRRD = Warp/Write Everything into Realistic Ridiculous Readable Distorted Dream Dimension Descriptions.

Wol-vriey blogs at:

http://odditfarm.wordpress.com

WOL-VRIEY
BIZARRO AND TRANSGRESSIVE FICTION

BOSTON POSH (BUD MALONE #1)

In 2028 AD, the USA is a nation ravaged by hungry dragons and dinosaurs. In Boston, Massachusetts, private eye Bud Malone is hired to rescue a kidnapped heiress. But nothing is as it seems.

Malone works to unravel a tangled web involving Boston Chinatown, a 200-year-old woman with a 9-year-old body, white robots, a human-liver-eating psychopath, a golem, a porcelain dragon, and a snake goddess with a crush on him. There's also a woman obsessed with chicken sex. Then Malone meets Posh Lane, a gorgeous call girl who's desperate to quit her pimp.

Romantic sparks ignite between Posh and Malone, but Posh's past suddenly catches up with her in a BIG way. To save Posh, Malone agrees to run a quest for Earth's new rulers, the Forks. But, Malone has no idea that agreeing to the Fork's odd request will send him on the weirdest trip he's ever been on in his life.

BOSTON CORPSE (BUD MALONE #2)

MAGIC CAN BE MURDER! - Drag queen Lucy Tang is back in Boston, and is hell-bent on settling her vindetta against casino owner Sookie Ling. And suddenly, Bud Malone, PI, has the case of his life to resolve.

When Boston's robot police force are baffled by a mind transfer case, they come to Malone for help. The one person who can likely help Malone out here is the witch Soledad Bathory. But Soledad seems to know a lot more than she's telling him. It's a case not made easier when Malone meets Soledad's beautiful cousin, Josephine 'Slave' Bailey. Slave has her own plans for Malone, most of which involve teaching him BDSM and making him her new Master.

Oh, and Rick Rogers owes Sookie Ling a whole lot of money, a gambling debt that's going to be literally Hell to pay!

BOSTON CORPSE - Not your average detective novel!

Burning Bulb
PUBLISHING

WOL-VRIEY
BIZARRO AND TRANSGRESSIVE FICTION

BOSTON LUST (BUD MALONE #3)

"Bless it, Father, for she has sinned."

Seven murdered gay women, all their bodies completely drained of blood. All also with large parts of their bodies dissolved away like acid has been pumped into their veins.

Bud Malone has to find the female vampire preying on Boston's lesbian population.

Then Malone meets the beautiful Trudi Carmen and the case gets even more tangled. Trudi needs Malone's help in recovering a ring that's gone missing. But how in the world is one little black ring related to either the dead women or their killer?

Resolving this case will lead Malone deep into Lucy Tang's legacy—The Abstracta. And then to the city of Genesis.

Boston Lust—Just when you thought Bean Town was safe to visit again.

HELL DANCER

Six people find themselves trapped in Detention, a nightmare realm where the demonic Schoolmaster is hell-bent on reforming them . . . until they die.

Porn superstar Venus Deluxe came to Springfield, MA to party, and next found her life hanging by a thread. One wrong answer will mean her death.

Suspended BPD detective Tanya Rockford was trying to stop one kind of violence, but found a terrifying another. With her and her companion's lives hanging in the balance, it's going to take all of her courage and resourcefulness to escape this hell she's stumbled into.

Porn stud Chad Cannon has made a career from his ten-inch penis. Here in Detention, however, it's his brains that matter. He'll soon be hoping all the pot he's smoked over the years hasn't completely messed up his memory.

The three students, Sherri, Jordan, and Mike? They were all just in the wrong place at the right time. Will anyone survive Detention? The evil Schoolmaster doesn't plan on letting that happen . . .

Burning Bulb
PUBLISHING

WOL-VRIEY
BIZARRO AND TRANSGRESSIVE FICTION

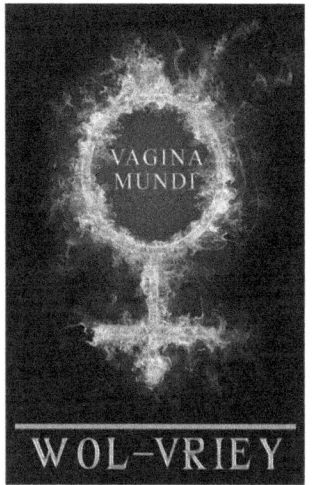

VAGINA MUNDI

Rachel Risk is a professional thief with super-strong hair that can stretch like tentacles to manipulate objects. Ashley Status has both a digitally augmented brain, and 'muscle-purses' in her arms and legs in which she stores inflatable objects—cars, guns, rocket launchers, etc.

When Raye is framed as the fall girl in a jewel robbery, the pair flee Chicago's vengeful robot gangsters and take refuge in the Hotel Bizarre, where the gorgeous 'vagina singer,' Femina, is performing for a week.

But the Hotel Bizarre is even stranger than its name suggests, and very soon Raye and Ash are involved in an deadly adventure, a struggle for survival the likes of which they'd never imagined possible—with loads of deviant sex, drugs, music, and violence at every turn. And just what is the old woman in the skin desert really doing with all those cats glued to her walls?

VAGINA MUNDI—a Bizarro Hymn in praise of WOMAN!

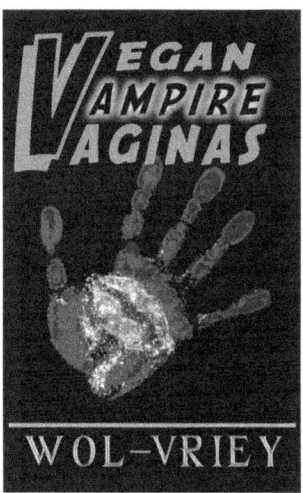

VEGAN VAMPIRE VAGINAS

The biggest bank heist in US history. And Tom Palmer can't remember pulling it off. And no, this isn't your standard case of amnesia. After a one-night-stand gone horribly wrong, Boston salesman Tom Palmer wakes up with a vagina implanted in his left hand. Then his day gets worse.

Tom is transported across space-time to a nightmare version of Boston, one where the Bizarro virus has transformed half the population into cannibals. Worst of all, Tom discovers that in this new Boston, he's the infamous gangster Pussypalm, wanted for robbing the Federal Reserve Bank of Boston a year ago. He also learns that the vagina in his hand is prophetic, i.e. it talks . . . after sex.

With 130 people left dead during his bank heist and six billion dollars missing, Tom knows he's living on borrowed time. It is in his best interests not to remember anything. Because once he does . . .

Burning Bulb
PUBLISHING

WOL-VRIEY
BIZARRO AND TRANSGRESSIVE FICTION

Dr. Orgasm

Courtney Taylor is young, intelligent, beautiful, and successful. She also has a boyfriend who loves her deeply. The problem is, no matter what Courtney does, she can't climax during sex.

When Florence Rigid's communist forces destroy the city of Metaphor, Courtney and her friends Teresa, Highball, Miki, and Heather are cast into the midst of a quest to find the only person able to save the land of Innuendo—Dr. Carol Orgasm, wanted by the communists for developing the O-Pill, a wonder drug that grants women sexual ecstasy on demand.

The communists will do anything to get their hands on the O-Pill and prevent its reaching the millions of Innuendo's women. But Courtney desperately wants that pill too. And so it's now a race between Courtney and the communists to find Dr. Orgasm first.

And Courtney has no choice but to win this race. She must win it: For her own orgasm . . . and for the freedom of female sexuality everywhere.

PUSSY TRANSMISSION

Pussy Transmission were the most decadent Pop Art ensemble of the 90's. Led by the beautiful painter Isis Lynch, the trio revolutionized the art world. Then suddenly, without explanation, Pussy Transmission vanished into historical obscurity. Now, twenty years later, three women come to Lynch Place. Lily and Nina are journalists desperate to interview Isis Lynch. Raven, on the other hand, wants to find her boyfriend, who's gone missing inside Isis's house. Raven's worried—she's heard that Pussy Transmission broke up because Isis began dabbling in black magic . . . with devastating results. All three women will shortly wish they'd never left home. Particularly once the rats in Lynch Place start warning them that they're going to die . . . and Raven meets Betty Butcher, the bouncy supernatural psycho who's intent on chopping her into bits. Pussy Transmission, Baby! Just because . . .

Burning Bulb
PUBLISHING

WOL-VRIEY
BIZARRO AND TRANSGRESSIVE FICTION

VEGAN ZOMBIE APOCALYPSE

In the post-apocalypse worlderness, zombies rule the earth. They're allergic to meat, and brains literally make them explode. Zombies now eat blood potatoes, parasitic tubers grown in the flesh of humancows corralled in maximum security farms. Two fugitives meet in the ancient ruins of Texas. The first is Soil 15-f, a womancow who's escaped her farm a week before she's due to be killed and her blood potato crop harvested. The second fugitive is Able Kane, former head necros food technician, now sentenced to death for heresy. But Soil is no ordinary humancow.

Unknown to herself, she's the vegan zombie agricultural revolution, and the zombies desperately want her back. And the necros equally desperately want Able Kane dead. He's fled with a forbidden discovery which will reshape the world for the worse if used. And Able is just hardheaded/misguided enough to use it.

MELANIE NEMESIS CATCHPOLE

In Springfield, Massachusetts, Melanie Catchpole is hired to fetch back a magic teddy bear worth millions of dollars from a warehouse across town. Problem is, the warehouse is down in Springfield's O-Zone-that totally weird sector of the city where Bizarro fell to Earth. The 'O' is a fairytale land, a place where dreams and nightmares literally live and breathe.

Worse still, the gingers—mutant cannibals—prowl the O. The gingers have already eaten everyone else Melanie's employers sent to get back the magic teddy bear.

Accompanied by the handsome but ruthless Doug Fisher (who she finds sexy but doesn't dare entrust her heart to), Melanie enters the O-Zone. Melanie and Doug are instantly caught up in an adventure they'd never have believed credible even if written as fiction . . . and Melanie's used to experiencing the very weird as the norm.

And now, additionally, there's a mystery to unravel: What does the dark, freezing-cold being called The Fixer want with Mary, the barkeep's daughter?

Burning Bulb
PUBLISHING

WOL-VRIEY
BIZARRO AND TRANSGRESSIVE FICTION

BIG TROUBLE IN LITTLE ASS

From Bizarro master storyteller Wol-vriey comes a truly weird western tale that will leave you awe-struck and on the edge of your seat...

In the town named Little Ass, tight-assed prostitute Rosa overhears a gunslinger's plans to assassinate rancher Edison Bennett. Once the badass Bennett learns of the plot, he ensures there'll be hell to pay for any attempt on his life!

Yes, it's going to take all of gunslinger Jude's shooting prowess, his eclectic collection of strange firearms, a trusty horse that requires an owners' manual, and the help of the lovely and invigorating Nell (who's EXTREMELY odd when the going gets weird), to survive the Bizarro hell that Edison Bennett unleashes in order to hold onto the land that he'd stolen from Madam Zizi.

BIZARRO 101 (A BASIC PRIMER)

Welcome to the strange place:

A collection of 37 flash fiction stories designed to introduce one to the Bizarro/New Weird Genre.

Weird, dreamy, nightmarish, absurd, sad, surreal, humorous . . . this collection of tales is all this and more.

***

"This primer is the very essence of any and all styles and types of Bizarro writing. Wol-vriey collects, distills, and bottles up these 37 tiny stories for your sensory enjoyment. This is an absolute must-read for anyone new to the genre, because it demonstrates the scope of what Bizarro is, and what it can be."
—Teresa Pollack, Bizarro commentator and blogger

Burning Bulb
PUBLISHING

WOL-VRIEY
BIZARRO AND TRANSGRESSIVE FICTION

GIRLS ARE NOT SMILING

Welcome To The Road Trip From Hell

Pagan is demon-possessed.

Lori is suicidal.

Britt is just terminally pissed off.

Meet three young Boston women on the run from the law, each with problems that will fuse into more than the sum of their individual parts, becoming a holocaust of sex and violence and terror, a literal rain of blood and horror and gore and evil.

And if that wasn't already bad enough, Pagan's pet demon is slowly transforming her into something both unspeakable and unholy. Truly, these girls aren't smiling.

BRAINCHEW

It was supposed to be a simple jewel heist, but it went badly wrong. Chuck got shot and died.

Lance hid his friend's corpse in the Pleasant Street Cemetery. But that was a big mistake—there was something undead, something extremely hungry . . . something eXXXtremely horrible, buried in the Pleasant Street Cemetery.

And Lance had just woken it up.

They called the monster Brainchew because it ate brains. Human brains. And it preferred those brains fresh from the heads . . . of the living.

And now it was awake again, Brainchew planned on feeding big-time tonight. Oh hell yes, it did.

Burning Bulb
PUBLISHING

OTHER GREAT TITLES FROM

Burning Bulb
PUBLISHING

WWW.BURNINGBULBPUBLISHING.COM

BELLY TIMBER

From the writers of Darkened Hills, Detour to Armageddon and Night of the Living Dead comes a novel unlike any other...

In the 1800's, ordinary people learned the secret of the Kala and undertook extraordinary measures to rid the earth of this evil. This is their story.

For John McCormick, life on the Indiana frontier held nothing but promise. His settlement along the White River would soon become the crossroads of America. Friends and family from back in Ohio and other points east were all making plans to see what all the fuss was about in the newly-formed city of Indianapolis. Yes, things were good. John had his general store and his friend George Pogue had his blacksmith business. Claims were being staked and relations with the native Indians were amicable. The town was growing and nothing could be better... or so he thought.

In Ohio, an evil was brewing. The Lecky Family, a group of ruthless Mongolian nomads, had made their way to America and were practicing their cannibalistic religion of Kala with reckless abandon. No one was safe, not even John McCormick's family.

Burning Bulb
PUBLISHING

BOB GRAY'S ATTACK OF THE MELONHEADS

"Melonheads is what I love. Give me a body count and gore, but don't forget the laughs. Anytime that I can be reminded of what makes Horror great it is a good thing. Melonheads does that and is something we should all support. Consider it highly recommended."
—*Screamsine.us*

Fifty years ago, a doctor sought to cure a terrible disease. Hidden from the world, Doctor Malcolm Crowe toiled in the dead of night while the world was sleeping, creating a new breed of mutant—all in the name of science.

Yes, he thought he could cure the sick children. But he was wrong.

Today, the results of his cruel and unconventional experiments have manifested into an evil never before seen.

Now, in Kirtland, Ohio, the town's unsuspecting residents are about to encounter the full onslaught of this unimaginable terror.

Can something be done before it's too late?

Burning Bulb
PUBLISHING

EVERYTHING HERE IS A NIGHTMARE
Collected Works Vol 1.

"Pyles makes it look easy. His characters come instantly alive with the cocksure verve and swagger of rock stars."
- Daniel Knauf, creator of HBO's "Carnivale,"
Executive Producer/Writer, ABC's "The Blacklist."

The critically acclaimed author of Demons, Dolls and Milkshakes returns with fifteen tales of horror and suspense with Everything Here is a Nightmare.

From zombies in the old west, to a young boy tempted by the Devil. From vampires with romantic longing, to an abandoned lighthouse haunted by vengeful spirits. From a serial killer getting unholy justice, to a haunted English race car, Nelson W Pyles invites you to explore a landscape of fear, suspense and horror.

Take his hand and hold on tight. Remember that whatever you find here, whatever you see, no matter what you might think it could be... know this: Everything Here is a Nightmare.

Burning Bulb
PUBLISHING

ANTHOLOGIES
BIZARRO AND TRANSGRESSIVE FICTION

THE BIG BOOK OF BIZARRO

The Big Book of Bizarro brings together the peculiar prose of an international cast of the most grotesquely-gonzo, genre-grinding modern writers who ever put pen to paper (or mouse to pad), including:

NIGHT OF THE LIVING DEAD horror writers John Russo & George Kosana; HUSTLER MAGAZINE erotica contributors Eva Hore, Andrée Lachapelle, & J. Troy Seate and established Bizarro genre authors D. Harlan Wilson, William Pauley III, Wol-vriey, Laird Long, Richard Godwin and so many more!

From Alien abductions to Zombie sex, The Big Book of Bizarro contains OVER FIFTY STORIES of the most outrélandish transgressive fiction that you'll ever lay your capricious and curious hands upon!

WESTWARD HOES

Nine outlaw writers rode into town from obscurity to pen nine tantalizing tales of horror and fantasy, and leaving once they branded their own personal marks on the weird western genre and became living legends of the American Frontier experience.

Like drunken Indian scouts, the writers fervidly tracked down and captured the Western genre, tore off its fashionable veneer and ravished its exposed essence.

So belly up to the bar with your favorite soiled dove and enjoy perusing these thrilling tales of Old West debauchery, danger and desire; compiled by the publisher of The Big Book of Bizarro and featuring the bizarro novella *Big Trouble in Little Ass* by Wol-vriey.

Burning Bulb
PUBLISHING

ANTHOLOGIES
BIZARRO AND TRANSGRESSIVE FICTION

THE BIG BOOK OF BIZARRO SPECIAL KINDLE EDITIONS

OTHER AWESOME COLLECTIONS

GARY LEE VINCENT'S
DARKENED
THE WEST VIRGINIA VAMPIRE SERIES

DARKENED HILLS

When evil descends on a small West Virginia town, who will survive?

Jonathan did not start out his life to become a rambler, it justworked out that way. William was a troubled youth with something to hide. Both were from Melas, a small town tucked away in the West Virginia hills... a town where disappearances are happening more and more frequently.

After the suicide of a wanted serial killer, the townsfolk thought the nightmare was over. But when a centuries-old vampire is discovered they find out the hard way it's just getting started. Dark secrets can only stay hidden for so long and when the devil comes to collect, there will be hell to pay. Can Jonathan and William find a way to stop the vampire before it's too late? Find out in *Darkened Hills!*

DARKENED HOLLOWS

In the heart-stopping sequel to the award-winning *Darkened Hills*, Jonathan and William must return to West Virginia to face possible criminal charges stemming from their last visit to the damned town of Melas, where both had narrowly escaped the clutches of a vampire seethe.

And as livestock start mysteriously getting murdered with all of their blood drained, worried farmers are searching for answers - leaving the local Sheriff and his deputy racing against time to learn the cause before a more violent crime is committed.

Burning Bulb
PUBLISHING

WWW. DARKENEDHILLS.COM

GARY LEE VINCENT'S
DARKENED
THE WEST VIRGINIA VAMPIRE SERIES

DARKENED WATERS

When the world goes to hell, the chosen must arise!

As Talman Cane orchestrates a flood of epic proportions in this third installment of the *Darkened* series the towns of Melas and Tarklin are caught completely off guard by the deluge. Hell-bent on finishing what they started, the evil brothers return to the lunatic asylum to take care of the witnesses and add to the ever-growing army of the undead.

Aided by Lucifer himself and the insane vampire demon Legion, the stage is set to channel all of the forces of hell to come forth. In an all-out race to survive, Jonathan, William, and Amanda soon discover they are up against impossible odds as Lucifer opens the Gateway to Hell, ushering in the zombie apocalypse and the End Times.

Find out who will survive this cosmic battle of the ages in *Darkened Waters*!

DARKENED SOULS

Melas and the Madison House are about to be rebuilt.
True evil is about to be reborne!

Young ex-priest and vampire-killer William is drawn back to the West Virginian town that almost killed him, where his vampire arch-enemy Victor Rothenstein still stalks the earth.

The town of Melas lies destroyed after the battle of the End of Days. But why is wealthy Jackie Nixon so eager to rebuild it using the bone dust of murdered souls?

Terrible evil has visited before, but the Gateway to Hell is about to be reopened in a horrific climax. And this time – it's personal.

WWW.*DARKENEDHILLS*.COM

Burning Bulb
PUBLISHING

DAVID J. FAIRHEAD

THE FALL

Hopelessness... How do you protect your loved ones when Hell itself opens its insidious mouth?
Horror... Nightmarish Creatures invade your world and there is nowhere to hide.
Blood... How long can you hold out before they come for you?
Pain... Where do you run to avoid being eaten alive by monsters with a voracious appetite for your flesh?
Screams... While you selfishly run for your own life.
Questions... Who is to blame? Where did they come from? How many people survived...and how does the human race find the means to fight back?

THE FALL OF TOMORROW is man's last tale of desperation told by those that are striving to salvage some hope against a ravenous bastion of evil beasts bent on ruling our world.

DWELLING IN THE DARK

From David J. Fairhead, author of the FALL OF TOMORROW, comes DWELLING IN THE DARK- A soulful anthology of creeping terror to keep you up in the small hours with horror set in the past, present and future. Overlapping bits of puzzle fitting each other, before and after The Fall of Tomorrow.

A place where three children facing a monstrous foe can only pray that their bloody summer would just come to an end. Go back to the 1960's- THE COMMUNE where overindulging hippies use a mage's diary to control the end of the world, only to see first-hand that their drug induced visions have horrific ramifications. Where a young boy's visit to a haunted house becomes a lesson in RESIDUAL morality. The story, DEEPER- plunges two brothers into a sinkhole only to find they were being hunted by an insidious creature from its depths. Visit the old west as hero Dekker Collins battles evil gunslingers in DEMONEYE.

And so much more...!

Burning Bulb
PUBLISHING

WWW.FAIRLYDARKPRODUCTIONS.COM

THE BOOBY HATCH

With NIGHT OF THE LIVING DEAD, John Russo helped blaze a path in the horror genre that has never been equalled. In this hillarious erotic novel, he blazes a path through the wild, zany Sex Revolution of the 1970s.

Sweet, innocent Cherry Jankowski works for Joyful Novelties, where she tests sex toys ranging from the ridiculous to the sublime. But she can't find love or peace of mind and her efforts are hampered by a Peeping Tom, an exhibitionist, a cross-dressing boyfriend, a quack psychiatrist, and even her own product-testing partner, Marcello Fettucini, who can't get it up anymore and is scared of losing his job!

www.TheJohnRusso.com

Burning Bulb
PUBLISHING

WEST VIRGINIA-THEMED HUMORROROTICA

BY RICH BOTTLES JR.

HELLHOLE WEST VIRGINIA

From the heights of Mothman's perch high atop the Silver Bridge in Point Pleasant to the depths of Hellhole Cavern in Pendleton County, evil lurks within the shadows as the sun sets upon the haunted hills and hollows of West Virginia.

Bizarro author Rich Bottles Jr. blows the coffin lid off horror genre clichés with this tour de force cast of Eco-friendly vampires, beach-yearning zombies and sex-starved she-devils.

LUMBERJACKED

If you are easily offended or do not possess a truly depraved sense of humor, this story may not be the light summer reading fare you desire. As for the four feisty female freshmen stranded on top of West Virginia's third highest mountain, they have no choice but to experience the sick, twisted debauchery and perverted mayhem described deep inside the tight unbroken bindings of this horrific missive.

Lumberjacked takes the reader to a nightmarish world where character development and aesthetic integrity are prematurely cut short by the swinging axes of maniacal lumberjacks, who are hell bent on death and destruction in the remote forests of Appalachia. And at the climax, when paranoia crosses over to the paranormal, Lumberjacked makes Deliverance look like a family raft trip down the Lower Gauley.

THE MANACLED

What happens when twin brothers lease out the former West Virginia State Penitentiary with the false purpose of filming a documentary on supernatural phenomena, but their true intention is to make a pornographic movie?

Chaos ensues as the disturbed spirits of murdered convicts, along with the reanimated dead from the neighboring Indian Burial Mound, take their vengeance on the unwary and undressed trespassers.

Zombies, ghosts, mobsters and porn collide in this bizarro tale from horror author Rich Bottles Jr.

Burning Bulb
PUBLISHING

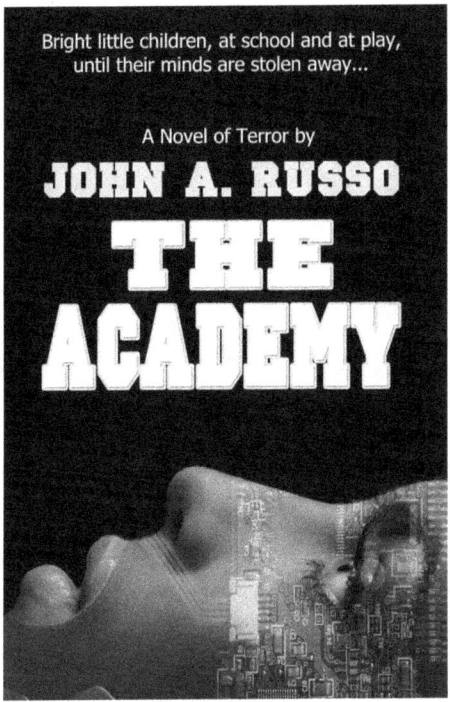

Bright little children, at school and at play,
until their minds are stolen away...

A Novel of Terror by
JOHN A. RUSSO
THE ACADEMY

THE ACADEMY

The Academy. It's every parent's dream, turning their little darlings into geniuses, superachievers, perfect little children.

And if there's a problem, the Academy fixes that too. It's a simple operation. Just a little device. Then a teeny pink scar on a tender little skull . . .

One boy knows the secret. Now he wants his mind back. But it's much, much too late. Too late for anything but the ugly feelings. The bad feelings. The messy sexy feelings. The knife-cold hatred, the murderous rage, for total, screaming, blood-drenching revenge . . .

www.TheJohnRusso.com

Burning Bulb
PUBLISHING

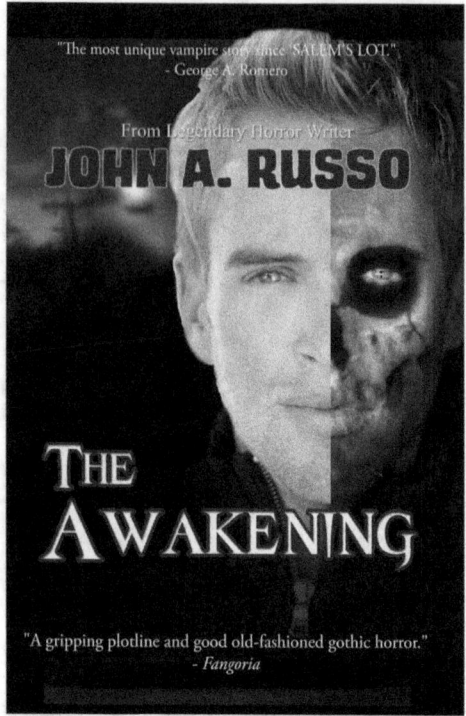

THE AWAKENING

For two hundred years, he has rested. Now he rises. Now he will be satisfied. Nothing can stop him. No one can resist him.

Benjamin Latham is young and handsome, his eighteenth-century mind wakened to a bizarre twentieth-century world. And there is the need deep within . . . an animal need, frightening, murderous, unholy . . . a vital need that must be fed.

And with his need comes a power over men and women to do his bidding, to quiet his dark craving . . .

Until the murders begin. And the inquiries. All suggesting the same hideous truth.

Now Benjamin must find a sanctuary: a lover, a partner, a friend. Someone who can share his darkness. Someone he can lead to . . . The Awakening.

www.TheJohnRusso.com

Burning Bulb
PUBLISHING

DEALEY PLAZA

From legendary horror and suspense writer JOHN RUSSO comes a harrowing tale where no one is safe!

Dealey Plaza is one of the most notorious places in America, and when youthful conspiracy buffs go there in 1964 to stage their own reenactment of the Kennedy Assassination, four of them are brutally murdered ~ the first victims of a hate-filled legacy that continues for four more decades.

The survivors of that long-ago Dallas trip, each of them now icons of the American way of life, are about to be honored ~ or killed.

Who will live and who will die? Will it be country-western star Lori McCoy? Her loving husband? Her scheming ex-husband? Or the case-hardened FBI agent and longtime friend who risks his life trying to protect them?

www.DealeyPlazaBook.com

Burning Bulb
PUBLISHING

LIMB TO LIMB

SUCH A PRETTY GIRL . . .
Tiffany Blake was a beautiful long-limbed dancer with a glorious future and the backing of a rich benefactor. Then a monstrous accident severed her leg at the hip.

SUCH A COLD, CRUEL KNIFE . . .
And now her fellow dancers are disappearing without a trace. One by one they fall victim to a dark and deadly pattern of evil – caught by the bloody, brutal logic that would have them pay with their lovely bodies for the cruel fate of another . . .victims of the sadistic madman whose flashing knife will make them writhe a gruesome new dance.

www.TheJohnRusso.com

Burning Bulb
PUBLISHING

"A sense of infectious fun, straight from the author's pen."
– Nightmare Library

From Legendary Horror Writer
JOHN A. RUSSO

LIVING THINGS

"Russo carries his talent for the horrific neatly over into the novel form."
– West Coast Review of Books

LIVING THINGS

Beneath the shimmering Miami sun sprawls one of the Mafia's biggest empires, a glittering world of lavish beachfront mansions, neon-painted nightclubs, beautiful women, expensive cars—and absolute control over the state's billion-dollar drug trade. But, one by one, its ganglords and henchmen are falling prey to a new rival. His powers are fueled by monstrous ancient rituals; his hellish undead legions slaughter mobsters and innocent citizens alike, his unholy lust for power is virtually unstoppable.

Now a burned-out ex-detective and a brilliant anthropologist must enter a gruesome, nightmare world to fight this master of malevolence and illusion. Their time is short, their weapons few, and they face an ultimate, terrifying choice - annihilation or the loss of their souls to the eternal torment of those who never die. . .

www.TheJohnRusso.com

Burning Bulb
PUBLISHING

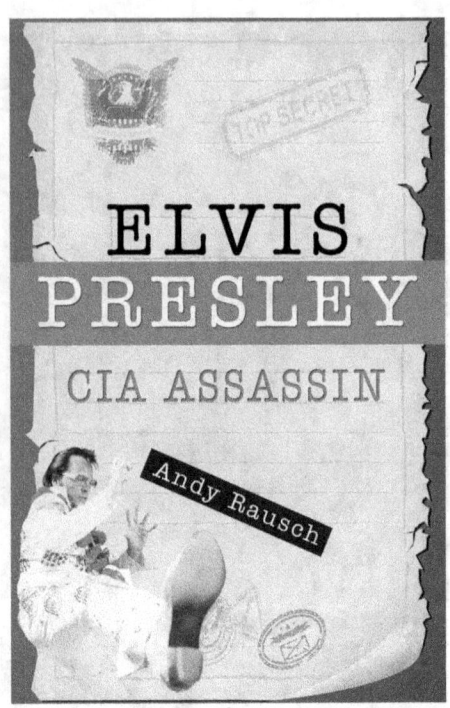

ELVIS PRESLEY, CIA ASSASSIN BY ANDY RAUSCH

"I can guarantee you. Read this book and you'll never look at Elvis the same way again!"
~ Douglas Brode, author of ELVIS CINEMA AND POPULAR CULTURE

SOON TO BE A MAJOR MOTION PICTURE

In 1970, singer Elvis Presley secretly met with President Richard Nixon. This new comedic novel imagines that Presley became a Central Intelligence Agency operative, eventually moving up through the ranks to become a skilled assassin.

Presented in an oral history fashion, the book tells us about Presley's secret transformation by the people who knew him best.

Did he fake his death in 1977? Was Presley involved with the Watergate scandal? The Iran hostage crisis? Communicating with aliens?

Read this book to find out the answers to these and many more questions.

Burning Bulb
PUBLISHING

THE TAILSMAN

From the creators of *The Big Book of Bizarro* and *Westward Hoes* comes a new comic unlike anything you have ever seen!

He's hot on the trail, looking for some *tail...*

Sly Franko was a man of the West, a forger of the wild frontier. Like the Country Western song that would be written years after he died, the words, "Faster horses, younger women, and more money," seemed to be the anthem of this horn dog cowboy.

Franko would ride into town on a blazing saddle, find the closest saloon to wet the whistle, belly up to a good card game, and find him a hot-loving hussy to get his cowpoke on with.

However, Sly might have met his match when a visit to bathroom leads to terror and death. Can Sly and his poker buddies solve the mystery before more of the townsfolk are murdered? Find out in this exciting premier issue of *The Tailsman*!

WWW.BURNINGBULBCOMICS.COM

THE HAGS OF BLACK COUNTY

by Michelle Bowser

Ruled by a committee of Hags, and fueled by toothless rivalries, Black County lurks just far enough out of the way to be completely unnoticed by the rest of civilization. Its inhabitants have been mentally warped for generations and the land itself seems to have the power to drive anyone unlucky enough to visit into ridiculous hillbilly madness. When a construction Company needs to bury a pipeline through its ludicrous hills and valleys, a twisted charm goes to work and every aspect of already bizarre Black County life takes a gory turn for the hysterical. Take a preposterous trip along with its citizens, both native and new, through escapades such as the Hag parade, the grand opening of Madame Skunk's House of Ill Repute, the demolition derby riot and the rabid, zombie clown apocalypse.

THE ABANDONED SOUL

by Daniel Sellers

After spending most of his 20s in a drug and alcohol fueled daze, a young man finally hits rock bottom. Having used up his friends and their good graces, he ends up squatting in an abandoned house. Forcibly sobering he begins to realize that he is not alone in this abandoned house. Left with one last friend and a mountain of regrets, he must decide if this presence is a guilty conscience, or a malicious hunter.

WE WISH YOU A HAPPY KILLDAY

by Jason Heroux

"We Wish You a Happy Killday" is the story of an international beloved holiday called "Killday" where one day a year everyone over the age of fifteen is permitted to register for a license allowing them to kill one other person. But this year Chad Ovenstock doesn't feel like killing anyone. His friends and family urge him to participate in the festivities, but he can't seem to get into the holiday spirit. On the day before Killday Chad comes in contact with Ambrose, an old friend who suffered a nervous breakdown and is now part of The One Ant Army, a mysterious cult dedicated to making the future disappear. When the holiday finally arrives Chad refuses to participate and tries to survive on his own, surrounded by constant gunfire, countless corpses, and the nagging suspicion that Ambrose may have secretly brainwashed him into becoming a member of The One Ant Army cult.

Burning Bulb
PUBLISHING